George Alfred Henty—1832–1902

HUNTING DOG SAVES JERRY FROM THE RAPIDS

CARRY READS UNCLE HARRY'S LETTER.

JERRY GIVES TOM A LESSON IN SHOOTING.

" LEAPING HORSE MOUNTED, AND RODE ACROSS THE STREAM."

" A MOMENT LATER THE INDIAN FELL FORWARD ON HIS FACE."

" THERE IS ANOTHER AVALANCHE, KEEP YOUR BACKS
TO THE WALL, BOYS."

" THEY WENT OUT TO LOOK AT THE INDIAN THE CHIEF HAD SHOT. "

"NO GOOD FIGHT HERE," SAID LEAPING HORSE.

Polyglot Press Henty Series

In the Heart of the Rockies

A Story of Adventure in Colorado

George A. Henty

Polyglot
Press

Philadelphia

THIS IS A POLYGLOT PRESS HENTY EDITION

Published in the United States by Polyglot Press, Inc.

A member of Polyglot Press Alliance

Philadelphia • Barcelona • Bejing • Rio de Janeiro • Toronto • London •
Sydney • Cairo • Tel Aviv • Mexico DF • Moscow • Trivandrum

Copyright ©2003 by Polyglot Press, Inc.

In the Heart of the Rockies, A Story of Adventure in Colorado
by George A. Henty, Trade Paperback.
ISBN: 1-4115-0174-8

Polyglot Press, the portrayal of the parrot on a perch, and the portrayal of a magnifying glass with the words "high legibility typeface" in the lens, and the portrayal of a computer monitor with the words "custom typeset" on the screen are all trademarks of Polygot Press, Inc.

This book is printed on acid-free paper. Designed for readability using Adobe Minion type family.

Library of Congress

Cataloging-in-Publication Data

1. G. A. Henty • 2. Authors, American-19th century.3. Literature •

4. English Writers • 5. Fiction

First edition—Blackie and Son Ltd., 1894

Composition by Polyglot Press, Inc., Philadelphia, PA. www.polyglotpress.com

Polyglot Mission Statement

Polyglot Press brings hard-to-find books and manuscripts back to print, making previously scarce and rare literary and historical information available to scholars, modern libraries and the general public at affordable prices.

Polyglot digitally restores (recovers, edits and proofs); custom typesets; and republishes comprehensive collections by well known authors in a high-legibility optical font. Each title is simultaneously printed in paperback, hard-cover, library, collectors and large print editions.

Polyglot also digitally restores the covers, frontispieces and illustrations accompanying the original and reprint editions of these works, selecting the most representative examples available from public and private collections.

Polyglot Literary Collections feature sixteenth to nineteenth century Northern European, North American and Australasian novelists and historians writing in English; and Mediterranean and Latin American novelists and historians writing in Spanish, Portuguese, French and Italian—with selected titles also available in translation.

Polyglot Historical Collections highlight scholarship on Mediterranean culture from late antiquity through the Renaissance.

Care is taken to insure that the complete originally published work is present, including author prefaces and dedications.

On each credits page, Polyglot catalogs the original publisher and publication dates; serialization publishers and dates; and available illustrator information.

Polyglot also includes, as faithfully as possible, original author introductions and dedications as well as appendices with a comprehensive list of published works.

Polyglot will augment each literary collection with previously published and unpublished short stories, poetry and essays as acquired.

To make this possible, Polyglot relies on special grants, numerous volunteers and cooperating institutions worldwide.

Polyglot staff, friends and contributors join libraries and museums dedicated to this important tradition, from the ancient libraries at Alexandria and Cordoba to the great collections of today.

Polyglot welcomes inquiries from cooperating author societies about reissuing comprehensive collections of currently out of print titles.

David A. Scott Publishing

Acknowledgements

In appreciation of those who made the
Polyglot Press G. A. Henty Series possible:

Harland Eastman

Horatio Alger Society
Robert E. Kasper, Executive Director

Northern Illinois University
Arthur P. Young, Dean of Libraries

Free Library of Philadelphia
Mary Wood Fischer, Chief, Collection Development Office

Polyglot G. A. Henty books are available in
Paperback, Hard Cover, Large Print
and Collector's Editions.

Beginning in 2003 Polyglot Press will offer a range of fine art
reproductions, posters, as well as note, greeting and playing
cards based on the original cover art and illustrations from the
Horatio Alger, Jr. and George A. Henty collections.

* *

Polyglot Press titles are available in Large Print.

* *

Polyglot Press collections include rare as well as scarce titles.

For a complete list of authors, titles, special offers, discounts and
future products visit

www.polyglotpress.com

Introduction
G. A. Henty

Henty, George Alfred (1832-1902) English war correspondent and author, helped set the standard for 19th Century boys' literature, primarily through his prodigious output of 77 historical novels for boys plus 11 intended for a more adult audience. Henty also produced numerous short stories and edited two short-lived boys' magazines, "The Union Jack" and "Beeton's Boy's Own Magazine." Henty's stories were influential on the generation that fought World War I—F. Scott Fitzgerald describes his protagonist in "This Side of Paradise" as having "all the Henty biases in history"—and continued to reach and inspire later readers, including historians A.J.P. Taylor and Barbara Tuchman and novelist Mordecai Richler.

G. A. Henty pioneered at the same time, adventure and historical fiction. He combined the two into a remarkable series of action novels and short stories that accurately portrayed the background of the British Empire in its glory years while weaving in a young hero whose interaction with large world events entertained the reader while educating. He followed on the heels of Walter Scott, and developed his special genre to a point where scores of others looked to him for a blueprint.

Henty did even more than developing a great literary contribution. He brought the Empire to its citizens all over the globe. Through reading his novels, friends of England learned of the breath of the Empire and the moral values of loyalty, courage, dedication, and honesty. Later critics complain of denigration towards the real and imagined enemies of British power, and certainly various books reflect the lack of tolerance for cultural diversity endemic in the course of world domination by victorious armies carrying the Union Jack.

The exhilaration produced by the tales still inspire new generations of readers both young and old, not to mention collectors and educators. During the 1880's Henty books started to appear with regularity and create much anticipation among the large readership of older boys.

The man behind the books lived the life he wrote about. His life (1832-1902) closely paralleled the reign of Queen Victoria (1837-1901). His works addressed many of her accomplishments, and certainly the spirit of her rule. During his school years at Westminster School and Cambridge University, he participated in a rigorous program of study and physical activity that included boxing, wrestling and rowing.

His experience with war started with his entry in the Crimean War, and then later as a war correspondent in Europe and Africa. He covered the Garibaldi revolution in Italy, the Franco-Prussian War, Austro-Italian War, Turkish-Serbian Wary, and the Spanish conflict with the Carlists. During the Italian skirmishes, troops from that country took Henty prisoner, thinking him an Austrian spy. The sentenced him to death, but his convincing argument to a commanding general won him release.

Henty's travels also took him to India, where he accompanied the Prince of Wales (Edward VII), and to the California gold fields. With these experiences, Henty was well prepared to relate the adventures of war and history.

He did just that, first to his own children, where he would continue a story sometimes for days, adding facts of battles to interloping activities of young heroes. The man was a natural storyteller. And write he did.

He completed over 144 books, plus numerous short stories and articles. He wrote at a frenetic pace, keeping a group of secretaries extremely active. Henty himself jotted down his approach to organizing a tale:

"When I have once fixed, not on the story but on the epoch, I send up to a London library and procure ten books on the subject. I glance through these. Perhaps only two of them will suit my purpose, so I send the others back and get another batch, until I have got everything I want. I get these books about ten days before I start writing. Then I have on my shelves at least a dozen atlases, some of them being amongst the earliest printed. These are very useful to me for stories of the Middle Age, as I get the roads and coastlines that then existed, and which in many places have changed materially during the last three hundred years. I have, of course, a number of encyclopedias from which I glean a lot of information about the character of the country, its population, products, and so on. Thus equipped I am able to start off on the story without having to pause to look up information. I sit on my sofa and smoke with two or three books open before me, the sofa being shared by three or four of my five dogs.'

With his books, Henty stirred many a youth's interest in history. As an amateur historian, he drew varied appraisals ranging from acceptability to criticism of his sources and then his representations of actual events. As a writer of prose, however, the evidence speaks for itself. He won over 25 million readers and became perhaps the first blockbuster author.

Some similarities abound in the novels. Most feature a male hero in his middle to late teens. There are varieties of family misfortune, timely acts to save a life, rescues of young girls, captures, escapes, rewards, legacies, battles, and liaisons with historic figures. Happy endings abound, and the hero often ends up the husband of a fair damsel.

In sea stories, the boys often start as midshipmen, and in land campaigns they might take on the duties of drummer boys. Medieval boys serve as pages, but in practically all cases the hero is of British descent.

A number of publishers worked with Henty, and his best connection might have been with Blackie & Son, where conscientious editing prepared quality copy for printing. Some of the criticism for his history came from Henty's sparse credits to his sources and the limited number of those sources used for reference. The other complaints against Henty amount to charges of racism and imperialism.

He might cheerfully admit to his praise and unabashed imperialist proclivity. Against imperialism lie the charges of domination and inconsideration towards conquered peoples. These accusations do contain merit. The other side of the argument, however, is that Imperialism, at least the British variety, educated, cared for, introduced law to, and uplifted countless peoples. These debates go on endlessly and find themselves thrust into every political foray imaginable, both local and international.

The charge of racism is more serious and merited, for slaves, Irish, Asians, and others can lodge objections to the Henty perspective. He reflected an era when slavery still persisted legally in the world, and where racist attitudes prevailed. Not that they have been eliminated by any means, but the reader or instructor can take the historic context into consideration.

In sum total G. A. Henty inspired six or seven generations to a study of history. He entertained millions and fathered a literary genre that features adventure and history combined into a historic novel. He wrote many more books than even the most prolific of authors and lived a life of adventure and danger that gave him license to speak of war and action. At least another six or seven generations will eagerly read Henty books.

Preface

My Dear Lads,

Until comparatively late that portion of the United States in which I have laid this story was wholly unexplored. The many windings canyons of the Colorado River extend through a country absolutely bare and waterless, and have the tales told by a few hunters or gold-seekers who, pressed by Indians, made the ascent of some of them, but little was known regarding this region it was not until 1869 that a thorough exploration of the canyons was made by a government expedition under the command of Major Powell. This expedition passed through the whole of the canyons from those high upon the Green River to the point where the Colorado issues out onto the plains. Four years were occupied by the party in making a detailed survey of the course of the main river and its tributaries. These explorations took place some eight or nine years after the date of my story. The country in which the Big Wind River has its source among the mountain chains contained in it, were almost unknown until, after the completion of the railway to California, the United States government was forced to send an expedition into it to punish the Indians for their raids upon settlers in the plains. For details of the geography and scenery I have relied upon the narrative of Mr. F... rol... nan who paid several visits to the country in 1878 and the following years in quest of sport, and was the first white man to penetrate the recesses of the higher mountains. At that time the Indians had almost entirely deserted the country. For the details of the dangers and difficulties of the passage through the canons I am indebted to the official report of Major Powell, published by the United States government.

Yours sincerely,
G. A. Henty.

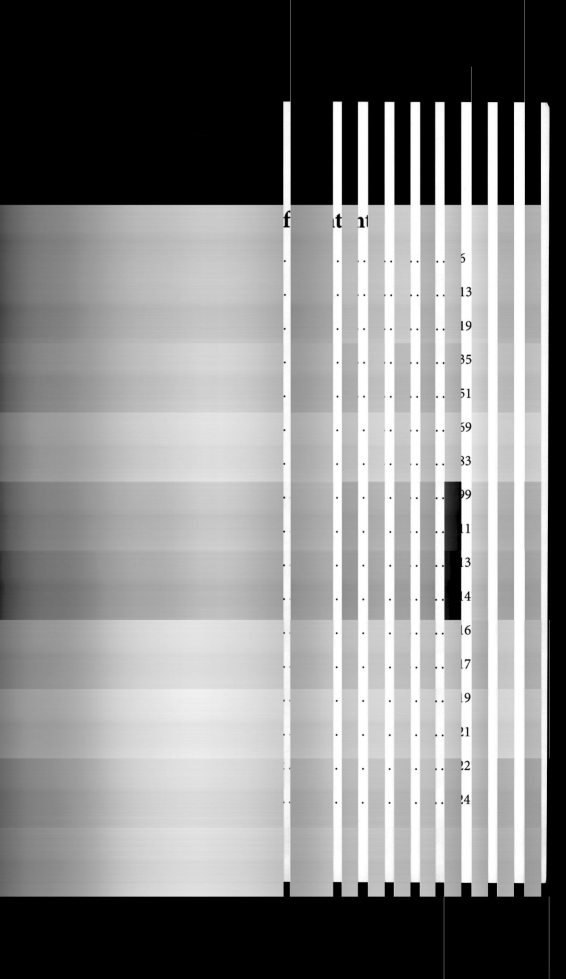

Chapter XVI. - Afloat in Canoes 259

Chapter XVII. - The Grand Canon 275

Chapter XVIII. - Back to Denver 291

G. A. Henty Catalogue Titles 324

e
i

Chapter I

Tom's Choice

"...can be of no use here, ... What ... I good ...? Why ... could ... earn money enough to pay for my own food even if ... who would help me to get clerks... I am too young ... rather go before the mast ... take a place in a shop ... even to enlist. I know just about as much as other boys at ... and I certainly have no talent any ways ... as I can see... sell a boat, and I ... the swimming ... sergeant who gives us lessons in single-stick and ... considers me his best pupil ... with the gloves, but all these things ... together would not bring me in sixpence a week. I don't want to ... away, and nothing would induce me to do so ... I should be of the slightest use to you here. What can I do ... any use? What is there ... to look forward to ... I say? I am sure that you would ... be ... worrying over me if I did get some sort of situation ... you ... know father and mother would not have liked to ... in, ... you seem to offer no chance for the future ... there is ... it ... would not matter what I did ... and while I ... could ... on ... to you."

The speaker was a lad of ... His and his sister who was ... his senior, were both dressed in deep mourning, and were sitting on ... bench near ... southeast ... looking across to Spithead and the ... Wight stretching away behind. They had ... their ... for ... weeks ... their mother to the grave, and had ... beside their father, a ... officer of the navy, who had died two years before. This was their first ...

19

had left the house, where remained their four sisters—Janet, who came between Carry and Tom; Blanche, who was fourteen; Lucie, twelve; and Harriet, eight. Tom had proposed the walk.

"Come out for some fresh air, Carry," he had said. "You have been shut up for a month. Let us two go together;" and Carry had understood that he wanted a talk alone with her. There was need, indeed, that they should look the future in the face. Since Lieutenant Wade's death their means had been very straitened. Their mother had received a small pension as his widow, and on this, eked out by drafts reluctantly drawn upon the thousand pounds she had brought him on her marriage, which had been left untouched during his lifetime, they had lived since his death. Two hundred pounds had been drawn from their little capital, and the balance was all that now remained. It had long been arranged that Carry and Janet should go out as governesses as soon as they each reached the age of eighteen, but it was now clear that Carry must remain at home in charge of the young ones.

That morning the two girls had had a talk together, and had settled that, as Janet was too young to take even the humblest place as a governess, they would endeavour to open a little school, and so, for the present at any rate, keep the home together. Carry could give music lessons, for she was already an excellent pianist, having been well taught by her mother, who was an accomplished performer, and Janet was sufficiently advanced to teach young girls. She had communicated their decision to Tom, who had heartily agreed with it.

"The rent is only twenty pounds a year," he said, "and, as you say, the eight hundred pounds bring in thirty-two pounds a year, which will pay the rent and leave something over. If you don't get many pupils at first it will help, and you can draw a little from the capital till the school gets big enough to pay all your expenses. It is horrible to me that I don't seem to be able to help, but at any rate I don't intend to remain a drag upon you. If mother had only allowed me to go to sea after father's death I should be off your hands now, and I might even have been able to help a little. As it is, what is there for me to do here?" And then he pointed out how hopeless the prospect seemed at Portsmouth.

Carry was silent for a minute or two when he ceased speaking, and sat looking out over the sea.

"Certainly, we should not wish you to go into a shop, Tom, and what you say about going into an office is also right enough. We have no sort of interest, and the sort of clerkship you would be likely to get here would not lead to anything. I know what you are thinking about—that letter of Uncle Harry's; but you know that mother could not bear the thought of it, and it would be dreadful for us if you were to go away."

"I would not think of going, Carry, if I could see any chance of helping you here, and I don't want to go as I did when the letter first came. It seems such a cowardly thing to run away and leave all the burden upon your shoulders, yours and Janet's, though I know it will be principally on yours; but what else is there to do? It was not for my own sake that I wanted before to go, but I did not see what there was for me to do here even when I grew up. Still, as mother said it would break her heart if I went away, of course there was an end of it for the time, though I have always thought it would be something to fall back upon if, when I got to eighteen or nineteen, nothing else turned up, which seemed to me very likely would be the case. Certainly, if it came to a choice between that and enlisting, I should choose that; and now it seems to me the only thing to be done."

"It is such a long way off, Tom," the girl said in a tone of deep pain; "and you know when people get away so far they seem to forget those at home and give up writing. We had not heard from uncle for ten years when that letter came."

"There would be no fear of my forgetting you, Carry. I would write to you whenever I got a chance."

"But even going out there does not seem to lead to anything, Tom. Uncle has been away twenty-five years, and he does not seem to have made any money at all."

"Oh, but then he owned in his letter, Carry, that it was principally his own fault. He said he had made a good sum several times mining and chucked it away; but that next time he strikes a good thing he was determined to keep what he made and to come home to live upon it. I sha'n't chuck it away if I make it, but shall send every penny home that I can spare."

"But uncle will not expect you, Tom, mother refused so positively to let you go. Perhaps he has gone away from the part of the country he wrote from, and you may not be able to find him."

"I shall be able to find him," Tom said confidently. "When that letter went, I sent one of my own to him, and said that though mother would not hear of my going now, I might come out to him when I got older if I could get nothing to do here, and asked him to send me a few words directed to the post-office telling me how I might find him. He wrote back saying that if I called at the Empire Saloon at a small town called Denver, in Colorado, I should be likely to hear whereabouts he was, and that he would sometimes send a line there with instructions if he should be long away."

"I see you have set your mind on going, Tom," Carry said sadly.

"No, I have not set my mind on it, Carry. I am perfectly ready to stop here if you can see any way for me to earn money, but I cannot stop here idle, eating and drinking, while you girls are working for us all."

"If you were but three or four years older, Tom, I should not so much mind, and though it would be a terrible blow to part with you, I do not see that you could do anything better; but you are only sixteen."

"Yes, but I am strong and big for my age; I am quite as strong as a good many men. Of course I don't mean the boatmen and the dockyard maties, but men who don't do hard work. Anyhow, there are lots of men who go out to America who are no stronger than I am, and of course I shall get stronger every month. I can walk thirty miles a day easy, and I have never had a day's illness."

"It is not your strength, Tom; I shall have no fears about your breaking down; on the contrary, I should say that a life such as uncle wrote about, must be wonderfully healthy. But you seem so young to make such a long journey, and you may have to travel about in such rough places and among such rough men before you can find Uncle Harry."

"I expect that I shall get on a great deal easier than a man would," Tom said confidently. "Fellows might play tricks with a grown-up fellow who they see is a stranger and not up to things, and might get into quarrels with him, but no one is likely to interfere with a boy. No, I don't think that there is anything in that, Carry,—the only real difficulty is in going away so far from you, and perhaps being away for a long time."

"Well, Tom," the girl said after another pause, "it seems very terrible, but I own that I can see nothing better for you. There is no way that you can earn money here, and I am sure we would rather think of you as mining and hunting with uncle, than as sitting as a sort of boy-clerk in some dark little office in London or Portsmouth. It is no worse than going to sea anyhow, and after all you may, as uncle says, hit on a rich mine and come back with a fortune. Let us be going home. I can hardly bear to think of it now, but I will tell Janet, and will talk about it again this evening after the little ones have gone to bed."

Tom had the good sense to avoid any expression of satisfaction. He gave Carry's hand a silent squeeze, and as they walked across the common talked over their plans for setting to work to get pupils, and said no word that would give her a hint of the excitement he felt at the thought of the life of adventure in a wild country that lay before him. He had in his blood a large share of the restless spirit of enterprise that has been the main factor in making the Anglo-Saxons the dominant race of the world. His father and his grandfather had both been officers in the royal navy, and a great-uncle had commanded a merchantman that traded in the Eastern seas, and had never come back from one of its voyages; there had been little doubt that all on board had been massacred and the ship burned by Malay pirates. His Uncle Harry had gone away when little more than a boy to seek a fortune in America, and had, a few years after his landing there, crossed the plains with one of the first parties that started out at news of the discovery of gold in California.

Tom himself had longed above all things to be a sailor. His father had not sufficient interest to get him into the royal navy, but had intended to obtain for him a berth as apprentice in the merchant service; but his sudden death had cut that project short, and his mother, who had always been opposed to it, would not hear of his going to sea. But the life that now seemed open to him was in the boy's eyes even preferable to that he had longed for. The excitement of voyages to India or China and back was as nothing to that of a gold-seeker and hunter in the West, where there were bears and Indians and all sorts of adventures to be encountered. He soon calmed down, however, on reaching home. The empty chair, the black dresses and pale faces of the girls, brought back in its full force the sense of loss.

In a short time he went up to his room, and sat there thinking it all over again, and asking himself whether it was fair of him to leave his sisters, and whether he was not acting selfishly in thus choosing his own life. He had gone over this ground again and again in the last few days, and he now came to the same conclusion, namely, that he could do no better for the girls by stopping at home, and that he had not decided upon accepting his uncle's invitation because the life was just what he would have chosen, but because he could see nothing that offered equal chances of his being able permanently to aid them at home.

When he came downstairs again Carry said:

"The others have gone out, Tom; you had better go round and see some of your school-fellows. You look fagged and worn out. You cannot help me here, and I shall go about my work more cheerfully if I know that you are out and about."

Tom nodded, put on his cap and went out; but he felt far too restless to follow her advice and call on some of his friends, so he walked across the common and lay down on the beach and went all over it again, until at last he went off to sleep, and did not wake up until, glancing at his watch, he found that it was time to return to tea. He felt fresher and better for his rest, for indeed he had slept but little for the past fortnight, and Carry nodded approvingly as she saw that his eyes were brighter, and the lines of fatigue and sleeplessness less strongly marked on his face.

Two hours later, when the younger girls had gone to bed, Carry said: "Now we will have a family council. I have told Janet about our talk, Tom, and she is altogether on your side, and only regrets that she is not a boy and able to go out with you. We need not go over the ground again; we are quite agreed with you that there seems no prospect here of your obtaining work such as we should like to see you at, or that would lead to anything. There are only two things open to you, the one is to go to sea, the other to go out to Uncle Harry. You are old to go as an apprentice, but not too old, and that plan could be carried out; still, we both think that the other is better. You would be almost as much separated from us if you went to sea as you would be if you went out to America. But before you quite decide I will read uncle's letter, which I have found this afternoon among some other papers."

She took out the letter and opened it.

"'My dear Jack,—I am afraid it is a very long time since I wrote last; I don't like to think how long. I have been intending to do so a score of times, but you know I always hated writing, and I have been waiting to tell you that I had hit upon something good at last. Even now I can only tell you that I have been knocking about and getting older, but so far I cannot say I have been getting richer. As I told you when I wrote last I have several times made good hauls and struck it rich, but somehow the money has always slipped through my fingers. Sometimes I have put it into things that looked well enough but turned out worthless; sometimes I have chucked it away in the fool's manner men do here. I have just come back from a prospecting tour in the country of the Utes, where I found two or three things that seemed good; one of them first-rate, the best thing, I think, I have seen since I came out here.

"'Unfortunately I cannot do anything with them at present, for the Utes are getting troublesome, and it would be as much as one's life is worth to go back there with a small party; so that matter must rest for a bit, and I must look out in another quarter until the Utes settle down again. I am going to join a hunting party that starts for the mountains next week. I have done pretty nearly as much hunting as mining since I came out, and though there is no big pile to be made at it, it is a pretty certain living. How are you all getting on? I hope some day to drop in on your quiet quarters at Southsea with some big bags of gold-dust, and to end my days in a nook by your fireside; which I know you will give me, old fellow, with or without the gold bags.

"'I suppose your boy is thirteen or fourteen years old by this time. That is too young for him to come out here, but if in two or three years you don't see any opening for him at home, send him out to me, and I will make a man of him; and even if he does not make a fortune in gold-seeking, there are plenty of things a young fellow can turn his hand to in this country with a good certainty of making his way, if he is but steady. You may think that my example is not likely to be of much benefit to him, but I should do for an object lesson, and seriously, would do my very best to set him in a straight path. Anyhow, three or four years' knocking about with me would enable him to cut his eye-teeth, and hold his own in the world. At the end of that time he could look round and see what line he would take up, and I need not say that I would help him to the utmost of my power, and though I have not done any good for myself I might do good for him.

"'In the first place, I know pretty well every one in Colorado, Montana, and Idaho; in the next place, in my wanderings I have come across a score of bits of land in out-of-the-way places where a young fellow could set up a ranche and breed cattle and horses and make a good thing of it; or if he has a turn for mechanics, I could show him places where he could set up saw-mills for lumber, with water-power all the year round, and with markets not far away. Of course, he is too young yet, but unless he is going to walk in your steps and turn sailor he might do worse than come out to me in three or four years' time. Rough as the life is, it is a man's life, and a week of it is worth more than a year's quill-driving in an office. It is a pity your family have run to girls, for if one boy had made up his mind for the sea you might have spared me another.'

"That is all. You know mother sent an answer saying that dear father had gone, and that she should never be able to let you go so far away and take up such a rough and dangerous life. However, Tom, as you wrote to uncle, her refusal would not matter, and by his sending you instructions how to find him, it is evident that he will not be surprised at your turning up. In the first place, are you sure that you would prefer this to the sea?"

"Quite sure, Carry; I should like it much better. But the principal thing is that I may soon be able to help you from there, while it would be years before I should get pay enough at sea to enable me to do so."

"Then that is settled, Tom. And now, I suppose," and her voice quivered a little, "you will want to be off as soon as you can?"

"I think so," Tom replied. "If I am to go, it seems to me the sooner I go the better; there is nothing that I can do here, and we shall all be restless and unsettled until I am off."

Carry nodded. "I think you are right, Tom; we shall never be able to settle to our work here when we are thinking of your going away. The first thing to do will be to draw some money from the bank. There will be your outfit to get and your passage to pay to America, and a supply of money to take you out West, and keep you until you join uncle."

"That is what I hate," Tom said gloomily. "It seems beastly that when I want to help you I must begin by taking some of your money."

"That can't be helped," Carry said cheerfully. "One must not grudge a sprat to catch a whale, and besides it would cost ever so much more if we had to apprentice you to the sea, and get your outfit. You will not want many clothes now. You have enough for the voyage and journey, and I should think it would be much better for you to get what you want out there, when you will have uncle to advise what is necessary. I should really think some flannel shirts and a rough suit for the voyage will be the principal things."

"I should think so, certainly," Tom agreed. "The less baggage one travels with the better, for when I leave the railway I shall only want what I can carry with me or pack on horses. Anything else would only be a nuisance. As to a rough suit for the voyage, the clothes I had before I put these on" (and he glanced at his black suit) "will do capitally. Of course I shall go steerage. I can get out for four or five pounds that way, and I shall be quite as well off as I should be as an apprentice. I know I must have some money, but I won't take more than is absolutely necessary. I am all right as far as I can see for everything, except three or four flannel shirts. I don't see that another thing will be required except a small trunk to hold them and the clothes I have on, which I don't suppose I shall ever wear again, and a few other things. You know

I would only allow you to have this one black suit made. I was thinking of this, and it would have been throwing away money to have got more. Of course, I don't know what I shall want out there. I know it is a long way to travel by rail, and I may have to keep myself for a month before I find uncle. I should think five-and-twenty pounds when I land would be enough for everything."

"I shall draw fifty pounds," Carry said positively. "As you say, your outfit will really cost nothing; ten pounds will pay for your journey to Liverpool and your passage; that will leave you forty pounds in your pocket when you land. That is the very least you could do with, for you may find you will have to buy a horse, and though I believe they are very cheap out there, I suppose you could not get one under ten pounds; and then there would be the saddle and bridle and food for the journey, and all sorts of things. I don't think forty pounds will be enough."

"I won't have a penny more, anyhow," Tom said. "If I find a horse too expensive I can tramp on foot."

"And you must be sure not to get robbed," Janet said, breaking in for the first time. "Just fancy your finding yourself without money in such a place as that. I will make you a belt to wear under your things, with pockets for the money."

"I hope I should not be such a fool as that, Janet, but anyhow I will be as careful as I can. I shall be very glad of the belt. One does not know what the fellows might be up to, and I would certainly rather not have my money loose in my pocket; but even if I were robbed I don't think it would be as desperate as you think. I expect a boy could always find something to do to earn his living, and I should try and work my way along somehow, but as that would not be pleasant at all I shall take good care of my money, you may be sure."

For an hour they sat talking, and before the council broke up it was agreed that they should look in the newspaper in the morning for a list of vessels sailing for America, and should at once write and take a passage.

There was no time lost. Carry felt that it would be best for them all that the parting should be got over as soon as possible. Letters were written the next morning to two steamship companies and to the owners of two sailing vessels asking the prices of steerage passages, agreeing that if there was not much difference it would be better to save perhaps a fortnight by taking the passage in a steamship.

The replies showed that the difference was indeed trifling, and a week after their receipt Tom Wade started from Portsmouth to Liverpool. Even at the last moment he was half-inclined to change his plans, it seemed so hard to leave his sisters alone; but Carry and Janet had both convinced themselves that his scheme was the best, and would not hear of his wavering now. They kept up a show of good spirits until the last, talked confidently of the success of their own plans, and how they should set about carrying them out as soon as they were free to act. The younger girls, although implored by the elders not to give way to their grief at the departure of their brother, were in a state of constant tearfulness, and were in consequence frequently got rid of by being sent on errands. Tom, too, took them out for hours every day, and by telling them stories of the wild animals he should hunt, and the Indians he should see, and of the stores of gold he should find hidden, generally brought them home in a more cheerful state of mind.

At last the parting was over, and after making heroic efforts to be cheerful to the end, Tom waved a last adieu with his handkerchief to the five weeping figures on the platform, and then threw himself back in his seat and gave free vent to his own feelings. Two girls sitting beside him sniggered at the sight of the strong-built young fellow giving way to tears, but a motherly-looking woman opposite presently put her hand on his knee.

"Don't be ashamed of crying, my lad," she said. "I have got a son years older than you, and we always have a good cry together every time he starts on a long voyage. Are you going far? I suppose those are your sisters? I see you are all in black. Lost someone dear to you, no doubt? It comes to us all, my boy, sooner or later."

"I am going to America," Tom replied, "and may not be back for years. Yes, those are my sisters, and what upsets me most is that I have to leave them all alone, for we have lost both our parents."

"Dear, dear, that is sad indeed! No wonder you are all upset. Well, well, America is not so very far away—only a ten days' voyage by steamer, they tell me, and my boy is away in a sailing ship. He is in China, I reckon, now; he sailed five months ago, and did not expect to be home under a year. I worry about him sometimes, but I know it is of no use doing that. The last thing he said when I bade good-bye to him was, 'Keep up your spirits, mother'; and I try to do so."

The old lady went on talking about her son, and Tom, listening to her kindly attempts to draw him out of his own troubles, grew interested, and by the time they reached Winchester, where she left the train, he had shaken off his first depression. It was a long journey with several changes, and he did not arrive in Liverpool until six o'clock in the evening, having been nearly twelve hours on the road. Carry's last injunction had been, "Take a cab when you get to Liverpool, Tom, and drive straight down to the docks, Liverpool is a large place, and you might get directed wrong. I shall be more comfortable if I know that, at any rate, you will go straight on board."

Tom had thought it an unnecessary expense, but as he saw that Carry would be more comfortable about him if he followed her advice, he promised to do so, and was not sorry for it as he drove through the streets; for, in spite of cutting down everything that seemed unnecessary for the voyage and subsequent journey, the portmanteau was too heavy to carry far with comfort, and although prepared to rough it to any extent when he had once left England, he felt that he should not like to make his way along the crowded streets with his trunk on his shoulder.

The cabman had no difficulty in finding the *Parthia*, which was still in the basin. Tom was, however, only just in time to get on board, for the men were already throwing off the warps, and ten minutes later she passed out through the dock-gates, and soon anchored in the middle of the river. Tom had been on board too many ships at Portsmouth to feel any of that bewilderment common to emigrants starting on their first voyage. He saw that at present everyone was too busy to attend to him, and so he put his portmanteau down by the bulwark forward, and leaning on the rail watched the process of warping the ship out of the docks. There were a good many steerage passengers forward, but at present the after-part of the ship was entirely deserted, as the cabin passengers would not come on board until either late at night or early next morning. When the anchor had been let drop he took up his trunk and asked a sailor where he ought to go to.

"Show me your ticket. Ah! single man's quarters, right forward."

There he met a steward, who, after looking at his ticket, said: "You will see the bunks down there, and can take any one that is unoccupied. I should advise you to put your trunk into it, and keep the lid shut. People come and go in the morning, and you might find that your things had gone too. It would be just as well for you to keep it locked through the voyage. I see that you have got a cord round it. Keep it corded; the more things there are to unfasten to get at the contents the less chance there is of anyone attempting it."

The place was crowded with berths, mere shallow trays, each containing a straw mattress and pillow and two coloured blankets. They were in three tiers, one above the other, and were arranged in lines three deep, with a narrow passage between. He saw by the number into which bags and packets had been thrown that the upper berths were the favourites, but he concluded that the lower tiers were preferable. "It will be frightfully hot and stuffy here," he said to himself, "and I should say the lower berths will be cooler than the upper." He therefore placed his trunk in one of those next to the central passage and near the door, and then went up on deck.

The *Parthia* was a Cunarder, and although not equal in size to the great ships of the present day, was a very fine vessel. The fare had been somewhat higher than that for which he could have had a passage in a sailing ship, but in addition to his saving time, there was the advantage that on board the steamers, passengers were not obliged to provide their own bedding, as they had to do in sailing vessels, and also the food was cooked for them in the ship's galleys.

The first meal was served soon after the anchor dropped, and consisted of a bowl of cocoa and a large piece of bread. Half an hour later a tender came alongside with the last batch of steerage passengers, and Tom was interested in watching the various groups as they came on board—men, women, and children.

"Well," he said to himself, "I do think I am better fitted to make my way out there than most of these people are, for they look as helpless and confused as a flock of sheep. I pity those women with children. It will be pretty crowded in our quarters, but there is a chance of getting a fair night's sleep, while in a place crowded with babies and children it would be awful."

Being a kind-hearted lad he at once set to work to help as far as he could, volunteering to carry children down below, and to help with boxes and bundles.

In many cases his assistance was thankfully accepted, but in some it was sharply refused, the people's manner clearly showing their suspicions of his motive. He was not surprised at this after all the warnings Carry had given him against putting any confidence in strangers, but was satisfied, after an hour's hard work, that he had rendered things somewhat easier for many a worried and anxious woman. It was getting dusk even on deck by the time he had finished.

"Thank you, lad," a man, who went up the companion ladder with him, said as they stepped on to the deck. "You have done my missis a good turn by taking care of those three young ones while we straightened up a bit, and I saw you helping others too. You are the right sort, I can see. There ain't many young chaps as puts themselves out of the way to do a bit of kindness like that. My name is Bill Brown; what is yours?"

"Tom Wade. I had nothing to do, and was glad to be of a little help. People who have never been on board ship before naturally feel confused in such a crowd."

"Have you been to sea?"

"Not on a voyage, but I have lived at Portsmouth and have often been on board troopships and men-of-war, so it does not seem so strange to me."

"Are you by yourself, or have you friends with you?"

"I am alone," Tom replied. "I am going out to join an uncle in the States."

"I have been across before," the man said. "I am a carpenter, and have worked out there six months, and came home six weeks back to fetch the others over. I have got a place, where I was working before, to go to as soon as I land. It makes a lot of difference to a man."

"It does indeed," Tom agreed. "I know if I were going out without any fixed object beyond taking the first work that came to hand, I should not feel so easy and comfortable about it as I do now."

"I have got two or three of my mates on board who are going out on my report of the place, and three families from my wife's village. She and the youngsters have been staying with her old folk while I was away. So we are a biggish party, and if you want anything done on the voyage you have only got to say the word to me."

Chapter II.
Finding Friends

The weather was fine, and Tom Wade found the voyage more pleasant than he had expected. The port-holes were kept open all the way, and the crowded quarters were less uncomfortable than would have been the case had they encountered rough weather. There were some very rough spirits among the party forward, but the great majority were quiet men, and after the first night all talking and larking were sternly repressed after the lights were out. The food was abundant, and although some grumbled at the meat there was no real cause of complaint. A rope across the deck divided the steerage passengers from those aft, and as there were not much more than one-half the emigrants aboard that the *Parthia* could carry, there was plenty of room on deck.

But few of the passengers suffered from sea-sickness, and the women sat and chatted and sewed in little groups while the children played about, and the men walked up and down or gathered forward and smoked, while a few who had provided themselves with newspapers or books sat in quiet corners and read. Tom was one of these, for he had picked up a few books on the United States at second-hand bookstalls at Portsmouth, and this prevented him from finding the voyage monotonous. When indisposed to read he chatted with Brown the carpenter and his mates, and sometimes getting a party of children round him and telling them stories gathered from the books now standing on the shelves in his room at Southsea. He was glad, however, when the voyage was over; not because he was tired of it, but because he was longing to be on his way west. Before leaving the ship he took a very hearty farewell of his companions on the voyage, and on landing was detained but a few minutes at the custom-house, and then entering an omnibus that was in waiting at the gate, was driven straight to the station of one of the western lines of railway.

From the information he had got up before sailing he had learnt that there were several of these, but that there was very little difference either in their speed or rates of fare, and that their through-rates to Denver were practically the same. He had therefore fixed on the Chicago and Little Rock line, not because its advantages were greater, but in order to be able to go straight from the steamer to the station without having to make up his mind between the competing lines. He found on arrival that the emigrant trains ran to Omaha, where all the lines met, and that beyond that he must proceed by the regular trains. An emigrant train was to leave that evening at six o'clock.

"The train will be made up about four," a good-natured official said to him, "and you had best be here by that time so as to get a corner seat, for I can tell you that makes all the difference on a journey like this. If you like to take your ticket at once you can register that trunk of yours straight on to Denver, and then you won't have any more trouble about it."

"Of course we stop to take our meals on the way?"

"Yes; but if you take my advice you will do as most of them do, get a big basket and lay in a stock of bread and cooked meat, cheese, and anything you fancy, then you will only have to go out and get a cup of tea at the stopping-places. It comes a good bit cheaper, and you get done before those who take their meals, and can slip back into the cars again quick and keep your corner seat. There ain't much ceremony in emigrant trains, and it is first come first served."

"How long shall we be in getting to Denver?"

"It will be fully a week, but there ain't any saying to a day. The emigrant trains just jog along as they can between the freight trains and the fast ones, and get shunted off a bit to let the expresses pass them."

Thanking the official for his advice, Tom took his ticket, registered his trunk, and then went out and strolled about the streets of New York until three o'clock. He took the advice as to provisions, and getting a small hamper laid in a stock of food sufficient for three or four days. The platform from which the train was to start was already occupied by a considerable number of emigrants, but when the train came up he was able to secure a corner seat. The cars were all packed with their full complement of passengers. They were open from end to end, with a passage down the middle. Other cars were added as the train filled up, but not until all the places were already occupied. The majority of the passengers were men, but there were a considerable number of women, and still more children; and Tom congratulated himself on learning from the conversation of those around him that a good many were not going beyond Chicago, and that almost all would leave the train at stations between that place and Omaha.

The journey to Chicago was the most unpleasant experience Tom had ever gone through. The heat, the dust, and the close confinement seemed to tell on the tempers of everyone. The children fidgeted perpetually, the little ones and the babies cried, the women scolded, and the men grumbled and occasionally quarrelled. It was even worse at night than during the day; the children indeed were quieter, for they lay on the floor of the passage and slept in comparative comfort, but for the men and women there was no change of position, no possibility of rest. The backs of the seats were low, and except for the fortunate ones by the windows there was no rest for the head; but all took uneasy naps with their chins leaning forward on their chest, or sometimes with their heads resting on their neighbour's shoulder. Tom did not retain his corner seat, but resigned it a few hours after starting to a weary woman with a baby in her arms who sat next to him. He himself, strong as he was, felt utterly worn out by the fatigue and sleeplessness.

Beyond Chicago there was somewhat more room, and it was possible to make a change of position. Beyond Omaha it was much better; the train was considerably faster and the number of passengers comparatively few. He now generally got a seat to himself and could put his feet up. The people were also, for the most part, acquainted with the country, and he was able to learn a good deal from their conversation. There were but few women or children among them, for except near the stations of the railway, settlements were very rare; and the men were for the most part either miners, ranchemen, or mechanics, going to the rising town of Denver, or bound on the long journey across the plains to Utah or California. It was on the eighth day after starting that Denver was reached.

Before leaving the ship Tom had put on his working clothes and a flannel shirt, and had disposed of his black suit, for a small sum, to a fellow-passenger who intended to remain at New York. This had somewhat lightened his portmanteau, but he was glad when he found that there were vehicles at the station to convey passengers up the hill to Denver, which was some three miles away, and many hundred feet above it. He was too tired to set about finding the Empire Saloon, but put up at the hotel at which the omnibus stopped, took a bath and a hearty meal, and then went straight to bed. After breakfast the next morning he at once set out. He had no difficulty in finding the whereabouts of the Empire Saloon, which he learned from the clerk of the hotel was a small place frequented almost entirely by miners. Its appearance was not prepossessing. It had been built in the earliest days of Denver, and was a rough erection. The saloon was low, its bare rafters were darkly coloured by smoke, a number of small tables stood on the sanded floor, and across the farther end of the room ran a bar. On shelves behind this stood a number of black bottles, and a man in his shirt sleeves was engaged in washing up glasses. Two or three rough-looking men in coloured flannel shirts, with the bottoms of their trousers tucked into high boots, were seated at the tables smoking and drinking.

"I am expecting a letter for me here," Tom said to the man behind the bar. "My name is Wade."

"The boss is out now," the man said. "He will be here in an hour or so. If there is anything for you he will know about it."

"Thank you. I will come again in an hour," Tom replied. The man nodded shortly, and went on with his work. When Tom returned, the bar-tender said to a man who was sitting at one of the tables talking to the miners, "This is the chap I told you of as was here about the letter."

"Sit right down," the man said to Tom, "I will talk with you presently; "and he continued his conversation in a low tone with the miners. It was nearly half an hour before he concluded it. Then he rose, walked across the room to Tom, and held out his hand.

"Shake, young fellow," he said; "that is, if you are the chap Straight Harry told me might turn up here some day."

"I expect I am the fellow," Tom said with a smile. "My uncle's name is Harry Wade."

"Yes, that is his name; although he is always called Straight Harry. Yes, I have got a letter for you. Come along with me." He led the way into a small room behind the saloon, that served at once as his bed-room and office, and motioned to Tom to sit down on the only chair; then going to a cupboard he took out a tin canister, and opening it shook out half a dozen letters on to the table.

"That is yourn," he said, picking one out.

It was directed to Tom, and contained but a few lines. *"If you come I have gone west. Pete Hoskings will tell you all he knows about me and put you on the line. Your affectionate uncle."*

"Are you Mr. Hoskings?" he asked the landlord.

"I am Pete Hoskings," the man said. "There ain't been no Mister to my name as ever I can remember."

"My uncle tells me that you will be able to direct me to him, and will put me on the line."

"It would take a darn sight cuter fellow than I am to direct you to him at present," the man said with a laugh. "Straight Harry went away from here three months ago, and he might be just anywhere now. He may be grubbing away in a mine, he may be hunting and trapping, or he may have been wiped out by the Indians. I know where he intended to go, at least in a general sort of way. He did tell me he meant to stay about there, and it may be he has done so. He said if he moved away and got a chance he would send me word; but as there ain't nary a post-office within about five hundred miles of where he is, his only chance of sending a letter would be by a hunter who chanced to be going down to the settlements, and who, like enough, would put it into his hunting-shirt and never give it another thought. So whether he has stayed there or not is more nor I can say."

"And where is *there*?" Tom asked.

"It is among the hills to the west of the Colorado River, which ain't much, seeing as the Colorado is about two thousand miles long. However, I can put you closer than that, for he showed me on a map the bit of country he intended to work. He said he would be back here in six months from the time he started; and that if you turned up here I was either to tell you the best way of getting there, or to keep you here until he came back. Well, I may say at once that there ain't no best way; there is only one way, and that is to get on a pony and ride there, and a mighty bad way it is. The only thing for you to do is to keep on west along the caravan tract. You have to cross the Green River,—that is the name of the Colorado on its upper course. Fort Bridger is the place for you to start from, but you have got to wait there until you sight some one or other bound south; for as to going by yourself, it would be a sight better to save yourself all trouble by putting that Colt hanging there to your head, and pulling the trigger. It is a bad country, and it is full of bad Indians, and there ain't many, even of the oldest hands, who care to risk their lives by going where Straight Harry has gone.

"I did all I could to keep him from it; but he is just as obstinate as a mule when he has made up his mind to a thing. I know him well, for we worked as mates for over a year down on the Yuba in California. We made a good pile, and as I had got a wife and wanted to settle I came back east. This place had a couple of dozen houses then; but I saw it was likely to boom, so I settled down and set up this saloon and sent for my wife to come west to me. If she had lived I should have been in a sight bigger place by this time; but she died six months after she got here, and then I did not care a continental one way or the other; and I like better to stop here, where I meet my old mates and can do as I like, than to run a big hotel. It ain't much to look at, but it suits me, and I am content to know that I could buy up the biggest place here if I had a fancy to. I don't take much money now, but I did when the place was young; and I bought a few lots of land, and you may bet they have turned out worth having. Well, don't you act rashly in this business. Another three months your uncle will turn up, if he is alive; and if he don't turn up at all I dare say I can put you into a soft thing. If you go on it is about ten to one you get scalped before you find him. Where are you staying?"

"At the Grand. The omnibus stopped there last night."

"Well, you stay there for a week and think it over. You have got to learn about the country west of the Colorado. You had best come here to do that. You might stay a month at the Grand and not find a soul who could tell you anything worth knowing, but there ain't a day when you couldn't meet men here who have either been there themselves or have heard tell of it from men who have."

"Are the natives friendly now?" Tom asked. "In a letter he wrote two years ago to us, my uncle said that he should put off going to a part of the country he wanted to prospect until the Indians were quiet."

"The darned critters are never either friendly or quiet. A red-skin is pizen, take him when you will. The only difference is, that sometimes they go on the war-path and sometimes they don't; but you may bet that they are always ready to take a white man's scalp if they get a chance."

"Well, I am very much obliged to you for your advice, which I will certainly take; that is, I will not decide for a few days, and will come in here and talk to the miners and learn what I can about it."

"You can hear at once," the landlord said. He stepped back into the saloon, and said to the two men with whom he had been talking: "Boys, this young chap is a Britisher, and he has come out all the way to join Straight Harry, who is an uncle of his. Straight Harry is with Ben Gulston and Sam Hicks, and they are prospecting somewhere west of the Colorado. He wants to join them. Now, what do you reckon his chances would be of finding them out and dropping in on their camp-fire?"

The men looked at Tom with open eyes.

"Waal," one of them drawled, "I should reckon you would have just about the same chance of getting to the North Pole if you started off on foot, as you would of getting to Straight Harry with your hair on."

Tom laughed. "That is not cheering," he said.

"It ain't. I don't say as an old hand on the plains might not manage it. He would know the sort of place Harry and his mates would be likely to be prospecting, he would know the ways of the red-skins and how to travel among them without ever leaving a trail or making a smoke, but even for him it would be risky work, and not many fellows would care to take the chances even if they knew the country well. But for a tenderfoot to start out on such a job would be downright foolishness. There are about six points wanted in a man for such a journey. He has got to be as hard and tough as leather, to be able to go for days without food or drink, to know the country well, to sleep when he does sleep with his ears open, to be up to every red-skin trick, to be able to shoot straight enough to hit a man plumb centre at three hundred yards at least, and to hit a dollar at twenty yards sartin with his six-shooter. If you feel as you have got all them qualifications you can start off as soon as you like, and the chances aren't more'n twenty to one agin your finding him."

"I haven't anyone of them," Tom said.

"Waal, it is something if you know that, young chap. It is not every tenderfoot who would own up as much. You stick to it that you don't know anything, and at the same time do your best to learn something, and you will do in time. You look a clean-built young chap, and you could not have a better teacher than Straight Harry. What he don't know, whether it is about prospecting for gold or hunting for beasts, ain't worth knowing, you bet. What is your name, mate?"

"Tom Wade."

"Waal, let us drink. It ain't like you, Pete, to keep a stranger dry as long as you have been doing."

"He ain't up to our customs yet," the landlord said, as he moved off towards the bar.

"It is a custom everywhere," the miner said reprovingly, "for folks to stand drink to a stranger; and good Bourbon hurts no man."

The landlord placed a bottle and four glasses on the counter. Each of the miners filled his glass for himself, and the bottle was then handed to Tom, who followed their example, as did Hoskings.

"Here is luck to you," the miner said, as he lifted his glass. Three glasses were set down empty, but Tom had to stop half-way with his to cough violently.

"It is strong stuff," he said apologetically, "and I never drank spirits without water before. I had a glass of grog-and-water on board a ship sometimes, but it has always been at least two parts of water to one of spirits."

"We mostly drink our liquor straight out here," the miner said. "But I am not saying it is the best way, especially for one who ain't used to it, but you have got to learn to do it if you are going to live long in this country."

"Standing drinks round is a custom here," Pete Hoskings explained, seeing that Tom looked a little puzzled, "and there ain't no worse insult than to refuse to drink with a man. There have been scores of men shot, ay, and hundreds, for doing so. I don't say that you may not put water in, but if you refuse to drink you had best do it with your hand on the butt of your gun, for you will want to get it out quick, I can tell you."

"There is one advantage in such a custom anyhow," Tom said, "it will keep anyone who does not want to drink from entering a saloon at all."

"That is so, lad," Pete Hoskings said heartily. "I keep a saloon, and have made money by it, but for all that I say to every young fellow who hopes to make his way some time, keep out of them altogether. In country places you must go to a saloon to get a square meal, but everyone drinks tea or coffee with their food, and there is no call to stay in the place a minute after you have finished. Calling for drinks round has been the ruin of many a good man; one calls first, then another calls, and no one likes to stand out of it, and though you may only have gone in for one glass, you may find you will have to drink a dozen before you get out."

"Why, you are a downright temperance preacher, Pete," one of the miners laughed.

"I don't preach to a seasoned old hoss like you, Jerry. I keep my preaching for those who may benefit by it, such as the youngster here; but I say to him and to those like him, you keep out of saloons. If you don't do that, you will find yourself no forwarder when you are fifty than you are now, while there are plenty of openings all over the country for any bright young fellow who will keep away from liquor."

"Thank you," Tom said warmly; "I will follow your advice, which will be easy enough. Beyond a glass of beer with my dinner and a tot of grog, perhaps once in three months when I have gone on board a ship, and did not like to say no, I have never touched it, and have no wish to do so."

"Stick to that, lad; stick to that. You will find many temptations, but you set your face hard against them, and except when you come upon a hard man bent on kicking up a muss, you will find folks will think none the worse of you when you say to them straight, 'I am much obliged to you all the same, but I never touch liquor.'"

Tom remained four days at the hotel, spending a good deal of his time at the saloon, where he met many miners, all of whom endorsed what the first he had spoken to had said respecting the country, and the impossibility of anyone but an old hand among the mountains making his way there.

On the fourth evening he said to Pete Hoskings: "I see that your advice was good, and that it would be madness for me to attempt to go by myself, but I don't see why I should not ride to Fort Bridger; not of course by myself, but with one of the caravans going west. It would be a great deal better for me to do that and to learn something of the plains and camping than to stay here for perhaps three months. At Fort Bridger I shall be able to learn more about the country, and might join some hunting party and gain experience that way. I might find other prospectors going up among the hills, and even if it were not near where my uncle is to be found, I should gain by learning something, and should not be quite a greenhorn when I join him."

"Well, that is sensible enough," Pete Hoskings said, "and I don't know as I can say anything against it. You certainly would not be doing any good for yourself here, and I don't say that either an hotel or a saloon is the best place for you. I will think it over, and will let you know when you come round in the morning; maybe I can put you a little in the way of carrying it out."

The next morning when Tom went to the saloon, Jerry Curtis, one of the miners he had first met there, was sitting chatting with Pete Hoskings.

"I had Jerry in my thoughts when I spoke to you last night, Tom," the latter said. "I knew he was just starting west again, and thought I would put the matter to him. He says he has no objection to your travelling with him as far as Fort Bridger, where maybe he will make a stay himself. There ain't no one as knows the plains much better than he does, and he can put you up to more in the course of a month than you would learn in a year just travelling with a caravan with farmers bound west."

"I should be very much obliged indeed," Tom said delightedly. "It would be awfully good of you, Jerry, and I won't be more trouble than I can help."

"I don't reckon you will be any trouble at all," the miner said. "I was never set much on travelling alone as some men are. I ain't much of a talker, but I ain't fond of going two or three months without opening my mouth except to put food and drink into it. So if you think you will like it I shall be glad enough to take you. I know Straight Harry well, and I can see you are teachable, and not set upon your own opinions as many young fellows I have met out here are, but ready to allow that there are some things as men who have been at them all their lives may know a little more about than they do. So you may take it that it is a bargain. Now, what have you got in the way of outfit?"

"I have not got anything beyond flannel shirts, and rough clothes like these."

"They are good enough as far as they go. Two flannel shirts, one on and one off, is enough for any man. Two or three pairs of thick stockings. Them as is very particular can carry an extra pair of breeches in case of getting caught in a storm, though for myself I think it is just as well to let your things dry on you. You want a pair of high boots, a buffalo robe, and a couple of blankets, one with a hole cut in the middle to put your head through; that does as a cloak, and is like what the Mexicans call a poncho. You don't want a coat or waistcoat; there ain't no good in them. All you want to carry you can put in your saddle-bag. Get a pair of the best blankets you can find. I will go with you and choose them for you. You want a thing that will keep you warm when you sleep, and shoot off the rain in bad weather. Common blankets are no better than a sponge. Then, of course, you must have a six-shooter and a rifle. No man in his senses would start across the plains without them. It is true there ain't much fear of red-skins between here and Bridger, but there is never any saying when the varmint may be about. Can you shoot?"

"No; I never fired off a rifle or a pistol in my life."

"Well, you had better take a good stock of powder and ball, and you can practise a bit as you go along. A man ain't any use out on these plains if he cannot shoot. I have got a pony; but you must buy one, and a saddle, and fixings. We will buy another between us to carry our swag. But you need not trouble about the things, I will get all that fixed."

"Thank you very much. How much do you suppose it will all come to?"

"Never you mind what it comes to," Pete Hoskings said roughly. "I told your uncle that if you turned up I would see you through. What you have got to get I shall pay for, and when Straight Harry turns up we shall square it. If he don't turn up at all, there is no harm done. This is my business, and you have got nothing to do with it."

Tom saw that he should offend Hoskings if he made any demur, and the kind offer was really a relief to him. He had thirty pounds still in his belt, but he had made a mental calculation of the cost of the things Jerry had considered essential, and found that the cost of a horse and saddle, of half another horse, of the rifle, six-shooter, ammunition, blankets, boots, and provisions for the journey, must certainly amount up to more than that sum, and would leave him without any funds to live on till he met his uncle.

He was so anxious to proceed that he would have made no excuse, although he saw that he might find himself in a very difficult position. Pete's insistence, therefore, on taking all expenses upon himself, was a considerable relief to him; for although determined to go, he had had an uneasy consciousness that it was a foolish step. He therefore expressed his warm thanks.

"There, that is enough said about it," the latter growled out. "The money is nothing to me one way or the other, and it would be hard if I couldn't do this little thing for my old mate's nephew. When are you thinking of making a start, Jerry?"

"The sooner the better. I have been four months here already and have not struck a vein, that is, not one really worth working, and the sooner I make a fresh start the better. To-day is Wednesday. There will be plenty of time to get all the things to-day and to-morrow, and we will start at daylight on Friday. You may as well come with me, Tom, and learn something about the prices of things. There are some Indians camped three miles away. We will walk over there first and pick up a couple of ponies. I know they have got a troop of them, that is what they come here to sell. They only arrived yesterday, so we shall have the pick of them."

Before starting there was a short conversation between Jerry and the landlord, and then the former put on his broad-brimmed hat.

"Have you seen any red-skins yet?"

"I saw a few at some of the stations the train stopped at between this and Omaha."

"Those fellows are mostly Indians who have been turned out of their tribes for theft or drunkenness, and they hang about the stations to sell moccasins and other things their squaws make, to fresh arrivals.

"The fellows you are going to see are Navahoes, though not good specimens of the tribe, or they would not be down here to sell ponies. Still, they are a very different sort from those you have seen."

An hour's walking took them to a valley, in which the Indians were encamped. There were eight wigwams. Some women paused in their work and looked round at the newcomers. Their dogs ran up barking furiously, but were driven back by a volley of stones thrown by three or four boys, with so good an aim that they went off with sharp yelps. Jerry strolled along without paying any attention to the dogs or boys towards a party of men seated round a fire. One of them rose as they approached.

"My white brothers are welcome," he said courteously. "There is room by the fire for them," and he motioned to them to sit down by his side. A pipe, composed of a long flat wooden stem studded with brass nails, with a bowl cut out of red pipe-stone, was now handed round, each taking a short puff.

"Does my brother speak the language of the Navahoes?" the chief asked in that tongue.

"I can get along with it," Jerry said, "as I can with most of your Indian dialects."

"It is good," the chief said. "My brother is wise; he must have wandered much."

"I have been a goodish bit among your hills, chief. Have you come from far?"

"The moon was full when we left our village."

"Ah, then you have been a fortnight on the road. Well, chief, I have come here to trade. I want to buy a couple of ponies."

The chief said a word or two to a boy standing near, and he with four or five others at once started up the valley, and in a few minutes returned with a drove of Indian ponies.

"They are not a bad lot," Jerry said to Tom.

"They don't look much, Jerry."

"Indian ponies never look much, but one of those ponies would gallop an eastern-bred horse to a stand-still."

Jerry got up and inspected some of the horses closely, and presently picked out two of them; at a word from the chief two of the lads jumped on their backs and rode off on them at full speed, and then wheeling round returned to the spot from where they started.

"My white brother is a judge of horses," the chief said; "he has picked out the best of the lot."

"There are three or four others quite as good," Jerry said carelessly. "Now, chief, how many blankets, how much powder and lead, and what else do you want for those two horses?"

The chief stated his demands, to which Jerry replied: "You said just now, chief, that I was a wise man; but it seems that you must regard me as a fool."

For half an hour an animated argument went on. Two or three times Jerry got up, and they started as if to quit the village, but each time the chief called them back. So animated were their gestures and talk that Tom had serious fears that they were coming to blows, but their voices soon fell and the talk became amicable again. At last Jerry turned to Tom.

"The bargain is struck," he said; "but he has got the best of me, and has charged an outrageous sum for them." Then, in his own language, he said to the chief:

"At noon to-morrow you will send the ponies down to the town. I will meet them at the big rock, half a mile this side of it, with the trade goods."

"They shall be there," the chief said, "though I am almost giving them to you."

As they walked away, Tom said:

"So you have paid more than you expected, Jerry?"

"No, I have got them a bargain; only it would never have done to let the chief know I thought so, or the horses would not have turned up to-morrow. I expect they have all been stolen from some other tribe. The two I have got are first-rate animals, and the goods will come to about fourteen pounds. I shall ride one of them myself, and put our swag on my own pony. That has been a very good stroke of business; they would never have sold them at that price if they had been honestly come by."

Chapter III.
On the Plains

The purchase of a buffalo robe, blankets, boots, and a Colt's revolver occupied but a short time, but the rifle was a much more difficult matter.

"You can always rely upon a Colt," the miner said, "but rifles are different things; and as your life may often depend upon your shooting-iron carrying straight, you have got to be mighty careful about it. A gun that has got the name of being a good weapon will fetch four times as much as a new one."

Denver was but a small place; there was no regular gunsmith's shop, but rifles and pistols were sold at almost every store in the town. In this quest Jerry was assisted by Pete Hoskings, who knew of several men who would be ready to dispose of their rifles. Some of these weapons were taken out into the country and tried at marks by the two men. They made what seemed to Tom wonderful shooting, but did not satisfy Hoskings.

"I should like the youngster to have a first-rate piece," he said, "and I mean to get him one if I can. There are two of these would do if we can't get a better, but if there is a first-rate one to be had in this township I will have it." Suddenly he exclaimed, "I must have gone off my head, and be going downright foolish! Why, I know the very weapon. You remember Billy the scout?"

"In course I do, everyone knew him. I heard he had gone down just before I got back here."

"That is so, Jerry. You know he had a bit of a place up in the hills, four or five miles from here, where he lived with that Indian wife of his when he was not away. I went out to see him a day or two afore he died. I asked him if there was anything I could do for him. He said no, his squaw would get on well enough there. She had been alone most of her time, and would wrestle on just as well when he had gone under. He had a big garden-patch which she cultivated, and brought the things down into the town here. They always fetch a good price. Why more people don't grow them I can't make out; it would pay better than gold-seeking, you bet. He had a few hundred dollars laid by, and he said they might come in handy to her if she fell sick, or if things went hard in winter. Well, you remember his gun?"

"In course—his gun was nigh as well known as Billy himself. He used to call it Plumb-centre. You don't mean to say she hasn't sold it?"

"She hasn't; at least I should have been sure to hear if she had. I know several of the boys who went to the funeral wanted to buy it, and offered her long prices for it too; but she wouldn't trade. I will ride over there this evening and see what I can do about it. She will sell to me if she sells to anyone, for she knows I was a great chum of Billy's, and I have done her a few good turns. She broke her leg some years back when he was away, and luckily enough I chanced to ride over there the next day. Being alone and without anyone to help, she would have got on badly. I sent a surgeon up to her, and got a red-skin woman to go up to nurse her. I don't wonder she did not like to sell Billy's piece, seeing he was so famous with it, and I feel sure money would not do it; but perhaps I can talk her into it." The next morning the articles agreed upon as the price of the horses were packed on Jerry's pony, and they went out to the meeting-place.

"It is twenty minutes early," Jerry said, as Tom consulted his watch, "and the red-skins won't be here till it is just twelve o'clock. A red-skin is never five minutes before or five minutes after the time he has named for a meeting. It may have been set six months before, and at a place a thousand miles away, but just at the hour, neither before nor after, he will be there. A white man will keep the appointment; but like enough he will be there the night before, will make his camp, sleep, and cook a meal or two, but he does not look for the red-skin till exactly the hour named, whether it is sunrise or sunset or noon. Red-skins ain't got many virtues,—least there ain't many of them has, though I have known some you could trust all round as ready as any white man,—but for keeping an appointment they licks creation."

A few minutes before twelve o'clock three Indians were seen coming down the valley on horseback. They were riding at a leisurely pace, and it was exactly the hour when they drew rein in front of Tom and his companion. Jerry had already unloaded his pony and had laid out the contents of the pack. First he proceeded to examine the two ponies, to make sure that they were the same he had chosen.

"That is all right," he said; "they would hardly have tried to cheat us over that—they would know that it would not pay with me. There, chief, is your exchange. You will see that the blankets are of good quality. There is the keg of powder, the bar of lead, ten plugs of tobacco, the cloth for the squaws, and all the other things agreed on."

The chief examined them carefully, and nodded his satisfaction. "If all the pale-faces dealt as fairly with the red man as you have done there would not be so much trouble between them," he said.

"That is right enough, chief; it can't be gainsaid that a great many, ay, I might say the most part, of the traders are rogues. But they would cheat us just the same as they would you, and often do take us in. I have had worthless goods passed off on me many a time; and I don't blame you a bit if you put a bullet into the skull of a rogue who has cheated you, for I should be mightily inclined to do the same myself."

No more words were wasted; the lads who had ridden the ponies down made up the goods in great bundles and went up the valley with their chief, while Jerry and Tom took the plaited leather lariats which were round the ponies' necks and returned to Denver. A saddle of Mexican pattern, with high peak and cantle, massive wooden framework, huge straps and heavy stirrups, was next bought. Jerry folded a horse-rug and tried it in different positions on the horse's back until the saddle fitted well upon it.

"That is the thing that you have got to be most particular about, Tom. If the saddle does not sit right the horse gets galled, and when a horse once gets galled he ain't of much use till he is well again, though the Indians ride them when they are in a terrible state; but then they have got so many horses that, unless they are specially good, they don't hold them of any account. You see the saddle is so high that there is good space between it and the backbone, and the pressure comes fair on the ribs, so the ponies don't get galled if the blankets are folded properly. The Indians do not use saddles, but ride either on a pad or just a folded blanket, and their ponies are always getting galled."

"The saddle is tremendously heavy."

"It is heavy, but a few pounds don't make much difference to the horse one way or the other, so that he is carrying it comfortably. The saddles would be no good if they were not made strong, for a horse may put his foot in a hole and come down head over heels, or may tumble down a precipice, and the saddle would be smashed up if it were not pretty near as strong as cast-iron. Out on the plains a man thinks as much of his saddle as he does of his horse, and more. If his horse dies he will put the saddle on his head and carry it for days rather than part with it, for he knows he won't be long before he gets a horse again. He can buy one for a few charges of powder and ball from the first friendly Indians he comes across, or he may get one given to him if he has nothing to exchange for it, or if he comes across a herd of wild horses he can crease one."

"What is creasing a horse?" Tom asked.

"Well, it is a thing that wants a steady hand, for you have got to hit him just on the right spot—an inch higher, you will miss him; half an inch lower, you will kill him. You have got to put a bullet through his neck two or three inches behind the ears and just above the spine. Of course if you hit the spine you kill him, and he is no good except to give you a meal or two if you are hard-up for food; but if the ball goes through the muscles of the neck, just above the spine, the shock knocks him over as surely as if you had hit him in the heart. It stuns him, and you have only got to run up and put your lariat round his neck, and be ready to mount him as soon as he rises, which he will do in two or three minutes, and he will be none the worse for the shock;

in fact you will be able to break him in more easily than if you had caught him by the rope."

Jerry then adjusted his own saddle to the other Indian horse.

"Can you ride?" he asked.

"No, I have never had any chance of learning at home."

"Well, you had better have a lesson at once. This is a good way for a beginner; "and he took a blanket, and having rolled it up tightly, strapped it over the peak of the saddle and down the flaps.

"There," he said. "You get your knees against that, and what with the high peak and the high cantle you can hardly be chucked out anyhow, that is, if the horse does not buck; but I will try him as to that before you mount. We will lead them out beyond the town, we don't want to make a circus of ourselves in the streets; besides, if you get chucked, you will fall softer there than you would on the road. But first of all we will give them a feed of corn. You see they are skeary of us at present. Indian horses are always afraid of white men at first, just as white men's horses are afraid of Indians. A feed of corn will go a long way towards making us good friends, for you may be sure they have never had a feed in their lives beyond what they could pick up for themselves."

The horses snuffed the corn with some apprehension when it was held out towards them, backing away from the sieves with their ears laid back; but seeing that no harm came to them they presently investigated the food more closely, and at last took a mouthful, after which they proceeded to eat greedily, their new masters patting their necks and talking to them while they did so. Then their saddles and bridles were put on, and they were led out of the stable and along the streets. At first they were very fidgety and wild at the unaccustomed sights and sounds, but their fear gradually subsided, and by the time they were well in the country they went along quietly enough.

"Now you hold my horse, Tom, and I will try yours."

Jerry mounted and galloped away; in ten minutes he returned.

"He will do," he said as he dismounted. "He is fresh yet and wants training. I don't suppose he has been ridden half a dozen times, but with patience and training he will turn out a first-rate beast. I could see they were both fast when those boys rode them. I don't wonder the chief asked what, for an Indian pony, was a mighty long price, though it was cheap enough for such good animals. He must have two or three uncommon good ones at home or he would never have parted with them, for when an Indian gets hold of an extra good pony no price will tempt him to sell it, for a man's life on the plains often depends on the speed and stay of his horse. Now, I will take a gallop on my own, and when I come back you can mount and we will ride on quietly together.

"There is not much difference between them," he said on his return. "Yours is a bit faster. Pete told me to get you the best horse I could find, and I fixed upon yours, directly my eye fell upon him, as being the pick of the drove. But this is a good one too, and will suit me as well as yours, for he is rather heavier, and will carry me better than yours would do on a long journey. Now climb up into your saddle."

Jerry laughed at the difficulty Tom had in lifting his leg over the high cantle. "You will have to practise presently putting your hands on the saddle and vaulting into it. Half a minute in mounting may make all the difference between getting away and being rubbed out. When you see the red-skins coming yelling down on you fifty yards away, and your horse is jumping about as scared as you are, it is not an easy matter to get on to its back if you have got to put your foot in the stirrup first. You have got to learn to chuck yourself straight into your seat whether you are standing still or both on the run. There, how do you feel now?"

"I feel regularly wedged into the saddle."

"That is right. I will take up the stirrups a hole, then you will get your knees firmer against the blanket. It is better to learn to ride without it, even if you do get chucked off a few times, but as we start to-morrow you have no time for that. In a few days, when you get at home in the saddle, we will take off the blanket, and you have got to learn to hold on by your knees and by the balance of your body. Now we will be moving on."

As soon as the reins were slackened the horses started together at an easy canter.

"That is their pace," Jerry said. "Except on a very long journey, when he has got squaws and baggage with him, a red-skin never goes at a walk, and the horses will keep on at this lope for hours. That is right. Don't sit so stiffly; you want your legs to be stiff and keeping a steady grip, but from your hips you want to be as slack as possible, just giving to the horse's action, the same way you give on board ship when vessels are rolling. That is better. Ah! here comes Pete. I took this way because I knew it was the line he would come back by—and, by gosh, he has got the rifle, sure enough!"

Pete had seen them, and was waving the gun over his head.

"I've got it," he said as he reined up his horse when he met them. "It was a stiff job, for she did not like to part with it. I had to talk to her a long time. I put it to her that when she died the gun would have to go to someone, and I wanted it for a nephew of Straight Harry, whom she knew well enough; that it was for a young fellow who was safe to turn out a great hunter and Indian fighter like her husband, and that he would be sure to do credit to Plumb-centre, and make the gun as famous in his hands as it had been in her husband's. That fetched her. She said I had been kind to her, and though she could not have parted with the gun for money, she would do it, partly to please me, and partly because she knew that Straight Harry had been a friend of her husband's, and had fought by his side, and that the young brave I spoke of, would be likely to do credit to Plumb-centre. Her husband, she said, would be glad to know that it was in such good hands. So she handed it over to me. She would not hear of taking money for it; indeed, I did not press it, knowing that she would feel that it was almost a part of her husband; but I will make it up to her in other ways. There, Tom; there is as good a shooting-iron as there is in all the territories."

"Thank you very much indeed, Pete. I shall value it immensely, and I only hope that some day I shall be able to do credit to it, as the poor woman said."

There was nothing particular in the appearance of the rifle. It was a plainly-finished piece, with a small bore and heavy metal.

"It don't look much," Jerry said, "but it is a daisy, you bet."

"We will try a shot with it, Jerry. She gave me the bag of bullets and a box of patches and his powder-horn with it. We will see what it will do in our hands, we are both pretty good shots."

He loaded the rifle carefully.

"You see that bit of black rock cropping out of the hill-side. I guess it is about two hundred and fifty yards away, and is about the size a red-skin's head would be if he were crawling through the grass towards us. Will you shoot first or shall I?"

"Fire away, Pete."

Hoskings took a steady aim and fired.

"You have hit it," Jerry exclaimed. "Just grazed it at the top."

They walked across to the rock; there was a chip just on the top.

"It was a good shot, Pete; especially considering how you are out of practice. If it had been a red-skin it would have stunned him sure, for I doubt whether it is not too high by a quarter of an inch or so, to have finished him altogether."

"It would have cut his top-knot off, Jerry, and that is all. I doubt whether it would have even touched his skin."

They returned to the spot where Pete had fired, and Jerry threw himself down on the grass and levelled his rifle.

"That is not fair, Jerry," Pete protested.

"It would not be fair if I was shooting against you, but we are only trying the rifle, and if that rock were a red-skin you may be sure that I should be lying down."

He fired; and on going to the stone again they found that the bullet had struck it fair, within an inch of its central point.

"That is something like a rifle," Jerry said delighted. "Now, Tom, you shall have a shot."

As they walked to the shooting-point, Jerry showed the lad how to hold the rifle, instructed him as to the backsight, and showed him how to get the foresight exactly on the nick of the backsight. "You must just see the bead as if it were resting in the nick, and the object you aim at must just show above the top point of the bead." He showed him how to load, and then told him to lie down, as he had done, on his chest, and to steady the rifle with the left arm, the elbow being on the ground. "You must be quite comfortable," he said; "it is of no use trying to shoot if you are in a cramped position. Now, take a steady aim, and the moment you have got the two sights in a line on the rock, press the trigger steadily. Press pretty hard; it is only a pull of about two pounds, but it is wonderful how stiff a trigger feels the first time you pull at it. You need not be at all afraid of the kick. If you press the butt tightly against your shoulder you will hardly feel it, for there is plenty of weight in the barr'l, and it carries but a small charge of powder. You won't want to shoot at anything much beyond this range, but sometimes you may have to try at four or five hundred yards when you are in want of a dinner. In that case you can put in a charge and a half of powder. Now, are you comfortable? You need not grip so hard with your left hand, the gun only wants to rest between your thumb and fingers. That is better. Now take a steady aim, and the moment you have got it press the trigger. Well done! that is a good shot for a first. You hit the dust an inch or two to the right of the stone. If it had been a red-skin you would have hit him in the shoulder. You will do, lad, and by the time we get to Fort Bridger I guess you will bring down a stag as clean as nine out of ten hunters."

"Don't get into the way of waiting too long before you fire, Tom," Pete Hoskings said. "Better to try to shoot too quick to begin with than to be too long about it. When you have made up your mind that you are going to shoot, get your bead on your mark and fire at once. You may want to hit a red-skin's head as he looks out from behind a tree, and to do that you must fire the instant you see him or he will be in again. One of the best shots I ever saw never used to raise his gun to his shoulder at all. He just dropped his piece into the hollow of his left hand, and would fire as he touched it. He did not seem to take any aim at all, but his bullet was sartin to hit the thing he wanted to, even if it were no bigger than an orange. He could not tell himself how he did it. 'I seen the thing and I fired, Pete,' he would say; 'the gun seems to point right of its own accord, I have not anything to say to it.' You see, shooting is a matter of eye. Some men may shoot all their lives, and they will never be more than just respectable, while others shoot well the first time that a gun is put in their hands. Want of nerve is what spoils half men's shooting; that and taking too long an aim. Well, it is time for us to be mounting and getting back. I have got to see that the dinner is all ready. I never can trust that black scoundrel, Sam, to do things right while I am away."

The preparations for the journey were completed by the evening. "Now mind, Tom," Pete Hoskings said the last thing before going to bed, "if you don't find your uncle, or if you hear that he has got wiped out, be sure you come right back here. Whether you are cut out for a hunter or not, it will do you a world of good to stick to the life until you get four or five years older and settle as to how you like to fix yourself, for there ain't no better training than a few years out on the plains, no matter what you do afterwards. I will find a good chum for you, and see you through it, both for the sake of my old mate, Straight Harry, and because I have taken a liking to you myself."

"Why do you call my uncle Straight Harry?" Tom asked, after thanking Pete for his promise. "Is he so very upright?"

"No, lad, no; it ain't nothing to do with that. There are plenty more erect men than him about. He is about the size of Jerry, though, maybe a bit taller. No; he got to be called Straight Harry because he was a square man, a chap everyone could trust. If he said he would do a thing he would do it; there weren't no occasion for any papers to bind him. When he said a thing you could bet on it. You could buy a mine on his word: if he said it was good you need not bother to take a journey to look at it, you knew it was right there, and weren't a put-up job. Once when we were working down on the Yuba we got to a place where there were a fault in the rock, and the lode had slipped right away from us. Everyone in camp knew that we had been doing well, and we had only got to pile up a few pieces of rock at the bottom, and no one who would have seen it would have known that the lode was gone. That is what most chaps would have done, and a third chap who was working with us was all for doing it. Anyone would have given us five hundred ounces for it. Well, I didn't say nothing, it was what pretty nigh anyone on the mines would have done if he had the chance, but Harry turned on our partner like a mountain lion. 'You are a mean skunk, New Jersey,' says he. 'Do you think that I would be one to rob a man only because he would be fool enough to take a place without looking at it? We've worked to the edge of the claim both ways, and I don't reckon there is a dollar's worth of gold left in it, now that it has pettered out at the bottom, and if there was I would not work another day with a man who proposed to get up a swindle.' So as soon as he got up to the surface he told everyone that the lode had gone out and that the claim weren't worth a red cent. He and New Jersey had a big fight with fists that evening. The other was bigger than Harry, and stronger, but he were no hand with his pistol, and Harry is a dead shot; so he told New Jersey he would fight him English fashion, and Harry gave him the biggest licking I ever saw a man have. I felt pretty mean myself, you bet, for having thought of planting the thing off; but as I hadn't spoken, Harry knew nothing about it. If he had, I doubt if he would ever have given me his hand again. Yes, sir, he is a straight man all round, and there is no man better liked than Harry. Why, there are a score of men in this town who know him as I do, and, if he came to them and said, 'I have struck it rich, I will go halves with you if you will plank down twenty thousand dollars to open her up,' they would pay down the cash without another word; and, I tell you, there ain't ten men west of the Missouri of whom as much could be said."

The next morning at daybreak Jerry and Tom started. They rode due north, skirting the foot of the hills, till they reached the emigrant route, for the railway had not been carried farther than Wabash, from which point it ran south to Denver. It was a journey of some five hundred miles to Fort Bridger, and they took a month to accomplish it, sometimes following the ordinary line of travel, sometimes branching off more to the north, where game was still abundant. "That is Fort Bridger, Tom. It ain't much of a place to look at; but is, like all these forts, just a strong palisading, with a clump of wooden huts for the men in the middle. Well, the first stage of your journey is over, and you know a little more now than when you left Denver; but though I have taught you a good bit, you will want another year's practice with that shooting-iron afore you're a downright good shot; but you have come on well, and the way you brought down that stag on a run yesterday was uncommon good. You have made the most of your opportunities, and have got a steady hand and a good eye. You are all right on your horse now, and can be trusted to keep your seat if you have a pack of red-skins at your heels. You have learnt to make a camp, and to sleep comfortable on the ground; you can frizzle a bit of deer-flesh over the fire, and can bake bread as well as a good many. Six months of it and you will be a good plain's-man. I wish we had had a shot at buffalo. They are getting scarcer than they were, and do not like crossing the trail. We ain't likely to see many of them west of the Colorado; the ground gets too hilly for them, and there are too many bad lands."

"What are bad lands, Jerry?"

"They are just lands where Nature, when she made them, had got plenty of rock left, but mighty little soil or grass seed. There are bad lands all over the country, but nowhere so bad as the tract on both sides of the Green and Colorado rivers. You may ride fifty miles any way over bare rock without seeing a blade of grass unless you get down into some of the valleys, and you may die of thirst with water under your feet."

"How do you mean, Jerry?"

"The rivers there don't act like the rivers in other parts. Instead of working round the foot of the hills they just go through them. You ride along on what seems to be a plain, and you come suddenly to a crack that ain't perhaps twenty or thirty feet across, and you look down, if you have got head enough to do it, and there, two thousand feet or more below you, you see a river foaming among rocks. It ain't one river or it ain't another river as does it; every little stream from the hills cuts itself its canon and makes its way along till it meets two or three others, then they go on together, cutting deeper and deeper until they run into one of the arms of the Green River or the Colorado or the Grand.

"The Green and the Colorado are all the same river, only the upper part is called the Green. For about a thousand miles it runs through great canons. No one has ever gone down them, and I don't suppose anyone ever will; and people don't know what is the course of the river from the time it begins this game till it comes out a big river on the southern plains. You see, the lands are so bad there is no travelling across them, and the rapids are so terrible that there is no going down them. Even the Indians never go near the canons if they can help it. I believe they think the whole thing is the work of an evil spirit."

"But you said some of the valleys had grass?"

"Yes; I have gone down one or two myself from the mountains of Utah, where the stream, instead of cutting a canon for itself, has behaved for a bit in the ordinary way and made a valley. Wonderfully good places they were— plenty of grass, plenty of water, and no end of game. I have spent some months among them, and got a wonderful lot of skins, beavers principally of course, but half a dozen mountain lions and two grizzlies. I did not bring home their skins, you bet. They were too heavy, and I should not have troubled them if they had not troubled me. There was good fish, too, in the streams, and I never had a better time. The red-skins happened to be friendly, and I was with a hunter who had a red-skin wife and a dozen ponies. If it hadn't been for that I should soon have had to quit, for it ain't no good hunting if you can't carry away the skins. As it was I made a good job of it, for I got nigh a thousand dollars for my skins at Utah.

"Well, here we are at the fort. I guess we may as well make our camp outside. If you go in you have got to picket your horse here and put your baggage there and come in at gun-fire, and all sorts of things that troubles a man who is accustomed to act as he likes."

The horses were soon picketed. "I will go in first and see who is here, Tom. There are usually a lot of loafing Indians about these forts, and though it is safe enough to leave our traps, out on the plain, it will not do here. We must stay with them, or at any rate keep them in sight; besides, these two horses would be a temptation to any red-skin who happened to want an animal."

"I will wait willingly, Jerry; I should know nobody inside the fort if I went in. I will see to making a fire and boiling the kettle, and I will have supper ready at seven o'clock."

"I shall be sure to be back by that time; like enough I sha'n't be a quarter of an hour away."

It was but half an hour, indeed, before Tom saw him returning, accompanied by a tall red-skin.

"This is a friend of mine, Tom. He was a chief of the Senecas, but his tribe are nearly wiped out, and he has been all his life a hunter, and there are few of us who have been much out on the plains who don't know him. Chief, this is Straight Harry's nephew I was telling you of, who has come out here to join his uncle. Sit down, we have got some deer-flesh. Tom here knocked one over on the run at two hundred and fifty yards by as good a shot as you want to see; while it is cooking we can smoke a pipe and have a chat."

The chief gravely seated himself by the fire.

"What have you been doing since I last saw you up near the Yellowstone?"

"Leaping Horse has been hunting," the Indian said quietly, with a wave of his hand, denoting that he had been over a wide expanse of country.

"I guessed so," Jerry put in.

"And fighting with 'Rappahoes and Navahoes."

"Then you've been north and south?"

The Indian nodded. "Much trouble with both; they wanted our scalps. But four of the 'Rappahoe lodges are without a master, and there are five Navahoe widows."

"Then you were not alone?"

"Garrison was with me among the 'Rappahoes; and the Shoshone hunter, Wind-that-blows, was with me when the Navahoes came on our trail."

"They had better have left you alone, chief. Do you know the Ute country?"

"The Leaping Horse has been there. The Utes are dogs."

"They are troublesome varmint, like most of the others," Jerry agreed. "I was telling you Straight Harry is up in their country somewhere. Tom here is anxious to join him, but of course that can't be. You have not heard anything of him, I suppose?"

"The Leaping Horse was with him a week ago."

"You were, chief! Why did you not tell me so when I was saying we did not know where he was?"

"My white brother did not ask," the chief said quietly.

"That is true enough, chief, but you might have told me without asking."

The Indian made no reply, but continued to smoke his hatchet pipe tranquilly, as if the remark betrayed such ignorance of Indian manners that it was not worth replying to.

Tom took up the conversation now.

"Was it far from here that you saw him?"

"Five days' journey, if travel quick."

"Was he hunting?" Jerry asked. "Hunting, and looking for gold."

"Who had he with him?"

"Two white men. One was Ben Gulston. Leaping Horse had met him in Idaho. The other was called Sam, a big man with a red beard."

"Yes, Sam Hicks; he only came back from California a few months back, so you would not be likely to have met him before. Were they going to remain where you left them?"

The Indian shook his head. "They were going farther north."

"Farther north!" Jerry repeated. "Don't you mean farther south?"

"Leaping Horse is not mistaken, he knows his right hand from his left."

"Of course, of course, chief," the miner said apologetically; "I only thought that it was a slip of the tongue. Then if they were going farther north they must have come back in this direction."

"They were on the banks of the Big Wind River when Leaping Horse met them."

"Jerusalem!" the miner exclaimed. "What on airth are they doing there? Why, we thought they had gone down to the west of the Colorado. I told you so, chief, when I talked to you about it; and instead of that, here they are up in the country of the 'Rappahoes and Shoshones."

"They went south," the Indian said quietly, "and had trouble with the Utes and had to come back again, then they went north."

"Ah, that accounts for it. I wonder Harry didn't send word to Pete Hoskings that he had gone up to the Big Wind River. I ain't heard of there being any gold in that region, though some think that coming down through the big hills from Yellowstone Valley on the northwest, metal might be struck."

"Going to look for gold a little," the chief said, "hunt much; not stay there very long, mean to go down south again after a bit. Leaping Horse go with them."

"Oh, I see. The Utes had come upon them, and they knew that if they stopped there they would lose their scalps sooner or later, so they came up here and made north for a bit to hunt and fossick about in the hills, and then go back when the Utes had quieted down."

The chief nodded.

"Well, well, that alters the affair altogether. Whereabouts did you leave them?"

"Near the Buffalo Lake."

"Don't know it. Where does it lie?"

"On a stream that runs into the river from the west, from a valley running up near Fremont's Buttes. They were going up so as to follow the Rivière de Noir, and then either strike up across the hills to the Upper Yellowstone, or go out west and come down over the Grosventre range on to the Wyoming range, and then down through Thompson's Pass, or else skirt the foot-hills on to the Green River."

"Waal, chief, I reckon that among all those hills and mountains, one would have just about the same chance of lighting on them as you would have of finding a chipmunk in a big pine-forest."

"Couldn't find," the chief said, "but might follow. If they go fast never catch them; if wait about, hunt beaver, look for gold and silver, then might come up to them easy enough, if 'Rappahoes not catch and kill. Very bad place. Leaping Horse told them so. White brother said he think so too; but other men think they find gold somewhere, so they go on. They have got horses, of course. Three horses to ride, three horses to carry beaver-traps and food. Leaping Horse came back here to sell his skins. He had promised to meet a friend here, or he would not have left Straight Harry, who is a good man and a friend of Leaping Horse. Three men not enough in bad country."

"Do you think there would be any chance of my finding them?" Tom asked eagerly.

A slight gleam of amusement passed over the Indian's face.

"My brother is very young," he said. "He will be a brave warrior and a great hunter some day, but his eyes are not opened yet. Were he to try he would leave his scalp to dry in the 'Rappahoes' lodges."

"That is just what I told him, chief. It would be sheer madness."

The Indian made no reply, and Jerry turned the conversation.

"You don't drink spirits, chief, or I would go and get a bottle from the fort."

"Leaping Horse is not a madman," the Indian said scornfully, "that he should poison his brain with fire-water."

"Yes; I remembered, chief, that you had fallen into our ways and drink tea."

"Tea is good," the Indian said. "It is the best thing the white man has brought out on to the plains."

"That is so, chief, except tobacco. We did not bring that; but I reckon you got it from the Spaniards long ago, though maybe you knew of it before they came up from the south."

The meat was now cooked, and Tom took it off the fire and handed the pieces on the ramrod, that had served as a spit, to the others, together with some bread, poured out the tea from the kettle, and placed a bag of sugar before them. There was little talk until after the meal was over. Then the Indian and Jerry smoked steadily, while Tom took a single pipe, having only commenced the use of tobacco since he had left Denver. Presently the Indian arose.

"In the morning I will see my white friends again," he said, and without further adieu turned and walked gravely back to the fort.

Chapter IV.
Leaping Horse

"He is a fine fellow," Jerry said, after the Indian had left him. "You must have a talk with him one of these days over his adventures among the 'Rappahoes and Navahoes, who are both as troublesome rascals as are to be found on the plains. An Indian seldom talks of his adventures, but sometimes when you can get him in the right humour you may hear about them."

"He talks very fair English," Tom said.

"Yes; he has been ten years among us. He was employed for two or three years supplying the railway men with meat; but no Indian cares to hunt long in one place, and he often goes away with parties of either hunters or gold-seekers. He knows the country well, and is a first-rate shot; and men are always glad to have him with them. There is no more trusty red-skin on the plains, and he will go through fire and water for those whom he regards as his special friends. I should say he is about the one man alive who could take you to your uncle."

"Do you think he would?" Tom asked eagerly.

"Ah, that is another matter; I don't know what his plans are. If he is engaged to go with another party he will go, for he would not fail anyone to whom he had made a promise. If he isn't engaged he might perhaps do it. Not for pay, for he has little use for money. His hunting supplies him with all he wants. It gives him food, and occasionally he will go with a bundle of pelts to the nearest town, and the money he gets for them will supply him with tea and tobacco and ammunition, and such clothes as he requires, which is little enough. Buckskin is everlasting wear, and he gets his worked up for him by the women of any Indian tribe among whom he may be hunting. If he were one of these fort Indians it would be only a question of money; but it would never do to offer it to him. He does not forget that he is a chief, though he has been away so many years from what there is left of his old tribe. If he did it at all it would be for the sake of your uncle. I know they have hunted together, and fought the Apaches together. I won't say but that if we get at him the right way, and he don't happen to have no other plans in his mind, that he might not be willing to start with you."

"I should be glad if he would, Jerry. I have been quite dreading to get to Fort Bridger. I have had such a splendid time of it with you that I should feel awfully lonely after you had gone on."

"Yes, I dare say you would feel lonesome. I should have felt lonesome myself if I did not light upon some mate going the same way. We got on very well together, Tom. When Pete Hoskings first put it to me whether I would be willing to take you with me as far as this, I thought that though I liked you well enough, it would not be in my way to be playing a sort of schoolmaster business to a young tenderfoot; but I had got to like the notion before we left Denver, and now it seems to me that we have had a rare good time of it together."

"We have indeed, Jerry; at least I have had. Even if the Indian would agree to take me I should miss you awfully."

Jerry made no reply, but sat smoking his pipe and looking into the fire. As he was sometimes inclined to be taciturn, Tom made no attempt to continue the conversation; and after moving out and shifting the picket-pegs so as to give the horses a fresh range of grass to munch during the night, he returned to the fire, wrapped himself in his blankets and lay down, his "Good-night, Jerry," meeting with no response, his companion being evidently absorbed in his own thoughts.

"You are not going on to-day, Jerry, are you?" Tom said, as he threw off his blankets and sat up in the morning. The sun was not yet up, but Jerry had already stirred up the embers, put some meat over them to cook, and put the kettle among them.

"No, I shall stop here for a day or two, lad. I am in no special hurry, and have no call to push on. I have not made up my mind about things yet."

They had scarcely finished breakfast when Leaping Horse came down from the fort.

"Tom here has been asking me, chief, whether there was any chance of getting you to guide him to his uncle. I said, of course, that I did not know what your plans were; but that if you had nothing special before you, possibly you might be willing to do so, as I know that you and Straight Harry have done some tall hunting and fighting together."

The Indian's face was impassive.

"Can my young brother ride day after day and night after night, can he go long without food and water, is he ready to run the risk of his scalp being taken by the 'Rappahoes? Can he crawl and hide, can he leave his horse and travel on foot, can he hear the war-cry of the red-skins without fear?"

"I don't say that I can do all these things, chief," Tom said; "but I can do my best. And, anyhow, I think I can promise that if we should be attacked you shall see no signs of my being afraid, whatever I may feel. I am only a boy yet, but I hope I am not a coward."

"You have come a long way across the sea to find my brother, Straight Harry. You would not have come so far alone if your heart had been weak. Leaping Horse is going back to join his white brother again, and will take you to him."

Tom felt that any outburst of delight would be viewed with distaste by this grave Indian, and he replied simply: "I thank you with all my heart, chief, and I am sure that my uncle will be grateful to you."

The chief nodded his head gravely, and then, as if the matter were settled and no more need be said about it, he turned to Jerry:

"Which way is my white friend going?"

"I'm dog-goned if I know. I had reckoned to go down past Utah, and to go out prospecting among the hills, say a hundred miles farther west; then while I journeyed along with Tom I got mixed in my mind. I should like to have handed him over safe to Harry; but if Harry had gone down to the Ute hills with an idea of trying a spot I have heard him speak of, where he thought he had struck it rich, he might not have cared to have had me come there, and so I concluded last night it was best the lad should wait here till Harry got back. Now the thing is altered; they are just hunting and prospecting, and might be glad to have me with them, and I might as well be there as anywhere else; so as you are going back there, I reckon I shall be one of the party."

"That will be capital, Jerry," Tom said. "With you as well as the chief we shall be sure to get through; and it will be awfully jolly having you with us."

"Don't you make any mistake," the miner said, "I should not be of much more use in finding them than you would. I ain't been up among the mountains all these years without learning something, but I ain't no more than a child by the side of the chief. And don't you think this affair is going to be a circus. I tell you it is going to be a hard job. There ain't a dozen white men as have been over that country, and we shall want to be pretty spry if we are to bring back our scalps. It is a powerful rough country. There are peaks there, lots of them, ten thousand feet high, and some of them two or three thousand above that. There are rivers, torrents, and defiles. I don't say there will be much chance of running short of food, if it wasn't that half the time one will be afraid to fire for fear the 'tarnal Indians should hear us. We ain't got above a month afore the first snows fall. Altogether it is a risky business, look at it which way you will."

"Well, Jerry, if it is as bad as that, I don't think it will be right for you and the chief to risk your lives merely that I should find my uncle. If he is alive he is sure to come back here sooner or later; or if he goes some other way back to Denver he will hear from Pete that I am here, and will either write or come for me."

"It ain't entirely on your account, lad, as I am thinking of going; and I am pretty sure the chief would tell you that it is the same with him. You see, he tried to persuade your uncle to turn back. My opinion is, that though he had to come here to keep the appointment, he had it in his mind to go back again to join your uncle. Haven't I about struck your thoughts, chief?"

The chief nodded. "My white brother Harry is in danger," he said. "Leaping Horse had to leave him; but would have started back to-day to take his place by his side. The Hunting Dog will go with him."

"I thought so, chief; I am dog-goned if I did not think so. It was Hunting Dog you came back here to meet, I suppose."

"Hunting Dog is of my tribe," he said; "he is my sister's son. He came across the plains to join me. He has hunted in his own country; this is the first time he has come out to take his place as a man. Leaping Horse will teach him to be a warrior."

"That is good; the more the better, so that there ain't too many. Well, what is your advice, chief? Shall we take our pack pony with the outfit?"

The chief shook his head decidedly. "Must travel quick and be able to gallop fast. My white brothers must take nothing but what they can carry with them."

"All right, chief; we will not overload ourselves. We will just take our robes and blankets, our shooting-irons, some tea and sugar, and a few pounds of flour. At what time shall we start?"

"In an hour we will ride out from the fort."

"We shall be ready. Ten minutes would fix us, except that I must go into the fort and sell my critter and what flour and outfit we sha'n't want, to a trader there.

"I ain't done badly by that deal," Jerry said when he returned. "I have sold the pony for more than I gave for him; for the red-skins have been keeping away from the fort of late, and the folks going by are always wanting horses in place of those that have died on the way. The other things all sold for a good bit more than we gave for them at Denver. Carriage comes mighty high on these plains; besides, the trader took his chances and reckoned them in."

"How do you mean, Jerry?"

"Waal, I told him we was going up to the Shoshone Sierra, and intended to hunt about and to come back, maybe by the Yellowstone and then by the Bear rivers, and that we would take the price of the goods out in trade when we got back. That made it a sort of lottery for him, for if we never came back at all he would never have to pay, so he could afford to take his risks and offer me a good price. I reckon he thinks he has got them at a gift. He has given two pieces of paper, one for you and one for me, saying that he owes the two of us the money; so if I should go under and you should get back, you will draw it all right."

They at once proceeded to pack their ponies. Divided between the saddle-bags of the two animals were four pounds of tea, eight of sugar, and thirty-six of flour. Each took a good store of ammunition, an extra pair of breeches, a flannel shirt, and a pair of stockings. The rest of their clothes had been packed, and taken up by Jerry to the traders to lie there until their return.

"That is light enough for anything," Jerry said, when the things were stowed into the saddle-bags. "Four-and-twenty pounds of grub and five pounds of ammunition brings it up to nine-and-twenty pounds each, little enough for a trip that may last three months for aught we know."

In addition to the ammunition in the saddle-bags, each carried a powder-horn and a bag of bullets over his shoulder. The revolvers were in their belts, and the rifles slung behind them. While Jerry was away at the fort Tom had made and baked three loaves, which were cut up and put in the holsters.

"Now we are ready, Tom; the Indians will be out in a minute or two. The sun is just at its highest."

Two minutes later the chief and his companion rode out from the gate of the fort. Jerry and Tom mounted their horses and cantered over to meet them. As they came up, Tom looked with interest at the young Indian. He judged him to be about nineteen, and he had a bright and intelligent face. He was, like his uncle, attired in buckskin; but the shirt was fringed and embroidered, as was the band that carried his powder-horn, a gift, doubtless, from some Indian maiden at his departure from his village. No greetings were exchanged; but the chief and Jerry rode at once side by side towards the northeast, and Tom took his place by the side of the young Indian.

"How are you?" he said, holding out his hand. The young Indian took it and responded to the shake, but he shook his head.

"Ah, you don't speak English yet?" Hunting Dog again shook his head. "That is a pity," Tom went on; "it would have been jolly if we could have talked together."

The chief said something to Jerry, who turned around in his saddle. "His uncle says he can talk some. He has taught him a little when he has paid visits to the village, but he has had no practice in speaking it. He will get on after a time."

All were well mounted, and they travelled fast. Just before sunset they crossed the Green River at a ford used by the emigrants, and some fifty miles northeast of Fort Bridger. They had seen a herd of deer by the way, and the two Indians had dismounted and stalked them. The others lost sight of them, but when two rifle-shots were heard Jerry said, "We will take the horses along to them, you may be sure they have got meat; the chief is a dead shot, and he says that his nephew has also gifts that way." As they expected, they found the Indians standing beside two dead deer. Hunting Dog laid open the stomachs with a slash of his knife, and removed the entrails, then tying the hind legs together swung the carcasses on to his horse behind the saddle, and the journey was at once renewed.

"You will make for Fremont's Buttes, I suppose, chief?" Jerry said, as after riding up the river for three or four miles so as to be able to obtain wood for their fire—as for a considerable distance on either side of the emigrant trail not a shrub was to be seen—they dismounted, turned the horses loose, lit a fire, and prepared a meal.

"Yes. We will go over the pass and camp at one of the little lakes at the head of the north fork, thence we will ride across the plain and ford Little Wind River, and then follow up the Sage Creek and make our camp at night on Buffalo Lake. From there we must follow their trail."

"And where shall we have to begin to look out for the 'Rappahoes?"

"They may be over the next rise; no one can say. The 'Rappahoes are like the dead leaves drifting before the wind. They come as far south as the emigrant trail, and have attacked caravans many times. After to-night we must look out for them always, and must put out our fires before dark."

Tom had noticed how carefully the young Indian had selected the wood for the fire; searching carefully along by the edge of the river for drift-wood, and rejecting all that contained any sap. He himself had offered to cut down some wood with the axe he carried strapped to his saddle, but Hunting Dog had shaken his head.

"No good, no good," he said. "Make heap smoke; smoke very bad."

Tom thought that the shrub he was about to cut would give out obnoxious smoke that would perhaps flavour the meat hanging over it, but when the Indian added, "Heap smoke, red-skins see a long way," he understood that Hunting Dog had been so careful in choosing the wood in order to avoid making any smoke whatever that might attract the attention of Indians at a distance from them. It was his first lesson in the necessity for caution; and as darkness set in he looked round several times, half expecting to see some crouching red-skins. The careless demeanour of his companions, however, reassured him, for he felt certain that if there was any fear of a surprise, they would be watchful.

After supper the Indian talked over with Jerry the route they would most probably have to pursue. The miner had never been in this part of the country before; indeed, very few white men, with the exception of trappers who had married Indian women and had been admitted into their tribes, had ever penetrated into this, the wildest portion of the Rocky Mountains. Vague rumours existed of the abundance of game there, and of the existence of gold, but only one attempt had been made to prospect on a large scale. This had taken place three years before, when a party of twenty Californian miners penetrated into the mountains. None of them returned, but reports brought down by Indians to the settlements were to the effect that, while working a gold reef they had discovered, they were attacked and killed to a man by a war party of Sioux.

"I was mighty nigh being one of that crowd," Jerry said when he told the story to Tom, as they sat over the camp fire that night. "I heard of their start when I got back to Salt Lake City, after being away for some time among the hills. I legged it arter them as fast as I could, but I found when I got to the last settlement that they had gone on ten days before, and as I did not know what line they had followed, and did not care to cross the pass alone, I gave it up. Mighty lucky thing it was, though I did not think so at the time."

"But why should my uncle's party have gone into such a dangerous country when they knew that the natives were so hostile?"

"It is a mighty big place, it is pretty nigh as big as all the eastern states chucked into one, and the red-skins are not thick. No one knows how many there are, but it is agreed they are not a big tribe. Then it ain't like the plains, where a party travelling can be seen by an Indian scout miles and miles away. It is all broken ground, canons and valleys and rocks. Then again, when we get on the other side of the Wind River they tell me there are big forests. That is so, chief, isn't it?"

The chief nodded. "Heap forests," he said, "higher up rocks and bad lands; all bad. In winter snow everywhere on hills. Red-skins not like cold; too much cold, wigwam no good."

"That's it, you see, Tom. We are here a long way above the sea-level, and so in the hills you soon get above the timber-line. It's barren land there, just rock, without grass enough for horses, and in winter it is so all-fired cold that the Indians can't live there in their wigwams. I reckon their villages are down in the sheltered valleys, and if we don't have the bad luck to run plump into one of these we may wander about a mighty long time before we meet with a red-skin. That is what you mean, isn't it, chief?"

Leaping Horse grunted an assent.

"What game is there in the country?"

"There are wapitis, which are big stag with thundering great horns, and there are big-horns. Them are mountain sheep; they are mostly up above the timber-line. Wapitis and big-horns are good for food, but their skins ain't worth taking off. There is beaver, heaps of them; though I reckon there ain't as many as there were by a long way, for since the whites came out here and opened trade, and the red-skins found they could get good prices for beaver, they have brought them down by thousands every year. Still, there is no doubt there is plenty left, and that trappers would do first-rate there if the red-skins were friendly. In course, there is plenty of b'ars, but unless you happen to have a thundering good chance it is just as well to leave the b'ars alone, for what with the chances of getting badly mauled, and what with the weight of the skin, it don't pay even when you come right side up out of a tussle."

"Are there any maps of the region?"

"None of any account. They are all just guess-work. You may take it that this is just a heap of mountains chucked down anyhow. Such maps as there are have been made from tales trappers who came in with pelts have told. Well, firstly they only knew about just where the tribe they had joined lived, and in the second place you may bet they warn't such fools as to tell anything as would help other fellows to get there; so you may put down that they told very little, and what they did tell was all lies. Some day or other I suppose there will be an expedition fitted out to go right through, and to punish these dog-goned red-skins and open the country; but it will be a long time arter that afore it will be safe travelling, for I reckon that soldiers might march and march for years through them mountains without ever catching a sight of a red-skin if they chose to keep out of their way. And now I reckon we had best get in atween our blankets."

The two Indians had already lain down by the fire. Tom was some time before he could get to sleep. The thought of the wild and unknown country he was about to enter, with its great game, its hidden gold treasures, its Indians and its dangers, so excited his imagination that, tired as he was with the long ride, two or three hours passed before he fell off to sleep. He was awoke by being shaken somewhat roughly by Jerry.

"Why, you are sleeping as sound as a b'ar in a hollow tree," the miner said. "You are generally pretty spry in the morning." A dip in the cold water of the river awoke Tom thoroughly, and by the time he had rejoined his comrades breakfast was ready. The ground rose rapidly as they rode forward. They were now following an Indian trail, a slightly-marked path made by the Indians as they travelled down with their ponies laden with beaver skins, to exchange for ammunition, blankets, and tobacco at the trading station. The country was barren in the extreme, being covered only with patches of sage brush. As they proceeded it became more and more hilly, and distant ridges and peaks could be seen as they crossed over the crests.

"These are the bad lands, I suppose?"

"You bet they are, Tom, but nothing like as bad as you will see afore you are done. Sage brush will grow pretty nigh everywhere, but there are thousands of square miles of rock where even sage brush cannot live."

The hills presently became broken up into fantastic shapes, while isolated rocks and pinnacles rose high above the general level. "How curiously they are coloured," Tom remarked, "just regular bands of white and red and green and orange; and you see the same markings on all these crags, at the same level."

"Just so, Tom. We reckon that this country, and it is just the same down south, was once level, and the rains and the rivers and torrents cut their way through it and wore it down, and just these buttes and crags and spires were left standing, as if to show what the nature of the ground was everywhere. Though why the different kinds of rocks has such different colours is more than I can tell. I went out once with an old party as they called a scientific explorer. I have heard him say this was all under water once, and sometimes one kind of stuff settled down like mud to the bottom, sometimes another, though where all the water came from is more nor I can tell. He said something about the ground being raised afterwards, and I suppose the water run off then. I did not pay much attention to his talk, for he was so choke-full of larning, and had got such a lot of hard names on the tip of his tongue, that there were no making head or tail of what he was saying."

Tom had learnt something of the elements of geology, and could form an idea of the processes by which the strange country at which he was looking had been formed.

"That's Fremont's Buttes," the Indian said presently, pointing to a flat-topped hill that towered above the others ahead.

"Why, I thought you said it was a fifty-mile ride to-day, Jerry, and we can't have gone more than half that."

"How far do you suppose that hill is off?"

"Three or four miles, I should think."

"It is over twenty, lad. Up here in the mountains the air is so clear you can see things plain as you couldn't make out the outlines of down below."

"But it seems to me so close that I could make out people walking about on the top," Tom said a little incredulously.

"I dare say, lad. But you will see when you have ridden another hour it won't seem much closer than it does now."

Tom found out that the miner was not joking with him, as he at first had thought was the case. Mile after mile was ridden, and the landmark seemed little nearer than before. Presently Hunting Dog said something to the chief, pointing away to the right. Leaping Horse at once reined in, and motioned to his white companions to do the same.

"What is it, chief?" Jerry asked.

"Wapiti," he replied.

"That is good news," the miner said. "It will be lucky if we can lay in a supply of deer flesh here. The less we shoot after we get through the pass the better. Shall we go with you, chief?"

"My white brothers had better ride on slowly," Leaping Horse said. "Might scare deer. No good lose time."

Tom felt rather disappointed, but as he went on slowly with Jerry, the miner said: "You will have plenty of chances later on, lad, and there is no time to lose in fooling about. The red-skins will do the business."

Looking back, Tom saw the two Indians gallop away till they neared the crest of a low swell. Then they leapt from their horses, and stooping low went forward. In a short time they lay prone on the ground, and wriggled along until just on the crest.

"I reckon the stag is just over there somewhere," Jerry said. "The young red-skin must have caught sight of an antler."

They stopped their ponies altogether now, and sat watching the Indians. These were half a mile away, but every movement was as clearly visible as if they were but a hundred yards distant. The chief raised himself on his arms and then on to his knees. A moment later he lay down again, and they then crawled along parallel with the crest for a couple of hundred yards. Then they paused, and with their rifles advanced they crept forward again.

"Now they see them," Jerry exclaimed.

The Indians lay for half a minute motionless. Then two tiny puffs of smoke darted out. The Indians rose to their feet and dashed forward as the sound of their shots reached the ears of their companions.

"Come on," Jerry said, "you may be sure they have brought down one stag anyhow. The herd could not have been far from that crest or the boy would not have seen the antler over it, and the chief is not likely to miss a wapiti at a hundred yards."

Looking back presently Tom saw that the Indian ponies had disappeared.

"Ay, Hunting Dog has come back for them. You may be sure they won't be long before they are up with us again."

In a quarter of an hour the two Indians rode up, each having the hind-quarters of a deer fastened across his horse behind the saddle, while the tongues hung from the peaks.

"Kill them both at first shot, chief?" Jerry asked; "I did not hear another report."

"Close by," the chief said; "no could miss."

"It seems a pity to lose such a quantity of meat," Tom remarked.

"The Indians seldom carry off more than the hindquarters of a deer, never if they think there is a chance of getting more soon. There is a lot more flesh on the hindquarters than there is on the rest of the stag. But that they are wasteful, the red-skins are, can't be denied. Even when they have got plenty of meat they will shoot a buffalo any day just for the sake of his tongue."

It was still early in the afternoon when they passed under the shadow of the buttes, and, two miles farther, came upon a small lake, the water from which ran north. Here they unsaddled the horses and prepared to camp.

Chapter V.
In Danger

There were no bushes that would serve their purpose near the lake; they therefore formed their camp on the leeward side of a large boulder. The greatest care was observed in gathering the fuel, and it burned with a clear flame without giving out the slightest smoke.

"Dead wood dries like tinder in this here air," the miner said. "In course, if there wur any red-skins within two or three miles on these hills they would make out the camp, still that ain't likely; but any loafing Indian who chanced to be hunting ten or even fifteen miles away would see smoke if there was any, and when a red-skin sees smoke, if he can't account for it, he is darned sartin to set about finding out who made it."

The horses fared badly, for there was nothing for them to pick up save a mouthful of stunted grass here and there.

"Plenty of grass to-morrow," the chief said in answer to a remark of Tom as to the scantiness of their feed. "Grass down by Buffalo Lake good."

Early the next morning they mounted and rode down the hills into Big Wind River valley. They did not go down to the river itself, but skirted the foot of the hills until they reached Buffalo Lake.

"There," the chief said, pointing to a pile of ashes, "the fire of my white brother." Alighting, he and Hunting Dog searched the ground carefully round the fire. Presently the younger Indian lightly touched the chief and pointed to the ground. They talked together, still carefully examining the ground, and moved off in a straight line some fifty yards. Then they returned.

"Indian here," Leaping Horse said, "one, two days ago. Found fire, went off on trail of white men."

"That is bad news, chief."

"Heap bad," the Indian said gravely.

"Perhaps he won't follow far," Tom suggested.

The Indian made no answer. He evidently considered the remark to be foolish.

"You don't know much of Indian nature yet, Tom," the miner said. "When a red-skin comes upon the trail of whites in what he considers his country, he will follow them if it takes him weeks to do it, till he finds out all about them, and if he passes near one of his own villages he will tell the news, and a score of the varmint will take up the trail with him. It's them ashes as has done it. If the chief here had stopped with them till they started this would not have happened, for he would have seen that they swept every sign of their fire into the lake. I wonder they did not think of it themselves. It was a dog-goned foolish trick to leave such a mark as this. I expect they will be more keerful arterwards, but they reckoned that they had scarce got into the Indian country."

"Do you think it was yesterday the red-skin was here, or the day before, chief?"

"Leaping Horse can't say," the Indian replied. "Ground very hard, mark very small. No rain, trail keep fresh a long time. Only find mark twice." He led them to a spot where, on the light dust among the rocks, was the slight impression of a footmark.

"That is the mark of a moccasin, sure enough," Jerry said; "but maybe one of the whites, if not all of them, have put on moccasins for the journey. They reckoned on climbing about some, and moccasins beat boots anyhow for work among the hills."

"Red-skin foot," the Indian said quietly.

"Well, if you say it is, of course it is. I should know it myself if I saw three or four of them in a line, but as there is only one mark it beats me."

"How would you know, Jerry?"

"A white man always turns out his toes, lad, an Indian walks straight-footed. There are other differences that a red-skin would see at once, but which are beyond me, for I have never done any tracking work."

The Indian without speaking led them to another point some twenty yards away, and pointed to another impression. This was so slight that it was with difficulty that Tom could make out the outline.

"Yes, that settles it," Jerry said. "You see, lad, when there was only one mark I could not tell whether it was turned out or not, for that would depend on the direction the man was walking in. This one is just in a line with the other, and so the foot must have been set down straight. Had it been turned out a bit, the line, carried straight through the first footprint, would have gone five or six yards away to the right."

It took Tom two or three minutes to reason this out to himself, but at last he understood the drift of what his companion said. As the line through one toe and heel passed along the centre of the other, the foot must each time have been put down in a straight line, while if the footprints had been made by a person who turned out his toes they would never point straight towards those farther on.

"Well, what is your advice, chief?" Jerry asked.

"Must camp and eat," the Indian replied, "horses gone far enough. No fear here, red-skin gone on trail."

"Do you think there have been more than one, chief?"

"Not know," Leaping Horse said; "find out by and by."

Tom now noticed that Hunting Dog had disappeared.

"Where shall we make the fire?"

The chief pointed to the ashes.

"That's it," Jerry said. "If any red-skin came along you see, Tom, there would be nothing to tell them that more than one party had been here."

The chief this time undertook the collection of fuel himself, and a bright fire was presently burning. Two hours later Hunting Dog came back. He talked for some time earnestly with the chief, and taking out two leaves from his wampum bag opened them and showed him two tiny heaps of black dust. Jerry asked no questions until the conversation was done, and then while Hunting Dog cut off a large chunk of deer's flesh, and placing it in the hot ashes sat himself quietly down to wait until it was cooked, he said:

"Well, chief, what is the news?"

"The Indian had a horse, Hunting Dog came upon the spot where he had left it a hundred yards away. When he saw ashes, he came to look at them. Afterwards he followed the trail quite plain on the soft ground at head of lake. Over there," and he pointed to the foot of the hills, "Indian stopped and fired twice."

"How on earth did he know that, chief?"

The chief pointed to the two leaves. The scout examined the powder. "Wads," he said. "They are leather wads, Tom, shrivelled and burnt. What did he fire at, chief?"

"Signal. Half a mile farther three other mounted redskins joined him. They stopped and had heap talk. Then one rode away into hills, the others went on at gallop on trail."

"That is all bad, chief. The fellow who went up the hills no doubt made for a village?"

The chief nodded. "The only comfort is that Harry has got a good start of them. It was a week from the time you left them before we met you, that is three days ago, so that if the red-skins took up the trail yesterday, Harry has ten days' start of them."

Leaping Horse shook his head. "Long start if travel fast, little start if travel slow."

"I see what you mean. If they pushed steadily on up the valley, they have gone a good distance, but if they stopped to catch beaver or prospect for gold they may not have got far away. Hadn't we better be pushing on, chief?"

"No good, horses make three days' journey; rest well to-day, travel right on to-morrow. If go farther to-night, little good to-morrow. Good camp here, all rest."

"Well, no doubt you are right, chief, but it worries one to think that while we are sitting here those 'tarnal red-skins may be attacking our friends. My only hope is that Harry, who has done a lot of Indian fighting, will hide his trail as much as possible as he goes on, and that they will have a lot of trouble in finding it."

The chief nodded. "My white brother, Harry, knows Indian ways. He did not think he had come to Indian country here or he would not have left his ashes. But beyond this he will be sure to hide his trail, and the 'Rappahoes will have to follow slow."

"You think they are 'Rappahoes, chief?"

"Yes, this 'Rappahoe country. The Shoshones are further north, and are friendly; the Bannacks and Nez pèrces are in northwest, near Snake River; and the Sioux more on the north and east, on other side of great mountains. 'Rappahoes here."

"Waal," Jerry said wrathfully, "onless they catch Harry asleep, some of the darned skunks will be rubbed out afore they get his scalp. It is a good country for hiding trail. There are many streams coming down from the hills into the Big Wind, and they can turn up or down any of them as they please, and land on rocky ground too, so it would be no easy matter to track them. By the lay of the country there does not seem much chance of gold anywheres about here, and, as I reckon, they will be thinking more of that than of beaver skins, so I think they would push straight on."

"Harry said he should get out of Big Wind River valley quick," Leaping Horse said. "Too many Indians there. Get into mountains other side. Go up Riviere de Noir, then over big mountains into Sierra Shoshone, and then down Buffalo through Jackson's Hole, and then strike Snake River. I told him heap bad Indians in Jackson's Hole, Bannacks, and Nez Percés. He said not go down into valley, keep on foot-hills. I told him, too bad journey, but he and other pale-faces thought could do it, and might find much gold. No good Leaping Horse talk."

"This is a dog-goned bad business I have brought you into, Tom. I reckoned we should not get out without troubles, but I did not calkerlate on our getting into them so soon."

"You did not bring me here, Jerry, so you need not blame yourself for that. It was I brought you into it, for you did not make up your mind to come till I had settled to go with Leaping Horse."

"I reckon I should have come anyhow," Jerry grumbled. "Directly the chief said where Harry and the others had gone my mind was set on joining them. It was a new country, and there wur no saying what they might strike, and though I ain't a regular Indian-fighter, leaving them alone when they leave me alone, I can't say as I am averse to a scrimmage with them if the odds are anyways equal."

"It is a wonderful country," Tom said, looking at the almost perpendicular cliffs across the valley, with their regular coloured markings, their deep fissures, crags, and pinnacles, "and worth coming a long way to see."

"I don't say as it ain't curous, but I have seen the like down on the Colorado, and I don't care if I never see no more of it if we carry our scalps safe out of this. I don't say as I object to hills if they are covered with forest, for there is safe to be plenty of game there, and the wood comes in handy for timbering, but this kind of country that looks as if some chaps with paint-pots had been making lines all over it, ain't to my taste noway. Here, lad; I never travel without hooks and lines; you can get a breakfast and dinner many a day when a gun would bring down on you a score of red varmints. I expect you will find fish in the lake. Many of these mountain lakes just swarm with them. You had better look about and catch a few bugs, there ain't no better bait. Those jumping bugs are as good as any," and he pointed to a grasshopper, somewhat to Tom's relief, for the lad had just been wondering where he should look for bugs, not having seen one since he landed in the States.

There were two lines and hooks in the miner's outfit, and Tom and Hunting Dog, after catching some grasshoppers, went down to the lake, while Jerry and the chief had a long and earnest conversation together. The baited hooks were scarcely thrown into the water when they were seized, and in a quarter of an hour ten fine lake trout were lying on the bank. Tom was much delighted. He had fished from boats, but had never met with much success, and his pleasure at landing five fish averaging four or five pounds apiece was great. As it was evidently useless to catch more, they wound up their lines, and Hunting Dog split the fish open and laid them down on the rock, which was so hot that Tom could scarce bear his hand on it.

Seeing the elder men engaged in talk Tom did not return to them, but endeavoured to keep up a conversation with the young Indian, whom he found to be willing enough to talk now they were alone, and who knew much more English than he had given him credit for. As soon as the sun set the fire was extinguished, and they lay down to sleep shortly afterwards. An hour before daylight they were in the saddle. Hunting Dog rode ahead on the line he had followed the day before. As soon as it became light Tom kept his eyes fixed upon the ground, but it was only now and then, when the Indian pointed to the print of a horse's hoof in the sand between the rocks, that he could make them out. The two Indians followed the track, however, without the slightest difficulty, the horses going at a hand gallop.

"They don't look to me like horses' footprints," Tom said to Jerry when they had passed a spot where the marks were unusually clear.

"I reckon you have never seen the track of an unshod horse before, Tom. With a shod horse you see nothing but the mark of the shoe, here you get the print of the whole hoof. Harry has been careful enough here, and has taken the shoes off his ponies, for among all the marks, we have not seen any made by a shod horse. The Indians never shoe theirs, and the mark of an iron is enough to tell the first red-skin who passes that a white man has gone along there. The chief and I took off the shoes of the four horses yesterday afternoon when you were fishing. We put them and the nails by to use when we get out of this dog-goned country."

After riding for two hours they came to the bank of a stream. The chief held up his hand for them to stop, while he dismounted and examined the foot-marks. Then he mounted again and rode across the stream, which was some ten yards wide and from two to three feet deep. He went on a short distance beyond it, leapt from his saddle, threw the reins on the horse's neck, and returned to the bank on foot. He went a short distance up the stream and then as much down, stooping low and examining every inch of the ground. Then he stood up and told the others to cross. "Leave your horses by mine," he said as they joined him. "Trail very bad, all rock." He spoke to the young Indian, who, on dismounting, at once went forward, quartering the ground like a spaniel in search of game, while the chief as carefully searched along the bank.

"Best leave them to themselves, Tom; they know what they are doing."

"They are hunting for the trail, Jerry, I suppose?"

"Ay, lad. Harry struck on a good place when he crossed where he did, for you see the rock here is as smooth as the top of a table, and the wind has swept it as clean of dust as if it had been done by an eastern woman's broom. If the horses had been shod there would have been scratches on the rock that would have been enough for the dullest Indian to follow, but an unshod horse leaves no mark on ground like this. I expect the red-skins who followed them were just as much puzzled as the chief is. There ain't no saying whether they crossed and went straight on, or whether they never crossed at all or kept in the stream either up or down."

It was half an hour before the two Indians had concluded their examination of the ground.

"Well, chief, what do you make of it?" Jerry asked when they had spoken a few words together.

"Hunting Dog has good eyes," the chief said. "The white men went forward, the red men could not find the trail, and thought that they had kept in the river, so they went up to search for them. Come, let us go forward."

The miner and Tom mounted their horses, but the Indians led theirs forward some three hundred yards. Then Hunting Dog pointed down, and the chief stooped low and examined the spot.

"What is it, chief?" Jerry asked; and he and Tom both got off and knelt down. They could see nothing whatever.

"That is it," Leaping Horse said, and pointed to a piece of rock projecting half an inch above the flat. "I am darned if I can see anything."

"There is a tiny hair there," Tom said, putting his face within a few inches of the ground. "It might be a cat's hair; it is about the length, but much thicker. It is brown."

"Good!" the chief said, putting his hand on Tom's shoulder. "Now let us ride." He leapt into his saddle, the others following his example, and they went on at the same pace as before.

"Well, chief," the miner said, "what does that hair tell you about it, for I can't make neither head nor tail of it?"

"The white men killed a deer on their way up here, and they cut up the hide and made shoes for horses, so that they should leave no tracks. One of the horses trod on a little rock and a hair came out of the hide."

"That may be it, chief," the miner said, after thinking the matter over, "though it ain't much of a thing to go by."

"Good enough," Leaping Horse said. "We know now the line they were taking. When we get to soft ground see trail plainer."

"What will the others do when they cannot find the trail anywhere along the bank?"

"Ride straight on," the chief said. "Search banks of next river, look at mouths of valleys to make sure white men have not gone up there, meet more of tribe, search everywhere closely, find trail at last."

"Well, that ought to give Harry a good start, anyhow."

"Not know how long gone on," the chief said gravely. "No rainfall. Six, eight—perhaps only two days' start."

"But if they always hide their trail as well as they did here I don't see how the Indians can find them at all—especially as they don't know where they are making for, as we do."

"Find camp. Men on foot may hide traces, but with horses sure to find."

"That is so," Jerry agreed, shaking his head. "An Indian can see with half an eye where the grass has been cropped or the leaves stripped off the bushes. Yes, I am afraid that is so. There ain't no hiding a camp from Indian eyes where horses have been about. It is sure to be near a stream. Shall you look for them, chief?"

The Indian shook his head. "Lose time," he said. "We go straight to Riviere de Noir."

"You don't think, then, they are likely to turn off before that?"

"Leaping Horse thinks not. They know Indian about here. Perhaps found Indian trail near first camp. Know, anyhow, many Indians. Think push straight on."

"That is the likeliest. Anyhow, by keeping on we must get nearer to them. The worst danger seems to me that we may overtake the red-skins who are hunting them."

The chief nodded.

"It is an all-fired fix, Tom," Jerry went on. "If we go slow we may not be in time to help Harry and the others to save their scalps; if we go fast we may come on these 'tarnal red-skins, and have mighty hard work in keeping our own ha'r on."

"I feel sure that the chief will find traces of them in time to prevent our running into them, Jerry. Look how good their eyes are. Why, I might have searched all my life without noticing a single hair on a rock."

After riding some fifteen miles beyond the stream, and crossing two similar though smaller rivulets, the chief, after a few words with Jerry, turned off to the left and followed the foot of the hills. At the mouth of a narrow valley he stopped, examined the ground carefully, and then led the way up it, carrying his rifle in readiness across the peak of the saddle. The valley opened when they had passed its mouth, and a thick grove of trees grew along the bottom. As soon as they were beneath their shelter they dismounted. The horses at once began to crop the grass. Hunting Dog went forward through the trees, rifle in hand.

"Shall I take the bits out of the horses' mouths, Jerry?" Tom asked.

"Not till the young Indian returns. It is not likely there is a red-skin village up there, for we should have seen a trail down below if there had been. Still there may be a hut or two, and we can do nothing till he comes back."

It was half an hour before Hunting Dog came through the trees again. He shook his head, and without a word loosened the girths of his horse and took off the bridle.

"He has seen no signs of them, so we can light a fire and get something to eat. I am beginning to feel I want something badly."

Thus reminded, Tom felt at once that he was desperately hungry. They had before starting taken a few mouthfuls of meat that had been cooked the day before and purposely left over, but it was now three o'clock in the afternoon, and he felt ravenous. The Indians quickly collected dried wood, and four of the fish were soon frizzling on hot ashes, while the kettle, hung in the flame, was beginning to sing.

"We have done nigh forty miles, Tom, and the horses must have a couple of hours' rest. We will push on as fast as we can before dark, and then wait until the moon rises; it will be up by ten. This ain't a country to ride over in the dark. We will hide up before morning, and not go on again till next night. Of course we shall not go so fast as by day, but we sha'n't have any risk of being ambushed. The chief reckons from what he has heard that the Indian villages are thick along that part of the valley, and that it will never do to travel by day."

"Then you have given up all hopes of finding Harry's tracks?"

"It would be just wasting our time to look for them. We will push on sharp till we are sure we are ahead of them. We may light upon them by chance, but there can be no searching for them with these red varmint round us. It would be just chucking away our lives without a chance of doing any good. I expect Harry and his party are travelling at night too; but they won't travel as fast as we do, not by a sight. They have got pack-ponies with them, and they are likely to lay off a day or two if they come upon a good place for hiding."

They travelled but a few miles after their halt, for the Indians declared they could make out smoke rising in two or three places ahead; and although neither Jerry nor Tom could distinguish it, they knew that the Indians' sight was much keener than their own in a matter of this kind. They therefore halted again behind a mass of rocks that had fallen down the mountain-side. Hunting Dog lay down among the highest of the boulders to keep watch, and the horses were hobbled to prevent their straying. The miner and the chief lit their pipes, and Tom lay down on his back for a sleep. A short time before it became dusk the call of a deer was heard.

"There are wapiti, chief. We can't take a shot at them; but it don't matter, we have meat enough for a week."

The chief had already risen to his feet, rifle in hand.

"It is a signal from Hunting Dog," he said, "he has seen something in the valley. My white brother had better get the horses together," and he made his way up the rocks. In a minute or two he called out that the horses might be left to feed, and presently came leisurely down to them. "Seen Indians—ten 'Rappahoes."

"Which way were they going?"

"Riding from Big Wind River across valley. Been away hunting among hills over there. Have got meat packed on horses, ride slow. Not have heard about white men's trail. Going to village, where we saw smoke." Tom was fast asleep when Jerry roused him, and told him that the moon was rising, and that it was time to be off.

They started at a walk, the chief leading; Jerry followed him, while Tom rode between him and Hunting Dog, who brought up the rear. Tom had been warned that on no account was he to speak aloud. "If you have anything you want to say, and feel that you must say it or bust," Jerry remarked, "just come up alongside of me and whisper it. Keep your eyes open and your rifle handy, we might come upon a party any minute. They might be going back to their village after following Harry's trail as long as they could track it, or it might be a messenger coming back to fetch up food, or those fellows Hunting Dog made out going on to join those in front. Anyhow we have got to travel as quiet as if there was ears all round us."

As they passed the clumps of trees where the Indian villages stood they could see the reflection of the fires on the foliage, and heard the frequent barking of dogs and an occasional shout. A quarter of a mile farther the chief halted and spoke to Hunting Dog, who at once dismounted and glided away towards the village.

"Gone to see how many men there," the chief said in explanation to Jerry. "Too much laugh, no good."

"He means the men must have gone off again, Tom. If there were men in the camp the boys would not be making a noise."

They were but a few hundred yards from the trees, and in a very short time the Indian returned.

"Men are gone," he said; "only squaws and boys there."

"How many lodges are there?" the chief asked. Hunting Dog held up both hands with extended fingers, and then one finger only.

"Eleven of them," Jerry said. "I expect they are all small villages, and they move their lodges across into the forests when winter comes on." As soon as they had mounted, the chief put his horse into a canter, and at this pace they went forward for some hours, breaking into a walk occasionally for a few minutes.

"I thought you said we should not go beyond a walk to-night, Jerry," Tom remarked on the first of these occasions.

"That is what we kinder agreed, lad; but you may be sure the chief has some good reason for going on faster. I dunno what it is, and I ain't going to ask. Red-skins hate being questioned. If he wants to tell us he will tell us without being asked."

A faint light was stealing over the sky when the chief halted his horse and sat listening. No sound, however, broke the stillness of the night.

"Did you think you heard anything, chief?"

"Leaping Horse heard nothing, but he stopped to listen. What does my white brother think of the 'Rappahoes having gone on directly they returned from the chase?"

"I thought that when they got the news that some white men had gone through, they might have started to join those following up the trail. Isn't that what you think, chief?"

"Only three white men, plenty Indians on trail; no hurry to follow; might have had feast after hunt and gone on in morning."

"So they might. You think the whites have been tracked, and are to be attacked this morning?"

"Perhaps attacked yesterday. Perhaps have got strong place, 'Rappahoes want more help to take it. White rifle shoot straight, perhaps want more men to starve them out."

They again went forward, at a gallop now. Jerry did not think much of the chief's idea. It seemed to him natural that the Indians should want to join in the hunt for scalps, and to get a share of the white men's goods, though he admitted that it was strange they should have gone on without taking a meal. Presently the chief reined in his horse again, and sat with head bent forward. Tom heard an angry grunt from between Hunting Dog's teeth. Listening intently also, he was conscious of a faint, far-away sound.

"You hear?" the chief said to Jerry.

"I heard something; but it might be anything. A waterfall in the hills miles away, that is what it sounds like."

"Guns," the chief said laconically.

"Do you think so?" Jerry said doubtfully. "There don't seem to me anything of guns in it. It is just a sort of murmur that keeps on and on."

"It is the mountains speaking back again," the chief said, waving his hand. "Hills everywhere. They say to each other, the red men who live in our bosoms are attacking the pale-face strangers."

"What do you think, Hunting Dog?" Tom whispered to the Indian.

"Gun-shot," he replied, in a tone of absolute conviction.

"Waal, chief, I will not gainsay your opinion," Jerry said. "How far do you think it is off?"

"The horses will take us there in two hours," the chief replied.

"Then we can put it at twenty miles at least. Let us be going; whatever the sound is, we shall know more about it before we have gone much farther."

"Not too fast," Leaping Horse said as the miner was urging his horse forward. "Maybe have to fight, maybe have to run. No good tire horse too much."

It was more than an hour before Tom could hear any distinct change in the character of the sound, but at last he was able to notice that, though seemingly continuous, the sound really pulsated; sometimes it almost died away, then suddenly swelled out again, and there were several vibrations close together. Jerry, more accustomed to the sound of firearms in the mountains, had before this come round to the chief's opinion.

"It is guns, sure enough, Tom; the chief has made no mistake about it. Waal, there is one comfort, they ain't been surprised. They are making a good fight of it, and we may be there in time to take a hand in the game."

"Shall we ride straight on and join them?"

"I reckon not, lad. We must wait until we see what sort of place Harry is in, and how we can best help him, before we fix on any scheme."

The sound became louder and clearer. The echo was still continuous, but the sound of the shots could be distinctly heard.

"It is over there, to the right," Jerry said, "They must have crossed the Big Wind River."

"And gone up the De Noir valley," the chief said. "We ought to be close to it now."

"Yes, I reckon it can't be far off, by what you told me about the distance."

"Better cross Big Wind at once. They no see us now."

"I agree with you, chief; it would not do for them to get sight of us. If they did our case would be worse than Harry's. I expect he has got strongly posted, or he would have been wiped out long ago; that is what would happen to us if they were to make us out and spy our numbers afore we get to some place where we and Harry's outfit can help each other."

They rode rapidly down to the river. With the exception of a few yards in the middle, where the horses had to swim, the depth was not great, and they were soon on the other side. They rode to the foot of the hills, and then kept along it. The sound of firing became louder and louder, and Tom felt his heart beat quickly at the thought that he might soon be engaged in a desperate fight with the Indians, and that with the odds greatly against his party. Presently the hills fell sharply away, and they were at the entrance of the valley of the Riviere de Noir, which is the principal arm of the Big Wind River at this point. The firing had very much died out during the last few minutes, and only an occasional shot was heard.

"They have beat off the attack so far," Jerry said to him encouragingly. "Now we have got to lie low a bit, while the chief sees how things stand."

Leaping Horse dismounted at the mouth of a narrow canon running up into the cliff beside them. A little stream trickled down its centre.

"Could not have been better," Jerry said. "Here is a place we four could hold against a crowd of red-skins for hours. There is water anyway, and where there is water there is mostly a little feed for horses. I will take your horse, chief, and Tom will take Hunting Dog's, if so be you mean him to go with you.

"Don't you worry yourself, lad," he went on, seeing how anxious Tom looked, as they started with the horses up the canon. "If Harry and his friends have beaten off the first attack, you may bet your boots they are safe for some time. It is clear the red-skins have drawn off, and are holding a pow-wow as to how they are to try next. They attacked, you see, just as the day was breaking; that is their favourite hour, and I reckon Harry must have been expecting them, and that he and his mates were prepared."

Chapter VI.
United

The canon showed no sign of widening until they had proceeded a quarter of a mile from the entrance, then it broadened suddenly for a distance of a hundred yards.

"There has been a big slip here both sides," the miner said, looking round. "It must have taken place a great many years ago, for the winter floods have swept away all signs of it, and there are grass and trees on the slopes. The horses can find enough to keep them alive here for a day or two, and that is all we shall want, I hope."

"It would be a nasty place to get out of, Jerry, for the cliffs are perpendicular from half-way up."

"It ain't likely as there is any place we could get out without following it to the upper end, which may be some fifty miles away. I don't know the country it runs through, but the red-skins are pretty certain to know all about it. If they were to track us here they would never try to fight their way in, but would just set a guard at the mouth and at the upper end and starve us out. It is a good place to hide in, but a dog-goned bad one to be caught in. However, I hope it ain't coming to that. It is we who are going to attack them, and not them us, and that makes all the difference. The red-skins can't have a notion that there are any other white men in this neighbourhood, and when we open fire on them it will raise such a scare for a bit that it will give us a chance of joining the others if we choose. That of course must depend on their position."

They walked back to the mouth of the canon, and had not to wait long for the return of the Indians.

"Come," Leaping Horse said briefly, at once turning and going off at a swift pace.

Jerry asked no questions, but with Tom followed close on the Indians' heels. There were bushes growing among the fallen rocks and debris from the face of the cliff, and they were, therefore, able to go forward as quickly as they could leap from boulder to boulder, without fear of being seen. A quarter of an hour's run, and the chief climbed up to a ledge on the face of the cliff where a stratum harder than those above it had resisted the effects of the weather and formed a shelf some twelve feet wide. He went down on his hands and knees, and keeping close to the wall crawled along to a spot where some stunted bushes had made good their hold. The others followed him, and lying down behind the bushes peered through them.

The valley was four or five hundred yards wide, and down its centre ran the stream. Close to the water's edge rose abruptly a steep rock. It was some fifty feet in height and but four or five yards across at the top. On the north and west the rocks were too perpendicular to be climbed, but the other sides had crumbled down, the stones being covered with brushwood. From the point where they were looking they could see the six horses lying among the bushes. They were evidently tightly roped, and had probably been led up there when the attack began and thrown at the highest point to which they could be taken, a spot being chosen where the bushes concealed their exact position from those below. The rock was about two hundred and fifty yards from the spot where the party was lying, and their position was about level with its top. Some twenty Indians were gathered a few hundred yards higher up the valley, and about as many some distance down it.

"Why didn't the varmint take their places here?" Jerry whispered to the chief.

"They came here. See," and he pointed to a patch of blood a few feet beyond him. "Indian guns not shoot far," he said, "powder weak; white man's rifles carry here, red-skin not able to shoot so far. When they found that, went away again."

"What are they going to do now, do you think?"

"Soon attack again."

Half an hour passed, and then a loud yell gave the signal and the two troops galloped towards the rock. They had evidently had experience of the accuracy of the white men's fire; not an Indian showed himself, each dropping over one side of his pony, with an arm resting in a rope round the animals' necks and one leg thrown over the back. So they dashed forward until close to the foot of the rocks. Another instant and they would have thrown themselves from their horses and taken to the bushes, but although hidden from the sight of the defenders of the position, they were exposed to the full view of the party on the ledge, from whom they were distant not more than two hundred yards. The chief fired first, and almost together the other three rifles flashed out. Three of the Indians fell from their horses, another almost slipped off, but with an effort recovered his hold with his leg. A yell of astonishment and fear broke from the Indians. As the two bands mingled together, some of the riders were exposed to those on the top of the rock, and three shots were fired. Two more of the 'Rappahoes fell, and the whole band in obedience to a shout from one of their chiefs galloped at full speed down the valley. The three men sprang to their feet, waving their hats, while the party on the ledge also leapt up with a shout. "It's you, chief, I see!" one of those on the rocks shouted. "I have been hoping ever since morning to hear the crack of your rifle, and I never heard a more welcome sound. We should have been rubbed out sure. Who have you got with you?"

"It's Jerry Curtis, Harry. I come up along with Leaping Horse, though I did not expect to find you in such a bad fix. This young Indian is Hunting Dog, and this young chap next to me is your nephew, Tom Wade. You did not expect to meet him like this, I reckon?"

While he had been speaking, all had reloaded their rifles.

"You had best go across and talk it over with Harry, chief, and consart measures with him for getting out of this fix. Those red-skins have got a bad scare, but you may bet they ain't gone far; and they have lost six of their bucks now beside what the others shot before, and it ain't in Indian natur for them to put up with such a loss as that." He had been looking at the rock as he spoke, and turning round uttered an exclamation of surprise, for the chief was no longer there. Looking down they saw that he had managed to make his way down the face of the cliff, and in another two minutes was ascending the rock. There he stood for some time in earnest conversation with the whites, and then returned to the ledge.

"Trouble over horses," he said.

"Ay, ay, I reckoned that was what you was talking over. There ain't no going back for them now."

The chief shook his head. "'Rappahoes keep watch," he said, "cannot go till night to fetch horses. All lie here to-day, go across to rock when darkness comes, then white men go up valley till get to trees an hour's march away; can see them from rock. Get in among trees and work up into hills. Leaping Horse and Hunting Dog cross river, go down other side past 'Rappahoes, then cross back and get into canon, drive horses up. White men meet them up in mountains."

"That seems a good plan enough, chief. That is, if you can get out at the other end of the canon."

"Canon little up high," the chief replied. "Find some place to climb."

"But they may find the horses to-day."

The Indian nodded. "May find, perhaps not."

"Why should we not go across to the rock at once, chief?"

"Indian count on fingers how many. They do not know we only four; much troubled in their mind where men come from, who can be. Redskins not like white men. Have many fancies. Fire come out of bush where 'Rappahoe had been killed; think that bad medicine, keep together and talk. Think if men here, why not go across to rock."

"I should not be surprised if you are right, chief. They are more likely to fancy we have come down from above than from below, for they must have reckoned for sure there were no other white men in the Big Wind valley, and our not showing ourselves will give them an all-fired scare."

"What does the chief mean by bad medicine, Jerry?" Tom asked.

"A red-skin is full of all sorts of ideas. Anything he can't make head nor tail of, is bad medicine; they think there is some magic in it, and that old Nick has had his finger in the pie. When they get an idea like that in their minds, even the bravest of them loses his pluck, and is like a child who thinks he has seen a ghost. It is a mighty good notion for us to lie low all day. The red-skins will reason it all out, and will say, if these are white men who killed our brothers why the 'tarnal don't they go and join the others, there ain't nothing to prevent them. If they ain't white men, who are they? Maybe they can move without our being able to see them and will shoot from some other place. No, I reckon it is likely they will keep pretty close together and won't venture to scatter to look for tracks, and in that case the chief's plan will work out all right. In course, a good deal depends on their chief; one of them is among those we shot, you can make out his feathers from here. If he is the boss chief, it may be that they will give it up altogether; the next chief will throw the blame on to him, and may like enough persuade them to draw off altogether. If it ain't the boss chief, then they are bound to try again. He would not like to take them back to their villages with the news that a grist of them had been killed and narry a scalp taken. I expect you will see this afternoon some of them come down to palaver with Harry."

The morning passed quietly and not unpleasantly, for they were lying in the shade, but before noon the sun had climbed up over the cliff behind them and shone down with great force, and they had to lie with their heads well under the bushes to screen them from its rays. Presently, Leaping Horse said:

"Indian chief come, no lift heads."

All shifted their position so as to look down the valley. An Indian chief, holding up his hands to show that he was unarmed, was advancing on foot, accompanied by another Indian also without arms.

"There is Harry going down to meet them," Jerry said.

Tom looked eagerly at the figure that came down from the rock and advanced to meet the Indians. It seemed strange to him that after having come so far to join his uncle they should remain for hours in sight of each other without meeting. It was too far to distinguish his features, but he saw by the light walk and easy swing of the figure that his uncle was a much more active man than he had expected to see. He had known indeed that he was but forty years old, but he had somehow expected that the life of hardship he had led would have aged him, and he was surprised to see that his walk and figure were those of a young man.

"Is it not rather dangerous, his coming down alone to meet two of them? They may have arms hidden."

"They have got arms, you may be sure," Jerry replied. "They have knives for certain, and most likely tomahawks, but I expect Harry has got his six-shooter. But it don't matter whether he has or not, there are his two mates up on that rock with their rifles, and we are across here. The 'Rappahoes would know well enough their lives wouldn't be worth a red cent if they were to try any of their games. They don't mean business; they will make out they have come to persuade. Harry and his mates to give up, which they know quite well they ain't fools enough to do. But what is really in their minds is to try and find out who we are, and where we have come from."

The conversation lasted a few minutes. Tom could see that questions were being asked about the concealed party, for the chief pointed to the ledge two or three times. When the talk was over the Indians went down the valley again at a slow pace, never once looking back, and the Englishman returned to the rocks.

"I don't suppose they have got much from Harry."

"I suppose uncle talks their language?"

"No, I don't reckon he knows the 'Rappahoe dialect. But the tribes on the western side of the plains can mostly understand each other's talk; and as I know he can get on well with the Utes, he is sure to be able to understand the 'Rappahoes' talk."

"Leaping Horse will go along the ledge," the chief said a few minutes later, after a short conversation with Hunting Dog. "The 'Rappahoes will try to find out who are here; not like to attack the rock till find out." The two Indians lay down flat on the ledge, and crawled along without raising themselves in the slightest until they reached a point where the cliffs projected somewhat. From here they could see down the valley, and they lay immovable, with their rifles in front of them.

"They are not more than fifty yards or so from those bushes where we got up on to the ledge. That is where the red-skins are likely to try crawling up, for there they would be out of sight of the rock."

"Surely they would never venture to come along the ledge in daylight, Jerry. They would have to pass along under the fire of uncle and his mates, and would have our rifles to meet in front."

"No, it would only be one, or at most, two scouts. They would reckon that from that point where the chief is lying they would get a view right along the ledge to here, and be able to make out what we are. It is the strangeness of the thing that has kept them quiet all these hours, and I expect their chief will want to prove that there are only a few of us, and that we are men for certain. I reckon they have sent off to the villages already, and there will be more of the varmint here to-night. The Indians are never fond of attacking in the dark; still, if they were sure about us, they might try it. They would know they could get up to the foot of that rock before being seen, and once among the bushes they would reckon they could make easy work of it."

A quarter of an hour later there was the crack of a rifle, followed instantly by an Indian yell.

"That is the chief's piece, Tom, and I reckon the lead has gone straight."

The silence remained unbroken for the next two hours, and then Leaping Horse crawled back as quietly as he had gone.

"What was it, chief?"

"It was a 'Rappahoe, who will scout no more," the chief said quietly. "He came up the bushes, but before he could step on to the ledge Leaping Horse fired, and he will take no tales back to his tribe."

"They won't try again, chief?"

Leaping Horse shook his head. "First take rock," he said, "then when they have the scalps of the white men they will watch us here. Will know we cannot stay here long without water."

"You are right there, chief, and no m'stake; my tongue is like a piece of leather now, and as soon as it gets dark I shall make a bee-line down to the river. I want to have a talk with Harry, but just at present I want a drink a blamed sight worse. If I had thought we were going to be stuck up here all day I would have brought my water-bottle with me."

The time passed very slowly, although the air became cooler as soon as the sun had gone down behind the opposite range. As soon as the light faded a little, the Indian crawled farther along the ledge, and returned in a short time saying that he had found a spot where the whites could descend. Two or three times Jerry urged that it was dark enough, before the chief consented to move. At last, however, he stood up and gave the cry of an owl, and they were in a minute or two joined by Hunting Dog, who had until now remained at his post. The chief at once led the way along the ledge until he reached the spot where the rock had crumbled away somewhat.

"We had better go down one at a time," Jerry said. "For if there was a slip or a tumble it might let down a gun-hammer, and we want our lead for the 'Rappahoes, and not for each other."

When it came to Tom's turn, he found it a very difficult place to get down in the semi-darkness, and two or three times he almost lost his footing. As soon as all were down they fell into Indian file, and crossed the valley to the rock, the chief giving the hoot of an owl twice as he approached it. Three men at once stepped out from the bushes at its foot.

"I began to wonder when you were coming, and was just going to get the ponies down before it was too dark to do it without running the risk of breaking their legs. Well, I am right glad to see you, Jerry; and you too, Tom, though it is too dark to see much of you. The chief has been telling me how he brought you along. There is no time to talk now, but I am right glad to see you, lad," and he shook Tom heartily by the hand. "Now, mates, let us get the horses down."

"I must make tracks for the water first, Harry, the young un and I are pretty near choking; and I expect the Indians are as bad, though it ain't their natur to talk about it."

"Get down horses first," the chief said. "Too dark soon."

"Waal, I suppose five minutes won't make much difference," Jerry grumbled, "so here goes."

"I have tied some hide over their hoofs," Harry said, "so as to make as little noise as possible about it."

"Must make no noise," the chief said urgently. "Red-skin scouts soon be crawling up."

One by one the horses were brought down, Harry leading them, and the others pushing aside the bushes as noiselessly as possible. Then their loads were carried down and packed upon them.

"You get on my horse, Jerry," Harry Wade whispered, "I will walk with Tom. I have had no time to say a word to him yet, or to ask about the people at home. Where is the chief?"

Leaping Horse and his companion had stolen away as soon as the loads had been adjusted. The others led the horses to the river, and allowed them to drink, while Jerry and Tom lay down and took a long draught of the water. The miners' bottles were filled, and they then started. "It is lucky the river makes such a roar among these rocks here," Harry said, "it will drown the sound of the horses' hoofs."

For half an hour they proceeded at a fast walk, then the skins were taken off the horses' feet and they went on at a trot, the two Wades taking hold of Jerry's stirrup-leathers and running alongside. In half an hour they entered the belt of trees, and dismounting, at once began to ascend the hill. They were some distance up when they heard a distant yell.

"You may yell as much as you like," Jerry panted, "you won't catch us now. They have been a mighty long time finding out we were gone."

"They could not make out about you," Harry said. "I could see by the chief's manner, and the glances the Indian with him kept giving to the place where you were lying, that they were puzzled and alarmed. They offered if we would surrender that they would allow us to return down the valley without hurt. I said, of course, that I preferred staying where I was; we had come up the valley and intended going farther; we didn't want to interfere with them, and if they had left us alone we should have left them alone; and they had only themselves to thank for the loss of some of their braves. 'We have,' I said, 'many friends, who will protect us, and much harm will fall on the Indians who venture to meddle with us.'

"'Are your friends white men?' the chief asked. 'Have they wings that they have flown down here from the hills?'

"'They have come, that is enough,' I said. 'You see, when they were wanted they were here, and if they are wanted again you will hear of them, and your braves will die, and you will gain nothing. You had best go back to your lodges and leave us to go away in peace. Whoever they are, they can shoot, as you have found out to your cost. They have no ill-will to the red-skins, providing the red- skins let us alone. They only fired four shots; if they had wished to, they could have killed many more.' When the chief saw that he could get nothing further from me he went away. As usual he spoke boastfully at last, and said that he had offered peace to us, and if war came, it would be our faults. I laughed, and said that we could take care of ourselves, and preferred doing so to trusting ourselves in the hands of the 'Rappahoes, when we had made some of their squaws widows."

"Would they have kept their word, uncle, do you think?" Tom asked.

"Not they. There are a few of the Indian tribes whose word can be taken, but as a rule words mean nothing with them, and if we had put ourselves in their power they would have tomahawked us instantly, or else taken us down and tortured us at their villages, which would have been a deal worse. I have no doubt they had a long talk after the chief returned to them, and that it was some time after it became dark before they could pluck up courage enough to climb the rock, though I expect they must have got close to it very soon after we left. I reckon they have been crawling up inch by inch. Of course, directly they got to where the horses had been tied they knew we had gone, and I expect that yell was a signal for a rush forward to the top. But we need not bother any more about them. They may ride as far as the foot of the forest, but when they find we have gained that safely they will give it up until morning; they will know well enough it is no good starting to search the woods in the dark. We may as well rest where we are until the moon is up, for we make so much noise crashing through this undergrowth that they could hear us down there."

"Now tell me, lad, about your mother and sisters, and how you came out after all."

Tom told his uncle of his mother's death, and the reason why he had left his sisters to come out to join him. "It is a very bad business, lad, and I take a lot of blame to myself. When I got your mother's letter, telling me of poor John's death, and that she would not hear of your coming out, I said some very hard things to myself. Here had I been knocking about for twenty years, and having had a fair share of luck, and yet I could not put my hand on five hundred dollars, and there was my brother's widow and children, and I, their nearest relative, could not help them. It made me feel a pretty mean man, I can tell you. Your mother did not say much about her circumstances, but it did not need that. I knew that John had retired from the navy with little besides his half-pay, and that her pension as his widow must be a mighty slim one. Altogether I had a pretty bad time of it. However, I took a tall oath that the next rich strike I made the dollars should not be thrown away. I reckoned that you would be out before long; for it was certain that if you were a lad of spirit you would not be staying there doing nothing. Your mother said that the girls all intended to take up teaching, and it was not likely that you would let them work for the family while you were loafing about at home. I know in my time it was hard enough to get anything to do there, and young fellows who have come out here to ranche tell me that it is harder than ever now. I thought you would fancy this life, and that in time you would talk your mother over into letting you come."

"I should never have got her to agree to it, uncle. I wanted to go to sea, but after father's death she would not hear of it. She said I was her only boy and that she could not spare me, and I had to promise to give up the thought. She was still more against your plan, but when I wrote to you I thought that possibly in time she might agree to it. But it was not long afterwards that her health began to fail, and I saw then that I must give up all thought of leaving her, and must, when I left school, take anything that offered; and it was only after her death that I talked it over with the girls, and they agreed that to come here was the best thing for me."

"And you left before my last letter arrived?"

"Yes; we had no letter after the one you wrote asking me to come out."

"No, I suppose you could not have had it. I wrote before I started out three months ago from Salt Lake City. I had struck a ledge of pretty good stuff, I and another. We sold out for a thousand dollars, and I sent my share off to your mother, telling her that I had been having bad luck since I got her letter, but that I hoped to do better in future, and I thought, anyhow, I could promise to send her as much once a year, and if I had a real stroke of luck she and her girls would have the benefit of it."

"That was good of you, uncle."

"Not good at all," Harry Wade grumbled. "I have behaved like a fool all along; it is true that when I did get letters from your father, which was not very often, he always wrote cheerfully, and said very little about how he was situated as to money. But I ought to have known—I did know, if I thought of it—that with a wife and six children it must be mighty hard to make ends meet on a lieutenant's half-pay, and there was I, often throwing away twice as much as his year's pension on a week's spree. When I heard he was gone you may pretty well guess how I felt. However, lad, if things turn out well I will make it up as far as I can. Now, let us join the others."

The others, however, were all sound asleep, having wrapped themselves in their blankets, and lain down as soon as the halt was decided upon. Jerry, having had no sleep the previous night, and but little for four or five days, had not even thought of asking the others for food, which they doubtless had on their saddles, although he had tasted nothing for twenty-four hours. Tom, however, less accustomed to enforced fasts, felt ravenous. "We have had nothing to eat to-day, uncle, except a crust left over from yesterday's baking, and I don't think I could get to sleep if I did not eat something."

"Bless me, I never thought of that, Tom. If I had I would have sent food across by the chief this morning. There is no bread, but there is plenty of cold meat. We cooked a lot yesterday evening, for we thought we might not get a chance of cooking to-day."

"Then you knew, uncle, the Indians were near?" Tom went on, when he had appeased his appetite and taken a drink of water, with a little whisky in it from his uncle's flask.

"Ay, lad; we guessed somehow we had been followed all along. We had done everything we could to throw them off the trail—travelling as much as we could in the course of streams, muffling the feet of our ponies, and picking out the hardest ground to travel on; but every morning before daybreak one of us went up the hillside, and twice we made out mounted Indians moving about down the valley. Yesterday morning ten of them came galloping up within easy shot. I don't think they thought that we were so near. They drew up their horses suddenly, had a talk, and then came riding after us. It didn't need their yells to tell us what their intention was. We knocked three of them out of their saddles, then threw our horses down and lay behind them.

"They galloped round and round us shooting, but we picked two more off, and then they rode away. We knew enough of them to be sure that they were not going to give it up, but would follow us 'till joined by enough of their tribe to attack us again. We made a long march, hoping to get to the timber before they could come up, but just as the sun was setting we saw them coming along, about fifteen of them; and we had just time to get up to that rock. As they rode past we opened a smart fire and dropped four of them; the others rode up the valley, so as to cut us off from going farther. We filled our water-skins and got the horses half-way up as you saw, and then lighted a fire and cooked. We kept watch all night, two down below and one at the top; but everything was quiet, and we guessed they were waiting for others to come up.

"About an hour before daylight we heard another gang arrive below us. They halted there, and it was not long before they began crawling up from above and below, and for a bit we shot pretty brisk. The odds were too much against them, with us on the height, and they drew off. Then for an hour they were pretty quiet while they were holding council, except that we did some shooting with a party who had climbed up to that ledge opposite; then we saw both bands mount, and reckoned they were going to make a dash for us. We knew if they did it in earnest we must go down, for once among the rocks and bushes there would be no keeping them from mounting up. We made up our minds that the end was not far off, though I fancy we should have accounted for a good many of them before they rubbed us out. When your four rifles spoke from the ledge we thought it was a party who had gone back there, for we felt sure that we had driven them all away, but it wasn't more than a moment before we saw it wasn't that. There was no mistaking the yell of astonishment from the Indians, and as the horses swerved round we saw that three of them had fallen. You may guess we didn't stop to argue who it was, but set to work to do our share; but it seemed to us something like a miracle when the red-skins rode off.

"We had been talking of Leaping Horse during the night, for he had promised to come back to join us, and I knew him well enough to be able to bet all creation that he would come. He had only left us to keep an appointment with his nephew, who was to join him at Fort Bridger. If there had only been two guns fired we should have put it down to him, but being four I don't think either of us thought of him till he stood up and shouted. Now, lad, you had better take a sleep. We shall be moving on as soon as the moon is fairly up, and it won't be over that hill behind us till two or three. I will watch till then, but I don't think there is the least chance of their following us to-night; they have been pretty roughly handled, and I don't think they will follow until they have solved the mystery of that ledge. They searched it, no doubt, as soon as they found the rock was empty, and at daybreak they will set about tracing the trail up. That will be easy enough for them when they have once got rid of the idea that there was something uncanny about it, and then we shall have them on our heels again and on the chief's too. The first thing for us to do will be to make along the hill till we get to the edge of the canon, where Leaping Horse has gone for your ponies, and to follow it to its upper end."

"I will watch, uncle, if you will wake me in an hour. I shall be all right after a nap, but I can scarcely keep my eyes open now."

It seemed, however, to Tom that he had not been asleep five minutes when his uncle shook him. The others were already on their feet. The moon was shining down through the trees, and with cautious steps, and taking the utmost trouble to avoid the branches, they started on their upward climb. Not a word was spoken, for all knew how far sound travels on a still night. There was, however, a slight breeze moving among the tree tops when they started, and in an hour this had so far increased that the boughs were swaying and the leaves rustling.

"I reckon there ain't no occasion to keep our mouths shut no longer," one of the men said. "Now that the trees are on the move they would not hear us if they were only a hundred yards away." All were glad when daylight began to appear, Tom because the climbing would be much easier when the ground could be seen, the others because they were all longing for a pipe, but had hitherto not dared to light one, for the flash of a match could be seen far away. They had been bearing steadily to the right as they mounted, and shortly after daybreak they suddenly found themselves on the edge of a canon.

"Do you think this is the one, Jerry?" one of the men asked.

"That is more than I can tell, Ben. I did not see an opening in the valley as we came up it, but we might very well have missed one in the dark. I should think from the distance we have gone towards the right it must be the one where we left our horses. Anyhow, whether it is or not, we must follow it up to the top and wait there for a bit to see if the chief comes."

"I reckon he will be there before us," Harry said; "that is if he got round the red-skins all right and found the horses. There would be no reason for him to wait, and I expect he would go straight on, and is like enough to be waiting for us by this time."

Chapter VII.
Chased

The party pressed forward as rapidly as they could. The ground was rough and at times very steep, and those on foot were able to keep up with the horses without much difficulty.

"You think the Indians will follow, uncle?" Tom asked.

"They will follow, you may bet your boots, Tom; by this time they have got to the bottom of the mystery. The first thing this morning some of them will go up on to the ledge where you were, follow your tracks down to the canon where you left the horses, and find that you came up the valley and not down it. They will have made out that there were two whites and two red-skins, and that the two red-skins have gone up the canon with the horses. Directly the matter is all cleared up, they will be hotter than ever for our scalps, for there is nothing a red-skin hates worse than being fooled. Of course, they will know that it is a good deal harder to wipe out seven men than three, and I don't think they will attack us openly; they know well enough that in a fair fight two red-skins, if not three, are likely to go down for each white they rub out. But they will bide their time: red-skins are a wonderful hand at that; time is nothing to them, and they would not mind hanging about us for weeks and weeks if they can but get us at last. However, we will talk it all over when the Indians join us. I don't think there is any chance of fighting to-day, but whether we shall get out of these mountains without having another scrimmage is doubtful."

Tom noticed that in his talk with him his uncle dropped most of the western expressions which when speaking with the others he used as freely as they did. He was now able to have a fair look at him, and found that he agreed pretty closely with the ideas he had formed of him. There was a strong likeness between him and his brother. They were about the same height, but Harry was broader and more strongly built. His face was deeply bronzed by long exposure to the wind and sun. He had a large tawny beard, while Tom's father had been clean shaved. The sailor was five years the senior, but the miner looked far younger than Tom could ever remember his father looking, for the latter had never thoroughly recovered his health after having had a long bout of fever on the Zanzibar station; and the long stride and free carriage of his uncle was in striking contrast to the walk of his father. Both had keen gray eyes, the same outline of face, the same pleasant smile.

"Now that I can see you fairly, Tom," the miner said, when they halted once for the horses to come up to them, "I can make out that you are a good deal like your father as I can first remember him."

"I was thinking you were very like him, uncle."

"We used to be alike in the old days, but I reckon the different lives we led must have changed us both a great deal. He sent me once a photograph four or five years ago, and at first I should not have known it was he. I could see the likeness after a bit, but he was very much changed. No doubt I have changed still more; all this hair on my face makes a lot of difference. You see, it is a very long time since we met. I was but twenty when I left England, and I had not seen him for two or three years before that, for he was on the Mediterranean station at the time. Well, here are the horses again, and as the ground looks flatter ahead we shall have to push on to keep up with them." They were presently altogether beyond the forest, and a broad plateau of bare rock stretched away in front of them for miles.

"There they are," Jerry Curtis shouted. "I was beginning to feel scared that the 'Rappahoes had got them."

It was a minute or two before Tom could make out the distant figures, for his eyes were less accustomed to search for moving objects than were those of his companions.

"They are riding fast," Harry Wade said. "I reckon they have made out some Indians on their trail."

The little dark mass Tom had first seen soon resolved itself into two horsemen and two riderless animals. They were still three or four miles away, but in twenty minutes they reached the party advancing to meet them. The whites waved their hats and gave them a cheer as they rode up.

"So you have managed to get through them all right, chief?"

"The 'Rappahoes are dogs. They are frightened at shadows; their eyes were closed. Leaping Horse stood near their fires and saw them go forward, and knew that his white brothers must have gained the forest before the 'Rappahoes got to the rock. He found the horses safe, but the canon was very dark and in some places very narrow, with many rocks in the road, so that he had to stop till the moon was high. It was not until morning came that he reached the head of the canon, an hour's ride from here. Half an hour back Leaping Horse went to the edge and looked down. There were ten 'Rappahoes riding fast up the trail. Has my brother heard anything of the others?"

"Nothing whatever," Harry said. "I reckon they did not begin to move until daylight, and as we went on when the moon rose they must be a good two hours behind us. Which way do you think we had better go, chief?"

"Where does my brother wish to go?"

"It matters mighty little. I should say for a bit we had better travel along this plateau, keeping about the same distance from the timber-line. I don't think the 'Rappahoes will venture to attack us in the open. If we keep on here we can cross the divide and get into the Shoshones' country, and either go down the Buffalo and then up the Snake and so work down south, or go east and strike some of the streams running that way into the Big Horn."

The chief shook his head.

"Too far, too many bad Indians; will talk over fire tonight."

"That is it, chief. It is a matter that wants a good deal of talking over. Anyhow, we had better be moving on at once."

Tom was glad to find himself in the saddle again, and the party rode on at a steady pace for some hours, then they halted, lit a fire, and cooked a meal. Tom noticed that the Indians no longer took pains to gather dry sticks, but took the first that came to hand. He remarked this to Jerry.

"They know it is no use trying to hide our trail here; the two bands of Indians will follow, one up and one down, until they meet at the spot where the chief joined us. From there they can track us easy enough. Nothing would suit us better than for them to come up to us here, for we should give them fits, sartin. This is a good place. This little stream comes down from that snow peak you see over there, and we have got everything we want, for this patch of bushes will keep us in firing for a bit. You see, there are some more big hills in front of us, and we are better here than we should be among them. I expect we shall camp here for the night."

"Then you don't think the Indians will come up close?"

"Not they. They will send a spy or two to crawl up, you may be sure, but they will know better than to come within reach of our rifles."

"I am mighty glad to have my teeth into some deer-flesh again," Ben Gulston said. "We had two or three chances as we came along, but we dare not fire, and we have just been living on bread and bacon. Where did you kill these wapiti?"

"At our first halt, near Fremont's Pass. We got two."

"Well, you haven't eaten much, Jerry," Sam Hicks said. "I reckon four men ought pretty well to have finished off two quarters by this time."

"I reckon we should have finished one of the bucks, Sam; but we caught a grist of fish the same day, dried them in the sun, and I think we mostly ate them. They would not keep as well as the flesh. That is as good as the day we shot it, for up here in the dry air meat keeps a sight better than down in the plains. Give me some more tea, Sam."

"What do you think, mates, of camping here?" Harry Wade said. "The chief thinks we are better here than we should be if we moved on. He feels certain the red-skins won't dare attack us."

There was a cordial agreement in favour of a halt, for after the work they had gone through during the last week they were glad of a rest.

No one would have thought half an hour afterwards that the little party engaged in washing their shirts at the stream or mending their clothes, were in the heart of a country unknown to most of them, and menaced by a savage foe. The horses cropped the scanty tufts of grass or munched the young tops of the bushes, the rifles stood stacked by the fire, near which the two Indians sat smoking and talking earnestly together, Hunting Dog occasionally getting up and taking a long careful look over the plain. As the men finished their various jobs they came back to the fire. "Now, chief," Harry said, "let us hear your ideas as to what we had best do. We are all pretty old hands at mountaineering, but we reckon you know a great deal more about it than we do. You don't like the plans I proposed."

"No can do it," the chief said positively. "In a moon the snow will fall, and there will be no crossing mountains."

"That is true enough," Jerry said. "An old trapper who had lived among the Shoshones told me that nine months in the year they were shut up in the valleys by the snow on the passes."

"Then how can live?" the chief went on. "As long as we stay in this country the 'Rappahoes will watch us. They will tell the Bannacks and the Nez Percés, and they too would be on our trail. As long as we keep together and watch they will not come, they fear the white man's rifle; but we cannot live without hunting, and then they kill one, two, till all killed. At night must always watch, at day cannot hunt. How we live? What good to stay? If we stop all killed sure."

There was silence round the circle. Every one of them felt the truth of the Indian's words, and yet they hated the thought of abandoning their search for gold, or, failing that, of a return home with their horses laden with beaver skins.

Harry was the first to speak. "I am afraid these varmint have interfered with our plans, mates. If we had had the luck to drop into one of the upper valleys without being noticed we could have hunted and trapped there and looked for gold for months without much chance of being discovered, but this has upset it all. I am afraid that what the chief says is true. If we keep together we starve, if we break up and hunt we shall be ambushed and killed. I hate giving up anything I have set my mind on, but this time I don't see a way out of it. We ain't the first party that has come up here and had to go back again with empty hands, and we know what happened to that party of twenty old-time miners from California two years ago, though none of them ever got back to tell the tale. We knew when we started, it wur just a chance, and the cards have gone against us."

"That is so," Ben agreed; "if it had turned out well we might have made a good strike. It ain't turned out well, and as every day we stay here there will be more of those varmint swarming round us, I say the sooner we get out of this dog-goned country the better."

"You can count me in with you, Ben," Sam Hicks said. "We have gone in for the game and we don't hold hands, and it ain't no use bluffing against them red-skins. We sha'n't have lost much time arter all, and I reckon we have all learned something. Some day when the railroad goes right across, Uncle Sam will have to send a grist of troops to reckon up with the red-skins in these hills, and arter that it may be a good country for mining and trapping, but for the present we are a darned sight more likely to lose our scalps than to get skins."

"Well, Leaping Horse, which way would you advise us to take, then?"

"Go straight back to canon, ride down there, cross river, go up mountains other side, pass them north of Union Peak, come down on upper water Big Wind River. From there little way on to Green River. Leaping Horse never been there, but has heard. One long day's ride from here, go to upper waters of Green River."

"That sounds good," Jerry Curtis said. "If we could once strike the Green we should be out of the 'Rappahoe country altogether. I have known two or three men who have been up the Green nearly to its head, and there is good hunting and a good many beaver in the side streams. I should not have thought it would have come anywhere like as near as this, but I don't doubt the chief is right."

"Union Peak," the chief said, pointing to a crag rising among a tumble of hills to the south.

"Are you sure, chief?"

The Indian nodded. "Forty, fifty miles away," he said. "Leaping Horse has been to upper waters of Green River, seen the peak from other side."

"That settles it, then," Harry said. "That is our course, there cannot be a doubt. I should never have proposed the other if I had had an idea that we were within sixty or seventy miles of the Green River. And you think we had better take the canon you came up by, chief?"

The Indian nodded. "If go down through forest may be ambushed. Open ground from here back to canon. 'Rappahoes most in front. Think we go that way, not think we go back. Get good start. Once across river follow up little stream among hills other side, that the way to pass. If 'Rappahoes follow us we fight them."

"Yes, we shall have them at an advantage there, for they would have to come up under our fire, and there are sure to be places where half a dozen men could keep fifty at bay. Very well, chief, that is settled. When do you think we had better start?"

"When gets dark," the chief replied. "No lose time, more Indian come every hour. Keep fire burning well, 'Rappahoes think we camp here. Take horses a little way off and mount beyond light of fire."

"You think they will be watching us?"

"Sure to watch. First ride north half an hour, then turn and ride to canon. If spies see us go off take word to friends we gone north. Too dark to follow trail. They think they catch us easy to-morrow, and take up trail in morning; but too late then, we cross river before that."

There was a general murmur of assent. The thought of being constantly watched, and suddenly attacked when least expecting it, made them feel restless, and the thought of early action was pleasant to them.

"You don't think that there are any spies watching us now, uncle, do you?"

"Not close, Tom; they would know better than that. They could see us miles away if we were to mount and ride off, and it is only when it gets dark that they would venture to crawl up, for if one were sighted in the daytime he would not have a ghost of a chance of getting away, for we could ride him down sartin."

"Well, I reckon we may as well take a sleep," Sam Hicks said. "You lie down for one, anyhow, Harry, for you watched last evening. We will toss up which of us keeps awake."

"Leaping Horse will keep watch," the chief said quietly. "No fear of Indians, but better to watch."

Knowing the power of the red-skins to keep awake for an almost unlimited time, none of the others thought of refusing the offer, and in a few minutes all were sound asleep. Towards sunset they were on their feet again. Another meal was cooked and eaten, then as it became dusk the horses were gathered fifty yards away, and Hunting Dog and Tom took their places beside them.

"Keep your eyes open and your rifle handy, Tom," his uncle said. "It is like enough that some young brave, anxious to distinguish himself, may crawl up with the intention of stampeding the ponies, though I don't think he would attempt it till he thought most of us were asleep. Still, there is no saying."

The watch was undisturbed, and soon it became so dark that objects could no longer be seen fifty yards away. Tom began to feel nervous. Every tuft of ground, every little bush seemed to him to take the form of a crawling Indian, and he felt a great sense of relief when he saw the figures round the fire rise and walk towards him. "I am glad you have come, uncle," he said frankly; "I began to feel very uncomfortable several times. It seemed to me that some of the bushes moved."

"That is just what I thought you would be feeling, Tom. But it was just as well that your first watch should be a short one, without much chance of an ambush being on foot; and I knew that if your eyes deceived you, Hunting Dog was there. Next time you won't feel so nervous; that sort of thing soon passes off."

A fresh armful of brushwood had been thrown on to the fire before the men left it, and long after they had ridden away they could see the flames mounting high. After riding north for a quarter of an hour they changed their route and passed round, leaving the fire half a mile on their right. The light of the stars was quite sufficient for them to travel by, and after four hours' journey the chief, who was riding ahead, halted.

"Not far from canon now. Listen."

A very faint murmur came to their ears, so faint that had not his attention been drawn to it Tom would not have noticed it at all.

"What is that noise?" he asked.

"That is the stream down in the canon," his uncle replied. "How far are we from the head, chief?"

"Not far, must ride slow."

They proceeded at a walk, changing their course a little towards the east. Hunting Dog went on ahead, and in a quarter of an hour they heard his signal, the cry of an owl. It arose from a point still further east, and quickening their pace, in a few minutes they came up to the young Indian, who was standing by his horse at the edge of a steep descent, at the bottom of which Tom could see a stream of water.

"It looks very steep," Jerry said.

"Steep, but smooth," the Indian replied. "Came up here with horses this morning." All dismounted, and Tom went up to his horse's head. "That won't do, Tom. Never go before a horse down a steep place where you can't see your way, always drive it before you."

There was some trouble in getting the horses to commence the descent, but after a short time the chief's pony set the example; and tucking its hind legs under it until it sat down on its haunches, began to slide down, while the other animals, after staring into the darkness with ears laid back and snorting with fear, were half-persuaded, half-forced to follow its example, and the men went down after them. The descent was not so steep as in the darkness it looked, and the depth was not over fifty feet. As soon as they reached the bottom they mounted again, and the chief leading the way, they rode down the canon. At first they were able to proceed at a fair pace, but as the sides grew higher and more precipitous the darkness became more dense, and they were obliged to pick their way with great caution among the boulders that strewed the bottom of the ravine. Several times they had to dismount in order to get the horses over heavy falls, and it was four hours from the time they entered the canon before they approached its mouth. When they entered the little wood where they had first left the horses, the chief said, "Make fire, cook food here. Leaping Horse and Hunting Dog go on and scout, maybe 'Rappahoes left watch in valley."

"Very well, chief. It is seven hours since we started; I think the horses will be all the better for an hour's rest, and I am sure we shall be the better of a feed. Besides, when we are once out of this hole we may have to travel fast."

"You don't think it likely that the 'Rappahoes are on the look-out for us at the entrance?" Tom asked, as the Indians moved away.

"Not likely at all, Tom. Still, as they might reckon that if we gave their searching party the slip we must come down again by the river or through this canon, they may have left a party or sent down word to some of their villages to keep a watch in the valley."

It was more than an hour before the Indians returned.

"No 'Rappahoes in valley," the chief said, as he seated himself by the fire and began without loss of time to eat the meat they had cooked in readiness. "Better be going soon, must cross river and get on before light come; have seen fires, Indian villages up on hillsides. When light comes and 'Rappahoes find trail they come back quick."

"You may bet your boots they will, chief," Sam Hicks said. "They will be a pretty mad crowd when they make out that we have come down again by the canon. As soon as they see which way we have headed some of them will make a bee-line down here in hopes of cutting us off at the mouth, but by the time they are here we shall be half-way up the hill."

The Indian made no reply, but he and Hunting Dog ate their meal steadily, and as soon as they had finished rose to their feet, and saying "Time to go" went out to fetch in their horses.

"I don't think the chief is as confident we shall get off without a fight as Sam seemed to be," Tom said to his uncle.

"There is never any saying what an Indian thinks, Tom, even when he has fallen into white man's ways, as Leaping Horse has done. It may be that the sight of the fires he made out on the opposite hills has troubled him. It will be light before we are far up on the side, and we may be made out by some of the varmint there. They are always restless. Go into an Indian village when you will, you will find some of them smoking by the fire. Their ears are so 'tarnal sharp, they can hear sounds that would never catch our ears, not at half the distance. The clink of a couple of pans together, or a stone set rolling by a horse's tread, were it ever so faint, would bring them on their feet directly, especially now they know that a war-party is out."

The march was again resumed. Passing through the narrowest part of the canon they issued out into the valley and made for the river. Some time was lost here, for Sam Hicks, who was leading one of the pack-ponies, was carried down several hundred yards by the stream, and with difficulty effected his landing. The horse's load shifted and had to be repacked. As soon as this was done they followed the river down for two miles till they came upon a stream running into it from the southwest.

"You think this is the stream we have to follow, chief?"

"Must be him, no other came in on this side for a long way; right line for peak."

They turned up by the stream, and after riding a mile found themselves entering a mountain gorge. It was not a canon but a steep, narrow valley. They picked their way with the greatest caution for some time, then the two Indians stopped simultaneously.

"What is the matter, chief?" Harry, who was riding next to them, whispered.

"Smell smoke."

Harry sniffed the air.

"I can't say I smell it, chief, but if you say you do that settles it. Where do you think it comes from?"

"Up valley; wind light, but comes that way. Indian village up here."

"Well, so much the worse for the Indian village if it interferes with us," Harry said grimly; "there is one thing certain, we have got to go through. Probably most of the braves are away up in the hills."

They now went on with redoubled caution. The chief gave his bridle to Hunting Dog and went forward on foot. A hundred yards farther the valley made a sharp turn and then widened out considerably, and the glow of a fire was visible among some trees standing on the hillside some fifty feet above the level of the stream. The chief looked at the sky; a faint light was breaking, and without pausing he continued to lead the way. They passed under the Indian encampment, and had got a few yards higher when the pony Sam Hicks was leading gave a sharp neigh.

"Darn its old ears!" Tom heard Jerry growl. Harry at the same moment put his horse to a trot, and the others following clattered up the valley, knowing that concealment was no longer of any use; indeed, an answering neigh from above and hurried shouts were heard, followed a moment afterwards by a loud yell as an Indian running through the trees caught sight of them in the moonlight.

"We are in for it now, Tom; that is, if there are men enough in the village to attack us."

The horses broke into a gallop. They had gone but fifty yards when a rifle-shot was heard from behind, and Tom felt a shock as the ball struck his saddle. Almost immediately another shot was fired abreast of him, and an Indian yell rose loudly behind them. A moment later Leaping Horse with a shout of triumph bounded down the rocks and leapt on to his horse. Four or five more shots were fired from behind, but none of them were hit. A hundred yards farther they were in shelter of a belt of trees that extended down to the stream. As they entered it Harry looked back. He could now see the hills beyond the main valley.

"Look, chief!" he exclaimed. "The varmint up there are signalling far off above the timber-line."

Bright tongues of fire could be seen, two close together and one a short distance to the left.

"What does that mean, uncle?" Tom asked, as the chief gave a short exclamation of surprise and anger.

"It means, lad, that the red-skins have been sharper than we gave them credit for. When their spies brought them news that we had started they must have come down to the fire and followed our trail at once with torches, before we had got above an hour or two away. No doubt it was slow work, but they must have found where we changed our course, and made out that we were making for the head of the canon. I expect most of them lost no time in following the trail farther, but rode straight for the head of the canon, and like enough they weren't half an hour behind us when we came out. The others rode to the edge of the plateau and set those fires alight."

"But what do they mean, uncle?"

"They are a warning to all the villages that we have headed back, you may be sure of that, though I can't say what the message is, for every tribe has its own signals, but it will have set them on the watch up and down the valley; and like enough the signal has been repeated somewhere at a point where it can be seen straight down the Big Wind Valley. The shooting will tell them all which way we are making, and if the 'Rappahoes have come out of the canon, as I reckon they have, they need lose no more time in looking for our trail. I reckon in half an hour we shall have a hundred or so of the varmint after us. I only hope there are no more villages upon this line. I don't so much care about the fellows who are following us, we are sure to find some place where we can make a stand, but it would be awkward if we find our way barred."

"But if there is no one in front, uncle, I should think we might be able to keep ahead. Our horses are as good as they are likely to have."

"You and Jerry might be able to, Tom, for you have got hold of two first-rate ponies; but the Indians' are nothing out of the way, and our ponies ain't in it with you; besides, they and the pack-horses have all been doing hard work for the last week with none too much food, and many of the 'Rappahoes will be on fresh horses. I expect we have got some very tall climbing to do before we get up to the pass, and we have got to do our fighting before we get there."

The ground rose steeply, and was encumbered by fallen stones and boulders, and it was not long before the pack-horses began to show signs of distress, while those ridden by Harry and his two comrades were drawing their breath in short gasps. After emerging from the trees the ravine had run in almost a straight line for more than half a mile, and just as they reached the end of this stretch a yell was heard down the valley. Looking back they saw eight or ten mounted Indians emerging from the wood at the lower end.

"That is a signal," Harry exclaimed, as four rifles were fired in quick succession. "Well, we have got a bit of a start of them, and they won't venture to attack us until some more come up. We had better take it a bit quietly, chief, or our horses will give out. I expect we sha'n't be long before we come upon a place where we can make a stand."

The Seneca looked round at the horses. "You, Sam, Ben and pack-horses go on till you get to place where can fight. We four wait here; got good horses, and can ride on. We stop them here for a bit."

"That would be best. I don't like being out of it, but we will do our share presently."

No more words were necessary. Harry and his two mates rode on at a slower pace than before, while the two Indians, Jerry, and Tom dismounted, left their horses beyond the turn, and then coming back took up their positions behind four large boulders. The Indians had noticed their returning figures, for they suddenly drew up their horses and gathered together in consultation.

"Draw your bullet, Tom," Jerry said, "and drop in half a charge more powder; I reckon that piece of yours will send a bullet among them with the help of a good charge. Allow a bit above that top notch for extra elevation. It's a good big mark, and you ought to be able to plump a bullet among them."

Tom followed the instructions, and then resting the barrel on the top of the boulder took a steady aim and fired. There was a sudden stir among the group of Indians. A horse reared high in the air, almost unseating its rider, and then they all rode off at the top of their speed, and halted two or three hundred yards lower down the valley. The Senecas uttered a grunt of approval.

"That was a good shot, Tom, though I wish you had hit one of the red-skins instead of his critter. Still, it will give them a good lesson, and make them mighty keerful. They won't care about showing their ugly heads within range of a piece that will carry five hundred yards."

A quarter of an hour passed without any movement on the part of the Indians. Then a large party of horsemen appeared from the trees below, and were greeted by them with a yell of satisfaction.

"There must be well-nigh fifty of them," Jerry said. "I reckon it's the party that came down the hill. They must have picked up a good many others by the way. Now the fun is going to begin."

After five minutes' consultation some twenty of the Indians dismounted, and dividing into two parties ascended the slopes of the valley and began to move forward, taking advantage of every stone and bush, so that it was but occasionally that a glimpse of one of their bodies was obtained.

"They are going to skirmish up to us," Jerry said, "till they are near enough to make it hot for us if we show a head above the rocks to fire. As soon as they can do that, the others will charge. I think they are not more than four hundred yards off now, Tom. That is within your range, so you may as well begin to show them that we are awake. If you can bring one down it will check their pace."

Tom had just noticed three Indians run behind a clump of bushes, and he now levelled his rifle so that it bore on a spot a foot on one side of it. Half a minute later an Indian appeared at the bush and began to run forward. Tom pressed the trigger. The Indian ran a few steps, and then fell forward on his face.

"Bravo, Plumb-centre!" Jerry shouted. "We said that you would do the rifle credit, Tom, and Billy the Scout could not have done better himself."

"Young white man make great hunter," the chief remarked approvingly. "Got good eye and steady hand."

The lesson had its effect. The Indian advance was no longer rapid, but was conducted with the greatest caution, and it was only occasionally that a glimpse could be caught of a dusky figure passing from rock to rock. When they came within three hundred yards the two Indians and Jerry also opened fire. One fell to a shot from the chief, but neither of the others hit their marks. Tom indeed did not fire again, the movements of the Indians being so rapid that they were gone before he could bring his sight to bear upon any of them.

"Go now," the chief said. "'Rappahoes fire soon; run quick."

It was but a few yards to shelter. As they dashed across the intervening space two or three Indian rifles rang out, but the rest of the assailants had been too much occupied in sheltering themselves and looking for the next spot to make for, to keep an eye upon the defenders, and the hastily-fired shots all missed. A moment later the party mounted their horses and rode up the ravine, the yells of the Indians ringing in their ears.

Chapter VIII.
In Safety

"We have gained half an hour anyhow," Jerry said, as they galloped up the ravine, "and I reckon by the time we overtake them we shall find them stowed away in some place where it will puzzle the red-skins to dislodge us. The varmint will fight hard if they are cornered, but they ain't good at advancing when there are a few rifle-tubes, in the hands of white men, pointing at them, and they have had a lesson now that we can shoot."

The ravine continued to narrow. The stream had become a mere rivulet, and they were high up on the hillside.

"I begin to be afeared there ain't no place for making a stand." Here he was interrupted by an angry growl, as a great bear suddenly rose to his feet behind a rock.

"You may thank your stars that we are too busy to attend to you," Jerry said, as they rode past within a few yards of it. "That is a grizzly, Tom; and an awkward beast you would have found him if you had come upon him by yourself without your shooting-iron. He is a big one too, and his skin would have been worth money down in the settlements. Ah, there they are."

The ravine made an abrupt turn to the west, and high up on its side they saw their three companions with the five horses climbing up the precipitous rocks. "How ever did they get up there?" Jerry exclaimed.

"Found Indian trail," the chief said. "Let my brothers keep their eyes open."

They rode on slowly now, examining every foot of the steep hillside. Presently Hunting Dog, who was ahead, uttered an exclamation. Between two great boulders there was a track, evidently a good deal used.

"Let Hunting Dog go first," the chief said. "Leaping Horse will follow the white men."

"I reckon that this is the great Indian trail over the pass," Jerry said to Tom, who preceded him. "I have heard there ain't no way over the mountains atween that pass by Fremont's Buttes and the pass by this peak, which they calls Union Peak, and the red-skins must travel by this when they go down to hunt buffalo on the Green River. It is a wonder Harry struck on it."

"Leaping Horse told him to keep his eyes open," the chief said from the rear. "He knew that Indian trail led up this valley."

"Jee-rusalem! but it's a steep road," Jerry said presently. "I am dog-goned if I can guess how the red-skins ever discovered it. I expect they must have tracked some game up it, and followed to see where it went to."

The trail wound about in a wonderful way. Sometimes it went horizontally along narrow ledges, then there was a bit of steep climbing, where they had to lead their horses; then it wound back again, and sometimes even descended for a distance to avoid a projecting crag.

"Ah! would ye, yer varmint?" Jerry exclaimed, as a shot rang out from the valley below and a bullet flattened itself against a rock within a foot or two of his head. The shot was followed by a loud yell from below, as a crowd of mounted Indians rode at full gallop round the angle of the ravine.

"Hurry on, Hunting Dog, and get round the next corner, for we are regular targets here." A few yards farther a turn of the path took them out of sight of the Indians, but not before a score of bullets came whistling up from below.

"The varmint have been riding too fast to shoot straight, I reckon. It will be our turn directly."

Just as he spoke the chief called upon them to dismount. They threw their bridles on their horses' necks, and descending to the ledge they had just left, lay down on it.

"Get your revolver out, Tom, before you shoot," Jerry said. "They will be off before you have time to load your rifle again."

The Indians were some four hundred feet below them, and were talking excitedly, evidently hesitating whether to follow up the trail. The four rifles cracked almost together. Two Indians fell, and the plunging of two horses showed that they were hit. In an instant the whole mass were on their way down the valley, followed by bullet after bullet from the revolvers which Leaping Horse as well as the whites carried. Anything like accurate aim was impossible, and no Indian was seen to fall, but it was probable that some of the bullets had taken effect among the crowded horsemen.

"Go on quiet now," Leaping Horse said, rising to his feet. "'Rappahoes not follow any farther. One man with this"—and he touched his revolver—"keep back whole tribe here."

Half an hour later they joined the party who had halted at the top of the track.

"It air too bad our being out of it," Ben said. "I hope you have given some of the varmint grist."

"Only five or six of them," Jerry replied regretfully, "counting in the one Leaping Horse shot at the village. Tom here did a big shot, and brought one down in his tracks at a good four hundred yards—as neat a shot as ever I saw fired. The chief he accounted for another; then atween us we wiped out two down below; and I reckon some of the others are carrying some of our lead away. Waal, I think we have shook them off at last anyhow. I suppose there ain't no other road they can come up here by, chief?"

"Leaping Horse only heard of one trail."

"You may bet your life there ain't another," Harry remarked. "They would never have used such a dog-goned road as this if there had been any other way of going up."

"Camp here," the chief said. "Long journey over pass, too much cold. Keep watch here at head of trail."

"That is a very good plan. I have heard that the pass is over nine thousand feet above the sea, and it would never do to have to camp up there. Besides, I have been looking at the sky, and I don't much like its appearance. Look over there to the north."

There were, indeed, evident signs of an approaching change in the weather. On the previous day every peak and jagged crest stood out hard and distinct in the clear air. Now all the higher summits were hidden by a bank of white cloud.

"Snow" the Indian said gravely; "winter coming."

"That is just what I thought, chief. At any rate we know where we are here, and there is brushwood to be gathered not far down the trail; and even if we are shut up here we can manage well enough for a day or two. These early snows don't lie long, but to be caught in a snow-storm higher up would be a sight worse than fighting with red-skins."

From the spot where they were now standing at the edge of the ravine the ground sloped very steeply up for some hundreds of feet, and then steep crags rose in an unbroken wall; but from the view they had had of the country from the other side they knew that behind this wall rose a range of lofty summits. The Indian trail ran along close to the edge of the ravine. The chief looked round earnestly.

"No good place to camp," he said. "Wind blow down hills, horses not able to stand against it. Heap snow tumble down from there," and he pointed upwards. "Carry everything down below."

"Well, if you think we had better push on, let us do so, chief."

The Indian shook his head and pointed to the clouds again. "See," he said; "storm come very soon."

Even in the last two or three minutes a change was perceptible. The upper edge of the clouds seemed to be suddenly broken up. Long streamers spread out like signal flags of danger. Masses of clouds seemed to be wrenched off and to fly with great rapidity for a short distance; some of them sinking a little, floated back until they again formed a part of the mountain cap, while others sped onwards towards the south.

"No time," the chief repeated earnestly; "must look for camp quick." He spoke in the Indian tongue to Hunting Dog, and the two stood on a point where the ground jutted out, and closely examined the ravine up whose side they had climbed. The chief pointed farther along, and Hunting Dog started at a run along the Indian trail. A few hundred yards farther he paused and looked down, moved a few steps farther, and then disappeared from sight. In three or four minutes he returned and held up his arms.

"Come," the chief said, and taking his horse's rein led it along the path. The others followed his example, glad, indeed, to be in motion. Five minutes before they had been bathed in perspiration from their climb up the cliff; now they were conscious of the extraordinary change of temperature that had suddenly set in, and each had snatched a blanket from behind his saddle and wrapped it round him. They soon reached the spot where Hunting Dog was standing, and looked down. Some thirty feet below there was a sort of split in the face of the cliff, a wall of rock rising to within four or five feet of the level of the edge of the ravine. At one end it touched the face of the rock, at the other it was ten or twelve feet from it, the space between being in the form of a long wedge, which was completely filled up with trees and brushwood. A ledge ran down from the point where Hunting Dog was standing to the mouth of the fissure.

"Jee-rusalem, chief!" Ben exclaimed. "That air just made for us—we could not have found a better, not if we had sarched for a year. But I reckon we shall have to clear the place a bit before we take the critters down."

Two axes were taken from one of the pack-horses.

"Don't cut away the bigger stuff, Ben," Harry said as his two mates proceeded down the ledge, "their heads will shelter us from the snow a bit; and only clear away the bushes enough to give room for the horses and us, and leave those standing across the entrance to make a screen. While you are doing it we will fetch in as much more wood and grass as we can get hold of before the snow begins to fall."

The horses were left standing while the men scattered along the top of the ravine, and by the time Ben shouted that they were ready, a considerable pile of brushwood and a heap of coarse grass had been collected. The horses were then led down one by one, unsaddled, and packed together in two lines, having beyond them a great pile of the bushes that had been cut away.

"I am dog-goned if this ain't the best shelter I ever struck upon," Jerry said. "We could not have fixed upon a better if we had had it built special," the others cordially agreed.

The place they occupied was of some twelve feet square. On either side was a perpendicular wall of rock; beyond were the horses; while at the entrance the bush, from three to four feet high, had been left standing; above them stretched a canopy of foliage. Enough dry wood had been collected to start a fire.

"Don't make it too big, Jerry, we don't want to scorch up our roof," Harry Wade said. "Well, I reckon we have got enough fuel here for a week, for there is what you cut down and what we brought, and all that is left standing beyond the horses; and with the leaves and the grass the ponies should be able to hold out as long as the fuel lasts. We are short of meat, but we have plenty of flour; and as for water, we can melt snow."

Buffalo rugs were laid down on each side by the rock walls, and on these they took their seats and lighted their pipes.

"I have been wanting a smoke pretty bad," Jerry said; "I ain't had one since we halted in that there canon. Hello, here it comes!"

As he spoke a fierce gust of wind swayed the foliage overhead and sent the smoke, that had before risen quietly upwards, whirling round the recess; then for a moment all was quiet again; then came another and a stronger gust, rising and gathering in power and laden with fine particles of snow. A thick darkness fell, and Harry threw some more wood on the fire to make a blaze. But loud as was the gale outside, the air in the shelter was hardly moved, and there was but a slight rustling of the leaves overhead. Thicker and thicker flew the snow-flakes in the air outside, and yet none seemed to fall through the leaves.

"I am dog-goned if I can make this out," Sam Hicks said. "We are as quiet here as if we were in a stone house, and one would think there was a copper-plated roof overhead. It don't seem nat'ral."

The others were also looking up with an air of puzzled surprise, not unmingled with uneasiness. Harry went to the entrance and looked out over the breastwork of bushes. "Look here, Sam," he said.

"Why, Harry, it looks to me as if it were snowing up instead of down," the miner said as he joined him.

"That is just it. You see, we are in the elbow of the valley and are looking straight down it, into the eye of the wind. It comes rushing up the valley and meets this steep wall on its way, and pushed on by the wind behind has to go somewhere, and so it is driven almost straight up here and over the hilltops behind us. So you see the snow is carried up instead of falling, and this rock outside us shoots it clear up over the path we were following above. As long as the wind keeps north, I reckon we sha'n't be troubled by the snow in here."

The explanation seemed satisfactory, and there was a general feeling of relief.

"I remember reading," Tom said, as the others took their seats again, "that people can stand on the edge of a cliff, facing a gale, without feeling any wind. For the wind that strikes the cliff rushes up with such force that it forms a sort of wall. Of course, it soon beats down again, and not many yards back you can feel the gale as strongly as anywhere else. But just at the edge the air is perfectly still."

The miners looked at Tom as if they thought that he was making a joke at their expense. But his uncle said:

"Yes, I can quite believe that. You see, it is something like a waterfall; you can stand right under that, for the force shoots it outwards, and I reckon it is the same sort of thing here."

The chief nodded gravely. He too had been surprised at the lull in their shelter when the storm was raging so furiously outside, but Harry's illustration of the action of rushing water enlightened him more than his first explanation had done.

"But water ain't wind, Harry," Ben said.

"It is like water in many ways, Ben. You don't see it, but you can feel it just the same. If you stand behind a tree or round a corner it rushes past you, and you are in a sort of eddy, just as you would be if it was a river that was moving alongside of you. Wind acts just the same way as water. If it had been a big river coming along the valley at the same rate as the wind it would rush up the rocks some distance and then sweep round and race up the valley; but wind being light instead of being heavy is able to rush straight up the hill till it gets right over the crest."

"Waal, if you say it is all right I suppose it is. Anyhow, it's a good thing for us, and I don't care how long it goes on in the same way. I reckoned that before morning we should have those branches breaking down on us with the weight of snow; now I see we are like to have a quiet night."

"I won't answer for that, Ben; it is early in the day yet, and there is no saying how the wind may be blowing before to-morrow morning. Anyhow, now we have time we may as well get some of those bundles of bushes that we brought down, and pile them so as to thicken the shelter of these bushes and lighten it a bit. If we do that, and hang a couple of blankets inside of them, it will give us a good shelter even if the wind works round, and will help to keep us warm. For though we haven't got wind or snow in here, we have got cold."

"You bet," Jerry agreed; "it is a regular blizzard. And although I don't say as it is too cold sitting here by the fire, it won't cost us anything to make the place a bit warmer."

Accordingly the bundles of wood they had gathered were brought out, and with these the screen of bush was thickened, and raised to a height of five feet; and when this was hung inside with a couple of blankets, it was agreed that they could get through the storm comfortably even if it lasted for a month. They cooked their last chunk of deer's flesh, after having first prepared some bread and put it in the baking-pot among the embers, and made some tea from the water in the skins. When they had eaten their meal they covered themselves up in buffalo robes and blankets, and lighted their pipes. There was, however, but little talk, for the noise of the tempest was so great, that it was necessary to raise the voice almost to a shout to be heard, and it was not long before they were all asleep.

For hours there was no stir in the shelter, save when a horse pawed the ground impatiently, or when Hunting Dog rose two or three times to put fresh sticks on the fire. It seemed to Tom when he woke that it ought to be nearly morning. He took out his watch, and by the light of the fire made out to his surprise that it was but ten o'clock. The turmoil of the wind seemed to him to be as loud as before, and he pulled the blankets over his shoulder again and was soon sound asleep. When he next woke, it was with the sensation of coldness in the face, and sitting up he saw that the blankets and the ground were covered with a thick coating of fine snow. There was a faint light in addition to that given by the embers of the fire, and he knew that morning was breaking. His movement disturbed his uncle, who was lying next him. He sat up and at once aroused the others.

"Wake up, mates," he said; "we have had somewhere about eighteen hours' sleep, and day is breaking."

In a minute all were astir. The snow was first shaken off the blankets, and then Harry, taking a shovel, cleared the floor. Jerry took the largest cooking-pot, and saying to Tom, "You bring that horse-bucket along," pushed his way out through a small gap that had been left in the screen of bushes. The wind had gone down a good deal, though it was still blowing strongly. The snow had drifted against the entrance, and formed a steep bank there; from this they filled the pot and bucket, pressing the snow down. Tom was glad to get back again within the shelter, for the cold outside was intense. The fire was already burning brightly, and the pot and a frying-pan were placed over it, and kept replenished with snow as fast as their contents melted. "We must keep on at this," Harry said, "there is not a drop left in the skins, and the horses must have water."

As soon as enough had melted it was poured into the kettle. There was some bacon among the trappers' stores, as they had calculated that they would not be able to hunt until out of Big Wind Valley and far up among the forests beyond. The frying-pan was now utilized for its proper work, while the pail was placed close enough to the fire to thaw its contents, without risking injury to it. Within an hour of breakfast being finished enough snow had been thawed to give the horses half a bucket of water each. In each pail a couple of pounds of flour had been stirred to help out what nourishment could be obtained from the leaves, and from the small modicum of grass given to each animal.

"It will be a big journey over the pass, anyhow," Harry had said. "Now that we are making tracks for the settlements we need not be sparing of the flour; indeed, the lighter we are the better."

The day did not pass so pleasantly as that preceding it, for the air was filled with fine snow that blew in at the entrance and found its way between the leaves overhead; while from time to time the snow accumulating there came down with a crash, calling forth much strong language from the man on whom it happened to fall, and shouts of laughter from his comrades. The party was indeed a merry one. They had failed altogether in the objects of their expedition, but they had escaped without a scratch from the Indians, and had inflicted some damage upon them; and their luck in finding so snug a shelter in such a storm far more than counterbalanced their disappointment at their failure.

"Have you often been caught in the snow, uncle?"

"You bet, Tom; me and the chief here were mighty nigh rubbed out three years ago. I was prospecting among the Ute hills, while Leaping Horse was doing the hunting for us both. It was in the middle of winter; the snow was deep on the ground in the valleys and on the tops of the hills, but there was plenty of bare rock on the hillside, so I was able to go on with my work. While as for hunting, the cold drove the big-horns down from the heights where they feed in summer, and the chief often got a shot at them; and they are good eating, I can tell you.

"We hadn't much fear of red-skins, for they ain't fond of cold and in winter move their lodges down to the most sheltered valleys and live mostly on dried meat. When they want a change they can always get a bear or maybe a deer in the woods. We were camped in a grove of pines in a valley and were snug enough. One day I had struck what I thought was the richest vein I had ever come on. I got my pockets full of bits of quartz with the gold sticking thick in it, and you may bet I went down to the camp in high glee. A quarter of a mile before I got there I saw Leaping Horse coming to meet me at a lope. It didn't want telling that there was something wrong. As soon as he came up he said 'Utes.' 'Many of them, chief?' I asked. He held up his open hands twice.

"'Twenty of them,' I said; 'that is pretty bad. How far are they away?' He said he had seen them coming over a crest on the other side of the valley. 'Then we have got to git,' I said, 'there ain't no doubt about that. What the 'tarnal do the varmint do here?' 'War-party,' the chief said. 'Indian hunter must have come across our trail and taken word back to the lodges.' The place where he had met me was among a lot of rocks that had rolled down. There had been no snow for a fortnight, and of course the red-skins would see our tracks everywhere, going and coming from the camp. We were on foot that time, though we had a pack-horse to carry our outfit. Of course they would get that and everything at the camp. I did not think much of the loss, the point was how were we to save our scalps? We had sat down behind a rock as soon as he had joined me. Just then a yell came from the direction of our camp, and we knew that the red-skins had found it. 'They won't be able to follow your trail here, chief, will they? ' He shook his head. 'Trail everywhere, not know which was the last.' We could see the grove where the camp was, and of course they could see the rocks, and it was sartin that if we had made off up the hill they would have been after us in a squirrel's jump; so there was nothing to do but to lie quiet until it was dark. We got in among the boulders, and lay down where we could watch the grove through a chink.

"'I don't see a sign of them,' I said. 'You would have thought they would have been out in search of us.'

"'No search,' the chief said. 'No good look for us, not know where we have gone to. Hide up in grove. Think we come back, and then catch us.'

"So it turned out. Not a sign of them was to be seen, and after that first yell everything was as quiet as death. In a couple of hours it got dark, and as soon as it did we were off. We talked matters over, you may be sure. There weren't no denying we were cornered. There we were without an ounce of flour or a bite of meat. The chief had caught up a couple of buffalo rugs as soon as he sighted the red-skins. That gave us just a chance, but it wasn't more. In the morning the red-skins would know we had either sighted them or come on their trail, and would be scattering all over the country in search of us. We agreed that we must travel a good way apart, though keeping each other in sight. They would have noticed that the trails were all single, and if they came upon two together going straight away from the camp, would know for sure it was us making off.

"You may think that with so many tracks as we had made in the fortnight we had been there, they would not have an idea which was made the first day and which was made the last, but that ain't so. In the first place, the snow was packed hard, and the footprints were very slight. Then, even when it is always freezing there is an evaporation of the snow, and the footprints would gradually disappear; besides that, the wind on most days had been blowing a little, and though the drift does not count for much on packed snow, a fine dust is blown along, and if the prints don't get altogether covered there is enough drift in them to show which are old ones and which are fresh. We both knew that they could not make much mistake about it, and that they would be pretty sure to hit on the trail I had made in the morning when I went out, and on that of the chief to the rocks, and following mine back to the same place would guess that we had cached there till it was dark.

"I could have done that myself; one can read such a trail as that like a printed book. The worst of it was, there were no getting out of the valley without leaving sign. On the bare hillsides and among the rocks we could travel safe enough, but above them was everywhere snow, and do what we would there would be no hiding our trail. We agreed that the only thing was to cross the snow as quick as possible, to keep on the bare rock whenever we got a chance, and wherever we struck wood, and to double sometimes one way sometimes another, so as to give the red-skins plenty of work to do to follow our trail. We walked all that night, and right on the next day till early in the afternoon. Then we lay down and slept till sunset, and then walked again all night. We did not see any game. If we had we should have shot, for we knew the red-skins must be a long way behind. When we stopped in the morning we were not so very far from the camp we had started from, for if we had pushed straight back to the settlements we should have been caught sure, for the Utes would have been certain to have sent off a party that way to watch the valleys we should have had to pass through. We lay down among some trees and slept for a few hours and then set out to hunt, for we had been two days without food, and I was beginning to feel that I must have a meal.

"We had not gone far when we came across the track of a black bear. We both felt certain that the trail was not many hours old. We followed it for two miles, and found it went up to a slide of rocks; they had come down from a cliff some years before, for there were bushes growing among them. As a rule a black bear will always leave you alone if you leave him, and hasn't much fight in him at the best; so up we went, thinking we were sure of our bear-steak without much trouble in getting it. I was ahead, and had just climbed up on to a big rock, when, from a bush in front, the bear came out at me with a growl. I expect it had cubs somewhere. I had just time to take a shot from the hip and then he was on me, and gave me a blow on the shoulder that ripped the flesh down to the elbow.

"But that was not the worst, for the blow sent me over the edge, and I fell seven or eight feet down among the sharp rocks. I heard the chief's rifle go off, and it was some time after that before I saw or heard anything more. When I came to I found he had carried me down to the foot of the slide and laid me there. He was cutting up some sticks when I opened my eyes. 'Have you got the bear, Leaping Horse?' ' "The bear is dead,' he said. 'My brother is badly hurt.'

"'Oh, never mind the hurt,' I said, 'so that we have got him. What are you doing, chief? You are not going to make a fire here, are you? '

"'My brother's leg is broken,' he said. 'I am cutting some sticks to keep it straight.'

"That brought me round to my senses, as you may guess. To break one's leg up in the mountains is bad at any time, but when it is in the middle of winter, and you have got a tribe of red-skins at your heels, it means you have got to go under. I sat up and looked at my leg. Sure enough, the left one was snapt like a pipe-stem, about half-way between the knee and the ankle. 'Why, chief,' I said, 'it would have been a sight better if you had put a bullet through my head as I lay up there. I should have known nothing about it.'

"'The Utes have not got my white brother yet.'

"'No,' said I, 'but it won't be long before they have me; maybe it will be this afternoon, and maybe to-morrow morning.' The chief said nothing, but went on with his work. When he had got five or six sticks about three feet long and as many about a foot, and had cut them so that they each had one flat side, he took off his buckskin shirt, and working round the bottom of it cut a thong about an inch wide and five or six yards long. Then he knelt down and got the bone in the right position, and then with what help I could give him put on the splints and bandaged them tightly, a long one and a short one alternately. The long ones he bandaged above the knee as well as below, so that the whole leg was stiff. I felt pretty faint by the time it was done, and Leaping Horse said, 'Want food; my white brother will lie quiet, Leaping Horse will soon get him some.'

"He set to work and soon had a fire going, and then went up to the rocks and came down again with the bear's hams and about half his hide. It was not long before he had some slices cooked, and I can tell you I felt better by the time we had finished. We had not said much to each other, but I had been thinking all the time, and when we had done I said, 'Now, chief, I know that you will be wanting to stay with me, but I ain't going to have it. You know as well as I do that the Utes will be here to-morrow at latest, and there ain't more chance of my getting away from them than there is of my flying. It would be just throwing away your scalp if you were to stop here, and it would not do me a bit of good, and would fret me considerable. Now before you start I will get you to put me somewhere up among those stones where I can make a good fight of it. You shall light a fire by the side of me, and put a store of wood within reach and a few pounds of bear's flesh. I will keep them off as long as I can with the rifle, then there will be five shots with my Colt. I will keep the last barrel for myself; I ain't going to let the Utes amuse themselves by torturing me for a few hours before they finish me. Then you make straight away for the settlements; they won't be so hot after you when they have once got me. The next time you go near Denver you can go and tell Pete Hoskings how it all came about.'

"'My white brother is weak with the pain,' the chief said quietly; 'he is talking foolishly. He knows that Leaping Horse will stay with his friend. He will go and look for a place.' Without listening to what I had to say he took up his rifle and went up the valley, which was a steep one. He was away better than half an hour and then came back. 'Leaping Horse found a place,' he said, 'where he and his brother can make a good fight. Straight Harry get on his friend's back.' It was clear that there weren't no use talking to him. He lifted me up on to my feet, then he got me well up on to his back, as if I had been a sack of coal, and went off with me, striding along pretty near as quick as if I had not been there. It might have been half a mile, when he turned up a narrow ravine that was little more than a cleft in the rock that rose almost straight up from the valley. It did not go in very far, for there had been a slide, and it was blocked up by a pile of rocks and earth, forty or fifty feet high. It was a big job even for the chief to get me up to the top of them. The snow had drifted down thick into the ravine, and it was a nasty place to climb even for a man who had got nothing but his rifle on his shoulder. However, he got me up safely, and laid me down just over the crest. He had put my buffalo robe over my shoulders before starting, and he rolled me up in this and said, 'Leaping Horse will go and fetch rifles and bear-meat,' and he set straight off and left me there by myself."

Chapter IX.
A Bad Time

"Even to me," Harry went on, after refilling and lighting his pipe, "it did not seem long before the chief was back. He brought a heavy load, for besides the rifles and bear's flesh he carried on his back a big faggot of brushwood. After laying that down he searched among the rocks, and presently set to work to dig out the snow and earth between two big blocks, and was not long before he scooped out with his tomahawk a hole big enough for the two of us to lie in comfortably. He laid the bear's-skin down in this, then he carried me to it and helped me in and then put the robes over me; and a snugger place you would not want to lie in.

"It was about ten feet below the level of the crest of the heap of rocks, and of course on the upper side, so that directly the red-skins made their appearance he could help me up to the top. That the two of us could keep the Utes back I did not doubt; we had our rifles, and the chief carried a revolver as well as I did. After they had once caught a glimpse of the sort of place we were on, I did not think they would venture into the ravine, for they would have lost a dozen men before they got to the mound. I had looked round while the chief was away, and I saw that a hundred yards or so higher up, the ravine came to an end, the sides closing in, so there was no fear of our being attacked from there. What I was afraid of was that the Indians might be able to get up above and shoot down on us, though whether they could or not depended on the nature of the ground above, and of course I could not see beyond the edge of the rocks.

"But even if they could not get up in the daylight, they could crawl up at night and finish us, or they could camp down at the mouth of the ravine and starve us out, for there was no chance of our climbing the sides, even if my leg had been all right. I was mighty sorry for the chief. He had just thrown his life away, and it must come to the same in the end, as far as I was concerned. Even now he could get away if he chose, but I knew well enough it weren't any good talking to him. So I lay there, just listening for the crack of his rifle above. He would bring down the first man that came in, sartin, and there would be plenty of time after that to get me up beside him, for they would be sure to have a long talk before they made any move. I did not expect them until late in the afternoon, and hoped it might be getting dark before they got down into the valley. There had been a big wind sweeping down it since the snow had fallen, and though it had drifted deep along the sides, the bottom was for the most part bare. I noticed that the chief had picked his way carefully, and guessed that, as they would have no reason for thinking we were near, they might not take up the trail till morning. Of course they would find our fire and the dead bear, or all that there was left of him, and they would fancy we had only stopped to take a meal and had gone on again. They would see by the fire that we had left pretty early in the day. I heard nothing of the chief until it began to get dark; then he came down to me.

"'Leaping Horse will go out and scout,' he said. 'If Utes not come soon, will come back here; if they come, will watch down at mouth of valley till he sees Utes go to sleep.' 'Well, chief,' I said; 'at any rate you may as well take this robe; one is enough to sleep with in this hole, and I shall be as snug as a beaver wrapped up in mine. Half your hunting shirt is gone, and you will find it mighty cold standing out there.'

"In an hour he came back again. 'Utes come,' he said. 'Have just lighted fire and going to cook. No come tonight. Leaping Horse has good news for his brother. There are no stars.'

"'That is good news indeed,' I said. 'If it does but come on to snow to-night we may carry our scalps back to the settlement yet.'

"'Leaping Horse can feel snow in the air,' he said. 'If it snows before morning, good; if not, the Utes will tell their children how many lives the scalps of the Englishman and the Seneca cost.'

"The chief lay down beside me. I did not get much sleep, for my leg was hurting me mightily. From time to time he crawled out, and each time he returned saying, 'No snow.' I had begun to fear that when it came it would be too late. It could not have been long before daybreak when he said, as he crawled in: 'The Great Manitou has sent snow. My brother can sleep in peace.' An hour later I raised myself up a bit and looked out. It was light now. The air was full of fine snow, and the earth the chief had scraped out was already covered thickly. I could see as much as that, though the chief had, when he came in for the last time, drawn the faggot in after him. I wondered at the time why he did it, but I saw now. As soon as the snow had fallen a little more it would hide up altogether the entrance to our hole. Hour after hour passed, and it became impossible to get even a peep out, for the snow had fallen so thickly on the leafy end of the brushwood, which was outward, that it had entirely shut us in. All day the snow kept on, as we could tell from the lessening light, and by two o'clock only a faint twilight made its way in.

"'How long do you think we shall be imprisoned here, chief?' I asked.

"'Must not hurry,' he replied. 'There are trees up the valley, and the Utes may make their camp there and stay till the storm is over. No use to go out till my brother can walk. Wait till snow is over; then stay two or three days to give time for Utes to go away. Got bear's flesh to eat; warm in here, melt snow.' This was true enough, for I was feeling it downright hot. Just before night came on the chief pushed the end of his ramrod through the snow and looked out along the hole.

"'Snow very strong,' he said. 'When it is dark can go out if wish.'

"There is not much to tell about the next five days. The snow kept falling steadily, and each evening after dark the chief went outside for a short time to smoke his pipe, while I sat at the entrance and smoked mine, and was glad enough to get a little fresh air. As soon as he came in again the faggot was drawn back to its place, and we were imprisoned for another twenty-four hours. One gets pretty tired after a time of eating raw bear's flesh and drinking snow-water, and you bet I was pretty glad when the chief, after looking out through a peephole, said that the snow had stopped falling and the sun was shining. About the middle of that day he said suddenly: 'I hear voices.'

"It was some time before I heard anything, but I presently made them out, though the snow muffled them a good deal. They did not seem far off, and a minute or two later they ceased. We lay there two days longer, and then even the chief was of opinion that they would have moved off. My own idea was that they had started the first afternoon after the snow had stopped falling.

"'Leaping Horse will go out to scout as soon as it is dark,' he said. 'Go to mouth of ravine. If Utes are in wood he will see their fires and come back again. Not likely come up here again and find his traces.'

"That is what I had been saying for the last two days, for after some of them had been up, and had satisfied themselves that there was no one in the gully, they would not be likely to come through the snow again. When the chief returned after an hour's absence, he told me that the Utes had all gone. 'Fire cold,' he said; 'gone many hours. Leaping Horse has brought some dry wood up from their hearth. Can light fire now.' You may guess it was not long before we had a fire blazing in front of our den, and I never knew how good bear-steak really was till that evening.

"The next morning the chief took off the splints and rebandaged my leg, this time putting on a long strip of the bear's-skin, which he had worked until it was perfectly soft while we had been waiting there. Over this he put on the splints again, and for the first time since that bear had knocked me off the rock I felt at ease. We stayed there another fortnight, by the end of which time the bones seemed to have knit pretty fairly. However, I had made myself a good strong crutch from a straight branch with a fork at the end, that the chief had cut for me, and I had lashed a wad of bear's-skin in the fork to make it easy. Then we started, making short journeys at first, but getting longer every day as I became accustomed to the crutch, and at the end of a week I was able to throw it aside.

"We never saw a sign of an Indian trail all the way down to the settlements, and by the time we got there I was ready to start on a journey again. The chief found plenty of game on the way down, and I have never had as much as a twinge in my leg since. So you see this affair ain't a circumstance in comparison. Since then the chief and I have always hunted together, and the word brother ain't only a mode of speaking with us; "and he held out his hand to the Seneca, who gravely placed his own in it.

"That war a tight corner, Harry, and no blamed mistake. Did you ever find out whether they could have got on the top to shoot down on you?"

"Yes, the chief went up the day after the Utes had left. It was level up there, and they could have sat on the edge and fired down upon us, and wiped us out without our having a show."

"And you have never since been to that place you struck the day the Utes came down, Harry?" Jerry asked. "I have heard you talk of a place you knew of, just at the edge of the bad lands, off the Utah hills. Were that it?"

Harry nodded. "I have never been there since. I went with a party into Nevada the next spring, and last year the Utes were all the time upon the war-path. I had meant to go down this fall, but the Utes were too lively, so I struck up here instead; but I mean to go next spring whether they are quiet or not, and to take my chances, and find out whether it is only good on the surface and peters out to nothing when you get in, or whether it is a real strong lode. Ben and Sam, and of course the chief, will go with me, and Tom here, now he has come out, and if you like to come we shall be all glad."

"You may count me in," Jerry said, "and I thank you for the offer. I have had dog-goned bad luck for some time, and I reckon it is about time it was over. How are you going to share?"

"We have settled that. The chief and I take two shares each as discoverers. You four will take one share each."

"That is fair enough, Harry. Those are mining terms, and after your nearly getting rubbed out in finding it, if you and the chief had each taken three shares there would have been nothing for us to grunt at.

They are a 'tarnal bad lot are the Utes. I reckon they are bad by nature, but the Mormons have made them worse. There ain't no doubt it's they who set them on to attack the caravans. They could see from the first that if this was going to be the main route west there would be so many coming along, and a lot perhaps settle there, that the Gentiles, as they call the rest of us, would get too strong for them. What they have been most afeard of is, that a lot of gold or silver should be found up in the hills, and that would soon put a stop to the Mormon business. They have been wise enough to tell the red-skins that if men came in and found gold there would be such a lot come that the hunting would be all spoilt. There is no doubt that in some of the attacks made on the caravans there have been sham Indians mixed up with the real ones. Red-skins are bad enough, but they are good men by the side of scoundrels who are false to their colour, and who use Indians to kill whites. That is one reason I want to see this railway go on till it jines that on the other side. It will be bad for game, and I reckon in a few years the last buffalo will be wiped out, but I will forgive it that, so that it does but break up the Saints as they call themselves, though I reckon there is about as little of the saint among them as you will find if you search all creation."

"Right you are, Jerry," Sam Hicks said. "They pretty nigh wiped me out once, and if Uncle Sam ever takes to fighting them you may bet that I am in it, and won't ask for no pay."

"How did it come about, Sam?" Jerry asked. "I dunno as I have ever heard you tell that story."

"Waal, I had been a good bit farther east, and had been doing some scouting with the troops, who had been giving a lesson to the red-skins there, that it was best for them to let up on plundering the caravans going west. We had done the job, and I jined a caravan coming this way. It was the usual crowd, eastern farmers going to settle west, miners, and such like. Among them was two waggons, which kept mostly as far apart from the others as they could. They was in charge of two fellows who dressed in store clothes, and had a sanctimonious look about them. There was an old man and a couple of old women, and two or three boys and some gals. They did not talk much with the rest, but it got about that they were not going farther than Salt Lake City, and we had not much difficulty in reckoning them up as Mormons. There ain't no law perviding for the shooting of Mormons without some sort of excuse, and as the people kept to themselves and did not interfere with no one, nothing much was said agin them. On a v'yage like that across the plains, folks has themselves to attend to, and plenty to do both on the march and in camp, so no one troubles about any one else's business.

"I hadn't no call to either, but I happened to go out near their waggons one evening, and saw two or three bright-looking maids among them, and it riled me to think that they was going to be handed over to some rich old elder with perhaps a dozen other wives, and I used to feel as it would be a satisfaction to pump some lead into them sleek-looking scoundrels who had them in charge. I did not expect that the gals had any idea what was in store for them. I know them Mormons when they goes out to get what they call converts, preaches a lot about the prophet, and a good deal about the comforts they would have in Utah. So much land for nothing, and so much help to set them up, and all that kind of thing, but mighty little about polygamy and the chance of their being handed over to some man old enough to be their father, and without their having any say in the matter. Howsoever, I did not see as I could interfere, and if I wanted to interfere I could not have done it; because all those women believed what they had been taught, and if I a stranger, and an ill-looking one at that, was to tell them the contrary, they wouldn't believe a word what I had said. So we went on till we got within four or five days' journey of Salt Lake City, then one morning, just as the teams were being hitched up, two fellows rode into camp.

"As we were in Utah now, there weren't nothing curious about that, but I reckoned them up as two as hard-looking cusses as I had come across for a long time. After asking a question or two they rode to the Mormon waggons, and instead of starting with the rest, the cattle was taken out and they stopped behind. Waal, I thought I would wait for a bit and see what they were arter. It weren't no consarn of mine noways, but I knew I could catch up the waggons if I started in the afternoon, and I concluded that I would just wait; so I sat by the fire and smoked. When the caravan had gone on the Mormons hitched up their cattle again. They were not very far away from where I was sitting, and I could see one of the men in black pointing to me as he talked with the two chaps who had just jined them. With that the fellow walked across to where I was sitting.

"'Going to camp here? ' says he.

"'Waal,' I says, 'I dunno, as I haven't made up my mind about it. Maybe I shall, maybe I sha'n't.'

"'I allow it would be better for you to move on.'

"'And I allow,' says I, 'it would be better for you to attend to your own affairs.'

"'Look here,' says he, 'I hear as you have been a-spying about them waggons.'

"'Then,' says I, 'whosoever told you that, is an all-fired liar, and you tell him so from me.'

"I had got my hand on the butt of my Colt, and the fellow weakened.

"'Waal,' he said, 'I have given you warning, that is all.'

"'All right,' says I, 'I don't care none for your warnings; and I would rather anyhow be shot down by white skunks dressed up as red-skins, than I would have a hand in helping to fool a lot of innercent women.' "He swore pretty bad at this, but I could see as he wasn't real grit, and he went off to the waggons. There was considerable talk when he got there, but as the Mormons must have known as I had been a scout, and had brought a lot of meat into the camp on the way, and as the chap that came across must have seen my rifle lying handy beside me, I guess they allowed that I had better be left alone. So a bit later the waggons started, and as I expected they would, went up a side valley instead of going on by the caravan route. The fellow had riz my dander, and after sitting for a bit I made up my mind I would go arter 'em. I had no particular motive, it wur just out of cussedness. I was not going to be bluffed from going whar I chose. This air a free country, and I had as much right to go up that valley as they had."

"I should have thought yer had had more common sense, Sam Hicks," Jerry said reproachfully, "than to go a-mixing yourself up in a business in which you had no sort of consarn. Ef one of them women had asked you to help her, or if you had thought she was being taken away agin her will, you or any other man would have had a right to take a hand in the game; but as it was, you war just fooling with your life to interfere with them Mormons in their own country."

"That is so, Jerry, and I ain't a word to say agin it. It war just a piece of cussedness, and I have asked myself forty-eleven times since, what on arth made me make such a blame fool of myself. Afore that fellow came over to bluff me I hadn't no thought of following the waggons, but arter that I felt somehow as if he dared me to do it. I reckoned I was more nor a match for the two fellows who just jined them, and as for the greasy-faced chaps in black, I did not count them in, one way or the other. I had no thought of getting the gals away, nor of getting into any muss with them if they left me alone. It was just that I had got a right to go up that valley or any other, and I was not going to be bluffed out of it. So I took up my shooting-iron, strapped my blanket over my shoulder, and started. They war maybe a mile away when I turned into the valley. I wasn't hungry for a fight, so I didn't keep up the middle, but just skirted along at the foot of the hill where it did not seem likely as they would see me. I did not get any closer to them, and only caught sight of them now and then.

"As far as I could make out there was only one horseman with them, and I reckoned the other was gone on ahead; looking for a camping-ground maybe, or going on to one of the Mormon farms to tell them to get things ready there. What I reckoned on doing, so far as I reckoned at all, was to scout up to them as soon as it got dark and listen to their talk, and try to find out for certain whether the women war goin' willing. Then I thought as I would walk straight up to their fires and just bluff those four men as they tried to bluff me. Waal, they went on until late in the afternoon, unhitched the cattle, and camped. I waited for a bit, and now that I war cooled down and could look at the thing reasonable, I allowed to myself that I had showed up as a blamed fool, and I had pretty well made up my mind to take back tracks and go down the valley, when I heard the sound of some horses coming down fast from the camp.

"Then the thought that I was a 'tarnal fool came to me pretty strong, you bet. One of those fellows had ridden on and brought down some of the Regulators, as we used to call them in the mining camps, but I believe the Mormons call them Destroying Angels, though there is mighty little of angels about them. I hoped now that they had not caught sight of me during the day, and that the band were going right down to the waggon camp; but as I had not taken any particular pains to hide myself, I reckoned they must have made me out. It war pretty nigh dark, and as I took cover behind a bush I could scarce see them as they rode along. They went down about two hundred yards and then stopped, and I could hear some of them dismount.

"'You are sure we are far enough?' one said.

"'Yes; I can swear he was higher up than this when we saw him just before we camped.'

"'If you two fellows hadn't been the worst kind of curs,' a man said angrily, 'you would have hidden up as soon as you made out he was following you and shot him as he came along.'

"'I told you,' another voice said, 'that the man is an Indian fighter, and a dead shot. Suppose we had missed him.'

"'You could not have missed him if you had waited till he was close to you before you fired; then you might have chucked him in among the bushes and there would have been an end of it, and we should have been saved a twenty-mile ride. Now then, look sharp for him and search every bush. Between us and Johnson's party above we are sure to catch him.'

"I didn't see that, though I did wish the rocks behind had not been so 'tarnal steep. I could have made my way up in the daylight, though even then it would have been a tough job, but without light enough to see the lay of the ledges and the best places for getting from one to another, it was a business I didn't care about. I was just thinking of making across to the other side of the valley when some horsemen came galloping back.

"'You stop here, brother Ephraim, and keep your ears well open, as well as your eyes. You stop fifty yards higher up, Hiram, and the others at the same distance apart. When the men among the rocks come abreast of you, Ephraim, ride on and take your place at the other end of the line. You do the same, Hiram, and so all in turn; I will ride up and down.'

"It was clear they meant business, and I was doubting whether I would take my chance of hiding or make for the cliff, when I saw a light coming dancing down from the camp, and knew it was a chap on horseback with a torch. As he came up the man who had spoken before said: 'How many torches have you got, brother Williams? '

"'A dozen of them.'

"'Give me six, and take the other six down to the men below. That is right, I will light one from yours.'

"You may guess that settled me. I had got to git at once, so I began to crawl off towards the foot of the cliffs. By the time I had got there, there war six torches burning a hundred yards below, and the men who carried them were searching every bush and prying under every rock. Along the middle of the valley six other torches were burning fifty yards apart. There was one advantage, the torches were pitch-pine and gave a fairish light, but not so much as tarred rope would have done; but it was enough for me to be able to make out the face of the cliff, and I saw a break by which I could get up for a good bit anyhow. It was where a torrent came down when the snows were melting, and as soon as I had got to the bottom I made straight up. There were rocks piled at its foot, and I got to the top of these without being seen.

"I hadn't got a dozen feet higher when my foot set a boulder rolling, and down it went with a crash. There were shouts below, but I did not stop to listen to what they said, but put up the bed of the torrent at a two-forty gait. A shot rang out, and another and another, but I was getting now above the light of their torches. A hundred feet higher I came to a stand-still, for the rock rose right up in front of me, and the water had here come down from above in a fall. This made it a tight place, you bet. There war no ledge as I could see that I could get along, and I should have to go down a good bit afore I got to one. They kept on firing from below, but I felt pretty sure that they could not see me, for I could hear the bullets striking high against the face of the rock that had stopped me.

"You may bet I was careful how I went down again, and I took my time, for I could see that the men with the torches had halted at the foot of the heap of rocks below, not caring much, I expect, to begin to mount, while the horsemen kept on firing, hoping to hear my body come rolling down; besides, they must have known that with their torches they made a pretty sure mark for me. At last I got down to the ledge. It war a narrow one, and for a few yards I had to walk with my face to the rock and my arms spread out, and that, when I knew that at any moment they might make me out, and their bullets come singing up, warn't by no means pleasant. In a few yards the ledge got wider and there was room enough on it for me to lie down. I crawled along for a good bit, and then sat down with my back against the rock and reckoned the matter up. All the torches war gathered round where I had gone up. Four more men had come down from the camp on horseback, and five or six on foot with torches were running down the valley. They had been searching for me among the bushes higher up, and when they heard the firing had started down to jine the others. The leader was shouting to the men to climb up after me, but the men didn't seem to see it.

"'What's the use?' I heard one fellow say; 'he must be chock-full of bullets long ago. We will go up and find his carcass in the morning.'

"'But suppose he is not dead, you fool.'

"'Well, if he ain't dead he would just pick us off one after another as we went up with torches.' "'Well, put your torches out, then. Here, I will go first if you are afraid,' and he jumped from his horse.

"You can bet your boots that my fingers itched to put a bullet into him. But it warn't to be done; I did not know how far the ledge went or whether there might be any way of getting off it, and now I had once got out of their sight it would have been chucking away my life to let them know whar I lay. So I got up again and walked on a bit farther. I came on a place where the rock had crumbled enough for me to be able to get up on to the next ledge, and after a lot of climbing up and down I got to the top in about two hours, and then struck across the hills and came down at eight o'clock next morning on to the caravan track. I hid up till evening in case they should come down after me, and next morning I came up to the caravan just as they were hitching the teams up for a start."

"You got out of that better than you deserved," Harry said. "I wouldn't have believed that any man would have played such a fool's trick as to go meddling with the Mormons in their own country without any kind of reason. It war worse than childishness."

The other two miners assented vigorously, and Sam said: "Waal, you can't think more meanly of me over that business than I do of myself. I have never been able to make out why I did it, and you may bet it ain't often I tells the story. It war a dog-goned piece of foolishness, and, as Harry says, I didn't desarve to get out of it as I did. Still, it ain't made me feel any kind of love for Mormons. When about two hundred shots have been fired at a man it makes him feel kinder like as if he war going to pay some of them back when he gets the chance, and you may bet I mean to."

"Jee-rusalem!"

The exclamation was elicited by the fall of a heavy mass of snow on to the fire, over which the kettle had just begun to boil. The tripod from which it hung was knocked over. A cloud of steam filled the place, and the party all sprung to their feet to avoid being scalded.

"It might have waited a few minutes longer," Jerry grumbled, "then we should have had our tea comfortable. Now the fire is out and the water is spilt, and we have got to fetch in some more snow; that is the last lot there was melted."

"It is all in the day's work, Jerry," Harry said cheerfully, "and it is just as well we should have something to do. I will fetch the snow in if the rest of you will clear the hearth again. It is a nuisance about the snow, but we agreed that there is no help for it, and we may thank our stars it is no worse."

It was not long before the fire was blazing again, but it took some time before water was boiling and tea made, still longer before the bread which had been soddened by the water from the kettle was fit to eat. By this time it was dark. When the meal was over they all turned in for the night. Tom was just going off to sleep, when he was roused by Leaping Dog suddenly throwing off his buffalo robe and springing to his feet with his rifle in his hand.

"Hist!" he said in a low tone. "Something comes!"

The men all seized their rifles and listened intently. Presently they heard a soft step on the snow outside, then there was a snuffing sound.

"B'ar!" the Indian said.

A moment later a great head reared itself over the bushes at the entrance. Five rifles rang out, the two Indians reserving their fire; the report was followed by the dull sound of a heavy fall outside.

"Wait a moment," Harry said sharply, as the others were preparing to rush out, "let us make sure he is dead."

"He is dead enough," Jerry said. "I reckon even a grizzly cannot walk off with five bullets in his head." Harry looked over the screen. "Yes, he is dead enough; anyhow he looks so. Waal, this is a piece of luck." They all stepped out on to the platform.

"Is it a grizzly, uncle?" Tom asked excitedly.

"He is a grizzly, sure enough. You don't want to see his colour to know that. Look at his size."

"Why, he is as big as a cow."

"Ay, lad, and a big cow too. You go in and make up the fire while we cut off enough meat for supper."

The fact that they had eaten a meal but half an hour before, went for nothing; slices of bear-meat were soon frizzling, and as hearty a meal was eaten as if no food had been tasted since the previous day. The men were in the highest spirits; the fact that they were out of meat had been the greatest drawback to the prospect of being shut up for perhaps a week, for badly-baked bread is but a poor diet to men accustomed to live almost exclusively upon meat.

"What brought the bear down here?" Tom asked.

"Curiosity at first perhaps, and then hunger," his uncle replied. "I expect he was going along on the path above when he saw the light among the leaves, and then no doubt he smelt the bread, and perhaps us and the horses, and came down to see what he could get.

"Curiosity is a bad fault, Tom. You have had two lessons in that this evening. Bear in mind that in this part of the world the safest plan is always to attend strictly to your own business."

All thought of sleep was for the present dissipated; their pipes were again lighted, and it was midnight before they lay down. In the morning the bear was with some difficulty skinned and cut up, the joints being left outside to freeze through. The snow still fell steadily, but the wind had almost died down. Sallying out they cut five or six long poles, and with some difficulty fixed these from above across from the cliff to the outstanding rock, pushed the bear's-skin across them, and lashed it there, its bulk being sufficient to cover the space above the fire and a considerable portion of their dwelling room.

After breakfast snow was again melted for the horses, and the work for the day thus done they seated themselves contentedly round the fire.

Chapter X.
An Avalanche

"You don't think, chief," Harry asked, "that there is any chance of the 'Rappahoes taking it into their heads to come up to have a look round?"

"Indians keep in lodges, no like cold; they think we have gone on over pass. If weather gets fine perhaps they come to look for our guns and packs. They think sure we die in snow-storm when we up in pass. When snow stops falling, we make no more fire; but path from valley all shut up by snow now."

"Yes, I don't think anyone would try to climb it till the sun has cleared the track; it was a pretty bad place when we came up," Harry said. "I don't say that men on foot could not make their way up; but as you say, the red-skins are not likely to try it until the weather has cleared a bit, though I don't say that they wouldn't if they knew we were camped here close to the top."

"What noise is that?" Tom asked. "I have heard it several times before, but not so loud as that."

"Snow-slide," Leaping Horse said. "Snow come down from mountains; break off trees, roll rocks down. Bad place all along here."

"Yes. I saw that you looked up at the hills behind there before you looked over the edge here, chief," Ben Gulston said, "and I reckoned that you had snow-slides in your mind. I thought myself that it was like enough the snow might come tumbling over the edge of that high wall and then come scooting down over where we war, and there

163

would have been no sort of show for us if we had been camped whar the trail goes along."

"Leaping Horse has heard from his red brothers with whom he has spoken that trail from top of valley very bad when snow falls. Many Indians stopping too long at fort, to trade goods, have been swept away by snow-slides when caught in storm here."

"I thought it looked a bad place," Harry remarked. "There ain't no fooling with a snow-slide anyway. I have come across bones once or twice lying scattered about in snug-looking valleys—bones of horses and men, and it was easy to see they had been killed by a snow-slide coming down on them. Rocks were heaped about among them, some of the bones were smashed. They had been hunting or trapping, and sheltered up in a valley when the storm came on and the slide had fallen on them, and there they had laid till the sun melted the snow in summer, when the coyotes and the vultures would soon clean the bones." He broke off suddenly; there was a dull sound, and at the same moment a distinct vibration of the ground, then a rustling murmur mingled with a rumbling as of a waggon passing over a rocky ground.

"There is another one," Jerry exclaimed, "and it is somewhere just above us. Keep your backs to the wall, boys."

Louder and louder grew the sound; the tremor of the earth increased, the horses neighed with fright, the men stood with their backs against the rock next to the hill. Suddenly the light was darkened as a vast mass of snow mingled with rocks of all sizes leapt like a torrent over the edge of the cliff, the impetus carrying it over the outer wall of their shelter and down into the ravine. There was a mighty sound of the crashing of trees, mingled with a thumping and rolling of the rocks as they dashed against the side of the ravine and went leaping down into the valley. The ground shook with a continuous tremor, and then the light returned as suddenly as it had been cut off, and a few seconds later a dead stillness succeeded the deafening roar from below. The passage of the avalanche overhead had lasted but a minute, though to the men standing below it the time had seemed vastly longer. Instinctively they had pressed themselves against the rock, almost holding their breath, and expecting momentarily that one of the boulders in its passage would strike the top of the outside wall and fall in fragments among them. The silence that followed was unbroken for some seconds, and then Sam Hicks stepped a pace forward.

"Jee-rusalem!" he said, "that was a close call. I don't know how you felt, boys, but it seemed as if all the sand had gone out of me, and I weakened so that my knees have not done shaking yet."

The men, accustomed as they were to danger, were all equally affected. Tom felt relieved to see that the others all looked pale and shaken, for he was conscious that he had been in a terrible fright, and that his legs would scarcely support his weight.

"I am glad to hear you say so, Sam, for I was in an awful funk; but I should not have said so if you hadn't spoken."

"You needn't be ashamed of that, Tom," his uncle put in. "You showed plenty of pluck when we were in trouble with the red-skins, but I am sure there was not one of us that did not weaken when that snow-slide shot over us; and none of us need be ashamed to say so. A man with good grit will brace up, keep his head cool and his fingers steady on the trigger to the last, though he knows that he has come to the end of his journey and has got to go down; but it is when there is nothing to do, no fight to be made, when you are as helpless as a child and have no sort of show, that the grit runs out of your boots. I have fought red-skins and Mexicans a score of times; I have been in a dozen shooting scrapes in saloons at the diggings; but I don't know that I ever felt so scared as I did just now. Ben, there is a jar of whisky in our outfit; we agreed we would not touch it unless one of us got hurt or ill, but I think a drop of medicine all round now wouldn't be out of place."

There was a general assent. "But before we take it," he went on, "we will take off our hats and say 'Thank God' for having taken us safe through this thing. If He had put this shelter here for us express, He could not have planted it better for us, and the least we can do is to thank Him for having pulled us through it safe."

The men all took off their hats, and stood silent for a minute or two with bent heads. When they had replaced their hats Ben Gulston went to the corner where the pack-saddles and packs were piled, took out a small keg, and poured out some whisky for each of the white men. The others drank it straight; Tom mixed some water with his, and felt a good deal better after drinking it. Ben did not offer it to the Indians, neither of whom would touch spirits on any occasion.

"It is a good friend and a bad enemy," Harry said as he tossed off his portion. "As a rule there ain't no doubt that one is better without it; but there is no better medicine to carry about with you. I have seen many a life saved by a bottle of whisky. Taken after the bite of a rattlesnake, it is as good a thing as there is. In case of fever, and when a man is just tired out after a twenty-four hours' tramp, a drop of it will put new life into him for a bit. But I don't say as it hasn't killed a sight more than it has cured. It is at the bottom of pretty nigh every shooting scrape in the camps, and has been the ruin of hundreds of good men who would have done well if they could but have kept from it."

"But you ain't a temperance man yourself, Harry?"

"No, Sam; but then, thank God, I am master of the liquor, and not the liquor of me. I can take a glass, or perhaps two, without wanting more. Though I have made a fool of myself in many ways since I have come out here, no man can say he ever saw me drunk; if liquor were to get the better of me once, I would swear off for the rest of my life. Don't you ever take to it, Tom; that is, not to get so as to like to go on drinking it. In our life we often have to go for months without it, and a man has got to be very careful when he goes down to the settlements, else it would be sure to get over him."

"I don't care for it at all, uncle."

"See you don't get to care for it, Tom. There are plenty start as you do, and before they have been out here long they do get to like it, and from that day they are never any good. It is a big temptation. A man has been hunting or trapping, or fossicking for gold in the hills for months, and he comes down to a fort or town and he meets a lot of mates. One says 'Have a drink?' and another asks you, and it is mighty hard to be always saying 'no'; and there ain't much to do in these places but to drink or to gamble. A man here ain't so much to be blamed as folks who live in comfortable houses, and have got wives and families and decent places of amusement, and books and all that sort of thing, if they take to drink or gambling. I have not any right to preach, for if I don't drink I do gamble; that is, I have done; though I swore off that when I got the letter telling me that your father had gone. Then I thought what a fool I had made of myself for years. Why, if I had kept all the gold I had dug I could go home now and live comfortably for the rest of my life, and have a home for my nieces, as I ought to have. However, I have done with it now. And I am mighty glad it was the cards and not drink that took my dust, for it is a great deal easier to give up cards than it is to give up liquor when you have once taken to it. Now let us talk of something else; I vote we take a turn up on to the trail, and see what the snow-slide has done."

Throwing the buffalo robes round their shoulders the party went outside. The air was too thick with snow to enable them to perceive from the platform the destruction it had wrought in the valley below, but upon ascending the path to the level above, the track of the avalanche was plainly marked indeed. For the width of a hundred yards, the white mantle of snow, that covered the slope up to the point where the wall of cliff rose abruptly, had been cleared away as if with a mighty broom. Every rock and boulder lying upon it had been swept off, and the surface of the bare rock lay flat, and unbroken by even a tuft of grass. They walked along the edge until they looked down upon their shelter. The bear's hide was still in its place, sloping like a penthouse roof, from its upper side two or three inches below the edge of the rock, to the other wall three feet lower. It was, however, stripped of its hair, as cleanly as if it had been shorn off with a razor, by the friction of the snow that had shot down along it.

"That is the blamedest odd thing I ever saw," Sam Hicks said. "I wonder the weight of the snow didn't break it in."

"I expect it just shot over it, Sam," Harry said. "It must have been travelling so mighty fast that the whole mass jumped across, only just rubbing the skin. Of course the boulders and stones must have gone clean over. That shows what a narrow escape we have had; for if that outer rock had been a foot or so higher, the skin would have caved in, and our place would have been filled chock up with snow in a moment. Waal, we may as well turn in again, for I feel cold to the bones already."

On the evening of the fifth day the snow ceased falling, and next morning the sky was clear and bright. Preparations were at once made for a start. A batch of bread had been baked on the previous evening. Some buckets of hot gruel were given to the horses, a meal was hastily eaten, the horses saddled and the packs arranged, and before the sun had been up half an hour they were on their way. The usual stillness of the mountains was broken by a variety of sounds. From the valley at their feet came up sharp reports, as a limb of a tree, or sometimes the tree itself, broke beneath the weight of the snow. A dull rumbling sound, echoing from hill to hill, told of the falls of avalanches. Scarcely had the echoes of one ceased, than they began again in a fresh quarter. The journey was toilsome in the extreme, for the horses' hoofs sank deep in the freshly-fallen snow, rendering their progress exceedingly slow.

"If we had been sure that this weather would hold, chief, it would have been better to have waited a few days before making our start, for by that time the snow would have been hard enough to travel on."

The chief shook his head. "Winter coming for good," he said, waving his hand towards the range of snowy summits to the north. "Clouds there still; if stop, not able to cross pass till next summer."

"That is so; we agreed as to that yesterday, and that if we don't get over now the chances are we shall never get over at all. Yet, it is a pity we can't wait a few days for a crust to form on the snow."

Twice in the course of the next hour avalanches came down from the hills above them; the first sweeping down into the valley a quarter of a mile behind them, the next but two or three hundred yards ahead of them. Scarcely a word was spoken from end to end of the line. They travelled in Indian file, and each horse stepped in the footprints of its predecessor. Every few hundred yards they changed places, for the labour of the first horse was very much heavier than of those following. At the end of an hour the men drew together for a consultation. There was a wide break in the line of cliffs, and a valley ran nearly due south.

"What do you think, chief? This confounded snow has covered up all signs of the trail, and we have got to find our own way. There is no doubt this valley below is running a deal too much to the west, and that the trail must strike off somewhere south. It looks to me as if that were a likely valley through the cliff. There is no hiding the fact that if we take the wrong turn we are all gone coons."

"Leaping Horse knows no more than his brother," the chief said gravely. "He knows the pass is on the western side of the great peak. The great peak lies there," and he pointed a little to the west of the break in the hills up which they were looking.

"It may be that we must cross the hills into another valley, or perhaps this will turn west presently."

"I tell you what, Harry," Sam Hicks said, "my opinion is, that our best plan by a long chalk will be to go back to our last place and to stop there for a bit. We have got b'ar's flesh enough for another fortnight, and we may kill some more game afore that is done. Ef this is but a spell of snow it may melt enough in another ten days for us to make out the trail and follow it. Ef, as the chief thinks, we have got winter right down on us, we must wait till the snow crust hardens ef it is a month or double. Anything is better than going on like this. What with this soft snow and these 'tarnal snow-slides, there ain't no more chance of our getting over that pass in one day's journey, than there air in our flying right down to Salt Lake City. Ef the worst comes to the worst, I tell yer I would rather go back and take our chance of following the Big Wind River down, and fighting the red-skins, than I would of crossing over these dog-goned hills."

The other three men were of the same opinion.

"Well, what do you say, chief?" Harry asked the Indian.

"Leaping Horse thinks that the trail will not be found until next summer," the chief replied quietly. "Heap of hills in front and heap of snow. If snow-storm catch us in the hills no find way anywhere. Leaping Horse is ready to do whatever his white brother thinks."

"Well, I am with the others," Harry said. "I don't like the look of those clouds. They are quiet enough now, but they may begin to shift any time, and, as you say, if we are caught in a snow-storm on the hills there is an end of us. I think Sam is right. Even if we have to rustle all through the winter in that hut there, I would rather face it than keep on."

That settled it. The horses' heads were turned, and they retraced their steps until they reached the shelter. The bear's-skin had been left where it was, the fire was soon set going, and there was a general feeling of satisfaction as they laid out the robes and blankets again.

"Look here, boys," Harry said, "this is not going to be a holiday time, you bet. We have got to make this place a sight snugger than it is now, for, I tell you, when the winter sets in in earnest, it will be cold enough here to freeze a buffalo solid in an hour. We have got to set to work to make a roof all over this place, and we have got to hunt to lay in a big stock of meat. We have got to get a big store of food for the horses, for we must be mighty careful with our flour now. We can wait a fortnight to see how things go, but if it is clear then that we have got to fight it out here through the winter, we must shoot the pack-ponies at once, and I reckon the others will all have to go later. However, we will give them a chance as long as we can."

"Take them down into the valley," the chief said. "All Indian horses."

"Ah, I didn't think of that, chief. Yes, they are accustomed to rustle for their living, and they may make a shift to hold on down there. I don't think there is much fear of Indians coming up."

"No Indians," Leaping Horse said. "Indians go away when winter set in. Some go to forest, some go to lodges right down valley. No stop up here in mountains. When winter comes plenty game—big-horn, wapiti."

"Ah, that is a more cheerful look-out, chief. If we can get plenty of meat we can manage without flour, and can go down and give the ponies a pail of hot gruel once a week, which will help them to keep life together. The first thing, I take it, is to cut some poles for the roof. I am afraid we shall have to go down to the bottom for them."

"Waal, we needn't begin that till to-morrow," Sam Hicks said. "If we had them, we have got no skins to cover them."

"Cut brushwood," Indian said. "First put plenty of brushwood on poles, then put skins over."

"Yes, that is the plan, chief. Well, if we get down there we shall have to take our shovels and clear the snow off some of the narrow ledges. If we do that we can lead one of the horses down to pack the poles up here."

The chief went out on to the platform. "No use clear snow now. Clouds moving. In two hours snow fall again."

The others joined him outside. "I reckon you are right, chief," Jerry said. "It is mighty lucky we didn't go on. It can't be much worse here than it was before."

At three in the afternoon it began to snow heavily again. There was less wind than there had been on the previous occasion, and the snow drifted through the entrance less than before. Just as they were turning in for the night an ominous crack was heard above. All leapt from their blankets, and looking up they could see by the light of the fire that the poles supporting the skin were all bent in a curve downwards.

"Jee-rusalem!" Sam Hicks exclaimed, "the whole outfit will be coming down on us."

"That it will, Sam. You see, there is no wind as there was before, and one of our jobs will be keeping the roof clear of snow. Turn out, boys; we must get rid of it somehow."

They at once set to work to lash two poles, some eight feet long, to the handles of the shovels, and as soon as this was done they all turned out. On reaching the edge of the ravine above the roof, they first cleared away the snow down to the rock so as to have firm standing, and then proceeded to shovel the snow off the surface of the skin. It was easier work than they expected, for as soon as it was touched it slid down the incline, and in a very few minutes the whole was cleared off.

"I think that is good until morning now," Harry said. "As long as the snow lasts we shall have to do it every few hours. Directly we get a spell of fine weather we must put some more poles under it to strengthen it."

For six days the snow continued to fall without intermission. At daybreak, at mid-day, and the last thing before they turned in at night the snow was cleared off the hide. With this exception they did not stir out of the shelter. They had also each day to clear out the inner portion of the fissure, as the snow now frequently broke through the trees in masses, startling the horses, and keeping them in a state of restlessness. The sixth day it stopped snowing, and the next morning the sky was bright and clear. The whole party at once started out, two of them taking shovels, and the rest brooms that they had made during the long hours of their confinement. By the middle of the day they had cleared the path down into the valley, and on their way back to dinner each carried up a large bundle of faggots.

The meal was cooked and eaten hastily, and the whole of the horses were then led down into the valley. Here a couple of dozen stout poles for the roof were cut by the whites, the two Indians at once going up the valley in search of game. In half an hour two rifle-shots were heard, and presently Hunting Dog ran in with the news that they had killed two wapiti. Jerry and Sam Hicks at once went off with him, leading two horses, and presently returned with the dead deer fastened across their backs.

"They are very like pictures I have seen of moose," Tom said to his uncle as he examined the great stags.

"New-comers often call them moose, Tom; but there is a difference between them, though what the difference is I cannot tell you, for I have never hunted moose. I believe the wapiti are peculiar to the West. They often go in great herds of three or four hundreds together."

"The chief says there are a great many of them up the valley," Jerry put in. "They made off when he fired, but I could see their foot-tracks myself all about. He says they have been driven down here by the storm for shelter. He has gone round with the lad to head them back."

"That is good news, Jerry. The meat we have got already will last some time, but it is as well to lay in a good stock, and we want the skins badly to make our roof. You had better lead these horses to the foot of the path, and then we will all take our post behind trees across the valley."

An hour later they heard the reports of two rifles a long way up the valley, and all stood in readiness. A few minutes later there was a dull trampling sound, and almost directly afterwards a herd of wapiti came along at a heavy trot, ploughing their way but slowly through the snow.

"Don't use your revolvers, boys," Harry had said, "except to finish off a stag you have wounded with your rifle. The chance is all against your bringing them down, and the poor brutes would only get away to die."

One after another the rifles rang out. Tom and his uncle both had the satisfaction of seeing the stags they had aimed at, plunge forward before they had gone many yards farther, and roll over dead. The other three had each hit the animal they aimed at, but as these kept on their course they dashed out in pursuit, firing their Colts, which in their hands were as deadly weapons as a rifle, and the three stags all fell, although one got nearly half a mile down the valley before he succumbed. A carcass was hoisted on to each of the horses' backs, and the loaded animals were then led up the track.

"Shall I wait until the Indians come back, uncle, and tell them why you have gone up?"

"There is no occasion for that, Tom; they would hear the shots, and will have guessed what has happened."

The poles were divided among the men and carried up to the top of the path, and laid down just above the shelter. Harry and Sam Hicks at once proceeded to cut them up into proper lengths, while the others skinned and cut up the deer. A number of thongs were cut from one of the hides for lashing cross-poles across those that were to act as ridge-poles. The bear's-skin was removed and additional poles placed at that spot, and all working together the framework of the roof was completed by nightfall. The Indians had returned soon after the party began their work, and taking their horses down fetched up the deer they had killed.

In the morning the roof was completed, hides being stretched over the framework and securely lashed to it with thongs. The whole of the trees and brushwood were then chopped down close to the ground so as to leave a level floor. The foliage was given to the horses, and the wood cut up and piled for fuel. The chief reported that at the upper end of the valley there was a thick pine-wood, which would give good shelter to the horses. Near it were plenty of bushes, and a level tract which had been a beaver meadow, and was thickly covered with grass, as he could see where the wapiti had scratched away the snow to get at it. This was excellent news, for the question of how the horses could be fed through the winter had troubled them much more than that of their own maintenance. The joints of venison were hung up on a pole outside what they now called their hut, one or two hams being suspended from the rafters over the fire, to be smoked.

"We shall have to rig up a b'ar-trap outside," Ben said, "or we shall be having them here after the meat; and a b'ar's ham now and then will make a change. Wapiti flesh ain't bad, but we should get dog-goned tired of it arter a bit."

"You may bet we shall, Ben," Jerry agreed; "but I reckon that we shall be able to get a lot of game through the winter. That valley down there is just the place for them to shelter in, and I hope we shall get a big-horn now and then. It will be a difficult thing to make a b'ar-trap outside. A grizzly wants a pretty strong pen to keep him in, and though the horses might drag up some big beams from below, there ain't no fastening them in this rock."

"No; I don't think we can make that sort of trap," Harry said. "We must contrive something else. We need not do all our work at once; we have got plenty of time before us. We want three or four more skins to finish our hut."

"You mean to fill up the entrance?"

"Yes; we will sew them together, and make a curtain to hang from the edge of the roof to the ground. I tell you it is going to be mighty cold here, and besides, it will keep the snow from drifting in."

"I wish to goodness we could make a chimney," Tom said. "The smoke went up through the leaves all right, but my eyes are watering now, and if you fill up the end with skins it will be something awful."

"You will get accustomed to it, Tom; but, of course, we must make a hole at the top when we fill up the entrance. What do you think is the next thing to be done, chief?"

"Get wood," the chief said emphatically. "Must fill all the end of hut with wood."

"That will be a big job, chief, but there is no doubt we must lay in a great store of it. Well, there is plenty of timber down in the valley, and with ten horses we can bring up a tidy lot every day."

"Let us cut quick before snow comes again."

"We will begin to-morrow morning, chief. I agree with you, the sooner the better."

Accordingly the next morning they went down to the valley. They had but two axes, and Jerry and Sam Hicks, who had both done a good deal of wood-cutting, undertook this portion of the work. The others took the horses up to the beaver meadow, where they at once began scraping at the snow, and were soon munching away at the rich grass.

"Why do you call it a beaver meadow, uncle? I don't see any beavers."

"They have gone long ago, perhaps a hundred years. As we know, this valley is occupied by the Indians in summer, and they would soon clear out the beavers. But it is called a beaver meadow because it was made by them. They set to work and dammed up the stream, and gradually all this flat became a lake. Well, in time, you know, leaves from the woods above, and soil and dead wood and other things brought down by the stream, gradually filled up the bottom. Then the beavers were killed, and their dams went to ruin and the water drained off, and in a short time grass began to grow. There are hundreds, ay, and thousands of beaver meadows among the hills, and on the little streams that run into the big rivers, and nowhere is the grass so rich. You will often see an Indian village by one of these meadows. They grow their roots and plant their corn there. The horses will do first-rate here through the winter if the snow don't get too deep for them, and, anyhow, we can help them out with a bucket of gruel occasionally."

"It will be awfully cold for them, though."

"It will be coldish, no doubt, but Indian ponies are accustomed to it."

"I should think, uncle, it would not take much trouble to make them a sort of shed up among the trees there."

Sam laughed, and even the chief smiled.

"It would not be a bad plan, Tom," his uncle said; "not so much for the sake of the warmth, though there is no doubt that the warmer they are the less they can do with to eat, but if they have a place to go to they are less likely to wander away, and we shall not have the trouble of hunting for them. Well, we will think it over."

Following the valley up, they found that it extended some ten miles farther, for the last two of which it was but a narrow canon a few yards wide. They shot a black bear and four small deer, and returned carrying the skins, the hind-quarters of the deer, and the bear's hams.

"We seem to have got meat enough for anything," Tom remonstrated when they shot the deer.

"Seven men will get through a lot of meat, Tom, when they have nothing else to go with it; and we may be weeks before we can put our heads out of our hut. Besides, the skins will be useful. We shall want deer-skin shirts, trousers, and socks and caps; and the skin of these deer is softer and more pliable than that of the wapiti. I don't want to kill more than I can help, lad, for I hate taking life without there is a necessity for it, but we can do with a lot more skins before we are stocked."

When, driving the horses before them, they returned to the woodcutters, they found they had cut down and chopped into logs a number of trees; and Tom was quite astonished at the great pile of firewood that had been got ready by them in the course of a day's work. The logs were made up into bundles, each weighing about eighty pounds. These were tied together with the horses' lariats, and then secured, one on each side of the saddle, two of the horses carrying the meat. Harry took the bridle of his horse and started up the path, the others following at once.

"That is a good day's work," Harry said as the logs were piled at the inner end of the hut. "That is about half a ton of wood. If we have but a week of open weather we shall have a good store in our cellar."

The work continued steadily for a week. The horses were each day taken to feed at the meadow, the two wood-choppers continued their work, while the rest of the party hunted. The Indians had on the second day gone down the valley, and returned with the report that the Indian lodges had all disappeared and that the valley was entirely deserted. Eight more wapiti were killed during the week, and fourteen smaller deer. Of an evening they occupied themselves in sewing the skins together with thongs of leather, the holes being made with their knives; and a curtain at the mouth of the hut was completed and hung.

Four wide slabs of wood had been cut. These had been bound together with thongs so as to form a sort of chimney four feet high, and with a good deal of difficulty this was secured by props in its position over a hole cut through the skins above the fire. "The first avalanche will carry it away, Tom."

"Yes, uncle; but we have had one avalanche here, and it seems to me the chances are strongly against our having another in exactly the same place."

The skins of the smaller deer were carefully scraped with knives on the inner side, smeared with bears' fat, and then rubbed and kneaded until they were perfectly soft.

Chapter XI.
Winter

The erection of Tom's shed for the horses did not take long. The whole party, with the exception of the two Indians,—who, as usual, went hunting,—proceeded to the pine-wood above the beaver meadow. After a little search six trees were found conveniently situated with regard to each other. The axemen cut down three young firs. One was lashed by the others between the two central trees, to form a ridge-pole eight feet from the ground; the others against the other trees, at a height of three feet, to support the lower ends of the roof. They were but ten feet apart, so that the roof might have a considerable pitch. Numbers of other young trees were felled and fixed, six inches apart, from the ridge down to the eaves. On these the branches of the young fir-trees were thickly laid, and light poles were lashed lengthways over them to keep them in their places.

As the poles of the roof had been cut long enough to extend down to the ground, no side walls were necessary. The ends were formed of poles lashed across to the side trees, but extending down only to within four feet six of the ground, so as to allow the horses to pass under, and were, like the roof, thickly covered with boughs. The lower ends were left open for a width of four feet in the middle, uprights being driven into the ground and the sides completed as before.

"What do you want a doorway at both ends for?" Tom asked. "It would have been easier and quicker to have shut one end up altogether, and it would be a good deal warmer."

"So it would, Tom; but if a grizzly were to appear at the door, what would the horses do? They would be caught in a trap."

"Do you think they are likely to come, uncle?"

"The likeliest thing in the world, Tom. Horses can smell bear a good distance off, and if they heard one either coming down or going up the valley, they would bolt through the opposite door. They will do first-rate here; they will stand pretty close together, and the warmth of their bodies will heat the place up. They won't know themselves, they will be so comfortable. It has only taken us a day's work to make the shed; and though we laughed at your idea at first, I think now that the day has been well spent in getting them up such a good shelter. Jerry has got the big pail boiling over his fire, and we will put in a few handfuls of the flour we brought down. Bring the horses in from the meadow, and we will give them each a drink of gruel in the shed. They will soon learn that it is to be their home."

For two more days the open weather continued, and the horses took up three loads of wood each afternoon, as they had done the previous week. Then, as there were signs of change, they were given a good feed at their shed; the saddles were taken off and hung up on some cross-poles over their heads.

The party had scarcely returned to the hut when the snow began to fall. They were, however, weather-proof, and felt the immense additional comfort of the changes they had made. Their stock of firewood was now a very large one. At each journey the horses had brought up about fifteen hundredweight; and as the work had gone on for nine days, they had, they calculated, something like fourteen tons of firewood neatly stacked. They had also a stock of poles in case the roof should require strengthening. A certain amount of light found its way in at the edges of the curtain across the entrance, but they depended principally upon the fire-light. The smoke, however, was a serious grievance, and even the men were forced occasionally to go outside into the open air to allay the smarting of their eyes.

"Don't you think, uncle, we might do something to dry the wood?"

"I can't see that we can do more than we are doing, Tom. We always keep a dozen logs lying round the fire to dry a bit before they are put on."

"I should think we might make a sort of stage about four feet above the fire and keep some logs up there. We might pile them so that the hot air and smoke could go up through them. They would dry a great deal faster there than merely lying down on the ground."

"I think the idea is a very good one, Tom; but we shall have to make the frame pretty strong, for if it happened to come down it might break some of our legs."

The men all agreed that the idea was a capital one, and after some consultation they set to to carry it out. Two strong poles were first chosen. These were cut carefully to the right length, and were jambed between the rocks at a height of seven feet above the floor and five feet apart. They were driven in and wedged so tightly that they could each bear the weight of two men swinging upon them without moving. Then four upright poles were lashed to them, five feet apart, and these were connected with cross-poles.

"That is strong enough for anything," Jerry said when the structure had been so far completed. "If a horse were to run against one of the poles he would hardly bring the thing down."

Four other short poles were now lashed to the uprights three feet below the upper framework, and were crossed by others so as to form a gridiron. On this, the logs were laid in tiers crossing each other, sufficient space being left between them to allow for the passage of the hot air.

"That is a splendid contrivance," Harry said when they took their seats on the buffalo robes round the fire and looked up admiringly at their work. "The logs will get as dry as chips, and in future we sha'n't be bothered with the smoke. Besides, it will do to stand the pail and pots full of snow there, and keep a supply of water, without putting them down into the fire and running the risk of an upset."

They had occupation now in manufacturing a suit of clothes a-piece from the deer-skins. As the work required to be neater than that which sufficed for the making of the curtain, pointed sticks hardened in the fire were used for making the holes, and the thongs that served as thread were cut as finely as possible; this being done by the Indians, who turned them out no thicker than pack-thread.

There was no occasion for hurry, and there was much laughing and joking over the work. Their hunting-shirts and breeches served as patterns from which to cut out the skins; and as each strove to outvie the others, the garments when completed were very fair specimens of work. The hunting-shirts were made with hoods that, when pulled over the head, covered the whole face except the eyes, nose, and mouth. As they had plenty of skin, the hoods and shirts were made double, so that there was hair both inside and out. They were made to come down half-way to the knee, being kept close at the waists by their belts. The leggings were made of single thickness only, as they would be worn over their breeches; they were long and reached down below the ankle. The Indians made fresh moccasins for the whole party; they were made higher than usual, so as to come up over the bottom of the leggings. In addition each was provided with long strips of hide, which were to be wound round and round the leggings, from the knee to below the ankle, covering tightly the tops of the moccasins, and so preventing the snow from finding its way in there. Gloves were then manufactured, the fingers being in one and the thumb only being free.

The work occupied them a fortnight, broken only by one day's spell of fine weather, which they utilized by going down into the valley, taking with them their kettles and pail, together with a few pounds of flour. They found the horses out in the meadow, and these, as soon as they saw them, came trotting to meet them with loud whinnies of pleasure. A fire was lit near the shed, the snow melted, and an allowance of warm gruel given to each horse. At Tom's suggestion a few fir-boughs were hung from the bar over each entrance. These would swing aside as the horses entered, and would keep out a good deal of wind. When at the end of a fortnight the sky cleared, the chief said that he thought that there would be but little more snow.

"If storm come, sure to bring snow, but not last long. Winter now set in; soon snow harden. Now make snow-shoes."

The hunters had all been accustomed to use these in winter. They had found the last expedition through the deep snow a very toilsome one, and they embraced the idea eagerly. Some of the poles were split into eight feet lengths. These were wetted and hung over the fire, the process being repeated until the wood was sufficiently softened to be bent into the required shape. This was done by the chief. Two cross-pieces were added, to stiffen them and keep them in the right shape when they dried; and the wood was then trimmed up and scraped by the men. When it had dried and hardened, the work of filling up the frame with a closely-stretched network of leather was undertaken. This part of the work occupied three or four days. The straps were attached to go across the toe and round the heel, and they were then ready to set off.

The weather was now intensely cold, but as there was but little wind it was not greatly felt; at the same time they were glad of their furs when they ventured outside the hut. On the first day after their snow-shoes were finished, the rest of the party started off to visit the horses, Hunting Dog remaining behind to give Tom instructions in the use of the snow-shoes, and to help him when he fell down.

Tom found it difficult work at first, the toe of the shoe frequently catching in the snow, and pitching him head foremost into it, and he would have had great difficulty in extricating himself, had not the young Indian been at hand. Before the day was over, however, he could get on fairly well; and after two or three more days' practice had made such progress that he was considered capable of accompanying the rest.

The wood-drying apparatus had succeeded excellently. The wood was now dried so thoroughly before being put on to the fire that there was no annoyance from the smoke inside the hut, and scarce any could be perceived coming from the chimney. Upon Harry's remarking upon this with satisfaction the first time they went out after using the dry wood, Tom said:

"What does it matter? There are no Indians in the valley."

"That is so, Tom; but as soon as the weather sets in clear, the red-skins will be hunting again. Winter is their best time for laying in their stock of pelts for trading. At other times the game is all high up in the mountains, and it is very difficult to get within range of it. In the winter the animals come down to the shelter of the forests and valleys, and they can be shot in numbers; especially as the Indians in their snow-shoes can get along almost as quickly as the wapiti can plough through the snow. At present the red-skins think that we must have been overtaken by that first storm and have all gone under; but as soon as they begin to venture out of their lodges to hunt, a column of smoke here would be sure to catch their eyes, and then we should be having them up the valley to a certainty. The first thing they would do would be to find our horses and drive them off, and the next thing would be to set themselves to work to catch us."

"But we could hold the path against them, uncle."

"Yes; but we should have to keep watch every day, which would be a serious trouble. Besides, there must be other places they could get up. No doubt their regular trail comes up here, because it is the straightest way to the pass, and possibly there may be no other point at which loaded animals could mount anywhere about here. But there must be plenty of places where Indians could climb, and even if it took them a detour of fifty miles they would manage it. As long as there is no smoke we may hope they will not discover us here, though any hunting party might come upon the horses. That is what has bothered me all along; but the chief and I have talked it over a dozen times, and can see no way of avoiding the risk.

"We can't keep the horses up here because we can't feed them; and even if we were to bring ourselves to leave this comfortable place and to build a hut down in the valley, we might be surprised and rubbed out by the red-skins. Of course we might bring them up here every night and take them down again in the morning, but it would be a troublesome business. We have agreed that we won't do much more shooting down in the valley, and that in coming and going to the horses we will keep along close to the foot of the cliffs this side, so that if two or three Indians do come up they won't see any tracks on the snow, unless they happen to come close up to the cliff. Of course if they go up as far as the beaver flat they will light upon the horses.

There is no help for that; but the chief and I agreed last night that in future two of us shall always stay up here, and shall take it by turns to keep watch. It won't be necessary to stand outside. If the curtain is pulled aside three or four inches one can see right down the valley, and any Indians coming up could be made out. If the party is a strong one a gun would be fired as a signal to those away hunting, and some damp wood thrown on the fire. They might possibly push on up the valley to have a look at the place, but the two up here with their rifles would soon stop them. After that, of course, the horses would have to be brought up here at night, and a watch kept by night as well as by day."

Two or three mornings later they found on going out that two joints of venison had been carried off, and footprints in the snow showed that it had been done by a grizzly bear. This turned their attention again to the construction of a trap, which had not been thought of since the day it was first mentioned. A young tree of four or five inches in diameter was cut below and brought up. The butt was cut in the shape of a wedge, and this was driven strongly into a fissure in the rock. A rope with a running noose had been fastened to the tree, and this was bent down by the united strength of four men, and fixed to a catch fastened in the ground, the noose being kept open by two sticks placed across it.

A foot beyond the noose a joint of venison was hung, the rope passing over a pole and then down to the catch, so that upon the joint being pulled the catch would be loosened, when the tree would fly up and the noose catch anything that might be through it.

A week later they were disturbed by an outburst of violent growling. Seizing their rifles they rushed out. A huge bear was caught by one of his paws. The animal's weight was too great for it to be lifted from the ground, but it was standing upright with its paw above its head, making furious efforts to free itself. A volley of bullets at once put an end to its life. The tree was bent down again and the noose loosed, and they at once returned to their rugs, leaving the bear where it fell. Four times during the winter did they thus capture intruders, providing themselves with an ample supply of bear's flesh, while the skins would sell well down at the settlements.

Otherwise sport was not very good. No more wapiti came up, but black and white tail deer were occasionally shot, and five or six big-horn sheep also fell to their rifles. One day on approaching the beaver meadow the chief pointed to some deep footprints. No explanation was needed. All knew that they were made by a big grizzly, and that the animal was going up the valley. No horses were in view on the flat, and grasping their rifles they hurried towards the wood. Just as they reached it the horses came galloping to meet them, whinnying and snorting.

"They have been scared by the critter," Jerry said. "Do you see their coats are staring. Gosh, look at this pack-pony—the bear has had his paw on him!"

The animal's hind-quarters were indeed badly torn.

"I wonder how it got away," Harry said. "When a grizzly once gets hold, it don't often leave go."

"There is something in front of the hut," Tom exclaimed.

"It's the grizzly, sure enough," Harry said. "It is a rum place for it to go to sleep."

They advanced, holding their rifles in readiness to fire, when Leaping Horse said:

"Bear dead."

"What can have killed him?" Harry asked doubtfully. "Horses kill him," the chief replied. They hurried up to the spot. The bear was indeed dead, and there were signs of a desperate struggle. There was blood on the snow from a point near the door of the hut to where the animal was lying ten yards away. Round it the snow was all trampled deeply. The bear's head was battered out of all shape; its jaw was broken, and one of its eyes driven out. The Indians examined the ground closely.

"Well, what do you make of it, chief?" Harry asked.

"Bear walk round hut, come in other end. Horses not able to get out in time. Pack-horse last, bear catch him by hind-quarters. Horse drag him a little way and then fall. Then other horses come back, form ring round bear and kick him. Look at prints of fore-feet deep in snow. That is where they kick; they break bear's jaw, break his ribs, keep on kick till he dead."

"I suppose that is how it came about, chief. I should not have thought they would have done it."

The Seneca nodded. "When wild horses with young foals attacked by bear or mountain-lion, they form circle with colts in the middle, stand heads in and kick. Bears and mountain-lion afraid to attack them."

"Waal, I should hardly have believed if I had not seen it," Sam Hicks said, "that horses would come back to attack a grizzly."

"Not come back," the chief said, "if not for friend. Friend cry out loud, then horses come back, fight bear and kill him."

"Well, it was mighty plucky of them," Harry said. "I am afraid this pony won't get over it; he is terribly torn."

The chief examined the horse's wounds again. "Get over it," he said. "Cold stop wounds bleeding, get some fat and put in."

"I reckon you will find plenty inside the grizzly," Jerry said. The chief shook his head. "Bear's fat bad; other horses smell him, perhaps keep away from him, perhaps kick him. Leaping Horse will bring fat from the big-horn he shot yesterday."

The animal lay where it had fallen, a mile up the valley. They went up and tied the great sheep's feet together, and putting a pole through them brought it down to the hut. Partly skinning it, they obtained some fat and melted this in a kettle over the fire. Sam Hicks had remained behind at the fire, the horses all standing near him, excited at the prospect of their usual meal. As soon as the fat was melted it was poured into the horse's wounds. The mess of gruel was then prepared and given to the animals. The bear was skinned and the hams cut off, then by a united effort it was dragged some distance from the hut, and the carcass of the big-horn, the bear's flesh and hide, were afterwards carried up to the hut.

Early in February the cold reached its extreme point, and in spite of keeping up a good fire they had long before this been compelled to build up the entrance with a wall of firewood, the interstices being stuffed with moss; the hut was lighted by lamps of bear and deer fat melted down and poured into tin drinking-cups, the wicks being composed of strips of birch bark. A watch was regularly kept all day, two always remaining in the hut, one keeping watch through a small slip cut in the curtain before the narrow orifice in the log wall, that served as a door, the other looking after the fire, keeping up a good supply of melted snow, and preparing dinner ready for the return of the hunters at sunset. Of an evening they told stories, and their stock of yarns of their own adventures and of those they had heard from others, seemed to Tom inexhaustible.

Hunting Dog had made rapid advances with his English, and he and Tom had become great friends, always hunting together, or when their turn came, remaining together on guard. The cold was now so intense that the hunting party was seldom out for more than two or three hours. Regularly twice a week the horses were given their ration of hot gruel, and although they had fallen away greatly in flesh they maintained their health, and were capable of work if called upon to do it. It was one day in the middle of February, that Hunting Dog, who was standing at the peep-hole, exclaimed:

"'Rappahoes!"

Tom sprang up from the side of the fire, and running to the entrance pulled aside the curtain and looked out. Six Indians on snow-shoes were coming up the valley. He ran out on to the platform and fired his rifle. As the sound of the report reached the Indians' ears they stopped suddenly.

"Shall I throw some green wood on the fire, Hunting Dog?"

"No need," the Indian replied. "The others only gone an hour, not farther than horses' hut; hear gun plain enough. Perhaps 'Rappahoes go back."

The Indians remained for some time in consultation.

"Not know where gun fired," Hunting Dog said. "Soon see hut, then know."

After a time the red-skins continued their way up the valley, but instead of coming on carelessly in the centre they separated, and going to the other side crept along among the fallen boulders there, where they would have escaped observation had it not been for their figures showing against the white snow.

"Must fire now," the young Indian said, "then Leaping Horse know 'Rappahoes coming up."

They went out on to the platform and opened fire. They knew that their chance of hitting one of the Indians was small indeed; the other side of the valley was a quarter of a mile away, and the height at which they were standing rendered it difficult to judge the elevation necessary for their rifles. However, they fired as fast as they could load.

The Indians made no reply, for their guns would not carry anything like the distance. They occasionally gathered when they came upon a boulder of rock sufficiently large to give shelter to them all, and then moved on again one at a time. When opposite the lower end of the pathway they again held a consultation.

"No go further," Hunting Dog said. "Afraid we come down path and stop them. See, Leaping Horse among rocks."

It was some time before Tom could detect the Indian, so stealthily did he move from rock to rock.

"Where are the others?"

"No see, somewhere in bushes. Leaping Horse go on to scout; not know how many 'Rappahoes."

Presently they saw the chief raise his head behind a rock within a hundred yards of that behind which the 'Rappahoes were sheltering.

"He see them now," Hunting Dog said. "See, he going to fire." There was a puff of smoke and a sharp report, and almost simultaneously rose an Indian yell, and the war-cry of the Seneca. Then five Indians leapt out from behind the rock and made down the valley at full speed, while from a clump of trees two hundred yards above the spot from which the chief had fired the four white men hurried out rifle in hand. The chief waited until they joined him, for the bend in the valley prevented him from seeing that the 'Rappahoes were making straight down it, and it would have been imprudent to have ventured out until his white allies came up.

"They have gone right down," Tom shouted at the top of his voice. Harry waved his arm to show that he heard the words, and then the five men ran to the corner. The Indians were already a quarter of a mile away, and were just entering the wood below. The whites were about to fire, when the chief stopped them. "No use fire," he said. "Stand back behind rocks; no good let 'Rappahoes count our rifles."

"That is true enough, chief," Harry said, as they all sprang among the rocks. "All they know at present is, that there are two up on the top there and one down here. If we were sure that we could wipe them all out it would be worth following and making a running fight of it, but there would be no chance of that, and it is better to let them go without learning more about us. Well, I should say the first thing is to get up the horses."

The chief nodded.

"Get up," he said, "but no fear 'Rappahoes come back to-night. Many hours' journey down to villages, then great council. Next night scouts come up valley, look all about for sign, and then go back and tell friends."

"I dare say you are right, chief. Anyhow, I shall feel a great deal more comfortable when we have got the critters up."

It was late in the afternoon before they reached the hut. Some hours were spent in collecting tufts of grass in places sheltered from the snow, and in cutting off great bundles of young fir-branches and the heads of evergreen bushes, and the horses arrived almost hidden under the load of grass and foliage they carried. Little was said until some hot tea had been drunk and the bear steaks in readiness were disposed off, for although they had worked hard and kept themselves comparatively warm down in the valley, they had as they moved slowly up the path with the horses become chilled to the bone.

"Now then, chief," Harry said, when they had lighted their pipes with the mixture of tobacco and willow bark that they had taken to, as soon as they found that they were likely to be imprisoned all the winter, "we must hold a council. We have been longer than I expected without disturbance by these varmint, but it has come now, and the question is what are we to do? We have agreed all along that there is no getting over the pass till the spring comes."

"Too cold," the chief said, "deep drift snow. Indians all say no can pass over hills in winter."

"That air a fact," Jerry said. "Down in the valley there it is all right, but up here the cold pretty near takes one's breath away. We ain't sure about the way. We couldn't get over the pass in one day's tramp, and we should be all stiff before morning. There would be no taking the horses, and there is a hundred miles to be done over the snow before we reach the fort. It ain't to be thought of. I would a sight rather go down the valley and fight the hull tribe."

"I agree with you, Jerry. We might, with luck, get down the valley, but I don't think there is a possibility of our crossing the pass till the winter breaks."

"No can go down valley," Leaping Horse said; "they find trail on snow, sure."

"That is so, chief, and in that case it is evident that we have got to fight it out here."

"Good place to stop," the Seneca said; "no good place to fight."

This was self-evident. An enemy on the rock above would be able to fire down through the roof, without their having a chance of making an effectual reply.

"The only way I can see," Harry said after a long pause, "is to build a sort of fort up above. If we put it just at the top of this pathway, we should have them whether they came up by the trail from below or climbed up anywhere else and came along above. It need not be a very big place, only just big enough for us all to fire over. We might make a sort of shelter in it with a fire, and keep guard there by turns." The chief nodded, and there was a general exclamation of assent from the others.

"The worst of it is," Jerry said, "the ground is so 'tarnal hard that there will be no driving posts into it. We have cut down all the trees near the bottom of the pass, and it would be a risky thing to go up higher, when we might have the red-skins come whooping up the valley at any time."

"Why not make a snow fort?" Tom suggested. "There is four feet of snow up there, and with the shovels we could make a wall ten feet high in a very short time."

"So we might, Tom; that is a capital idea. The difficulty is, the snow does not bind in this bitter cold as it does in England."

"If it was hammered down it would, I should think, uncle. You know the Esquimaux make snow houses, and it is as cold there as it is here. The snow at the top is light enough, but I should think as it gets down it would be hard enough to cut out in blocks. We have plenty of water, and if we pour it over each layer of blocks it would freeze into solid ice directly. When we finish it we might pour more water down over the outside, and it would make a regular wall of ice that no one could climb up."

"Hooray! Bully for you, Tom!" Jerry shouted, while similar exclamations of approval broke from all the others, while the chief said gravely, "My young brother has the head of a man; he is able to teach warriors."

"You shall be engineer-in-chief, Tom," Harry said. "It is certain we may sleep quietly to-night; at daybreak to-morrow we will begin the job."

The first thing in the morning a semicircular line was traced out at the top of their pathway. It was thirty feet across, for, as Tom said, the walls ought to be at least four feet thick; and six feet would be better, as they would want a parapet at least two feet thick to fire over. It was agreed that the whites should use the two shovels by turns. The Indians were unaccustomed to the work, and were to undertake that of scouting along the hillside, and of watching by turns at night. The frying-pan was brought into requisition, a wooden handle being made for it. The hard upper crust was removed with the shovels, and the layer beneath this was sufficiently soft for the instrument to be used as a shovel. Below that it hardened, and could be cut out in great blocks. The loose snow was thrown inside of the line traced out.

As fast as the blocks were cut out they were carried and piled regularly to form the face. Tom's share of the work was to keep on melting snow, and to bring it up and pour between and over the blocks. As fast as a line of these were made the loose snow was thrown in behind it and trampled down hard. Except for meals there was no rest. The chief said that as there was little chance of the 'Rappahoes coming up so soon, Hunting Dog had better stay behind and help, and he lent his aid in carrying the blocks of snow on a rough stretcher they made for the purpose. By the time it became dark the wall had risen to a height of three feet above the general level of the snow, and was already sufficient to form an excellent breastwork.

At the end farthest from the side from which the Indians were likely to come, a gap was left between it and the edge of the ravine three feet wide, in order that if necessary the horses could pass out. When it became dark the chief returned. He had gone many miles along towards the main valley, but had seen no sign of any Indians. After supper was over he took one of the wapiti skins and his buffalo robe, went up to the "fort," as they had already called it, and laid the deer-skin down on the slope of snow behind the wall, wrapped the buffalo robe round him, and lay down upon it. Hunting Dog then threw another robe over him, projecting a foot beyond his head, so that he could from time to time raise it and look out over the snow. The night was a dark one, but any object moving across the unbroken white surface could be seen at a considerable distance.

"I feel sure I should go to sleep," Tom said, "if I were to lie down like that."

"I have no doubt you would, Tom, but there is no fear with the chief. An Indian never sleeps on the watch, or if he does sleep, it is like a dog: he seems to hear as well as if he were awake, and every minute or two his eyes open and he takes a look round. I would rather have an Indian sentry than half a dozen white ones, unless it is in the open, where there is no tree to lean against, and a man must keep moving."

Hunting Dog threw himself down as soon as he returned to the hut, and was almost instantly asleep. Three hours later he rose and went out, and Leaping Horse a minute or two later returned.

"All quiet," he said; and then after smoking for a short time also lay down.

Chapter XII.
The Snow Fort

The hut was quiet at an unusually early hour, for the men had done a very hard day's work, and felt the strain after the long weeks of inactivity. At daybreak they were up and about, but could remain out but a few minutes, for the cold was so intense that they felt unable to face it until they had taken some hot tea and eaten something. Half an hour sufficed for this early breakfast. Hunting Dog was again left behind by the chief when he started.

"Two eyes enough," the latter said. "Hunting Dog more use here."

The wall of blocks was raised three more feet during the day, as it was agreed to devote all their efforts to this, and to defer the work of thickening it until the next day, for the snow had now been cleared so far from its foot that it could no longer be thrown inside. Though but six feet above the snow level, it was at least three feet more above the level of the rock, and its face was a solid sheet of ice, Tom having, during the two days, made innumerable journeys backwards and forwards with snow-water.

"Another couple of feet and it will be high enough for anything," Harry said. "I don't believe that the Indians will venture to attack us, but it is just as well to have it so high that they can't help each other up to the top. If they knew how strong it is, I am sure they would not attack, and would leave us alone altogether, but if a hundred of them creep up in the dark and make a rush, they will do their best to try to climb it. Anyhow we sha'n't need to make the bank behind very high.

195

If it goes to within four feet and a half of the top, so that we can stand and fire over the wall, that is all that is wanted."

Leaping Horse returned at dusk as before. He uttered a warm approval of the work when he had examined it.

"Good fort," he said, "better than palisades. Indian no climb over it. No opening to fire through, good as wall of town house."

"I think they will be puzzled when they get here, chief."

"Must watch well to-night," the chief said. "Indian scout sure to come. Two men keep on watch; two better than one."

"That is so, chief; we will change every hour. But it will be mighty cold. I don't see why we shouldn't rig up a shelter against the wall, and have a bit of a fire there. Then the two on watch can take it by turns every few minutes to come in and get a warm."

With poles and skins a lean-to was speedily constructed against the wall. The snow was hammered down, and a hearth made of half a dozen logs packed closely together. Some brands were brought up from the fire in the hut, and the skins across the end of the lean-to dropped, so that the air within could get warm while they were at supper.

"Hunting Dog and Tom shall take the first watch," Harry said; "Sam and I will take the next, Jerry and Ben the third, then you, chief, can take the next."

"Leaping Horse watch by himself," the Seneca said; "his eyes will be open."

"Very well, chief. I know you are as good as any two of us, so that will give us each one hour out and three hours in bed." Wrapping buffalo robes round them, Tom and the young Indian went up to the fort. Tom drew aside one of the skins and looked into the shelter. The hearth was in a glow, and two logs lying on it were burning well. The night was very still, except for the occasional rumble of some distant snow-slide. For a few minutes they stood looking over the wall, but keeping far back, so that only their heads were above its level.

"Tom go in by the fire," the Indian said. "All white, no need for four eyes."

"Very well, I will go in first; but mind, you have got to go in afterwards. I sha'n't go in if you don't."

After waiting for a few minutes in the shelter Tom went out again, and Hunting Dog took his place. It was his first war-path, and nothing would have persuaded him to retire from the watch had he not felt sure that even white men's eyes could not fail to detect any dark object moving on the surface of the snow. But although all white the surface was not level; here and there were sudden elevations marking rises in the rock beneath. Still it seemed impossible to Tom that anyone could approach unseen.

In spite of the protection of the buffalo robe it was intensely cold outside, and he was glad each time when his turn came for a warm by the fire. The changes, too, made the time pass quickly, and he was quite surprised when his uncle and Sam came out to relieve them. The other two men and the chief were still smoking by the fire. There was tea in the kettle, and they evidently did not mean to lie down until after their first watch. Every few minutes the chief got up and went out to the platform, and stood listening there intently for a short time. Just before it was time to change the guard again he said when he returned:

"Indian down in valley."

"Have you heard them, chief?"

"Leaping Horse heard a dead stick crack."

"That might have been a deer," Ben suggested.

The chief shook his head. "'Rappahoe; heard gun strike tree."

"Then I reckon they will be up in our watch," Ben said. "Well, we shall be ready for them."

"Perhaps come, perhaps not come; perhaps scout up valley first see if some of us there, and look for horses. Perhaps some come up path; but crawl up slow, not know whether look-out there."

"Well, I don't envy them if they have got much crawling to do to-night; it is cold enough to freeze one's breath."

"'Rappahoe not like cold," the chief said, "but wants scalp bad; that makes his blood warm."

"I will let some of it out," Jerry said wrathfully, "if I get a chance to lay a bead on one of them. Don't you be afeard, chief; we will look out sharp enough, you bet. Waal, I reckon it is about our time to turn out, Ben."

"Jerry tells me that you have heard noises below, chief," Harry said when he came in. "We heard nothing, but it ain't easy to hear well with these hoods over one's head."

"Hoods bad for hear," the chief assented. "Leaping Horse heard plain, Indians down below."

"Well, it is only what we expected, chief. Anyhow, we are ready for them when they come."

Tom lay down now, and knew nothing more till Hunting Dog touched him.

"Time to go and watch," he said.

"Has everything been quiet?"

The Indian nodded. "No come yet."

Leaping Horse remained at his post after they came out to relieve him. Tom made no comment. Harry had impressed upon him the necessity for absolute silence.

"If they hear voices they will never come near us," he had said, "and we would rather they came than stopped away. The sooner we get this job over the better."

The chief stood with his head slightly bent forward and the hood of his hunting-shirt thrown back, listening attentively. Then he touched Hunting Dog, and stooping low down whispered something in his ear, and then both stood again listening. Tom, too, threw back his hood, but he could hear nothing whatever, and was soon glad to pull it forward over his ears again. He strained his eyes in the direction towards which they were listening, which was apparently towards the edge of the ravine where the Indian trail came up from below. All seemed to him to be white and bare.

Presently the chief's rifle went up to his shoulder; there was a sharp crack, a dark figure leapt up from the snow fifty yards away and then fell headlong down again. It seemed to Tom almost magical. His eyes had been fixed in that direction for the last five minutes, and he could have sworn that the surface of the snow was unbroken. A minute later the other four men came running up.

"What is it, chief?" Harry whispered.

Leaping Horse pointed to the dark figure stretched out on the snow.

"So you have got the varmint. Good! Do you think there are any more of them about?"

"More there sure," the chief said, pointing to the path up from below. "Perhaps more there," and he pointed to a broad black line from the foot of the cliffs to the edge of the ravine, where, three days before, an avalanche from the hills above had swept the rock clear of snow.

"They must have made sure that we were all asleep, or that fellow would never have shown himself on the snow," Harry said.

"He did not show himself, uncle. How he got there I don't know; but I was looking at the spot when the chief fired, and I saw no signs of him whatever. How he hid himself I don't know. If it had been anywhere else I should have said he must have had a white sheet over him."

"It certainly was not that whatever it was, Tom. However, we shall see in the morning. Well, we may as well turn in again. Will they try again, do you think, chief?"

"Not try to-night, too cold; if any there, will hide up till daybreak. Now they know we are awake, will not venture on snow."

Half an hour later a great fire was lighted out of gunshot range lower down the valley, and three or four figures could be seen round it.

"Too cold," Hunting Dog said to Tom. "All gone down to get warm."

The watches were relieved regularly through the night, but there was no further alarm until just after daylight had broken, when Sam Hicks suddenly discharged his rifle. The others all turned out at once. He had fired at a bush just at the point where the trail came up from below, and he declared that he had seen a slight movement there, and that some pieces of the snow had dropped from the leaves.

"We will make sure that there is no one there," Harry said, "and then we will turn out and have a look. It is like enough that one of the red-skins from below came up the path to have a look at us this morning."

He took a steady aim and fired.

"Fetch up an axe, Tom; we will cut that bush away at once. It is lucky that Sam caught sight of the red-skin. If he had not done so he might have got a bullet in his own head, for when the red-skin had finished taking a view of the fort he would certainly have picked off Sam or myself before he went down. It is a weak point, that from here one can't command the path. If they come in force we shall have to keep watch on the platform too. From there you can get a sight of two or three of its turnings." They went out together, and as they passed, stopped to look at the body of the Indian the chief had shot. He was a young brave of two- or three-and-twenty, and the manner of his advance so far unperceived was now evident. Favoured by a slight fall in the ground, he had crawled forward, scooping a trench wide enough for his body a foot in depth, pushing the snow always forward, so that it formed a sort of bank in front of him and screened him from the sight of those on watch. The chief's keen eye had perceived a slight movement of the snow, and after watching a moment had fired at the point where he judged anyone concealed by it must be. He had calculated accurately. The ball had struck on the shoulder close to the neck, and had passed down through the body. The Indian had brought no rifle with him, but had knife and tomahawk in his belt.

"Poor young fellow," Harry said. "He wanted to win a name for himself by a deed of desperate bravery. It has cost him his life, but as he would have taken ours if he had had a chance it is of no use regretting it."

They now went on to the bush.

"You were right, Sam," he went on, as they saw the impression on the snow made by a figure lying down behind it. "There was an Indian here sure enough, and here is the mark of the stock of his rifle, and no doubt he would have picked off one of us if you had not scared him. I don't expect you hit him; there are no signs of blood."

"Fire too high," the chief said, pointing to a twig that had been freshly cut off two feet from the ground. "Always shoot low at man behind bush. Man cannot float in air."

There was a general laugh at Sam, who replied: "I did not suppose he could, chief. I just fired where I saw the snow fall, without thinking about it one way or the other. I was an all-fired fool, but I shall know better next time."

The bush was cut down, and also two or three others that grew along by the edge of the ravine. On their way back to the hut Harry stopped by the dead Indian.

"Fetch me a shovel, Tom," he said. "I will dig a hole in the snow; it ain't a pleasant object to be looking at anyway."

Tom fetched the shovel. Harry dug down in the snow till he reached the rock, then he and Jerry laid the body in it and filled in the snow again. The chief looked on.

"Bears get him," he said when they had finished.

"That is like enough, chief, but we have done the best we can for him. There is no digging into the rock."

"I thought the Indians always scalped enemies they shot?" Tom afterwards said to his uncle.

"So they do, Tom; but you see the chief is a sort of civilized Indian. He has consorted for years with whites, and he knows that we don't like it. I don't say he wouldn't do it if he were on the war-path by himself, but with us he doesn't, at any rate not openly. I have no doubt it went against his grain to see the red-skin buried with his hair on, for the scalp would have been a creditable one, as it would not have been got without a clear eye and good judgment in shooting. I have no doubt he has got some scalps about him now, though he don't show them; but they will be hung up some day if he ever settles down in a wigwam of his own.

"Well, chief, and what do you think," he asked Leaping Horse, as, after returning to the hut, they sat down to breakfast, "will they come or won't they?"

"I think they no come," the chief said. "Scout behind bush will tell them fort too strong to take; must cross snow, and many fall before they get to it. Very hard to climb. No like cold, Leaping Horse thinks they will stop in wigwams."

"No fools either," Jerry agreed; "a man would be worse than a natural if he were to go fooling about in this weather, and run a pretty good big risk of getting shot and nothing much to gain by it. They know we have left their country now, and ain't likely to come back again either to hunt there or to dig gold, and that all we want is to get away as soon as we can. I allow that the chief is right, and that we sha'n't hear no more of them, anyhow not for some time."

The chief nodded. "If come again, not come now. Wait a moon, then think perhaps we sleep sound and try again; but more likely not try."

"Much more likely," Harry assented. "Unless they can do it by a surprise, Indians are not fond of attacking; they know we shoot straighter than they do and have better rifles. You remember that time when you and I and Jersey Dick kept off a party of Navahoes from sunrise till sunset down near the Emigrant trail? It was lucky for us that a post-rider who was passing along heard the firing, and took the news to a fort, and that the officer there brought out fifty troopers just as the sun went down, or we should have been rubbed out that night sure."

The Seneca nodded.

"How was it, Harry?" Sam Hicks asked.

"It was just the usual thing, Sam. We had left the trail two days before, and were hunting on our own account when the Navahoes came down. We had just time to throw the three horses and lie down behind them. They were within two hundred yards when I began and fetched the chief, who was leading them, out of his saddle. Leaping Horse brought down another one and Jersey Dick held his fire, and instead of keeping straight on they began to straggle round. And they kept at that all day. Sometimes they would get in pretty close, but each time they did the chief brought down a horse, and when his rider, who was of course hanging on the other side of him, got up to run, I fetched him down. Dick wasn't much of a shot, so we would not let him fire. It discourages red-skins mightily when they see that there is never a shot thrown away, and that it is sure death whenever one draws a trigger. So at last they got careful and held off, knowing as they would get us at night, when they could have crawled up on foot and made a rush when they got close to us.

"The worst of it was we hadn't struck water the evening before, and it was just one of the hottest days on the plains, and we were pretty nigh mad with thirst before evening. I believe when the soldiers rode up I was about as glad to get a drink from one of their bottles as I was that the Navahoes bolted when they saw them coming. No, the redskins ain't any good for an open attack; they would have lost fewer men by riding straight at us than they did by fooling round, but they could not bring themselves to do it, and I reckon that is what it will be here. They may, as the chief says, try, say six weeks on, when the frost begins to break, in hopes that we may have given up keeping watch; but if they find us awake they will never try an open attack, for they could not reckon on taking the place without losing a score of men in doing so. If the snow was off the ground it would be different. Then of a dark night they could crawl up close and make a rush."

After breakfast the chief and Hunting Dog went out scouting. When they returned they brought news that three Indians had come over the snow along the side of the hills, that three others had come up the valley, and that in a wood half a mile below where they had seen the fire, there had been a large party encamped.

"I reckoned that would be about it, chief. Three fellows came along over the hill, in case we should be keeping guard at the top of the path, and they had a big force somewhere down below, so that if the scouts reported that there was nothing to prevent them falling on us they would come up before morning and wipe us out. I suppose they have all ridden off?"

"All gone. Leaping Horse and Hunting Dog followed right down valley. No stop anywhere, gone back to lodges."

"Then in that case, Harry, we had best get the critters down to their shed again. They have eaten all that stuff they brought up three days ago, I gave them the last of it this morning. The Indians know that we keep a pretty sharp look-out during the day and there ain't no fear of their coming up here when it is light."

As the chief was also of opinion that there was no danger, the horses were taken down the path into the valley, where on having their bridles unbuckled they at once trotted off of their own accord towards the beaver meadow.

For the next six weeks a watch was kept regularly, but by only one man at a time. The horses were driven down to the valley every morning and brought up again before sunset. There was little hunting now, for they had as many skins as they could carry comfortably, and a supply of frozen meat sufficient to last well into the spring. In March the weather became perceptibly warmer, and the snow in the valley began to melt where the full power of the sun at mid-day fell upon it. Day by day the crashes of distant avalanches became more frequent, and they began to look forward to the time when they should be able to proceed on their journey.

One night towards the end of the month Tom was on watch, when he heard a rustling sound far up beyond the wall of cliff in front of him. It grew louder and rose to a roar, and then a white mass came pouring down over the cliff. Leaping from the wall he dashed down the path to the hut. It needed no word to call the men to their feet, for a deep rumbling filled the air and the rock seemed to quiver. The horses struggled to break their head-ropes and snorted with fright.

"Your backs to the wall!" Harry shouted, and as all leapt across at his order there was a crash overhead. The roof above them fell in and a mass of snow followed; a minute later a deep silence followed the deafening roar.

"Anyone hurt?" Harry shouted, and the replies came in muffled tones. Tom was jambed against the rock by the snow; he was nearest to the entrance, his uncle was next to him.

"I am all right at present, uncle, but I feel half smothered."

"All right, lad; I am pretty free, and I will soon clear you a bit."

The snow was pushed away from before Tom's face, his left arm was cleared, and then his uncle with a vigorous pull brought him back close to him. Here he was comparatively free, for a part of the roof had fallen close to the wall and had partially kept off the snow. Then Harry turned, and with some difficulty managed to get Jerry, who was next to him, freed from the snow.

"Now, Jerry, you work along that way and get at the others. Tom and I will try to burrow a way out."

It was a difficult task. Once through the passage in the log wall they pushed to the left towards the edge of the platform, taking it by turns to go first until the snow became lighter; then by a vigorous effort Harry rose to his feet, sending a mass of snow tumbling over the edge of the platform. As soon as Tom had joined him they set to work with hands and knives, and soon cleared a passage back to the entrance. Just as they did so Jerry crawled out from within.

"Are they all right, Jerry?"

"Yes, the others are coming; only about twelve feet of the roof caved in, and the two Indians and Sam soon got in among the horses. I had a lot of trouble with Ben; he had been knocked down, and I thought that he was gone when I got him out; but he is all right now, though he can't walk yet. The Indians and Sam have got the shovels, and are workng away to clear a passage along by the wall; there is no getting Ben out through that rabbit-hole you have made."

"Thank God we are all right," Harry said; "it does not matter a bit, now that we know no one is badly hurt. We will begin at this end, but we sha'n't be able to do much until we get the shovels, the snow will fall in as fast as we get it out."

They soon found that they could do nothing in this way.

"We will try to tunnel again," Harry said, "it is not more than ten feet along. If we get in and hump ourselves, we shall soon get it big enough to drag Ben out, then the others can follow, and we can set to work with the spades to clear the place."

After a good deal of effort they succeeded in enlarging the hole, and then got Ben through it, one crawling backwards and pulling him while the other shoved at his legs.

"How do you feel, Ben?" Harry asked him when they laid him down outside.

"I dunno, Harry; I am afraid my back is badly hurt. I don't seem to feel my legs at all. I expect they are numbed from the weight of snow on them."

"I will crawl into our store and fetch out the keg."

"I reckon a drop of whisky will do me good if anything will," Ben said. "I was crushed pretty near flat, and if my head hadn't been against the wall I should have been smothered. Are you all right, young Tom?"

"Yes, I am not hurt at all. The snow squeezed me against the rock, and I could not move an inch, but uncle managed to get me a little free and then pulled me out of it."

Harry soon came back with the whisky, and was followed by the Indians and Sam, who found that they could do nothing with the snow, which fell in as fast as they cleared it. Their first step was to dig out a buffalo robe to wrap Ben in. His voice was stronger after he had drank some spirit, and he said that he felt better already. The others at once set to work with the shovels. They first cleared the platform along by the wall to the entrance, and then attacked the snow which filled the space between the two rock walls to the top.

Two of them worked with poles, loosening the snow above, and bringing it down in masses, while those with shovels cast it out on to the platform, going out occasionally to throw it over into the ravine. Hunting Dog made his way up over the snow to the top of the path, and called down to say that the fort was entirely swept away, and the chief told him to take up his post at once at the top of the path leading from below.

"He need not have told us that the fort was gone," Jerry grumbled. "If it had been made of cast-iron it would not have stood. The sooner we get our rifles out the better."

This could not be done for a time, for the loosening of the snow above had caused that below to slip, and the passage along by the wall had fallen in. The Indians, however, who had slept beyond the part filled by snow, had brought their pieces out with them, and could have defended the path alone. Several times those at work were buried by falls of snow, and had to be dragged out by the others. By daylight a considerable gap had been made in the snow, and they were able to get into the space beyond the fall. A number of logs, and a joint of meat that had been taken in the day before to thaw, were brought out, and a fire was soon blazing on the platform.

"I wonder why the snow did not shoot over as it did before?" Ben, who was now able to sit up, remarked.

"I reckon it is the fort did it," Harry said. "Of course it went, but it may have checked the rush of the snow for a moment, and those thick walls couldn't have got the same way on as the rest of the snow had."

"But the fort wasn't over the roof, uncle," Tom remarked.

"No, but it may have blocked the slide a little, and thrown some of it sideways; you see it is only this end that gave, while it shot right over the rest of the roof just as before."

"It is mighty lucky it did not break in all along," Sam Hicks said, "for it would have left us without horses if it had; and it would have been mighty rough on us to have lost them, just as we are going to want them, after our taking such pains with them all through the winter."

The chief took Hunting Dog's place as soon as he had finished his meal, and remained on watch all day. The men worked without ceasing, but it was not until sunset that the snow was completely cleared away.

"I reckon that we shall have to be starting before long," Jerry said as they sat round the fire in what they before called their store-room, having driven the horses as far in as possible to make room. "We could have held out before as long as we liked, but it is different now. The rock's cleared now for a hundred yards on each side of us, our fort's gone, and there is nothing to prevent the red-skins from crawling close up the first dark night and making a rush. They are like enough to be sending scouts up the valley occasionally, and it won't be long before they hear that our fort has gone and the ground cleared of snow."

Leaping Horse nodded. "Two men must watch at top of path," he said.

"That is right enough, chief; but we know three of them came along the hills before, and it is like enough they will all come that way next time. They are safe to reckon that we shall hold the path."

"It is very unfortunate," Harry said; "in another month, we should have been able to travel. Anyhow, it seems to me that we have got to try now; it would never do to be caught in here by the red-skins. If we are to go, the sooner the better. All our meat has been carried over the edge. This is about the time we expected the Indians back, and it would be dangerous to scatter hunting. It is a big risk, too, taking the horses down to the meadow. No, I think we can manage to get over the pass. The snow gets softer every day when the sun is on it; but it freezes at night. We have the moon, too, so we shall be able to travel then; and even if we take three or four days getting over the divide we can sleep in the daytime."

"We must get a little more meat anyhow before we start," Jerry said. "This joint ain't more than enough for another square meal for us, and though I reckon the big-horns will be coming up to the hills again now, it won't do to risk that."

"We have the pack-horses, Jerry."

"Yes, I did not think of them. Horseflesh ain't so bad on a pinch; but I don't want to lose our skins."

"Better our skins than our hair," Sam laughed.

"That is right enough, Sam, but I would like to save both."

"Perhaps there is some of the meat under the snow," Tom suggested. "It hung near the wall, and the snow must have come straight down on it from above, as it did in here."

"That is so, Tom; we will have a look the first thing in the morning. I am so tired now I would not dig for it if it were gold."

As soon as it was light the next morning they began to clear the snow from the rest of the platform, and found to their great satisfaction four bear hams. The rest of the meat had been swept over the edge. The two Indians had not shared in the work, having started away early without saying where they were going. They returned to breakfast, each carrying a hind-quarter of venison, which they had found in the snow below.

It was agreed that a start should be made that evening. By sunset the horses were loaded, and half an hour later they moved away. Ben Gulston had to be assisted on to his horse, for although in other respects recovered, it was found that he had so severely strained his back across the loins that he was scarcely able to walk a foot. The moon was shining brightly, and as soon as they were on the snow they could see as plainly as if it were day. All were in high spirits that they had left the spot where for six months they had been prisoners. They had difficulty in restraining themselves from shouting and singing, but the chief before starting had warned them of the necessity for travelling silently.

"Snow-slides very bad now; shouting might set them going."

The others looked rather incredulous, but Harry said:

"I know he is right, boys; for I have heard that in the Alps the guides always forbid talking when they are crossing places exposed to avalanches. At any rate we may as well give the snow as little chance as may be of going for us."

They travelled in Indian file from habit rather than necessity, for the snow was firm and hard, and the horses made their way over it without difficulty. There had been some debate as to the way they should go; but they determined at last to take the valley through the cliff wall, and to strike to the right whenever they came upon a likely spot for crossing. Two such attempts were made in vain, the upper slopes of snow being found too steep for the horses to climb; but at the third, which was made just after morning broke, they succeeded in getting up the hill to their right, and, after great difficulty, descended into another valley. This they had little doubt was the one that led to the pass, for from the hill they could see the great peak along whose foot the trail ran.

It was ten o'clock before they got down into the valley. The snow was beginning to be soft on the surface, and the horses were tired out. They therefore halted, made a fire with two or three of the logs they had brought with them for the purpose, boiled water and had breakfast, and gave half a bucket of gruel to each of the animals. Then wrapping themselves in their buffalo robes they lay down and slept till late in the afternoon. The journey was resumed at sunset, and before morning they had crossed the divide; and when the sun rose obtained a view over the country far to the south.

Chapter XIII.
A Fresh Start

In the evening they camped on the banks of the Green River, here a stream of but small size, except when the melting snow swelled its waters into a torrent. At the spot where they halted a rivulet ran into the stream from a thickly-wooded little valley. It was frozen, but breaking the ice with their axes they found that water was flowing underneath. They had observed that there was a marked difference in temperature on this side of the mountains, upon which the strength of the southern sun had already in many places cleared away the snow.

"It is a comfort to be able to sit by a fire without the thought that redskins may be crawling up towards you," Sam Hicks said heartily, "and to sleep without being turned out to stand watch in the cold."

"You say the country ahead is bad, chief?"

"Bad lands both sides of Green River. Deep canons and bare rock."

"Well, we need not follow it; it don't make any difference to us whether we get down to the fort in a fortnight or six weeks."

"None at all," Harry said. "We have agreed that when summer fairly sets in we will try that place I hit on just as the Utes came down on us. It is the richest place I have ever seen, and if the Indians will but let us alone for a month we ought to bring back a big lot of dust; and if we do, we can sell our share in it for a big sum, and take down enough men to thrash the Utes out of their boots if they interfere with us. By our reckoning it is the end of March now, though we don't at all agree as to the day; but at any rate, it is there or thereabouts. That gives us a good six weeks, and if we start in the middle of May it will be time enough. So I propose that we strike more to the west, or to the east, whichever you think is the best, chief, and try and pick up a few more pelts so as to lay in a fresh stock of goods for our next trip."

"Bad hills everywhere," the chief said; "better go west, plenty of game there."

"No fear of Indians?"

"Indians there peaceable; make good trade with whites. Ten years ago fight, but lose many men and not get much plunder. Trappers here good friends with them. Traders bring up powder and cloth and beads. Indians no give trouble."

For the next six weeks, therefore, they travelled slowly, camping sometimes for two or three days on a stream, and then making a long march until they again came to water. The beaver traps had been left behind, but they were fortunate enough to come upon several beaver villages, and by exercising patience they were able to shoot a good many, getting in all some fifty skins. Tom used to go out in the evening and lie down to watch the beavers at work, but he would not take a gun.

"I could not shoot them down in cold blood, uncle. It is almost like looking at a village of human beings at work. One can shoot a man who is wanting to shoot you, without feeling much about it, but to fire at a man labouring in the fields is murder. Of course, if we wanted the flesh for food it would be different."

"I did not see you refuse that beaver-tail soup we had last night, Tom."

"No, and it was very good, uncle; but I would very much rather have gone without it than shoot the beaver the tail belonged to."

"Well, Tom, as we have all got guns, and as none of us have any scruples that way, there is no occasion whatever for you to draw a trigger on them. They take some shooting, for if you hit them in the water they sink directly, and you have got to kill them dead when they are on land, otherwise they make for the water at once and dive into their houses and die there."

They killed a good many other animals besides the beaver, including several wolverines, and by the time they got down to the fort in the middle of May they had had to give up riding and pack all the animals with the skins they had obtained. None of these were of any great value, but the whole brought enough to buy them a fresh outfit of clothes, a fresh stock of provisions and powder, and to give them a hundred dollars each.

The evening after the sale was effected Tom wrote home to his sisters, giving them a brief account of what had taken place since the letter he had posted to them before starting for the mountains, but saying very little of their adventures with Indians. "I am afraid you have been in a great fright about me," he said, "but you must never fidget when you don't get letters. We may often be for a long time away from any place where we can post them, or, as they call it here, mail them, though I certainly do not expect to be snowed up again for a whole winter. Owing to the Indians being hostile we did not do nearly so well as we expected, for we could not go down to hunt in the valleys. So after getting a fresh outfit for our next journey our share is only a hundred dollars each. I did not want to take a share, for of course I was not of much use to them, though I have learnt a lot in the last six months, and can shoot now as well as any of them, except the two Indians. "However, they all insisted on my having the same share as the rest. Uncle wanted me to take his hundred dollars and send them home to you with mine, but I told him that I would not do so, for I know you have money enough to go on with, even if your school has turned out a failure. So I think it would be as well for us to keep our money in hand for the present. There is never any saying what may happen; we may lose our horses and kit, and it would be very awkward if we hadn't the money to replace them. As soon as we get more we will send it off, as you know I always intended to do. I have still some left of what I brought out with me, but that and the two hundred dollars would not be more than enough to buy an entirely new outfit for us both.

"I hope you got the five hundred dollars uncle sent you. He told me he sent it off from Denver, and it ought to have got home a few weeks after I left. It is horrid to think that there may be letters from you lying at Denver, but it serves me right for being so stupid as not to put in the short note I wrote you from here before I started, that you had better direct to me at Fort Bridger, as I shall almost be sure to come back to it before I go to Denver. I like uncle awfully; it seems to me that he is just what I expected he would be. I suppose they all put in equal shares, but the other men quite look upon him as their leader. Sometimes when he is talking to me he speaks just as people do at home. When he talks to the men he uses the same queer words they do. He is taller than father was, and more strongly built. What I like in him is, he is always the same. Sometimes the others used to get grumbly when we were shut up so long, but it never seemed to make any difference in him.

"I told you when I wrote from Denver that he was called 'Straight Harry,' because he always acted straightforwardly, and now I know him I can quite understand their calling him so. One feels somehow that one could rely upon his always being the same, whatever happened. Leaping Horse is a first-rate fellow, and so is Hunting Dog, though of course he does not know nearly as much as the chief does, but he knows a lot. The other three are all nice fellows, too, so we were a very jolly party. They know a tremendous lot of stories about hunting and red-skins and that sort of thing. Some of them would make all you girls' hairs stand on end. We are going to start off in two or three days to hunt up a gold mine uncle found three years ago. The Indians are going, too; they will hunt while the rest of us work. It will be quite a different journey to the last, and I expect it will be just as hot this time as it was cold last. We may be away for four months, and perhaps we may not come back till the snow sets in, so don't expect a letter till you see it."

This was by far the longest letter Tom had ever written, and it took him several hours to get through. He had the room to himself, for the others were talking over their adventures with old friends they had met at the fort. His uncle returned about ten o'clock.

"Where are the others?" Tom asked.

"In the saloon; but they are not drinking, that is, not drinking much. I told them that if they were to get drunk one of them would be sure to blab as to where we were going, or at any rate to say enough to excite suspicion among some of the old miners, that we knew of a good thing, and in that case we should get a lot of men following us, and it would interfere with our plans altogether. A party as small as ours may live for months without a red-skin happening to light on us, but if there were many more they would be certain to find us. There would be too much noise going on, too much shooting and driving backward and forward with food and necessaries. We want it kept dark till we thoroughly prove the place. So I made them all take an oath this morning that they would keep their heads cool, and I told them that if one of them got drunk, or said a word about our going after gold, I would not take him with us. I have given out that we are going on another hunting party, and of course our having brought in such a lot of skins will make them think that we have hit on a place where game is abundant and are going back there for the summer."

Two more pack-ponies had been added to the outfit. They might be away for five or six months, and were determined to take a good supply of flour this time, for all were tired of the diet of meat only, on which they had existed for the last six months, having devoted by far the greater part of the flour to the horses.

When they started next day they turned their faces north, as if they intended to hunt in the mountains where they had wintered. They made but a short march, camped on a stream, and long before daybreak started again, travelling for some hours to the west and then striking directly south. For two days they travelled rapidly, Tom going out every morning with the Indians hunting, while the others kept with the pack-horses. Ben had now quite recovered from the strain which had crippled him for the first three weeks of their march down to Fort Bridger. They were now fairly among the Ute hills, and at their third camping-place Harry said:

"We must do no more shooting now till we get to our valley. We have got a supply of deer-flesh for a week at least, and we must be careful in future. We heard at the fort that several miners have been cut off and killed by the Utes during the winter, and that they are more set than ever against white men entering their country. Everyone says those rascally Saints are at the bottom of it. We must hide our trail as much as we can. We are just at the edge of the bad lands, and will travel on them for the next two days. The red-skins don't go out that way much, there being nothing either to hunt or to plunder, so there is little fear of their coming on our trail on the bare rocks, especially as none of the horses are shod. On the third day we shall strike right up into their mountains."

"Are you sure that you will know the place again, Harry?"

"I reckon I could find it, but I should not feel quite certain about it if I had not the chief with me. There is no fear of his going wrong. When a red-skin has once been to a place he can find his way straight back to it again, even if he were a thousand miles off."

"You said when we were talking of it among the hills, uncle," Tom said, as he rode beside him the next morning, "that Leaping Horse and you each took two shares. I wonder what he will do with his if it turns out well."

"He won't do anything with it, Tom. The chief and I are like brothers. He does not want gold, he has no use for it; and, besides, as a rule, Indians never have anything to do with mining. He and Hunting Dog really come as hunters, and he has an understanding with me that when the expedition is over I shall pay them the same as they would earn from any English sportsman who might engage them as guides and hunters, and that I shall take their shares in whatever we may make. I need not say that if it turns out as well as we expect, the Indians will get as many blankets and as much ammunition as will last them their lives. You can't get a red-skin to dig. Even the chief, who has been with us for years, would consider it degrading to do work of that kind; and if you see an Indian at mining work, you may be sure that he is one of the fellows who has left his tribe and settled down to loaf and drink in the settlements, and is just doing a spell to get himself enough fire-water to make himself drunk on.

"The Seneca would be just as willing to come and hunt for us for nothing. He would get his food and the skins, which would pay for his tobacco and ammunition, and, occasionally, a new suit of leggings and hunting-shirt, made by an Indian woman, and with this he would be happy and contented. He doesn't mind taking money in return for skins, and he and Hunting Dog had their full share in the division at the fort. When I last talked to him about this business, he said, 'Leaping

Horse doesn't want money. Of what use is it to him? He has got a bagful hidden at home, which he has been paid when he was scouting with the army, and for the skins of beasts he has shot. It is enough to buy many horses and blankets, and all that a chief can want. He is going with his friend to hunt, and to fight by his side if the Utes come; he wants none of the gold.' I explained the matter to him, and he said carelessly: ' Leaping Horse will take the two shares, but it will be for his brother, and that he may send it to the girls, the sisters of his friend Tom, of whom he spoke one night by the fire.'

"Hunting Dog is like Leaping Horse, he will take no gold. I have told the three men how matters stand. Of course, it makes no difference to them whether the Indians keep their share or hand it over to me, but at the same time I thought they ought to know how we stood. They said it was no business of theirs; that as I was the discoverer I had a right to sell the whole thing if I chose, and that they thought I had done the friendly thing by them in letting them in as partners. So you see it is all right and square. It is like enough, too, that we shall find some other lodes, and of course there they will come in on even terms with us. So they are pleased with the look-out, and know well enough it is likely to be the best strike they ever made in their lives."

They kept near the edge of the bad lands, as had they gone farther out they would have been obliged to make long detours to get round the head of the canons made by rivers running down into the Colorado. They had filled their water-skins at the last stream where they had camped, and had taken with them enough dried wood for their fires. These they lit each night in a hollow, as from the upper slopes of the Ute hills a view could be obtained for a great distance over the flat rocky plateau. Tom was heartily glad when the two days' journey was over. Not a living creature had met their eyes; there was no grass on which beasts could exist, no earth in which prairie-dogs could burrow; even birds shunned the bare waste of rock.

"It is a desolate country," he said, as they sat round the fire; "it would be enough to give one the horrors if one were alone. It is hot now, and in the height of summer the heat and glare from the rock must be awful."

"It is, Tom; many and many a man has died of thirst in the bad lands. And what makes it more terrible is, that they can perhaps see water a thousand feet below them and yet die from the want of it."

"When we were camped on the Green River, uncle, you said that no one had ever followed it down."

"That is so, lad. One knows whereabouts it goes, as men driven by thirst have followed canons down to it; and in some places it runs for many miles across low land before it plunges into another canon. Then it cuts its way for two or three hundred miles, perhaps, through the hills, with walls two or three thousand feet high. No one, so far as I know, has gone down these big canons, but it is certain there are rapids and whirlpools and rocks in them. Two or three parties have gone down through some of the shorter canons to escape Indians, and most of them have never been heard of again, but one or two have got down some distance and managed to escape.

"No one has followed the course by land. They could not do so unless they carried all their provisions, and drink and food for their animals, and even then the expedition would take months, perhaps years to do; for every spring from the hills runs down a canon to the river, sometimes fifty miles, sometimes a hundred long, and each time the party came upon one of these they would have to work up to the mountains to get round it. It is over a thousand miles in a straight line from the place where the Green River first enters a canon to where the Colorado issues out on to the plains, and it may be quite twice that distance if one could follow all its windings. Some day when the country fills up attempts will no doubt be made to find out something about it; but it will be a big job whenever it is tried, and may cost a lot of lives before the canons are all explored."

In the morning they started westward for the hills. The greatest care was observed on the march. They took advantage of every depression, and when obliged to pass over level ground moved at a distance apart, as a clump or string of moving animals would be made out at a distance from which a solitary one would be unnoticed. By noon they had left the bare rock, and were travelling up a valley clothed with grass and dotted with clumps of trees. In the first of these they halted.

"We will stay here until it begins to get dusk," Harry said, "and then move on as fast as we can go. If we don't lose our way we shall be there before morning."

There was no moon, but the stars shone brilliantly, and the mountains, with their summits still covered with snow, could be seen ahead. The chief went on in front. Sometimes they proceeded up valleys, sometimes crossed shoulders and spurs running down from the hills. They moved in Indian file, and at times proceeded at a brisk pace, at other times more slowly; but there was no halt or sign of hesitation on the part of their leader. At last, just as morning was breaking, the chief led them into a clump of trees. He moved a little distance in, and then reined in his horse and dismounted.

"Does my brother remember that?" he said to Harry, pointing to something on the ground.

"Jee-hoshaphat!" Harry exclaimed; "if that ain't my old pack-saddle! This is the very spot where we camped, boys. Well, chief, you are certainly a wonder. I doubt whether I could have found my way here in the daytime. Half a dozen times to-night it seemed to me that you were going in the wrong direction altogether, and yet you bring us as straight to the spot as if all the time you had been following a main road."

"Bully for the chief!" Jerry said warmly. "I am blamed if that ain't a fust-rate piece of tracking. Waal, here we are at our journey's end. Can we make a fire?"

"Make small fire, but must put screen round."

"Very well; we will leave the fire to you, and we will unpack the critters. There is a bundle of dry wood left, so we sha'n't have the bother of looking for it now."

Before lighting the fire the two Indians stretched some blankets some six feet above it, to prevent the light falling upon the foliage; then by their directions Sam cut a dozen short poles, and fixed them in a circle round the fire. Half a dozen more blankets were fastened to the poles, forming a wall round the fire, which the chief then lighted. The nights were, at that height above the sea-level, cool enough to make the heat pleasant, and there was just room for the seven men to sit between the blanket wall and the fire.

"Do you mean this to be our permanent camp, Harry?"

"What do you think, Leaping Horse?"

"Wait till me go up gold valley," the Seneca said. "If can't find a good place there better stay here; if go backwards and forwards every day make trail Indian squaw would notice."

"That is so, chief; but by what Harry says it is a mere gully, and the horses will have to range."

"Horses must feed," the chief said. "If we find a place up there, make hut, take saddles and outfit there. Tie up horses here, and let them loose to feed at night. No regular track then. But talk after sleep."

"It will be broad daylight by the time that we have finished our meal," Jerry said, "and I reckon none of us will be wanting to sleep till we have got a sight of Harry's bonanza."

As soon as they had finished their meal, the mining implements, which had been carefully hidden among the rest of their goods when they started from the fort, were brought out. Among these were a dozen light pick-heads and half a dozen handles, as many shovels, a flat iron plate for crushing ore upon, and a short hammer, with a face six inches in diameter, as a pounder; also a supply of long nails, to be used in fastening together troughs, cradles, or any other woodwork that might be required; three or four deep tin dishes, a bottle of mercury, a saw, and a few other tools. Three of the pick-heads were now fastened to their handles, and taking these, a couple of shovels, two of the tin basins, a sledge hammer, and some steel wedges, and the peculiar wooden platter, in shape somewhat resembling a small shield with an indentation in the middle, called a vanner, and universally used by prospectors, the five whites and Leaping Horse started from their camp for the spot where Harry had found the lode. It lay about a mile up a narrow valley, running into the larger one. A rivulet trickled down its centre.

"I reckoned on that," Harry said. "Of course it was frozen when we were here, but I could see that there was water in summer. You see this hollow runs right up into that wood, and there is sure to be water in it for the next three months anyhow."

They had gone but a short distance up when they stopped at a spot where the streamlet widened out into a pool. "Let us try here," Jerry said, "and see if there is any sign."

Half a shovelful of sand was placed in the vanner with a small quantity of water, and while Harry and Sam proceeded to wash some gravel roughly in the pans, Tom stood watching Jerry's operations. He gave a gentle motion to the vanner that caused its contents to revolve, the coarser particles being thrown towards the edges while the finer remained in the centre. The water was poured away and the rougher particles of gravel and sand swept off by the hand; fresh water was then added, and the process repeated again and again, until at last no more than a spoonful of fine sand remained in the centre. A sideway action of the vanner caused this to slope gradually down towards the edge. At the very bottom three tiny bits of yellow metal were seen. They were no bigger than pins' heads. It seemed to Tom that this was a miserably small return for five minutes' labour, but the others seemed well satisfied, and were still more pleased when, on the two pans being cleaned out, several little pieces of gold were found, one of which was nearly as large as a small pea.

"That is good enough," Ben said; "it will run a lot richer when we get down on to the rock."

At two other places on their way up they tried the experiments, with increasingly good results.

"There is some tall work to be done here with washing," Harry said. "Now come on to the vein. I only saw one of them, but there must be a lot more or you would not find so much metal in the sand. However, the one I saw is good enough for anything." They went on again to a point where the rock cropped boldly out on both sides of the valley; Harry led them a few paces up the side, and pointed to some white patches in the rock. "That is where I chipped it off, lads, three years ago."

The face of the lode, discoloured by age and weather, differed but little from the rock surrounding it; but where it had been broken off it was a whitish yellow, thickly studded with little bits of dull yellow metal sticking out of it. Tom was not greatly impressed, but he saw from the faces of his companions that they were at once surprised and delighted.

"By gosh, Harry, you have done it this time!" Sam Hicks exclaimed. "You have struck it rich, and no mistake. I thought from the way you talked of it it must be something out of the way, but I am blamed if I thought it was like this."

"Stand back, you chaps," Jerry said, lifting the heavy sledge hammer; "let me get a drive at it. Here is a crack. Put one of them wedges in, Ben."

The wedge was placed in the fissure, and Ben held it while Jerry gave a few light blows to get it firmly fixed.

"That will do, Ben; take away your hand and let me drive at it." Swinging the hammer round his head Jerry brought it down with tremendous force on the head of the wedge. Again and again the heavy hammer rose and fell, with the accuracy of a machine, upon the right spot, until the wedge, which was nine inches long, was buried in the crevice.

"Now another one, Ben. Give me a longer one this time."

This time Ben held the wedge until it was half buried, having perfect confidence in Jerry's skill. It was not until the fourth wedge had been driven in that a fragment of rock weighing four or five hundredweight suddenly broke out from the face. All bent eagerly over it, and the miners gave a shout of joy. The inner surface, which was white, but slightly stained with yellow, with blurs of slate colour here and there, was thickly studded with gold. It stuck out above the surface in thin, leafy plates with ragged edges, with here and there larger spongy masses. "I reckon that is good enough," Jerry said, wiping the sweat from his forehead. "Ef there is but enough of it, it is the biggest thing that ever was struck. There ain't no saying how rich it is, but I will bet my boots it's over five hundred ounces to the ton. It ain't in nature that it is going to run far like that, but it is good enough for anything. Well, what is the next thing, Harry?"

"We will break it up," Harry said, "and carry it down with us to the camp. If the Utes came down on us to-morrow, and we could get off with it, that would be plenty to show if we want to make a sale."

It took them a long time to break up the rock, for the quartz was hard, and was so bound together by the leafy gold running through it that each of the four men had several spells with the hammer before it was broken up into fragments weighing some twenty pounds apiece. As soon as this was done the men collected earth, filled up the hole in the face of the rock, and planted several large tufts of grass in it, and poured four or five tins of water over them; then they smeared with mud the patches where Harry had before broken pieces off.

"What is all that for, Jerry?" Tom asked.

"It is to hide up the traces, lad. We may have to bolt away from here to-morrow morning for anything we know, and before we come back again someone else may come along, and though we shall locate our claims at the mining register, there would be a lot of trouble if anyone else had taken possession, and was working the vein when we got back."

"It is not likely that anyone else would come along here, Jerry."

"Waal, I reckon that is so, but one ain't going to trust to chance when one has struck on such a place as this."

The Seneca had been the only unmoved person in the party. "What do you think of that, chief?" Harry asked him.

"If my white brother is pleased Leaping Horse is glad," he replied. "But the Indian does not care for gold. What can he do with it? He has a good gun, he does not want twenty. He does not want many hunting suits. If he were to buy as many horses as would fill the valley he could not ride them all, and he would soon tire of sitting in his lodge and being waited upon by many wives. He has enough for his needs now. When he is old it will be time to rest."

"Well, that is philosophy, chief, and I don't say you are wrong from your way of looking at it. But that gold means a lot to us. It means going home to our people. It means living in comfort for the rest of our lives. It means making our friends happy."

"Leaping Horse is glad," the chief said gravely. "But he cannot forget that to him it means that the white brother, with whom he has so long hunted and camped and fought bad Indians, will go away across the great saltwater, and Leaping Horse will see him no more."

"That is so, chief," Harry said, grasping the Indian's hand warmly, "and I was a selfish brute not to think of it before. There is one thing I will promise you. Every year or so I will come out here and do a couple of months' hunting with you. The journey is long, but it is quickly made now, and I know that after knocking about for twenty years I shall never be content if I don't take a run out on the plains for a bit every summer. I will give you my word, Leaping Horse, that as long as I have health and strength I will come out regularly, and that you shall see your white brother's friendship is as strong as your own."

The Seneca's grave face lit up with pleasure. "My white brother is very good," he said. "He has taken away the thorn out of the heart of Leaping Horse. His Indian brother is all glad now." The quartz was placed in sacks they had brought with them to carry down samples, and they at once returned to the camp, where, after smoking a pipe, they lay down to sleep; but it was some time before all went off, so excited were they at the thought of the fortune that seemed before them.

In the afternoon they took one of the pieces of stone, weighing, by a spring balance, twenty pounds, and with the flat plate and the crushing-hammer went to the stream. The rock was first broken with the sledge into pieces the size of a walnut. These were pulverized on the iron plate and the result carefully washed, and when the work was finished the gold was weighed in the miner's scales, and turned the four-ounce weight.

"That is nearly five hundred ounces to the ton," Harry said, "but of course it is not going to run like that. I reckon it is a rich pocket; there may be a ton of the stuff, and there may be fifty. Now let's go up and have a quiet look for the lode, and see if we can trace it. We ought to see it on the rock the other side."

A careful search showed them the quartz vein on the face of the rock some fifty feet higher up the valley, and this showed them the direction of the run of the lode. It was here, however, only six inches wide instead of being two feet, as at the spot where it was first found. Some pieces were broken off: there was gold embedded in it, but it was evident that it was nothing like so rich as on the other side. A piece of ten pounds was pounded up, it returned only a little over a pennyweight of gold.

"About twelve ounces to the ton," Harry said. "Not bad, but a mighty falling off from the other. To-morrow morning we will follow the lode on the other side and see if we can strike an outcrop."

The next day they found the lode cropping up through the rock some thirty yards from their great find. It was about nine inches wide. They dug it out with their picks to a depth of two feet so as to get a fair sample. This when crushed gave a return at the rate of twenty ounces.

"That is rich enough again, and would pay splendidly if worked by machinery. Of course the question is, how far it holds on as rich as we found it at the face, and how it keeps on in depth? But that is just what we can't find. We want drills and powder, as picks are no sort of good on this hard quartz. Supposing it goes off gradually from the face to this point, there would be millions of dollars in it, even supposing it pinched in below, which there is no reason in the world to suppose. We may as well take a few of these chunks of rock, they will show that the gold holds fairly a good way back anyhow."

A few pieces were put aside and the rest thrown into the hole again, which was stamped down and filled up with dust. The party then went back to dinner, and a consultation was held as to what was next to be done.

"Of course we must stake out our claims at once," Harry said. "In the first place there are our own eight claims —two for each of the discoverers and one each for the others. Hunting Dog will not have a share, but will be paid the regular rate as a hunter. Then we will take twenty claims in the names of men we know. They wouldn't hold water if it were a well-known place, and everyone scrambling to get a claim on the lode; but as there is no one to cut in, and no one will know the place till we have sold it and a company sends up to take possession and work it, it ain't likely to be disputed. The question is, What shall we do now? Shall we make back to the settlements, or try washing a bit?"

"Try washing, I should say," Jerry said. "You may be some time before you can sell the place. Anyone buying will know that they will have to send up a force big enough to fight the Utes, and besides they will want someone to come up here to examine it before they close the bargain. I vote we stick here and work the gravel for a bit so as to take enough away to keep us till next spring. I reckon we shall find plenty of stuff in it as we go down, and if that is so we can't do better than stick to it as long as there is water in the creek."

"I agree with you there, Jerry; but it will never do to risk losing those first samples. I am ready to stay here through the summer, but I vote we sew them up in deer-hide, and put two or three thicknesses of skin on them so as to prevent accidents. Two of us had best go with them to the fort and ask the Major to let us stow them away in his magazine, then, if we have to bolt, we sha'n't be weighted down with them. Besides, we might not have time for packing them on the horses, and altogether it would be best to get them away at once, then come what might we should have proofs of the value of the mine."

This proposal was cordially agreed to, and it was settled that on the following morning Harry himself should, with Hunting Dog and two pack-horses, start for the fort, following the same route they came, while the rest should set to work to construct a cradle, and troughs for leading the water to it.

Chapter XIV.
An Indian Attack

A couple of trees were felled in the middle of the clump in which they were still encamped. They were first roughly squared and then sawn into planks, the three men taking it by turns to use the saw. The question of shifting the camp up to the spot where they intended to work was discussed the night before Harry started, but it was agreed at last that it would be better to remain where they were.

"If Utes come, sure to find traces," the chief said. "Many horses in valley make tracks as plain as noonday. Gold valley bad place for fight."

"That is so," Jerry agreed. "We should not have a show there. Even if we made a log-house,—and it would be a dog-goned trouble to carry up the logs,—we might be shut up in it, and the red-skins would only have to lie round and shoot us down if we came out. I reckon we had best stay here after all, Harry. We could keep them outside the range of our rifles anyhow by day."

"I don't see that that would be much good to us, Jerry; for if they came by day they would not find us here. Still I don't know that it ain't best for us to stay here; it would give us a lot of trouble to build a place. I reckon two of us had better stay here all the day with the horses. If the red-skins come, they can fire a couple of shots, and we shall hear them up at the washing-place. The red-skins would be safe to draw off for a bit to talk it over before they attacked, as they would not know how many there were among the trees. That would give the rest time to come down."

It took three days' hard work to saw the planks and make the cradle, and troughs sufficiently long to lead the water down into it from the stream higher up. These were roughly but strongly made, the joints being smeared with clay to prevent the water from running through. A dam was then made to keep back the water above the spot where they intended to begin, which was about fifty yards below the quartz vein, and from this dam the trough was taken along on strong trestles to the cradle.

The horses were brought into the camp at daybreak every morning and tied up to the trees, and were let out again at nightfall. Tom remained in camp, the chief being with him. The latter, however, was, during the time Harry was away, twice absent for a day on hunting excursions lower down the valley, which was there thickly wooded. The first time, he returned with the hams and a considerable portion of the rest of the flesh of a bear. The second time, he brought up the carcass of a deer.

"How far does the valley run?" Tom asked.

"Valley last ten miles. Sides get steep and high, then canon begin."

"That will run right down to the Colorado?"

The chief nodded. "Leaping Horse go no farther. Canon must go down to the river."

"How far is it before the sides of the valley get too steep to climb?"

"Two miles from here. Men could climb another mile or two, horses not."

"Is there much game down there, chief?"

The Seneca nodded. "That is a comfort; we sha'n't be likely to run out of fresh meat."

The chief was very careful in choosing the wood for the fire, so that in the daytime no smoke should be seen rising from the trees. When the dead wood in the clump of trees was exhausted he rode down the valley each day, and returned in an hour with a large faggot fastened behind him on the horse. He always started before daybreak, so as to reduce the risk of being seen from the hills. On the sixth day the men began their work at the gravel. The bottle of mercury was emptied into the cradle, the bottom of which had been made with the greatest care, so as to prevent any loss from leakage. Two of the men brought up the gravel in buckets and pans, until the cradle was half full. Then water was let in, and the third man rocked the machine and kept on removing the coarse stuff that worked up to the top, while the others continued bringing up fresh gravel.

"Well, what luck?" Tom asked, when they returned in the evening.

"We have not cleaned up yet; we shall let it run for three or four days before we do. We are only on the surface yet, and the stuff wouldn't pay for the trouble of washing out."

On the eighth day after their departure Harry and Hunting Dog returned.

"Well, boys, it is all stowed away safely," he said. "I know the Major well, and he let me have a big chest, which he locked up, after I had put the bags in, and had it stowed away in the magazine; so there is no fear of its being touched. Any signs of the red-skins?"

"Nary a sign. We have none of us been up the valley beyond this, so that unless they come right down here, they would find no trail. The horses are always driven down the valley at night."

"How is the work going on, Jerry?"

"We began washing two days ago; to-morrow night we shall clean up. We all think it is going to turn out pretty good, for we have seen gold in the sand several times as we have carried it up in the pails."

The next day Tom went up with the others, the Indians remaining in camp. Two men now worked at the cradle, while the other three brought up the sand and gravel. Towards evening they began the work of cleaning up. No more stuff was brought up to the machine, but the water was still run into it. As fast as the shaking brought the rough gravel to the top it was removed, until only a foot of sand remained at the bottom. The water was now stopped and the sand dug out, and carefully washed in the pans by hand. At the bottom of each pan there remained after all the sand had been removed a certain amount of gold-dust, the quantity increasing as the bottom was approached. The last two panfuls contained a considerable amount.

"It does not look much," Tom said when the whole was collected together.

"It is heavy stuff, lad," Harry replied. "What do you think there is, Jerry? About twelve ounces, I should fancy."

"All that, Harry; nigher fourteen, I should think."

The pan was now put at the bottom of the cradle, a plug pulled out, and the quicksilver run into it. A portion of this was poured on wash-leather, the ends of which were held up by the men so as to form a bag. Harry took the leather, and holding it over another pan twisted it round and round. As the pressure on the quicksilver increased it ran through the pores of the leather in tiny streams, until at last a lump of pasty metal remained. This was squeezed again and again, until not a single globule of quicksilver passed through the leather. The ball, which was of the consistency of half-dried mortar was then taken out, and the process repeated again and again until the whole of the quicksilver had been passed through the leather. Six lumps of amalgam about the size of small hens' eggs remained.

"Is that good, uncle?" Tom asked.

"Very fair, lad; wonderfully good indeed, considering we have not got down far yet. I should say we shall get a pound and a half of gold out of it."

"But how does the gold get into it, uncle?"

"There is what is called an affinity between quicksilver and gold. The moment gold touches quicksilver it is absorbed by it, just as a drop of water is taken up by a lump of salt. It thickens the quicksilver, and as it is squeezed through the leather the quicksilver is as it were strained out, and what remains behind becomes thicker and thicker, until, as you see, it is almost solid. It is no good to use more pressure, for if you do a certain amount of the gold would be squeezed through the leather. You see, as the stuff in the cradle is shaken, the gold being heavier than the sand finds its way down to the bottom, and every particle that comes in contact with the quicksilver is swallowed up by it."

"And how do you get the quicksilver out of those lumps?"

"We put them in one of those clay crucibles you saw, with a pinch of borax, cover them up, and put them in a heap of glowing embers. That evaporates the quicksilver, and leaves the gold behind in the shape of a button." This was done that evening, and when the buttons were placed in the scales they just turned the two-pound weight.

"Well, boys, that is good enough for anything," Harry said. "That, with the dust, makes a pound a day, which is as good as the very best stuff in the early days of California."

They worked steadily for the next seven weeks. Contrary to their expectations the gravel was but little richer lower down than they had found it at the end of the first wash-up, but continued about equally good, and the result averaged about a pound weight of gold a day. This was put into little bags of deer-skin, each containing five pounds' weight, and these bags were distributed among the saddle-bags, so that in case of sudden disturbance there would be no risk of their being left behind. The Indians took it by turns to hunt; at other times they remained on guard in camp, Tom only staying when one of them was away. One day when the mining party stopped work, and sat down to eat some bread and cold meat,—which they had from the first brought up, so as to save them the loss of time entailed by going to the camp and back,—the report of a gun came upon their ears. All started to their feet and seized their rifles, and then stood listening intently. A minute later two more shots were heard at close intervals.

"Redskins for sure!" Jerry exclaimed. "I thought as how our luck were too good to last." They started at a run down the little valley, and only paused when they reached its mouth. Harry then advanced cautiously until he could obtain a view of the main valley. He paused for a minute and then rejoined his companions.

"There are fifty of them," he said, "if there is one. They are Utes in their war-paint. They are a bit up the valley. I think if we make a rush we can get to the trees before they can cut us off."

"We must try anyhow," Sam Hicks said, "else they will get the two Indians and our horses and saddles and all. Just let us get breath for a moment, and then we will start."

"Keep close together as you run," Harry said, "and then if they do come up we can get back to back and make a fight of it." After a short pause they started. They had not gone twenty yards when a loud yell proclaimed that the Indians had seen them. They had, however, but three hundred yards to run, while the Utes were double that distance from the clump.

When the miners were within fifty yards of the trees two rifle-shots rang out, and two of the Utes, who were somewhat ahead of the rest, fell from their horses, while the rest swerved off, seeing that there was no hope of cutting the party off. A few more yards and the miners were among the trees.

"So the Utes have found us out, chief," Harry said as he joined Leaping Horse, who had just reloaded his rifle.

"Must have tracked us. They are a war-party," the Seneca replied. "Hunter must have found tracks and taken news back to the villages."

"Well, we have got to fight for it, that is clear enough," Harry said. "Anyhow, now they see there are seven of us they are not likely to attack until it gets dark, so we have time to think over what had best be done. We had just begun our meal when we heard your shot, and the best thing we can do is to have a good feed at once. We may be too busy later on."

The chief said a word to the young Indian, and, leaving him on the watch, accompanied the others to the fire. They had scarcely sat down when Hunting Dog came up.

"More Utes," he said briefly, pointing across the valley.

They at once went to the outer line of trees. On the brow of the rise opposite were a party of horsemen between twenty and thirty strong.

"That shows they have learnt all about our position," Harry said. "Those fellows have been lying in wait somewhere over the hill to cut us off if we took to our horses on seeing the main body. Let us have a look the other side."

Crossing the clump of trees, they saw on the brow there another party of Utes.

"I reckon they must have crossed that valley we were working in just after we got through," Jerry said. "It is mighty lucky they did not come down on us while we were washing, for they could have wiped us all out before we had time to get hold of our guns. Well, Harry, we are in a pretty tight fix, with fifty of them up the valley and five-and-twenty or so on each side of us. We shall have to be dog-goned smart if we are to get out of this scrape."

"Hand me your rifle, Tom," his uncle said, "it carries farther than mine, and I will give those fellows a hint that they had best move off a bit."

Steadying his piece against a tree, he took a careful aim and fired. One of the Indians swerved in his saddle, and then fell forward on the neck of his horse, which turned and galloped off with the rest.

"Now we will have our meal and take council, chief," Harry said as he turned away, "If we have got to fight there is no occasion to fight hungry."

The fire was made up; there was no need to be careful now. Strips of deer's flesh were hung over it, and the meal was soon ready. But little was said while it was being eaten, then they all lighted their pipes and each put a pannikin of hot tea beside him.

"Now, chief," Harry said, "have you arrived at any way out of this? It is worse than it was the last time we got caught in this valley."

The chief shook his head. "No good fight here," he said; "when night come they creep up all round."

"Yes, I see that we have got to bolt, but the question is, how? If we were to ride they would ride us down, that is certain. Jerry and Tom might possibly get away, though that ain't likely. Their critters are good, but nothing downright extraordinary, and the chances are that some of the Utes have got faster horses than theirs. As for the rest of us, they would have us before we had ridden an hour."

"That ain't to be thought of," Jerry said. "It seems to me our best chance would be to leave the critters behind, and to crawl out the moment it gets dark, and try and get beyond them."

"They will close in as soon as it gets dark, Jerry. They will know well enough that that is the time we shall be moving. I reckon we should not have a chance worth a cent of getting through. What do you say, chief?"

Leaping Horse nodded in assent.

"Well, then," Sam Hicks said, "I vote we mount our horses and go right at them. I would rather do that and get rubbed out in a fair fight than lie here until they crawl up and finish us."

No one answered, and for some minutes they smoked on without a word being spoken, then Harry said:

"There is only one chance for us that I can see, and that is to mount now and to ride right down the valley. The chief says that in some places it is not more than fifty yards wide, with steep cliffs on each side, and we could make a much better fight there, for they could only attack us in front. There would be nothing for them then but to dismount and close in upon us from tree to tree, and we could make a running fight of it until we come to the mouth of the cañon. There must be places there, that we ought to be able to hold with our seven rifles against the lot of them."

"Bully for you, Harry! I reckon that would give us a chance anyhow. That is, if we ain't cut off before we get to the wood."

"Let us have a look round and see what they are doing," Harry said. "Ah! here comes Hunting Dog. He will tell us all about it."

"Utes on hills all gone up and joined the others," the young Indian said as he came up.

"It could not be better news!" Harry exclaimed. "I reckon they have moved away to tempt us to make a start for the fort, for they know if we go that way they will have us all, sure. They have not reckoned on our riding down the valley, for they will be sure we must have found out long ago that there ain't any way out of it. Well, we had best lose no time. There is some meat ready, Hunting Dog, and you had best fill up while we get ready for a start."

The blankets and buffalo rugs were wrapped up and strapped behind the saddles, as soon as these were placed behind the horses. They had only a small quantity of meat left, as the chief was going out hunting the next morning, but they fastened this, and eighty pounds of flour that still remained, on to one of the pack-horses. They filled their powder-horns from the keg, and each put three or four dozen bullets into his holsters, together with all the cartridges for their pistols; the rest of the ammunition was packed on another horse. When all was completed they mounted.

"We may get a couple of hundred yards more start before we are seen," Harry said. "Anyhow, we have got five hundred yards, and may reckon on making the two miles to where the valley narrows before they catch us."

The instant, however, they emerged from the wood, two loud yells were heard from Indians who had been left lying down on watch at the top of the slopes on either side. Sam, who was the worst shot of the party, had volunteered to lead the string of pack-horses, while Ben was ready to urge them on behind.

"You may want to stop some of the leading varmint, and I should not be much good at that game, so I will keep straight on without paying any attention to them."

A loud answering yell rose from the Indians up the valley.

"We shall gain fifty yards or so before they are fairly in the saddle," Harry said as they went off at the top of their speed, the horses seeming to know that the loud war-cry boded danger. They had gone half a mile before they looked round. The Indians were riding in a confused mass, and were some distance past the grove the miners had left, but they still appeared as far behind as they had been when they started. Another mile and the mass had broken up; the best-mounted Indians had left the rest some distance behind, and considerably decreased the gap between them and the fugitives. Another five minutes and the latter reached the wood, that began just where the valley narrowed and the cliffs rose almost perpendicularly on each side. As soon as they did so they leapt from their horses, and each posting himself behind a tree opened fire at their pursuers, the nearest of whom were but two hundred yards away. Four fell to the first seven shots; the others turned and galloped back to the main body, who halted at once.

"They won't try a charge," Harry said; "it isn't in Indian nature to come across the open with the muzzles of seven rifles pointed at them. They will palaver now; they know they have got us in a trap, and they will wait till night. Now, chief, I reckon that you and I and Hunting

Dog had best stay here, so that if they try, as they are pretty sure to do, to find out whether we are here still, we can give them a hint to keep off. The other four had better ride straight down the canon, and go on for a bit, to find out the best place for making a stand, and as soon as it is dark we will go forward and join them. There will be no occasion for us to hurry. I reckon the skunks will crawl up here soon after it is dark; but they won't go much farther, for we might hide up somewhere and they might miss us. In the morning they will come down on foot, sheltering behind the trees as much as they can, till at last they locate us."

The chief nodded his approval of the plan, and Tom and the three miners at once started, taking the pack-horses with them. On the way down they came upon a bear. Ben was about to fire, but Jerry said: "Best leave him alone, Ben; we are only three miles down, and these cliffs would echo the sound and the red-skins would hear it and know that some of us had gone down the valley, and might make a rush at once." In an hour and a half they came down to a spot where the valley, after widening out a good bit, suddenly terminated, and the stream entered a deep canon in the face of the wall of rock that closed it in.

"I reckon all this part of the valley was a lake once," Jerry said. "When it got pretty well full it began to run over where this canon is and gradually cut its way out down to the Colorado. I wonder how far it is to the river."

They had gone but a hundred yards down the canon when they came to a place where a recent fall of rocks blocked it up. Through these the stream, which was but a small one, made its way.

"There is a grist of water comes down here when the snow melts in the spring," Ben remarked. "You can see that the rocks are worn fifty feet up. Waal, I reckon this place is good enough for us, Jerry."

"I reckon so, too," the latter agreed. "It will be a job to get our horses over; but we have got to do it anyhow, if we have to carry them." The animals, however, managed to scramble up the rocks that filled the canon to the height of some thirty feet. The distance between the rock walls was not more than this in width.

"We could hold this place for a year," Ben said, "if they didn't take to chucking rocks down from above."

"Yes, that is the only danger," Jerry agreed; "but the betting is they could not get nigh enough to the edge to look down. Still, they might do it if the ground is level above; anyhow, we should not show much at this depth, for it is pretty dark down here, and the rocks must be seven or eight hundred feet high."

It was, indeed, but a narrow strip of sky that they saw as they looked up, and although still broad daylight in the valley they had left, it was almost dark at the bottom of the deep gorge, and became pitch dark as soon as the light above faded.

"The first job in the morning," Jerry said, "will be to explore this place down below. I expect there are places where it widens out. If it does, and there are trees and anything like grass, the horses can get a bite of food; if not, they will mighty soon go under, that is if we don't come upon any game, for if we don't we sha'n't be able to spare them flour."

"It is almost a pity we did not leave them in the valley to take their chance," Tom said.

"Don't you make any mistake," Jerry said. "In the first place they may come in useful to us yet, and even if we never get astride of them again they may come in mighty handy for food. I don't say as we mayn't get a bear if there are openings in the canon, or terraces where they can come down, but if there ain't it is just horse-meat we have got to depend on. Look here, boys, it is 'tarnal dark here; I can't see my own hand. I vote we get a light. There is a lot of drift-wood jammed in among the stones where we climbed up, that will do to start a fire, and I saw a lot more just at the mouth of this gap. We know the red-skins ain't near yet, so I vote we grope our way up and bring some down. It will be a first-rate thing, too, to make a bit of fire half-way between here and the mouth; that would put a stop to their crawling up, as they are like enough to try to do, to make out whereabouts we are. Of course we shall have to damp our own fire down if they come, else we should show up agin the light if we went up on the rock."

The others agreed at once, for it was dull work sitting there in the black darkness. All had matches, and a piece of dry fir was soon found.

This was lighted, and served as a torch with which to climb over the rocks. Jammed in between these on the upper side was a large quantity of drift-wood. This was pulled out, made into bundles, and carried over the rock barrier, and a fire was soon blazing there. Then taking a brand and two axes they went up to the mouth of the gorge, cut up the arms of some trees that had been brought down by the last floods and left there as the water sank. The greater part of these were taken down to their camping-place; the rest, with plenty of small wood to light them, were piled half-way between the barrier and the mouth of the canon, and were soon blazing brightly.

They were returning to their camping-place, when Ben exclaimed that he heard the sound of horses' hoofs. All stopped to listen.

"There are not more than three of them," Ben said, "and they are coming along at a canter. I don't expect we shall hear anything of the red-skins until to-morrow morning."

They heard the horses enter the canon, then Jerry shouted: "Are you all right, Harry?"

"Yes; the red-skins were all quiet when we came away. Why, where are you?" he shouted again when he came up to the fire.

"A hundred yards farther on I will show you a light."

Two or three blazing brands were brought up. Harry and the Indians had dismounted at the first fire, and now led their horses up to the stone barrier.

"What on arth have you lit that other fire for, Jerry?" Harry asked as he stopped at the foot of the barrier.

"Because we shall sleep a dog-goned sight better with it there. As like as not they may send on two or three young warriors to scout. It is as black as a wolf's mouth, and we might have sat listening all night, and then should not have heard them. But with that fire there they dare not come on, for they would know they could not pass it without getting a bullet in them."

"Well, it is a very good idea, Jerry; I could not think what was up when I got there and did not see anybody. I see you have another fire over the other side. I could make it out clear enough as we came on."

"It will burn down a bit presently," Jerry said. "I should not try to get those horses up here now, Harry. It was a bad place to come up in daylight, and like enough they would break their legs if they tried it now. They will do just as well there as they would on this side, and you can get them over as soon as the day breaks."

"I would rather get them over, Jerry; but I see it is a pretty rough place."

Leaving the horses, Harry and the Indians climbed over the barrier, and were soon seated with the others round their fire, over which the meat was already frizzling.

"So the Indians kept quiet all the afternoon, Harry?"

"As quiet as is their nature. Two or three times some of them rode down, and galloped backwards and forwards in front of us to make out if we were there. Each time we let them fool about for a good long spell, and then when they got a bit careless sent them a ball or two to let them know we were still there. Hunting Dog went with the three horses half a mile down the valley soon after you had gone, so that they might not hear us ride off.

"As soon as it began to get dusk we started. We had to come pretty slow, for it got so dark under the trees we could not make out the trunks, and had to let the horses pick their own way. But we knew there was no hurry, for they would not follow till morning, though of course their scouts would creep up as soon as it was dark, and wouldn't be long before they found out that we had left."

"I reckon they will all come and camp in the wood and wait for daylight before they move, though I don't say two or three scouts may not crawl down to try and find out where we are. They will move pretty slow, for they will have to pick their way, and will know well enough that if a twig cracks it will bring bullets among them. I reckon they won't get here under four or five hours. It is sartin they won't try to pass that fire above. As soon as they see us they will take word back to the others, and we shall have the whole lot down here by morning."

"We shall have to get the horses over, the first thing. Two of us had best go down, as soon as it is light enough to ride without risking our necks, to see what the canon is like below."

"Yes, that is most important, Jerry; there may be some break where the red-skins could get down, and so catch us between two fires."

"I don't care a red cent for the Utes," Jerry said. "We can lick them out of their boots in this canon. What we have been thinking of, is whether there is some place where the horses can get enough to keep them alive while we are shut up here. If there is game, so much the better; if there ain't, we have got to take to horseflesh."

"How long do you suppose that the Indians are likely to wait when they find that they can't get at us?" Tom asked.

"There ain't no sort of saying," his uncle replied. "I reckon no one ever found out yet how long a red-skin's patience will last. Time ain't nothing to them. They will follow up this canon both sides till they are sartin that there ain't no place where a man can climb up. If there ain't, they will just squat in that valley. Like enough they will send for their lodges and squaws and fix themselves there till winter comes, and even then they might not go. They have got wood and water. Some of them will hunt and bring in meat, which they will dry for the winter; and they are just as likely to stay here as to go up to their villages."

A vigilant watch was kept up all night, two of them being always on guard at the top of the barrier. As soon as morning broke, the three horses were got over, and half an hour later Harry and Sam Hicks rode off down the canon, while the others took their places on guard, keeping themselves well behind the rocks, between which they looked out. They had not long to wait, for an Indian was seen to dart rapidly across the mouth of the canon. Two rifles cracked cut, but the Indian's appearance and disappearance was so sudden and quick that they had no reason to believe that they had hit him.

"They will know now that we are here, and are pretty wide awake," Ben said. "You may be sure that he caught sight of these rocks."

A minute or two later several rifles flashed from among the fallen stones at the mouth of the gorge.

"Keep your eyes open," Jerry said, "and when you see the slightest movement, fire. But don't do it unless you feel certain that you make out a head or a limb. We've got to show the Utes that it is sartin death to try and crawl up here."

Almost immediately afterwards a head appeared above the stones, the chief's rifle cracked, and at the same instant the head disappeared.

"Do you think you got him, chief?"

"Think so, not sure. Leaping Horse does not often miss his mark at two hundred yards."

Almost directly afterwards Tom fired. An Indian sprang to his feet and bounded away.

"What did you fire at, Tom?"

"I think it was his arm and shoulder," Tom replied. "I was not sure about it, but I certainly saw something move."

"I fancy you must have hit him, or he would not have got up. Waal, now I reckon we are going to have quiet for a bit. They must have had a good look at the place while they were lying there, and must have seen that it air too strong for them. I don't say they mayn't come on again to-night—that they may do, but I think it air more likely they won't try it. They would know that we should be on the watch, and with seven rifles and Colts we should account for a grist of them afore they got over. What do you say, chief?"

"Not come now," the Indian said positively. "Send men first along top see if can get down. Not like come at night; the canons of the Colorado very bad medicine, red-skins no like come into them. If no way where we can get up, then Utes sit down to starve us."

"That will be a longish job, chief. A horse a week will keep us for three months."

"If no food for horse, horse die one week."

"So they will, chief. We must wait till Harry comes back, then we shall know what our chances are."

It was six hours before Harry and Sam returned. There was a shout of satisfaction from the men when they saw that they had on their saddles the hind-quarters of a bear.

"Waal, what is the news, Harry?"

"It ain't altogether good, Ben. It goes down like this for about twelve miles, then it widens out sudden. It gets into a crumbly rock which has got worn away, and there is a place maybe about fifty yards wide and half a mile long, with sloping sides going up a long way, and then cliff all round. The bottom is all stones; there are a few tufts of coarse grass growing between them. On the slopes there are some bushes, and on a ledge high up we made out a bear. We had two or three shots at him, and at last brought him down. There may be more among the bushes; there was plenty of cover for them."

"There was no place where there was a chance of getting up, Harry?"

"Nary a place. I don't say as there may not be, but we couldn't see one."

"But the bear must have got down."

"No. He would come down here in the dry season looking for water-holes, and finding the place to his liking he must have concluded to settle there. It is just the place a bear would choose, for he might reckon pretty confident that there weren't no chance of his being disturbed. Well, we went on beyond that, and two miles lower the canon opened again, and five minutes took us down on to the bank of the Colorado. There was no great room between the river and the cliff, but there were some good-sized trees there, and plenty of bush growing up some distance. We caught sight of another bear, but as we did not want him we left him alone."

"Waal, let us have some b'ar-meat first of all," Jerry said. "We finished our meat last night, and bread don't make much of a meal, I reckon. Anyhow we can all do with another, and after we have done we will have a talk. We know what to expect now, and can figure it up better than we could before."

Chapter XV.
The Colorado

"Well, boys," Harry Wade began after they had smoked for some time in silence, "we have got to look at this matter squarely. So far we have got out of a mighty tight place better than we expected. Yesterday it seemed to us that there weren't much chance of our carrying our hair away, but now we are out of that scrape. But we are in another pretty nigh as bad, though there ain't much chance of the red-skins getting at us."

"That air so, Harry. We are in a pretty tight hole, you bet. They ain't likely to get our scalps for some time, but there ain't no denying that our chance of carrying them off is dog-goned small."

"You bet there ain't, Jerry," Sam Hicks said. "Them pizon varmint will camp outside here; for they know they have got us in a trap. They mayn't attack us at present, but we have got to watch night and day. Any dark night they may take it into their heads to come up, and there won't be nothing to prevent them, for the rustling of the stream among the rocks would cover any little noise they might make. The first we should know of it would be the yell of the varmint at the foot of this barrier, and afore we could get to the top the two on guard would be tomahawked, and they would be down on us like a pack of wolves. I would a'most as soon put down my rifle and walk straight out now and let them shoot me, if I knew they would do it without any of their devilish tortures, as go on night after night, expecting to be woke up with their war-yell in my ears.

"Of course they will be always keeping a watch there at the mouth of the canon,—a couple of boys are enough for that,—for they will know that if we ride out on our horses we must go right up the valley, and it is a nasty place to gallop through in the dark; besides, some of them will no doubt be placed higher up to cut us off, and if we got through, which ain't likely, they could ride us down in a few hours. If we crept out on foot and got fairly among the trees we should be no better off, for they would take up our trail in the morning and hunt us down. I tell you fairly, boys, I don't see any way out of it. I reckon it will come to our having to ride out together, and to wipe out as many of the Utes as possible afore we go down. What do you say, chief?"

"Leaping Horse agrees with his white brother, Straight Harry, whose mind he knows."

"Waal, go on then, Harry," Sam said. "I thought that you had made an end of it or I wouldn't have opened out. I don't see no way out of it at present, but if you do I am ready to fall in with it whatever it is."

"I see but one way out of it, boys. It is a mighty risky thing, but it can't be more risky than stopping here, and there is just a chance. I spoke to the chief last night, and he owned that it didn't seem to him there was a chance in that or any other way. However, he said that if I went he would go with me. My proposal is this, that we take to the river and try and get through the canons."

There was a deep silence among the men. The proposal took them by surprise. No man had ever accomplished the journey. Though two parties similarly attacked by Indians had attempted to raft clown some of the canons higher up; one party perished to a man, one survivor of the other party escaped to tell the tale; but as to the canons below, through which they would have to pass, no man had ever explored them. The Indians regarded the river with deep awe, and believed the canons to be peopled with demons. The enterprise was so stupendous and the dangers to be met with so terrible, that ready as the western hunters were to encounter dangers, no one had ever attempted to investigate the windings and turnings of the river that for two thousand miles made its way through terrific precipices, and ran its course some three thousand feet below the surrounding country, until it emerged on to the plains of Mexico.

"That was why I was so anxious to reach the river," Harry went on after a pause. "I wanted to see whether there were some trees, by which we could construct a raft, near its bank. Had there not been, I should have proposed to follow it up or down, as far as we could make our way, in hopes of lighting on some trees. However, as it is they are just handy for us. I don't say as we shall get through, boys, but there is just a chance of it. I don't see any other plan that would give us a show."

Jerry was the first to speak.

"Waal, Harry, you can count me in. One might as well be drowned in a rapid or carried over a fall as killed, or, wuss, taken and tortured by the red-skins."

"That is so, Jerry," Sam Hicks agreed. While Ben said: "Waal, if we git through it will be something to talk about all our lives. In course there ain't no taking the horses?"

"That is out of the question, Ben. We shall not have much time to spare, for the Utes may take it into their heads to attack us any night; and, besides, we have no means of making a big raft. We might tie two or three trunks together with the lariats and spike a few cross-pieces on them, we might even make two such rafts; that is the outside. They will carry us and our stores, but as for the horses, we must either leave them down in the hollow for the Indians to find, or put a bullet through their heads. I expect the latter will be the best thing for them, poor beasts."

"No want trees," the chief said. "Got horses' skins; make canoes."

"You are right, chief," Harry exclaimed; "I never thought of that. That would be the very thing. Canoes will go down the rapids where the strongest rafts would be dashed to pieces, and if we come to a bad fall we can make a shift to carry them round."

The others were no less pleased with the suggestion, and the doubtful expression of their faces as they assented to the scheme now changed to one of hopefulness, and they discussed the plan eagerly. It was agreed that not a moment should be lost in setting to work to carry it out, and that they should forthwith retreat to the mouth of the lower canon; for all entertained a secret misgiving that the Utes might make their attack that night, and felt that if that attack were made in earnest it would succeed. It was certain they would be able to find some point at which the lower gorge could be held; and at any rate a day would be gained, for at whatever hour of the night the Indians came up they would not venture farther until daybreak, and there would probably be a long palaver before they would enter the lower canon.

Tom had not spoken. He recognized the justice of Harry's reasoning, but had difficulty in keeping his tears back at the thought of his horse being killed. For well-nigh a year it had carried him well; he had tended and cared for it; it would come to his call and rub its muzzle against his cheek. He thought that had he been alone he would have risked anything rather than part with it.

"Don't you like the plan, Tom?" Harry said to him, as, having packed and saddled the horses, they rode together down the canon. "I don't suppose the passage is so terrible after all."

"I am not thinking of the passage at all, uncle," Tom said almost indignantly; "it will be a grand piece of adventure; but I don't like—I hate—the thought of my horse being killed. It is like killing a dear friend to save one's self."

"It is a wrench, lad," Harry said kindly; "I can quite understand your feelings, and don't like the thought myself. But I see that it has got to be done, and after all it will be better to kill the poor brutes than to let them fall into the hands of the Indians, who don't know what mercy to their beasts means, and will ride them till they drop dead without the least compunction."

"I know it is better, uncle, ever so much better—but it is horrible all the same. Anyhow, don't ask me to do it, for I could not."

"I will see to that, Tom. You shall be one of the guards of the canon. You would not be of much use in making the canoes, and you won't have to know anything about it till you go down and get on board."

Tom nodded his thanks; his heart was too full for him to speak, and he felt that if he said a word he should break down altogether. They rode rapidly along, passed through the little valley where the bear had been killed, without stopping, and went down the lower canon, carefully examining it to fix upon the most suitable point for defence. There had been no recent fall, and though at some points great boulders lay thickly, there was no one place that offered special facilities for defence.

"Look here, boys," Harry said, reining up his horse at a point within two hundred yards of the lower end, "we can't do better than fix ourselves here. An hour's work will get up a wall that will puzzle the red-skins to get over, and there is the advantage that a shot fired here by the guard will bring our whole force up in a couple of minutes. I vote we ride the horses down to the river and let them pick up what they can, and then come back here and build the wall. It will be getting dark in an hour's time, and we may as well finish that job at once. Ben and Sam, you may as well pick out a couple of young fir-trees and bring them down at once, then there will be no time lost. Five of us will be enough for the wall. Keep your eyes open. Likely enough there is a bear or two about, and it would be a great thing for us to lay in a stock of meat before we start."

As soon as they issued from the gorge the horses were unsaddled and the stores taken off the pack-animals. As they were doing this Harry said a few words in a low tone to Sam. He then carefully examined the trees, and picked out two young firs. Sam and Ben took their axes, and the other five went up the gorge again, and were soon hard at work collecting boulders and piling them in a wall.

"There is a gun, uncle," Tom exclaimed presently.

"Well, I hope they have got sight of a bear, we shall want a stock of meat badly."

A dozen shots were fired, but Tom thought no more of it as he proceeded with his work. The bottom of the cañon was but fifteen feet wide, and by the time it was dark they had a solid wall across it nearly six feet high, with places for them to stand on to fire over.

"Now then, Tom, you may as well take post here at once. I will send Sam or Ben up to watch with you. I don't think there is a shadow of chance of their coming to-night, but there is never any answering for red-skins. I would leave Hunting Dog with you, but we shall want him to help make the framework for the canoes; the Indians are a deal handier than we are in making lashings. I will send your supper up here, lad, and your buffalo robes. Then you can take it by turns to watch and sleep. I reckon we shall be at work all night; we have got to get the job finished as quick as we can."

A quarter of an hour later Sam Hicks came up.

"Have you got the trees down, Sam?"

"Lor' bless you, it didn't take a minute to do that. We got them down and split them up, then lit a fire and got the meat over it and the kettle, and mixed the dough."

"Did you kill another bear? We heard you firing."

"No; the critter was too high up, and I ain't much good at shooting. Perhaps they will get sight of him to-morrow, and Harry and the chief will bring him down if he is within range of their shooting-irons. It is 'tarnal dark up here."

In twenty minutes two lights were seen approaching, and Harry and Hunting Dog came up carrying pine-wood torches. Each had a great faggot of wood fastened on his back, and Harry also carried the frying-pan, on which were a pile of meat and two great hunks of bread, while Hunting Dog brought two tin pannikins of hot tea.

"That will make it more cheerful for you," Harry said, as he unfastened the rope that tied the faggot to his shoulders. "Now, Hunting Dog, get a good fire as soon as you can, and then come down again to us."

The fire was soon blazing merrily, and Tom and Sam sat down to enjoy their meal.

"Don't you think one of us ought to keep watch, Sam?"

"Not a bit of it," Sam said. "The red-skins will never dare to enter that canon until after dark, and if they started now and made their way straight on, they would not be here for another three or four hours. I would bet my boots they don't come at all to-night; even if they were not scared at us, they would be scared at coming near the river in the dark. No, we will just take our meal comfortable and smoke a pipe, and then I will take first watch and you shall take a sleep. We ain't closed an eye since the night before last."

Tom, indeed, was nearly asleep before he had finished his pipe, and felt that he really must get a nap. So saying to Sam, "Be sure and wake me in two hours," he rolled himself in his robe and instantly fell asleep.

It seemed to him that he had only just gone off when Sam roused him. He leapt to his feet, however, rifle in hand.

"Anything the matter, Sam?"

"Everything quiet," the miner replied.

"What did you wake me for then? I have not been asleep five minutes."

"According to my reckoning, mate, you have been asleep better'n five hours. It was about half-past eight when you went off, and I reckon it is two now, and will begin to get light in another hour. I would not have waked you till daybreak, but I found myself dropping off."

"I am awfully sorry," Tom began

"Don't you trouble, young un. By the time you have been as long in the West as I have you won't think anything of two nights' watch. Now you keep a sharp lookout. I don't think there is much chance of their coming, but I don't want to be woke up with a red-skin coming right down on the top of me."

"I see you have let the fire out, Sam," Tom said, with a little shiver.

"I put it out hours ago," Sam said, as he prepared to lie down. "It would never have done to keep it all night, for a red-skin would see my head over the top of the wall, while I should not get a sight of him till he was within arm's-length."

Tom took up his post, and gazed earnestly into the darkness beyond the wall. He felt that his sense of vision would be of no use whatever, and therefore threw all his faculties into that of listening. Slight as was the chance of the Indians coming, he yet felt somewhat nervous, and it was a satisfaction to him to see beyond the mouth of the canon the glow of the fire, by which, as he knew, the others were hard at work.

In an hour the morning began to break, and as soon as he could see well up the canon he relighted the fire, jumping up to take a look over the wall every minute or so. It was not long before he saw his uncle approaching with a kettle.

"I saw your smoke, Tom, and guessed that you would be glad of a mug of hot tea. You have seen no signs of Indians, I suppose?"

"We have heard nothing, uncle. As to seeing, up to half an hour ago there was no possibility of making out anything. But I have not even been listening; Sam went on guard directly we had finished supper, and I asked him to call me in two hours, but he did not wake me until two o'clock."

"He is a good fellow," Harry said. "Well, don't wake him now. I can't leave you the kettle, for we have to keep boiling water going, but you can put his tin into the ashes and warm it up when he wakes. Here are a couple of pieces of bread."

"Why do you have to keep the kettle boiling, uncle?"

"To bend the wood with. The piece we are working on is kept damp with boiling water. We hold it for a time over the fire, pouring a little water on as fast as it evaporates; that softens the wood, and we can bend it much more evenly than we could if we did it by force. Besides, when it is fastened into its position it remains, when it is dry, in that shape, and throws no strain on to anything."

"Are you getting on well?"

"Capitally. We should have done both the frames by now, but we were obliged to make them very strong so as to resist the bumps they are sure to get against rocks. When they are finished you might almost let them drop off the top of a house, they will be so strong and elastic. If the Indians will but give us time we shall make a first-rate job of them."

Three hours later Harry came up again with the kettle and some cooked meat. Sam had just woke up, and was quite angry with Tom for not rousing him before. "The others have been working all night," he said, "and here have I been asleep for five hours; a nice sort of mate they will think me."

"Well, but you were watching five hours, Sam; and I would a deal rather work all night than stand here for two hours in the dark, wondering all the time whether the Indians are crawling up, and expecting at any moment to hear a rush against the wall."

"I am going to take your place, Sam, when you have finished your breakfast," Harry said, as he came up. "If the Utes found out last night that we had gone, their scouts may be coming down before long. My rifle shoots a bit straighter than yours does."

"It ain't the rifle, Harry," Sam said good-temperedly; "it is the eye that is wrong, not the shooting-iron. I never had much practice with these long guns, but when it comes to a six-shooter, I reckon I can do my share as well as most. But they won't give me a chance with it."

"I hope they won't, Sam. I am sure they won't as long as there is light, and I hope that before it gets dark they will conclude to leave us alone."

A vigilant watch was kept now.

"I think I saw a head look out from that corner," Tom exclaimed suddenly, two hours after Sam had left them.

"I am quite sure I did, Tom. We must wait until he shows himself a bit more. I reckon it is a good three hundred yards off, and a man's Head is a precious small mark at that distance. Stand a bit higher and lay your rifle on the wall. Don't fire if he only puts his head out. They know we can shoot, so there is not any occasion to give them another lesson. I don't hold to killing, unless you have got to do it. Let him have a good look at us.

"When he goes back and tells the tribe that there is a three hundred yards' straight passage without shelter, and a strong wall across the end of it, and two white men with rifles ready to shoot, I reckon they will know a good deal better than to try to come up it, as long as there is light. Besides, they won't think there is any occasion to hurry, for they won't count on our taking to the river, and will know that we shall be keeping watch at night. So it may very well be that they will reckon on wearing us out, and that we may not hear of them for a week. There is the fellow's head again!"

The head remained visible round the corner of the rock for two or three minutes.

"He knows all about it now, Tom. You won't see any more of him to-day. I will go down and lend them a hand below."

Tom asked no questions about the horses; he had thought of them a score of times as he stood on guard, and the thought had occurred to him that it was possible the shots he had heard while they were building the wall on the previous afternoon, had been the death shots of the horses. It did not occur to him when Sam was telling the story about the bear, that this was a got-up tale, but when he came to think it over, he thought it probable that it was so. Sam himself was not much of a shot, but Ben, although inferior to Harry or either of the two Indians, shot as well as Jerry, and would hardly have missed a bear three or four times running. Each time the thought of the horses occurred to him he resolutely put it aside, and concentrated his mind upon the probable perils of the passage down the canons and the wonderful gorges they would traverse, and the adventures and excitement they were sure to pass through. He thought how fortunate it was they had taken the precaution of sending their specimens of quartz back to the fort; for were they in the canoes, the fruits of the journey would be irrevocably lost were these to upset; for now the Indians had twice discovered the presence of whites in the valley they would be sure to watch it closely, and it would not be possible to go up to the mine again unless in strong force.

The day passed quietly. Harry brought up Tom's meals, and late in the afternoon all hands came up, and the wall of stones was raised four feet, making it almost impregnable against a sudden attack. The two Indians took post there with Tom, and watched alternately all night. The Utes, however, remained perfectly quiet. They probably felt sure that the fugitives must sooner or later be forced to surrender, and were disinclined to face the loss that must occur before so strong a position, defended by seven men armed with rifles and revolvers, could be carried.

At three o'clock on the following afternoon Hunting Dog came up. "Tom go down and get dinner," he said, "Hunting Dog will watch."

Tom took his rifle and started down the canon.

"Come on, lad," his uncle shouted. "We are pretty near ready for a start, and have all had our dinner; so be quick about it. We want to get well away from here before night."

Tom went to the fire and ate his meal. As he sat down he saw that the stores, blankets, and robes had all been carried away. When he finished, his uncle led him down to the river. Two canoes were floating in the water, and the other men were standing beside them.

"There, Tom, what do you think of them?"

"They are splendid, uncle; it seems impossible that you can have built them in two days."

"Five hands can do a lot of canoe-building in forty-eight hours' work, Tom."

The canoes were indeed models of strength if not of beauty. They were each about twenty feet long and five feet wide. Two strong pieces of pine two inches square ran along the top of each side, and one of the same width but an inch deeper formed the keel. The ribs, an inch wide and three-quarters of an inch thick, were placed at intervals of eighteen inches apart. The canoes were almost flat-bottomed. The ribs lay across the keel, which was cut away to allow them to lie flush in it, a strong nail being driven in at the point of junction—these being the only nails used in the boat's construction. The ribs ran straight out to almost the full width of the canoe, and were then turned sharp up, the ends being lashed with thongs of hide to the upper stringers.

Outside the ribs were lashed longitudinal wattles of tough wood about an inch wide. They were placed an inch apart, extending over the bottom and halfway up the side. Over all was stretched the skin, five horses' hides having been used for each boat. They were very strongly sewed together by a double row of thongs, the overlaps having, before being sewed, been smeared with melted fat. Cross-pieces of wood at the top kept the upper framework in its place. The hair of the skin was outward, the inner glistened with the fat that had been rubbed into it.

"They are strong indeed," Tom said. "They ought to stand anything, uncle."

"Yes, I think they would stand a blow against any rock if it hadn't a cutting edge. They would just bound off as a basket would. Of course they are very heavy for canoes; but as they won't have to carry more than the weight of four men each, they will draw little over a couple of inches or so of water.

"That is why we made them so wide. We could not get strength without weight; and as there is no saying what shallows there may be, and how close in some places rocks may come up to the surface, we were obliged to build them wide to get light draught. You see we have made ten paddles, so as to have a spare one or two in case of breakage. We have two spare hides, so that we shall have the means of repairing damages."

Tom said nothing about the horses. Manufactured into a boat, as the skins were, there was not much to remind him of them; but he pressed his uncle's hand and said, "Thank you very much, uncle; I don't mind so much now, but I should not like to have seen them before."

"That is all right, Tom; it was a case of necessity. Sam and Ben shot them directly we got here."

The stores were all laid by the boats, being divided between them so that the cargoes were in all respects duplicates of each other. Before Tom came down some had already been placed in each boat, with a blanket thrown over them.

"You have got the gold, I suppose, uncle?"

"You may bet that we did not leave that behind. There is half in each boat, and the bags are lashed to the timbers, so that if there is an upset they cannot get lost."

"How are we going?"

"We have settled that you and I and the two Indians shall go together, and the rest in the other boat. The Indians know nothing of canoeing, and won't be of very much use. I know you were accustomed to boats, and I did some rowing when I was a young man. I wish we had a couple of Canadian Indians with us, or of half-breeds; they are up to this sort of work, and with one in the stern of each canoe it would be a much less risky business going down the rapids. However, no doubt we shall get handy with the paddles before long."

When everything was ready Harry fired his rifle, and in a couple of minutes Hunting Dog came running down. The others had already taken their seats. He stepped into Harry's boat, and they at once pushed off.

The river was running smoothly here, and Harry said, "Directly we get down a little way we will turn the boat's head up stream and practise for a bit. It would never do to get down into rough water before we can use the paddles fairly."

Tom sat in the bow of his boat, Hunting Dog was next to him, then came the chief, and Harry sat in the stern. A paddle is a much easier implement to manage for a beginner than is an oar, and it was not long before they found that they could propel the boats at a fair rate. In a short time they had passed the end of the shelf at the mouth of the cañon, and the cliffs on that side rose as abruptly as they did on the other. The river was some eighty yards wide.

"We will turn here," Harry said, "and paddle up. We sha'n't do more than keep abreast of these rocks now, for the stream runs fast though it is so smooth."

They found, indeed, that they had to work hard to hold their position.

"Now, Tom," Harry sang out, "it is you and I do the steering, you know. When you want the head to go to the right you must work your paddle out from the boat, when you want to go to the left you must dip it in the water rather farther out and draw it towards the boat. Of course when you have got the paddle the other side you must do just the contrary. You must sing out right or left according as you see rocks ahead, and I shall steer with my paddle behind. I have a good deal more power over the boat than you have, and you must depend upon me for the steering, unless there is occasion for a smart swerve."

At first the two boats shot backwards and forwards across the stream in a very erratic way, but after an hour's practice the steersmen found the amount of force required. An hour later Harry thought that they were competent to make a start, and turning they shot rapidly past the cliffs. In a couple of miles there was a break in the rocks to the left.

"We will land there," Harry said. "There are trees near the water and bushes farther up. We will make a camp there. There is no saying how far we may have to go before we get another opportunity. We have done with the Utes for good, and can get a sound night's sleep. If you, chief, will start with Hunting Dog as soon as we land, we will get the things ashore and light the fire. Maybe you will be able to get a bear for us."

They did not trouble to haul up the canoes, but fastened them by the head-ropes, which were made from lariats, to trees on the shore.

Daylight was beginning to fade as they lighted the fire. No time was lost before mixing the dough, and it was in readiness by the time that there were sufficient glowing embers to stand the pot in. The kettle was filled and hung on a tripod over the fire. In a short time the Indians returned empty-handed.

"No find bear," the chief said, "getting too dark to hunt. To-morrow morning try."

Harry got up and went to the boats, and returned directly with a joint of meat. Tom looked up in surprise.

"It is not from yours, Tom," Jerry said as he saw him looking at it. "We took the hind-quarters of the four pack-ponies, but left the others alone. It was no use bringing more, for it would not keep."

"So it is horseflesh!" Tom rather shrank from the idea of eating it, and nothing would have induced him to touch it had he thought that it came from his own favourite. Some steaks were cut and placed in the frying-pan, while strips were hung over the fire for those who preferred the meat in that way. Tom felt strongly inclined to refuse altogether, but when he saw that the others took their meat as a matter of course, and proceeded to eat with a good appetite, he did not like to do so. He hesitated, however, before tasting it; but Harry said with a laugh, "Fire away, Tom. You can hardly tell it from beef, and they say that in Paris lots of horseflesh is sold as beef."

Thus encouraged, Tom took a mouthful, and found it by no means bad, for from their long stay in the valley the animals were all in excellent condition, and he acknowledged to himself that he would not have known the flesh from beef.

"I call it mighty good for a change," Jerry said. "Out on the plains, where one can get buffalo, one would not take horse for choice, but as we have been eating deer and bear meat for about a year, horse-meat ain't bad by no means. What! You won't take another bit, Tom?"

"Not to-night, Jerry; next time I shall be all right. But it is my first trial, you know, and though I can't say it is not good, it gives me a queer feeling, so I will stick to the bread."

"Well, boys," Harry said presently, "we have made a first-rate start, and have got out of a big scrape, easier than I ever looked for. We could not have got two better canoes for our work if we had had them brought special from Canada, and it seems to me that they ought to go down pretty near anywhere without much damage. We shall get real handy with our paddles in two or three days, and I hope we sha'n't meet with any big rapids until we have got into the way of managing them well."

"You bet, Harry, we have got out well," said Jerry. "I tell you it looked downright ugly, and I wouldn't have given a continental for our chances. As for the rapids, I guess we shall generally find rocks one side or the other where we can make our way along, and we can let down the canoes by the ropes. Anyhow, we need not get skeery over them. After getting out of that valley with our hair on, the thought of them does not trouble me a cent."

Chapter XVI.
Afloat in Canoes

The two Indians were off long before daylight, and just as the others were having a wash at the edge of the river they heard the crack of a rifle some distance up the cliff.

"Bear!" Jerry exclaimed; "and I reckon they have got it, else we should have hard another shot directly afterwards. That will set us up in food for some time. Get the fire made up, Tom, you won't have to eat horse steak for breakfast unless you like."

The Indians returned half an hour later laden with as much bear-flesh as they could carry.

"I vote we stop here for two days," Harry said. "We have got a lot of meat now, but it won't keep for twenty-four hours in this heat, so I vote we cut it up and dry it as the Indians do buffalo-meat; it will keep any time. Besides, we deserve a couple of days' rest, and we can practise paddling while the meat dries. We got on very well yesterday, but I do want us to get quite at home in the boats before we get to a bad bit."

The proposal was agreed to, and as soon as breakfast was over the whole of the meat was cut up into thin slices and hung up on cords fastened from tree to tree.

"It ought to take three days to do it properly, and four is better," Harry said. "Still, as we have cut it very thin, I should think two days in this hot sun ought to be enough."

"Are there any fish in the river, uncle?"

"I have no doubt there are, Tom, grists of them, but we have got no hooks."

"Jerry has got some, he told me he never travelled without them, and we caught a lot of fish with them up in the mountains just after we started before. I don't know about line, but one might unravel one of the ropes."

"I think you might do better than that, Tom. The next small animal we shoot we might make some lines from the gut. They needn't be above five or six feet long. Beyond that we could cut a strip of thirty or forty feet long from one of the hides. However, we can do nothing at present in that way. Now let us get into the canoes and have a couple of hours' paddling. After dinner we will have another good spell at the work."

By evening there was a marked improvement in the paddling over that of the previous day, and after having had another day's practice all felt confident that they should get on very well. By nightfall on the second day, the meat was found to be thoroughly dried, and was taken down and packed in bundles, and the next morning they started as soon as it was light. It was agreed that the boats should follow each other at a distance of a hundred yards, so that the leader could signal to the one behind if serious difficulties were made out ahead, and so enable it to row to the bank in time. Were both drawn together into the suck of a dangerous rapid they might find themselves without either boats or stores, whereas if only one of the boats was broken up, there would be the other to fall back upon. Harry's boat was to take the lead on the first day, and Tom, as he knelt in the bows, felt his heart beat with excitement at the thought of the unknown that lay before them, and that they were about to make their way down passes probably unpenetrated by man. Passing between what had seemed to them the entrance to a narrow canon, they were surprised to find the river widen out. On their right a great sweep of hills bent round like a vast amphitheatre, the resemblance being heightened by the ledges running in regular lines along it, the cliff being far from perpendicular.

"I should think one could climb up there," Tom said, half-turning round to his uncle.

"It looks like it, Tom, but there is no saying; some of those steps may be a good deal steeper than they look. However, I have no doubt one could find places where it would be possible to climb if there were any use in doing so, but as we should only find ourselves up on bad lands we should gain nothing by it."

"I don't mean we should want to climb up now, uncle; but it seemed a sort of satisfaction to know that there are places where one could climb in case we got the boats smashed up."

"If we had to make our way up, lad, it would be much better to go by one of the lateral canons like the one we came down by. I can see at least half a dozen of them going up there. We should certainly find water, and we might find game, but up on the plateau we should find neither one nor the other."

On the left-hand bank of the river the cliffs fell still farther back in wide terraces, that rose one behind the other up to a perpendicular cliff half a mile back from the river. There was a shade of green here and there, and the chief pointed far up the hill and exclaimed "Deer!"

"That is good," Harry said. "There are sure to be more of these places, and I should think we are not likely to starve anyhow. We can't spare time to stop now; we want to have a long day's paddle to see what it is going to be like, and we have got meat enough for the present. If we happen to see a deer within rifle-shot, so that we can get at him without much loss of time, we will stop, for after all fresh meat is better eating than dry."

"I should think it would be, uncle," Tom said. "From the look of the stuff I should think it would be quite as tough as shoe leather and as tasteless."

"It needs a set of sharp teeth, Tom, but if you are hard set I have no doubt you will be able to get through it, and at any rate it constitutes the chief food of the Indians between the Missouri and the Rockies."

For the next three hours they paddled along on the quiet surface of the river. The other canoe had drawn up, since it was evident that here at least there was no reason why they should keep apart.

"I didn't expect we should find it as quiet as this, Harry," Jerry Curtis said. "It is a regular water-party, and I should not mind how long I was at it if it were all like this."

"We shall have rough water enough presently, Jerry, and I expect we shall look back on this as the pleasantest part of the trip. It seems to me that the hills close in more towards the end of this sweep. It has made a regular horseshoe."

"I reckon it depends upon the nature of the rock," Ben put in.

"That is it, you may be sure, Ben. Wherever it is soft rock, in time it crumbles away like this; where it is hard the weather don't affect it much, and we get straight cliffs. I expect it is there we shall find the rapids worst. Well, we shall soon make a trial of them, I fancy. It looks like a wall ahead, but the road must go through somewhere."

A quarter of an hour later Harry said: "You had better drop back now, Jerry, there is the gap right ahead. If you see me hold up my paddle you row ashore. When we come to a bad rapid we had better all get out, and make our way down on the rocks as far as we can, to see what it is like. It will never do to go at it blind. Of course we may find places where the water comes to the wall faces on both sides, and then there is nothing to do but to take our chance, but I don't propose to run any risks that I can avoid."

There was a perceptible increase in the rate of the current as they neared the gorge, and when they came within a short distance of it Harry gave the signal to the boat behind, and both canoes made for the shore. As they stepped out on to the rocks the chief pointed to a ledge far above them. "There will be time for Hunting Dog to shoot a deer," he said, "while we go down to see canon."

Tom in vain endeavoured to make out the object at which the Indian was pointing. Hunting Dog had evidently noticed it before landing, and upon Harry giving a nod of assent, started off with his rifle. The others waited until Jerry and his companions joined them, and then started along the rocks that had fallen at the foot of the cliffs. They were soon able to obtain a far better view of the gorge than they had done from the canoe. The river ran for a bit in a smooth glassy flood, but a short distance down, it began to form into waves, and beyond that they could see a mass of white foam and breakers. They made their way along the rocks for nearly two miles. It seemed well-nigh impossible to Tom that the boats could go down without being swamped, for the waves were eight or ten feet high, with steep sides capped with white. At last the gorge widened again, and although the cliff to the right rose perpendicularly, on the other side it became less steep, and seemed lower down to assume the same character as that above the gorge.

"It looks pretty bad," Harry said, speaking for almost the first time since they had started, for the roar of the water against the rocks, echoed and re-echoed by the cliffs, rendered conversation an impossibility. "It looks bad, but as far as I can see there are no rocks that come up near the surface, and the canoes ought to go through the broken water safely enough."

"It is an all-fired nasty-looking place," Jerry said; "but I have heard men who had been in the north talk about rapids they had gone through, and from what they said about them they must have been worse than this. We have got to keep as near the side as we can; the waves ain't as high there as they are in the middle, and we have got to keep the boat's head straight, and to paddle all we know. If we do that, I reckon the canoes will go through."

They retraced their steps up the gorge. Hunting Dog was standing by the boat with the dead deer at his feet. Jerry picked it up. "I had better take this, I reckon, Harry. You have got one man more than we have;" and he and his two companions went on to their boat.

"Now, what do you think, Tom?" his uncle said. "Can you trust your head to keep cool? It will need a lot of nerve, I can tell you, and if her head swerves in the slightest she will swing round, and over she will go, and it would want some tall swimming to get out of that race. You paddle as well as the chief,—better, I think,—but the chief's nerves are like iron. He has not been practising steering as you have, but as there seem to be no rocks about, that won't matter so much. I ought to be able to keep her straight, if you three paddle hard. It may need a turn of the paddle now and then in the bow, but that we can't tell. So it shall be just as you like, lad. If you think your nerves can stand it you take your usual place, but if you have doubts about it, it were best to let the chief go there."

"I think I could stand it, uncle, for I have been out in wherries in some precious rough seas at Spithead; but I think it would be best for the chief to take my place this time, and then I shall see how I feel."

Harry said a few words to the chief in his own language, and Leaping Horse without a word stepped into the bow, while Tom took the seat behind him.

"We sha'n't be long going down," Harry said. "I reckon the stream is running ten miles an hour, and as we shall be paddling, it will take us through in ten minutes. We had all better sit farther aft, so as to take her bow right out of water. She will go through it ever so much easier so."

They shifted their seats until daylight could be seen under the keel a foot from the bow.

"I think that is about the right trim," Harry said. "Now paddle all."

The boat shot off from the shore. A minute later it darted into the gorge, the Indian setting a long sweeping stroke. There were two or three long heaves, and then they dashed into the race. Tom held his breath at the first wall of water, but, buoyant and lightly laden as the canoe was, with fully a foot of free board, she rose like a feather over it, and darted down into the hollow beyond. Tom kept his eyes fixed on the back of the chief's head, clinched his teeth tightly, and paddled away with all his strength. He felt that were he to look round he should turn giddy at the turmoil of water. Once or twice he was vaguely conscious of Harry's shouts, "Keep her head in-shore!" or "A little farther out!" but like a man rowing a race he heeded the words but little. His faculties were concentrated on his work, but he could see a slight swerve of the Indian's body when he was obeying an order.

He was not conscious of any change of motion, either in the boat or in the water round, when Harry shouted, "Easy all!" and even then it was the chief's ceasing to paddle rather than Harry's shout which caused him to stop. Then he looked round and saw that the race was passed, and that the canoe was floating in comparatively quiet water.

"She is a daisy!" Harry shouted; "we could not do better if we had been all Canadian half-breeds, chief. Now, we had better set to and bale her out as quickly as we can."

Tom now for the first time perceived that he was kneeling in water, and that the boat was nearly half-full.

Their tea pannikins had been laid by their sides in readiness, and Hunting Dog touched him and passed forward his tin and the chief's, both of which had been swept aft. The Seneca at once began to throw out the water, but Tom for a minute or two was unable to follow his example. He felt as weak as a child. A nervous quivering ran through his body, and his hand trembled so that he could not grasp the handle of the tin.

"Feel bad, Tom?" his uncle asked cheerily from behind. "Brace up, lad; it was a pretty warm ten minutes, and I am not surprised you feel it. Now it is over I am a little shaky myself."

"I shall be all right presently, uncle." A look at the chief's back did more to steady Tom's nerves than his own efforts. While he himself was panting heavily, and was bathed in perspiration, the chief's breath came so quietly that he could scarce see his shoulders rise and fall, as he baled out the water with perfect unconcern. With an effort the boy took hold of his dipper, and by the time the boat was empty his nerves were gaining their steadiness, though his breath still came quickly. As he laid down his tin he looked round.

"Heap water," Hunting Dog said with a smile; "run like herd of buffalo."

The other boat lay twenty yards behind them, and was also engaged in baling.

"All right now, Tom?"

"All right, uncle; but it is lucky you put the chief in the bows. I should have made a mess of it; for from the time we got into the waves it seemed nothing but confusion, and though I heard your voice I did not seem to understand what you said."

"It was a trial to the nerves, Tom, but we shall all get accustomed to it before we get through. Well, thank God, we have made our first run safely. Now paddle on, we will stop at the first likely place and have a meal."

A mile farther they saw a pile of drift-wood on the left bank, and Harry at once headed the canoe to it, and drawing the boat carefully alongside they got out. A minute later the other canoe joined them.

"Jee-hoshaphat, Harry!" Jerry exclaimed as he stepped out; "that was worse nor a cyclone. I would rather sit on the back of the worst kind of bucker than jump over those waves again. If we are going to have much of this I should say let us find our way back and ask the Utes to finish us off."

"It was a rough bit, Jerry; but it might have been a deal worse if there had been rocks in the stream. All we had to do was to keep her straight and paddle."

"And a pretty big all, too," Jerry grumbled. "I felt skeered pretty nigh out of my wits, and the other two allow they were just as bad. If it hadn't been for your boat ahead I reckon we should never have gone through it, but as long as you kept on straight, there didn't seem any reason why we shouldn't. I tell you I feel so shaky that if there were a grizzly twenty yards off I am blamed if I could keep the muzzle of my rifle on it."

Tom had been feeling a good deal ashamed of his nervousness, and was much relieved at hearing that these seasoned men had felt somewhat the same as he had done.

"What do you say, boys," Harry asked when breakfast had been cooked and eaten, "if we stop here for to-day? Likely enough we may get some game, and if not it won't matter, for the deer will last us a couple of days."

"You bet," Ben Gulston said; "I think we have had enough of the water for to-day. I don't feel quite sure now I ain't going round and round, and I don't think any of us will feel right till we have had a night's sleep. Besides, all the rugs and blankets are wet and want spreading out in the sun for a bit, and the flour will want overhauling."

"That settles it, Ben; let us get all the outfit out of the boats at once."

After the things had been laid out to dry the two Indians went off in search of game; but none of the others felt any inclination to move, and they spent the rest of the day lying about smoking and dozing. The Indians brought back a big-horn, and the next morning the canoes dropped down the stream again. For some miles the river flowed quietly along a wide valley. At the end of that time it made an abrupt turn and entered the heart of the mountains. As before, Harry's canoe went in advance. The canon was here a deep gloomy chasm, with almost perpendicular sides, and for some distance the river ran swiftly and smoothly, then white water was seen ahead, so the two boats rowed in to the rocks at the foot of the precipice, and the occupants proceeded to explore the pass ahead. It was of a different character to the last. Black rocks rose everywhere above the surface, and among these the river flowed with extraordinary force and rapidity, foaming and roaring.

All agreed that it was madness to think of descending here, and that a portage was necessary. The contents of the boats were lifted out, and then one of them was carried down over the rocks by the united strength of the party. They had gone half a mile when they came to a spot where they could go no farther, as the water rushed along against the rock wall itself. Some fifty yards further down they could see that the ledge again began.

"We must go and fetch the other boat," Harry shouted above the din of the water, "and let them down one by one. There is no other way to do it."

The second boat was brought down, and another journey was made to bring down the stores. The lariats were then tied together.

"Let us sit down and smoke a pipe before we do anything more," Jerry said. "Three times up and down them rocks is worse nor thirty miles on a level."

All were glad to adopt this suggestion, and for half an hour they sat watching the rushing waters. As they did so they discussed how they had better divide their forces, and agreed that Harry's boat should, as before, go down first. Three men would be required to let the boat down, and it would need at least four to check the second boat when it came abreast of them. Although all felt certain that a single line of the plaited hide would be sufficient, they determined to use two lines to ensure themselves against risk.

"I should let them run out fast at first, Jerry, only keeping enough strain on them to keep her head well up stream. Begin to check her gradually, and let her down only inch by inch. When you see we are close to the rocks, hold her there while we get her alongside, and don't leave go till we lift her from the water. Directly we are out, fasten the ropes to the bow of your canoe, then launch her carefully; and whatever you do, don't let go of the rope. Launch her stern first close to the wall, then two get in and get well towards the stern, while the other holds the rope until the last moment. Then those two in the boat must begin to paddle as hard as they can, while the last man jumps in and snatches up his paddle. Keep her head close to the wall, for if the current catches it and takes her round she would capsize in a moment against those rocks. Paddle all you know; we shall haul in the rope as fast as you come down. When you come abreast two of us will check her, and the others will be on the rocks to catch hold of her side as she swings in."

The first canoe was launched stern foremost, the four men took their seats in her and began to paddle against the stream with all their strength, while Jerry and his companions let the lines run through their fingers. The boat glanced along by the side of the wall. The men above put on more and more strain, giving a turn of the ropes round a smooth water-worn rock they had before picked out as suitable for the purpose. The water surged against the bow of the canoe, lifting it higher and higher as the full strain of the rope came upon it. The chief was kneeling in the stern facing the rocks below, and as the canoe came abreast of them he brought her in alongside. Harry held up his paddle, the men above gave another turn of the ropes round the rock, and the canoe remained stationary. Hunting Dog sprang out on to the rocks, and taking hold of the blade of the chief's paddle, brought the canoe in so close that the others were able to step ashore without difficulty. The baggage was taken out, and the canoe lifted from the water, turned upside down, and laid on the rocks.

Harry held up his hand to show that they were ready, having before he did so chosen a stone round which to wind the lariats. The other boat was then launched. Sam and Ben took their places astern and began to paddle against the stream. As they were in the back-water below the ledge of rock they were able to keep her stationary while Jerry took his place and got out his paddle. When all were ready, they paddled her out from the back-water. As soon as the current caught her she flew past the cliff like an arrow, although the three men were now paddling at the top of their speed. Harry and the chief pulled in the rope hand over hand, while Hunting Dog and Tom went a short way down the rocks.

"Don't check her too suddenly, chief," Harry shouted. "Let the rope run out easy at first and bring the strain on gradually."

"The ropes will hold," the chief said. "One stop buffalo in gallop, two stop boat."

"Yes, but you would pull the head out of the canoe, chief, if you stopped her too suddenly."

The chief nodded. He had not thought of that. In spite of the efforts of the oarsmen the canoe's head was swerving across the stream just as she came abreast of them. A moment later she felt the check of the rope.

"Easy, chief, easy!" Harry shouted, as the water shot up high over the bow of the canoe. "Wait till she gets a bit lower or we shall capsize her."

The check of the bow had caused the stern to swerve out, and when they again checked her she was several lengths below them with her head inclined to shore. More and more strain was put on the ropes, until they were as taut as iron bars. A moment later Tom and Hunting Dog seized two paddles held out to them, and the boat came gently in alongside.

"Gosh!" Ben exclaimed, as he stepped ashore, "it has taken as much out of me as working a windlass for a day. I am blamed if I did not think the hull boat was coming to pieces. I thought it was all over with us for sure, Harry; when she first felt the rope, the water came in right over the side."

"It was touch and go, Ben; but there was a rock just outside you, and if we had not checked her a bit her head would have gone across it, and if it had, I would not have given a red cent for your lives."

All day they toiled on foot, and by nightfall had made but four miles. Then they camped for the night among the rocks. The next four days were passed in similar labour. Two or three times they had to cross the torrent in order to get on to fallen rocks on the other side to that which they were following. These passages demanded the greatest caution. In each case there were rocks showing above water in the middle of the channel. One of these was chosen as most suited to their purpose, and by means of the ropes a canoe was sheered out to it. Its occupants then took their places on the rock, and in turn dropped the other boat down to the next suitable point, the process being repeated, step by step, until the opposite bank was reached.

At the end of the fourth day the geological formation changed. The rock was softer, and the stream had worn a more even path for itself, and they decided to take to the boats again. There was no occasion for paddling now, it was only when a swell on the surface marked some hidden danger below that a stroke or two of the paddle was needed to sweep them clear of it. For four hours they were carried along at the rate of fully twelve miles an hour, and at the end of that time they shot out from between the overhanging walls into a comparatively broad valley. With a shout of delight they headed the boats for shore, and leapt out on to a flat rock a few inches above the water.

"If we could go on at that pace right down we should not be long before we were out of the mountains," Tom said.

"We could do with a bit slower, Tom; that is too fast to be pleasant. Just about half that would do—six miles an hour. Twelve hours a day would take us out of the canons in a fortnight or so. We might do that safely, but we could not calculate on having such good luck as we have had to-day, when going along at twelve miles an hour. The pace for the last four days has been just as much too slow as this is too fast. Four miles a day working from morning till night is heart-breaking. In spite of our run to-day, we cannot have made much over a hundred miles since we started. Well, there is one comfort, we are in no great hurry. We have got just the boats for the work, and so far as we can see, we are likely to find plenty of food. A job like this isn't to be reckoned child's play. So far I consider we have had good luck; I shall be well content if it averages as well all the way down. The fear is we may get to falls where we can neither carry nor let the boats down. In that case we should have to get out of the canon somewhere, pack as much flour as we could carry, and make our way across country, though how far we might have to travel there is no knowing. I hope it mayn't come to that; but at any rate I would rather go through even worse places than that canon above than have to quit the boats."

"Right you are, Harry," Jerry agreed. "I would rather tote the canoe on my back all the way down to Mexico, than have to try and make my way over the bad lands to the hills. Besides, when we get a bit farther we shall be in the Navahoe country, and the Utes ain't a sarcumstance to them. The Ute ain't much of a fighter anyway. He will kill white men he finds up in his hills, 'cause he don't want white men there, but he has to be five or six to one before he will attack him. The Navahoe kills the white man 'cause he is a white man, and 'cause he likes killing. He is a fighter, and don't you forget it. If it had been Navahoes instead of Utes that had caught us up in the hills, you may bet your bottom dollar our scalps would be drying in their lodges now."

"That is so, Jerry," Ben put in. "Besides, the Navahoes and the Apaches have got no fear of white men. They have been raiding Mexico for hundreds of years, and man to man they can whip Mexikins out of their boots. I don't say as they haven't a considerable respect for western hunters; they have had a good many lessons that these can out-shoot them and out-fight them; still they ain't scared of them as plain Indians are. They are a bad lot, look at them which way you will, and I don't want to have to tramp across their country noways. It was pretty hard work carrying that boat along them rocks, but I would rather have to do so, right down to the plains, then get into a muss with the Navahoes."

"How far does the Navahoe country come this way?"

"There ain't no fence, Tom, I expect. They reckon as it's their country just as far as they like to come. They don't come up as far north as this, but where they ends and where the Utes begin no one knows but themselves; and I reckon it shifts according as the Navahoes are busy with the Mexicans in the south, or have got a quiet spell, and take it into their heads to hunt this way."

For many days they continued their journey, sometimes floating quietly along a comparatively wide valley, sometimes carrying their boats past dangerous rapids, sometimes rushing along at great speed on the black, deep water, occasionally meeting with falls where everything had to be taken out of the canoes, and the boats themselves allowed to shoot over the falls with long ropes attached, by which they were drawn to shore lower down. It was seldom that they were without meat, as several big-horns and two bears were shot by the Indians. They had no doubt that they could have caught fish, but as a rule they were too tired when they arrived at their halting-place to do more than cook and eat their suppers before they lay down to rest.

"I reckon it won't be very long before we come upon a Mexican village," Harry said one day, after they had been six weeks on their downward course. "I have heard there is one above the Grand Cañon."

The scenery had varied greatly. In some of the valleys groves of trees bordered the river; sometimes not even a tuft of grass was to be seen. Occasionally the cliffs ran in an even line for many miles, showing that the country beyond was a level plateau, at other times rugged peaks and pinnacles resembling ruined castles, lighthouses, and churches could be seen. Frequently the cliffs rose three or four thousand feet in an almost unbroken line, but more often there were rounded terraces, where it would have been easy to ascend to the upper level. Everywhere the various strata were of different colours: soft grays and browns, orange, vermilion, purple, green, and yellow. They soon learned that when they passed through soft strata, the river ran quietly; where the rocks were hard there were falls and rapids; where the strata lay horizontal the stream ran smoothly, though often with great rapidity; where they dipped up stream there were dangerous rapids and falls.

Since the start the river had been largely swollen by the junctions of other streams, and was much wider and deeper than it had been where they embarked; and even where the rapids were fiercest they generally found comparatively quiet water close to the bank on one side or the other. Twice they had had upsets, both the boats having been capsized by striking upon rocks but an inch or two below the surface of the water. Little harm was done, for the guns and all other valuable articles were lashed to the sides of the boats, while strips of hide, zigzagged across the ends of the canoes at short distances apart, prevented the blankets and rugs and other bulky articles from dropping out when the boat capsized.

Since the river had become wider and the dangers less frequent, the boats always kept near each other. Upsets were therefore only the occasion for a hearty laugh; for it took but a few minutes to right the canoe, bale it out, and proceed on their way. Occasionally they had unpleasant visitors at their camp, and altogether they killed ten or twelve rattle-snakes. In some of the valleys they found the remains of the dwellings of a people far anterior to the present Indian races. Some of these ruins appeared to have been communal houses. At other points they saw cliff-dwellings in the face of the rock, with rough sculptures and hieroglyphics. The canons varied in length from ten to a hundred and fifty miles, the comparatively flat country between them varying equally in point of appearance and in the nature of the rocks. As they got lower they once or twice saw roughly-made rafts, composed of three or four logs of wood, showing where Indians had crossed the river. The journey so far had been much more pleasant than they had expected, for as the river grew wider the dangers were fewer and farther apart, and more easily avoided; and they looked forward to the descent of the Grand Canon, from which they knew they could not be far distant, without much fear that it would prove impracticable.

Chapter XVII.
The Grand Canon

Passing from a short canon, the boats emerged into a valley with flat shores for some distance from the river. On the right was a wide side canon, which might afford a passage up into the hills. Half a mile lower down there were trees and signs of cultivation; and a light smoke rose among them. At this, the first sign of human life they had seen since they took to the boats, all hands paddled rapidly. They were approaching the shore, when Leaping Horse said to Harry: "No go close. Stop in river and see, perhaps bad Indians. Leaping Horse not like smoke."

Harry called to the other canoe, and they bore out into the stream again. The chief stood up in the boat, and after gazing at the shore silently for a moment said:

"Village burnt. Burnt little time ago, post still burning." As he resumed his seat Harry stood up in turn.

"That is so, chief. There have only been five or six huts; whether Indian or white, one can't tell now."

Just at this moment an Indian appeared on the bank. As his eye fell on the boats he started. A moment later he raised a war-yell.

"Navahoe," the chief said. "Navahoe war-party come down, kill people and burn village. Must row hard."

The yell had been answered from the wood, and in two or three minutes as many score of Indians appeared on the banks. They shouted to the boats to come to shore, and as no attention was paid, some of them at once opened fire. The river was about a quarter of a mile wide, and although the shots splashed round them the boats were not long in reaching the farther bank, but not unharmed, for Ben had dropped his paddle and fallen back in the boat.

"Is he badly hurt?" Harry asked anxiously, as the canoes drew alongside each other near the bank, and Sam turned round to look at his comrade.

"He has finished his journey," Sam said in a hoarse voice. "He has gone down, and a better mate and a truer heart I never met. The ball has hit him in the middle of the forehead. It were to be, I guess, for it could only have been a chance shot at that distance."

Exclamations of sorrow and fury broke from the others, and for a few minutes there was no thought of the Indians, whose bullets were still falling in the water, for the most part short of the boats. A sharp tap on the side of Harry's canoe, followed by a jet of water, roused them.

"We mustn't stop here," Harry said, as Hunting Dog plugged the hole with a piece of dried meat, "or poor Ben won't be the only one."

"Let us have a shot first," Jerry said. "Young Tom, do you take a shot with Plumb-centre. It is about four hundred and fifty yards as near as I can reckon, and she will carry pretty true that distance."

"We will give them a shot all round," Harry said, as he took up his rifle.

Six shots were discharged almost at the same moment. One of the Indians was seen to fall, the rest bounded away to a short distance from the bank. Then Hunting Dog at a word from the chief stepped into the other canoe. Keeping close under the bank they paddled down. The Indians had ceased firing, and had disappeared at a run.

"What are they up to now, chief?"

"Going down to mouth of canon, river sure to be narrow; get there before us."

"Wait, Jerry," Harry shouted to the other boat, which was some twenty yards ahead. "The chief thinks they have gone to cut us off at the head of the canon, which is likely enough. I don't suppose it is fifty yards wide there, and they will riddle us if we try to get through in daylight. We had better stop and have a meal and talk it over."

The boats were rowed ashore, and the men landed and proceeded to light a fire as unconcernedly as if no danger threatened them. Ben's death had cast a heavy gloom over them, and but few words were spoken, until the meal was cooked and eaten.

"It is a dog-goned bad business," Jerry said. "I don't say at night as we mayn't get past them without being hit, but to go rushing into one of those canons in the dark would be as bad as standing their fire, if not wuss. The question is—could we leave the boats and strike across?"

"We could not strike across this side anyhow," Harry said. "There are no settlements west of the Colorado. We know nothing of the country, and it is a hundred to one we should all die of thirst even if we could carry enough grub to last us. If we land at all it must be on the other side, and then we could not reckon on striking a settlement short of two hundred miles, and two hundred miles across a country like this would be almost certain death."

"As the Navahoes must have ridden down, Harry, there must be water. I reckon they came down that canon opposite."

"Navahoe on track in morning," the chief said quietly. "When they see we not go down river look for boat, find where we land and take up trail. Canon very plain road. Some go up there straight, take all our scalps."

No one spoke for a moment or two. What the Seneca said was so evident to them that it was useless to argue. "Well, chief, what do you advise yourself?" Harry asked at length.

"Not possible go on foot, Harry. Country all rocks and canons; cannot get through, cannot get water. Trouble with Navahoes too. Only chance get down in boat to-night. Keep close under this bank; perhaps Indians not see us, night dark."

"Do you think they can cross over to this side?"

"Yes, got canoe. Two canoes in village, Leaping Horse saw them on bank. When it gets dark, cross over."

"We will get a start of them," Harry said. "Directly it is dark we can be off too. The shore is everywhere higher than our heads as we sit in the canoes, and we can paddle in the shadow without being seen by them on the other side, while they won't venture to cross till it is pitch dark.

As the stream runs something like three miles an hour, I reckon that they are hardly likely to catch us. As for the rapids, they don't often begin until you are some little distance in. At any rate we shall not have to go far, for the red-skins will not dare to enter the cañon, so we can tie up till morning as soon as we are a short distance in. We have got to run the gauntlet of their fire, but after all that is better than taking our chances by leaving the boats. If we lie down when we get near them they may not see us at all; but if they do, a very few strokes will send us past them. At any rate there seems less risk in that plan than in any other."

The others agreed.

"Now, boys, let us dig a grave," he went on, as soon as the point was settled. "It is a sort of clay here and we can manage it, and it is not likely we shall find any place, when we are once in the cañon, where we can do it." They had neither picks nor shovels with them, for their mining tools had been left at the spot where they were at work, but with their axes and knives they dug a shallow grave, laid Ben's body in it, covered it up, and then rolled a number of boulders over it.

Ben's death affected Tom greatly. They had lived together and gone through many perils and risks for nearly a year, and none had shown more unflagging good-humour throughout than the man who had been killed. That the boats might upset and all might perish together, was a thought that had often occurred to him as they made their way down the river, but that one should be cut off like this had never once been contemplated by him. Their lives from the hour they met on the Big Wind River had seemed bound up together, and this sudden loss of one of the party affected him greatly. The others went about their work silently and sadly, but they had been so accustomed to see life lost in sudden frays, and in one or other of the many dangers that miners and hunters are exposed to, that it did not affect them to the same extent as it did Tom.

Except two or three men who remained on watch on the opposite bank, though carefully keeping out of rifle-range, they saw no signs of the Navahoes during the day. As soon as it became so dark that they were sure their movements could not be seen from the other side, they silently took their places in the boats, and pushed off into the current. For a quarter of an hour they lay in the canoes, then at a signal from Harry knelt up, took their paddles and began to row very quietly and cautiously, the necessity for dropping their paddles noiselessly into the water and for avoiding any splashing having been impressed on all before starting.

"There is no occasion for haste," Harry said. "Long and gentle strokes of the paddle will take us down as fast as we need go. If those fellows do cross over, as I expect they will, they will find it difficult to travel over the rocks in the dark as fast as we are going now, and there is no fear whatever of their catching us if we go on steadily."

After an hour's rowing they could make out a dark mass rising like a wall in front of them, and Harry passed the word back to the other canoe, which was just behind them, that they should now cease paddling, only giving a stroke occasionally to keep the head of the canoe straight, and to prevent the boat from drifting out from under the shelter of the bank. In the stillness of the night they could hear a low roaring, and knew that it was caused by a rapid in the canon ahead. Higher and higher rose the wall of rock, blotting out the stars in front of them till the darkness seemed to spread half-way over the sky.

They could see that the boat was passing the shore more rapidly, as the river accelerated its course before rushing into the gorge. Suddenly there was a shout on the right, so close that Tom was startled, then there was a rifle-shot, and a moment later a wild outburst of yells and a dozen other shots. At the first shout the paddles dipped into the water, and at racing speed the boats shot along. Eight or ten more rifle-shots were fired, each farther behind them.

"Anyone hurt?" Harry asked.

There was a general negative.

"I don't believe they really saw us," Harry said. "The first fellow may have caught sight of us, but I expect the others merely fired at random. Now let us row in and fasten up, for judging from that roaring there must be a big rapid close ahead."

The boats were soon fastened up against the rocks, and the chief stepped ashore, saying:

"Leaping Horse and Hunting Dog will watch. Navahoes may come down here. Don't think they will be brave enough to enter canon, too dark to see. Still, better watch."

"Just as you like, chief," Harry said, "but I have no belief that they will come down here in the dark; it would be as much as they would dare do in broad daylight. Besides, these rocks are steepish climbing anyway, and I should not like myself to try to get over them, when it is so dark that I can't see my own hand, except by putting it up between my eyes and the stars."

"If it was not for that," Jerry said, "I would crawl along to the mouth and see if I couldn't get a shot at them varmint on the other side."

"You would not find them there, Jerry. You may be sure that when they saw us go through they would know it was of no use waiting there any longer. They would flatter themselves that they had hit some of us, and even if they hadn't, it would not seem to matter a cent to them, as the evil spirit of the canon would surely swallow us up."

"Well, they have been wrong in their first supposition, uncle," Tom said, "and I hope they will be equally wrong in the second."

"I hope so, Tom. Now we may as well go to sleep. As soon as there is any light we must explore as far as we can go, for by the noise ahead it must be either a fall or a desperately bad rapid."

When daylight broke, the whites found Hunting Dog sitting with his rifle across his knees on a rock above them.

"Where is the chief?" Harry asked him.

"Leaping Horse went up the rocks to see if Navahoes have gone."

"Very well. Tell him when he comes back we have gone down to have a look at the rapid. Tom, you may as well stay here. There is plenty of drift-wood among those rocks, and we will breakfast before we start down. I reckon we shall not have much time for anything of that sort after we are once off."

Tom was by no means sorry to be saved a heavy climb. He collected some wood and broke it up into suitable pieces, but at the suggestion of Hunting Dog waited for the chief's return before lighting it. The chief came down in a few minutes.

"Navahoes all gone," he said briefly. "Then I can light a fire, chief?"

Leaping Horse nodded, and Tom took out the tightly-fitting tin box in which he kept his matches. Each of the party carried a box, and to secure against the possibility of the matches being injured by the water in case of a capsize, the boxes were kept in deer's bladders tightly tied at the mouth. The fire was just alight when the others returned.

"It is better ahead than we expected," Harry said; "the noise was caused by the echo from the smooth faces of the rocks. It is lucky we hauled in here last night, for these rocks end fifty yards on, and as far as we can see down, the water washes the foot of the wall on both sides. We were able to climb up from them on to a narrow ledge, parallel with the water, and went on to the next turn, but there was no change in the character of the river. So we shall make a fair start anyway."

More wood was put on the fire, and in a quarter of an hour the kettle was boiling and slices of meat cooked. Half an hour later they took their places in the canoes and started. The canon was similar to the one they had last passed; the walls were steep and high, but with irregular shelves running along them. Above these were steep slopes, running up to the foot of smooth perpendicular cliffs of limestone. The stream was very rapid, and they calculated that in the first half-hour they must have run six miles. Here the walls receded to a distance, and ledges of rock and hills of considerable heights intervened between the river and the cliffs. They checked the pace of their canoes just as they reached this opening, for a deep roar told of danger ahead. Fortunately there were rocks where they were able to disembark, and a short way below they found that a natural dam extended across the river.

"There has been an eruption of trap here," Harry said, looking at the black rock on either side. "There has been a fissure, I suppose, and the lava was squeezed up through it. You see the river has cut a path for itself some hundreds of feet deep. It must have taken countless ages, Tom, to have done the work."

Over this dam the water flowed swiftly and smoothly, and then shot down in a fall six feet high. Below for a distance of two or three hundred yards was a, furious rapid, the water running among black rocks. With considerable difficulty they made a portage of the boats and stores to the lower end of the rapid. This transit occupied several hours, and they then proceeded on their way. Five more miles were passed; several times the boats were brought to the bank in order that falls ahead might be examined. These proved to be not too high to shoot, and the boats paddled over them. When they had first taken to the river they would never have dreamt of shooting such falls, but they had now become so expert in the management of the boats, and so confident in their buoyancy, that the dangers which would then have appalled them were now faced without uneasiness.

They now came to a long rapid, presenting so many dangers that they deemed it advisable to let down the boats by lines. Again embarking they found that the wall of rocks closed in and they entered a narrow gorge, through which the river ran with great swiftness, touching the walls on each side. Great care was needed to prevent the boats being dashed against the rock, but they succeeded in keeping them fairly in the middle of the stream. After travelling four miles through this gorge it opened somewhat, and on one side was a strip of sand.

"We will land there," Harry said. "It looks to me like granite ahead, and if it is we are in for bad times, sure."

The boats were soon pulled up, and they proceeded to examine the cliffs below. Hitherto the danger had been in almost exact proportion to the hardness of the rock, and as they were entering a far harder rock than they had before encountered, greater difficulties than those they had surmounted were to be expected.

They could not see a long distance down, but what they saw was enough to justify their worst anticipations. The canon was narrower than any they had traversed, and the current extremely swift. There seemed but few broken rocks in the channel, but on either side the walls jutted out in sharp angles far into the river, with crags and pinnacles.

"Waal, it is of no use looking at it," Jerry said after a pause. "It is certain we can't get along the sides, so there is nothing to do but to go straight at it; and the sooner it is over the better."

Accordingly they returned to the boats, and soon darted at the speed of an arrow into the race. Bad as it was at starting it speedily became worse: ledges, pinnacles, and towers of rock rose above the surface of the stream breaking it into falls and whirlpools. Every moment it seemed to Tom that the boat must inevitably be dashed to pieces against one of these obstructions, for the light boats were whirled about like a feather on the torrent, and the paddlers could do but little to guide their course. The very strength of the torrent, however, saved them from destruction, the whirl from the rocks sweeping the boat's head aside when within a few feet of them, and driving it past the danger before they had time to realize that they had escaped wreck. Half an hour of this, and a side canon came in. Down this a vast quantity of boulders had been swept, forming a dam across the river, but they managed to paddle into an eddy at the side, and to make a portage of the boats to the water below the dam, over which there was a fall of from thirty to forty feet high. Three more similar dams were met with. Over one the canoes were carried, but on the others there was a break in the boulder wall, and they were able to shoot the falls. After three days of incessant labour, they heard, soon after starting from their last halting-place, a roar even louder and more menacing than they had yet experienced. Cautiously they got as close as possible to the side, and paddling against the stream were able to effect a landing just above the rapid. On examining it they found that it was nearly half a mile long, and in this distance the water made a fall of some eighty feet, the stream being broken everywhere with ledges and jagged rocks, among which the waves lashed themselves into a white foam. It seemed madness to attempt such a descent, and they agreed that at any rate they would halt for the day. The rocks through which the canon ran were fully a thousand feet high, but they decided that, great as the labour might be, it would be better to make a portage, if possible, rather than descend the cataract.

"There is a gulch here running up on to the hill," Tom said. "Hunting Dog and I will start at once and see if it is possible to get up it, and if so how far it is to a place where we can get down again."

Harry assented; Leaping Horse without a word joined the explorers, and they set off up the gulch. It was found that the ravine was steep, but not too steep to climb. When they were nearly at the top Hunting Dog pointed to the hillside above them, and they saw a big-horn standing at the edge of the rock. The three fired their rifles simultaneously, and the wild sheep made a spring into the air and then came tumbling down the side of the ravine. As fresh meat was beginning to run short this was a stroke of good fortune, and after reloading their guns they proceeded up the ravine until they reached the crest of the hill. The soil was disintegrated granite, and tufts of short grass grew here and there. After walking about a mile, parallel to the course of the river, they found that the ground descended again, and without much difficulty made their way down until they reached the foot of a little valley; following this they were soon standing by the side of the river. Above, its surface was as closely studded with rocks as was the upper cataract; below, there was another fall that looked impracticable, except that it seemed possible to pass along on the rocks by the side. It was getting dark by the time they rejoined their comrades.

"Your report is not a very cheerful one," Harry said, "but at any rate there seems nothing else to be done than to make the portage. The meat you have got for us will re-stock our larder, and as it is up there we sha'n't have the trouble of carrying it over."

The next day was a laborious one. One by one the canoes were carried over, but the operation took them from daybreak till dark. The next morning another journey was made to bring over the rugs and stores, and they were able in addition to these to carry down the carcass of the sheep, after first skinning it and cutting off the head with its great horns. Nothing was done for the rest of the day beyond trying whether another portage could be made. This was found to be impracticable, and there was nothing for them but to attempt the descent. They breakfasted as soon as day broke, carried the boats down over the boulder dam with which the rapids commenced, and put them into the water. For some little distance they were able to let them down by ropes, then the rocks at the foot of the cliffs came to an end. Fortunately the seven lariats furnished them with a considerable length of line, and in addition to these the two Indians had on their way down plaited a considerable length of rope, with thongs cut from the skins of the animals they had killed.

The total available amount of rope was now divided into two lengths, the ends being fastened to each canoe. One of the boats with its crew on board was lowered to a point where the men were able to get a foothold on a ledge. As soon as they had done so the other boat dropped down to them, and the ropes were played out until they were in turn enabled to get a footing on a similar ledge or jutting rock, sometimes so narrow that but one man was able to stand. So alternately the boats were let down. Sometimes when no foothold could be obtained on the rock wall, the pinnacles and ledges in the stream were utilized. All the work had to be done by gesture, for the thunder of the waters was so tremendous that the loudest shout could not be heard a few yards away. Hour passed after hour. Their progress was extremely slow, as each step had to be closely considered and carried out with the greatest care.

At last a terrible accident happened. Harry, Leaping Horse, and Tom were on a ledge. Below them was a fall of three feet, and in the foaming stream below it, rose several jagged rocks. Jerry's canoe was got safely down the fall, but in spite of the efforts of the rowers was carried against the outer side of one of these rocks. They made a great effort to turn the boat's head into the eddy behind it, but as the line touched the rock its sharp edge severed the rope like a knife, and the boat shot away down the rapid. Those on the ledge watched it with breathless anxiety. Two or three dangers were safely passed, then to their horror they saw the head of the canoe rise suddenly as it ran up a sunken ledge just under the water. An instant later the stern swept round, bringing her broadside on to the stream, and she at once capsized.

"Quick!" Harry exclaimed, "we must go to their rescue. Keep close to the wall, chief, till we see signs of them. It is safest close in."

In an instant they were in their places, and as they released the canoe she shot in a moment over the fall. For a short distance they kept her close to the side, but a projecting ledge threw the current sharply outwards, and the canoe shot out into the full force of the rapid. The chief knelt up in the bow paddle in hand, keeping a vigilant eye for rocks and ledges ahead, and often with a sharp stroke of the paddle, seconded by the effort of Harry in the stern, sweeping her aside just when Tom thought her destruction inevitable. Now she went headlong down a fall, then was caught by an eddy, and was whirled round and round three or four times before the efforts of the paddlers could take her beyond its influence. Suddenly a cry came to their ears. Just as they approached a rocky ledge some thirty feet long, and showing a saw-like edge a foot above the water, the chief gave a shout and struck his paddle into the water.

"Behind the rock, Tom, behind the rock!" Harry exclaimed as he swept the stern round. Tom paddled with all his might, and the canoe headed up stream. Quickly as the movement was done, the boat was some twelve yards below the rock as she came round with her nose just in the lower edge of the eddy behind it, while from either side the current closed in on her. Straining every nerve the three paddlers worked as for life. At first Tom thought that the glancing waters would sweep her down, but inch by inch they gained, and drove the boat forward from the grasp of the current into the back eddy, until suddenly, as if released from a vice, she sprang forward. Never in his life had Tom exerted himself so greatly. His eyes were fixed on the rock in front of him, where Hunting Dog was clinging with one hand, while with the other he supported Jerry's head above water. He gave a shout of joy as the chief swept the head of the canoe round, just as it touched the rock, and laid her broadside to it.

"Stick your paddle between two points of the rock, Tom," Harry shouted, "while the chief and I get them in. Sit well over on the other side of the boat."

With considerable difficulty Jerry, who was insensible, was lifted into the boat. As soon as he was laid down Hunting Dog made his way hand over hand on the gunwale until close to the stern, where he swung himself into the boat without difficulty.

"Have you seen Sam?" Harry asked.

The young Indian shook his head. "Sam one side of the boat," he said, "Jerry and Hunting Dog the other. Boat went down that chute between those rocks above. Only just room for it. Jerry was knocked off by rock. Hunting Dog was near the stern, there was room for him. He caught Jerry's hunting-shirt, but could not hold on to boat. When came down here made jump at corner of rock. Could not hold on, but current swept him into eddy. Then swam here and held on, and kept calling. Knew his brothers would come down soon."

"Here is a spare paddle," Harry said, as he pulled one out from below the network, "there is not a moment to lose. Keep your eyes open, chief." Again the boat moved down the stream. With four paddles going the steersman had somewhat more control over her, but as she flew down the seething water, glanced past rocks and sprang over falls, Tom expected her to capsize every moment. At last he saw below them a stretch of quiet water, and two or three minutes later they were floating upon it, and as if by a common impulse all ceased rowing.

"Thanks be to God for having preserved us," Harry said reverently. "We are half-full of water; another five minutes of that work and it would have been all over with us. Do you see any signs of the canoe, chief?"

The chief pointed to a ledge of rock extending out into the stream. "Canoe there," he said. They paddled across to it. After what the young Indian had said they had no hopes of finding Sam with it, but Harry gave a deep sigh as he stepped out on to the ledge.

"Another gone," he said. "How many of us will get through this place alive? Let us carry Jerry ashore." There was a patch of sand swept up by the eddy below the rock, and here Jerry was taken out and laid down. He moaned as they lifted him.

"Easy with him," Harry said. "Steady with that arm. I think he has a shoulder broken, as well as this knock on the head that has stunned him."

As soon as he was laid down Harry cut open his shirt on the shoulder. "Broken," he said shortly. "Now, chief, I know that you are a good hand at this sort of thing. How had this better be bandaged?"

"Want something soft first."

Tom ran to the canoe, brought out the little canvas sack in which he carried his spare flannel shirt, and brought it to the chief. The latter tore off a piece of stuff and rolled it into a wad. "Want two pieces of wood," he said, holding his hands about a foot apart to show the length he required. Harry fetched a spare paddle, and split a strip off each side of the blade. The chief nodded as he took them. "Good," he said. He tore off two more strips of flannel and wrapped them round the splints, then with Harry's aid he placed the shoulder in its natural position, laid the wad of flannel on the top of it, and over this put the two splints. The whole was kept in its place by flannel bandages, and the arm was fastened firmly across the body, so that it could not be moved. Then the little keg of brandy was brought out of the canoe, a spoonful poured into the pannikin, with half as much water, and allowed to trickle between Jerry's lips, while a wad of wet flannel was placed on his head.

"There is nothing more we can do for him at present," Harry said. "Now we will right the other boat, and get all the things out to dry."

Three or four pounds of flour were found to be completely soaked with water, but the main store was safe, as the bag was sewn up in bearskin. This was only opened occasionally to take out two or three days' supply, and then carefully closed again. On landing, Hunting Dog had at once started in search of drift-wood, and by this time a fire was blazing. A piece of bear's fat was placed in the frying-pan, and the wetted flour was at once fried into thin cakes, which were tough and tasteless; but the supply was too precious to allow of an ounce being wasted. Some slices of the flesh of the big-horn were cooked.

"What is my white brother going to do?" the chief asked Harry.

"There is nothing to do that I can see, chief, but to keep on pegging away. We agreed that it would be almost impossible to find our way over these barren mountains. That is not to be thought of, now that one of our number cannot walk. There is no choice left, we have got to go on."

"Leaping Horse understand that," the chief said. "He meant would you take both canoes? One is big enough to take five."

"Quite big enough, chief, but it would be deeper in the water, and the heavier it is the harder it will bump against any rock it meets; the lighter they are the better. You see, this other canoe, which I dare say struck a dozen times on its way down, shows no sign of damage except the two rents in the skin, that we can mend in a few minutes. Another thing is, two boats are absolutely necessary for this work of letting down by ropes, of which we may expect plenty more. If we had only one, we should be obliged to run every rapid. The only extra trouble that it will give us is at the portages. I think we had better stay here for two or three days, so as to give Jerry a chance of coming round. No doubt we could carry him over the portages just as we can carry the boats, but after such a knock on the head as he has had, it is best that he should be kept quiet for a bit. If his skull is not cracked he won't be long in getting round. He is as hard as nails, and will pull round in the tenth of the time it would take a man in the towns to get over such a knock. It is a pity the halt is not in a better place. There is not a shadow of a chance of finding game among these crags and bare rocks."

From time to time fresh water was applied to the wad of flannel round Jerry's head.

"Is there any chance, do you think, of finding poor Sam's body?"

The chief shook his head. "No shores where it could be washed up, rocks tear it to pieces; or if it get in an eddy, might be there for weeks. No see Sam any more."

The fire was kept blazing all night, and they took it by turns to sit beside Jerry and to pour occasionally a little brandy and water between his lips. As the men were moving about preparing breakfast the next morning Jerry suddenly opened his eyes. He looked at Tom, who was sitting beside him.

"Time to get up?" he asked. "Why did you not wake me?" And he made an effort to move. Tom put his hand on him.

"Lie still, Jerry. You have had a knock on the head, but you are all right now."

The miner lay quiet. His eyes wandered confusedly over the figures of the others, who had, when they heard his voice, gathered round him.

"What in thunder is the matter with me?" he asked. "What is this thing on my head? What is the matter with my arm, I don't seem able to move it?"

"It is the knock you have had, Jerry," Harry said cheerfully. "You have got a bump upon your head half as big as a cocoa-nut, and you have damaged your shoulder. You have got a wet flannel on your head, and the chief has bandaged your arm. I expect your head will be all right in a day or two, but I reckon you won't be able to use your arm for a bit."

Jerry lay quiet without speaking for a few minutes, then he said: "Oh, I remember now; we were capsized. I had hold of the canoe, and I remember seeing a rock just ahead. I suppose I knocked against it."

"That was it, mate. Hunting Dog let go his hold and caught you, and managed to get into an eddy and cling to the rocks till we came down and took you on board."

Jerry held out his hand to the Indian. "Thankee," he said. "I owe you one, Hunting Dog. If I ever get the chance you can reckon on me sure, whatever it is. But where is Sam? Why ain't he here?"

"Sam has gone under, mate," Harry replied. "That chute you went down was only just wide enough for the boat to go through, and no doubt he was knocked off it at the same time as you were; but as the Indian was on your side, he saw nothing of Sam. I reckon he sank at once, just as you would have done if Hunting Dog hadn't been behind you."

Jerry made no reply, but as he lay still, with his eyes closed, some big tears made their way through the lids and rolled down his bronzed face. The others thought it best to leave him by himself, and continued their preparations for breakfast.

Chapter XVIII.
Back to Denver

"Then are you going to make a start again?" Jerry asked, after drinking a pannikin of tea.

"We are not going on to-day; perhaps not to-morrow. It will depend on how you get on."

"I shall be a nuisance to you anyway," the miner said, "and it would be a dog-goned sight the best way to leave me here; but I know you won't do that, so it ain't no use my asking you. I expect I shall be all right to-morrow except for this shoulder, but just now my head is buzzing as if there was a swarm of wild bees inside."

"You will be all the better when you have had a good sleep; I reckon we could all do a bit that way. Young Tom and Hunting Dog are going to try a bit of fishing with those hooks of yours. We talked about it when we started, you know, but we have not done anything until now. We want a change of food badly. We may be a month going down this canon for anything I know, and if it keeps on like this there ain't a chance of seeing a head of game. It ought to be a good place for fish at the foot of the rapids —that is, if there are any fish here, and I reckon there should be any amount of them. If they do catch some, we will wait here till we can dry a good stock. We have nothing now but the dried flesh and some of the big-horn. There ain't above twenty pounds of flour left, and we could clear up all there is in the boat in a week. So you need not worry that you are keeping us."

Half an hour later Hunting Dog and Tom put out in one of the canoes, and paddling to the foot of the rapids let the lines drop overboard, the hooks being baited with meat. It was not many minutes before the Indian felt a sharp pull. There was no occasion to play the fish, for the line was strong enough to hold a shark, and a trout of six pounds weight was soon laid in the bottom of the boat.

"My turn now," Tom said; and the Indian with a smile took the paddle from his hand, and kept the boat up stream while Tom attended to the lines. Fish after fish was brought up in rapid succession, and when about mid-day a call from below told them that it was time for dinner, they had some thirty fish averaging five pounds' weight at the bottom of the boat.

There was a shout of satisfaction from Harry as he looked down into the canoe, and even the chief gave vent to a grunt that testified his pleasure.

"Hand me up four of them, Tom; I did not know how much I wanted a change of food till my eyes lit on those beauties. We saw you pulling them out, but I did not expect it was going to be as good as this."

The fish were speedily split open, and laid on ramrods over the fire.

"I reckon you will want another one for me," Jerry, who had been asleep since they started, remarked. "I don't know that I am good for one as big as those, but I reckon I can pick a bit anyhow."

A small fish was put on with the others, and as soon as they were grilled, all set to at what seemed to Tom the best meal he had ever eaten in his life. He thought when he handed them to Harry that two would have been amply sufficient for them all, but he found no difficulty whatever in disposing of a whole one single-handed. "Now, Tom, the chief and I will take our turn while you and Hunting Dog prepare your catch. He will show you how to do it, it is simple enough. Cut off the heads, split and clean them, run a skewer through to keep them flat, and then lay them on that rock in the sun to dry. Or wait, I will rig up a line between two of the rocks for you to hang them on. There is not much wind, but what there is will dry them better than if they were laid flat."

Jerry went off to sleep again as soon as the meal was finished, and the bandages round his head re-wetted. The paddle from which the strips had been cut furnished wood for the skewers, and in the course of half an hour the fish were all hanging on a line. Twenty-two more were brought in at sunset. Some of these, after being treated like the others, were hung in the smoke of the fire, while the rest were suspended like the first batch.

The next morning Jerry was able to move about, and the fishing went on all day, and by night a quantity, considered sufficient, had been brought ashore.

"There are over four hundred pounds altogether," Harry said, "though by the time they are dried they won't be more than half that weight. Two pounds of dried fish a man is enough to keep him going, and they will last us twenty days at that rate, and it will be hard luck if we don't find something to help it out as we go down."

They stopped another day to allow the drying to be completed. The fish were taken down and packed on board that evening, and at daylight they were afloat again. For the next ten days their labours were continuous. They passed several rapids as bad as the one that had cost them so dear; but as they gained experience they became more skilful in letting down the boats. Some days only two or three miles were gained, on others they made as much as twelve. At last they got out of the granite; beyond this the task was much easier, and on the fifteenth day after leaving their fishing ground, they emerged from the canon.

By this time Jerry had perfectly recovered, and was with great difficulty persuaded to keep his arm bandaged. He had chafed terribly at first at his helplessness, and at being unable to take any share in the heavy labours of the others; but after the rapids were passed he was more contented, and sat quietly at the bottom of the boat smoking, while Harry and Tom paddled, the two Indians forming the crew of the other canoe. The diet of fish had been varied by bear's flesh, Leaping Horse having shot a large brown bear soon after they got through the rapids. A shout of joy was raised by the three whites as they issued from the gorge into a quiet valley, through which the river ran, a broad tranquil stream. Even the Indians were stirred to wave their paddles above their heads and to give a ringing whoop as their companions cheered. The boats were headed for the shore, and the camp was formed near a large clump of bushes.

Their joy at their deliverance from the dangers of the cañon was dashed only by the thought of the loss of their two comrades. The next day three short cañons were passed through, but these presented no difficulties, and in the afternoon they reached the mouth of the Rio Virgen, and continuing their journey arrived five days later at Fort Mojarve. This was a rising settlement, for it was here that the traders' route between Los Angeles and Sante Fé crossed the Colorado. Their appearance passed almost unnoticed, for a large caravan had arrived that afternoon and was starting east the next morning.

"We had best hold our tongues about it altogether," Harry said, as soon as he heard that the caravan was going on the next morning. "In the first place they won't believe us, and that would be likely to lead to trouble; and in the next place we should be worried out of our lives with questions. Besides, we have got to get a fresh outfit, for we are pretty near in rags, and to buy horses, food, and kit. We can leave the boats on the shore, no one is likely to come near them."

"I will stop and look after them," Tom said. "There are the saddles, buffalo-robes, blankets, and ammunition. This shirt is in rags, and the last moccasins Hunting Dog made me are pretty nearly cut to pieces by the rocks. I would rather stay here and look after the boats than go into the village; besides, it will save you the trouble of carrying all these bags of gold about with you."

Harry nodded, cut two of the little bags free from their lashings and dropped them into his pocket, and then went up to the Fort with Jerry and the Indians. Tom cut the other bags loose and put them on the ground beside him, threw a buffalo-robe over them, and then sat for some hours watching the quiet river and thinking over all they had gone through. It was almost dark when the others returned.

"It has taken us some time, Tom," his uncle said as they threw some bundles down beside him; "the stores and clothes were easy enough, but we had a lot of trouble to find horses. However, we did not mind much what we paid for them, and the traders were ready to sell a few at the prices we offered. So we have got five riding horses and two pack-ponies, which will be enough for us. That bundle is your lot, riding breeches and boots, three pairs of stockings, two flannel shirts, a Mexican hat, and a silk neck handkerchief. We may as well change at once and go up to the village."

The change was soon effected. Harry and Jerry Curtis had clothes similar to those they had bought for Tom, while the Indians wore over their shirts new deer-skin embroidered hunting-shirts, and had fringed Mexican leggings instead of breeches and boots. They, too, had procured Mexican sombreros. Taking their rifles and pistols, and hiding their stock of ammunition, the gold, and their buffalo-robes and blankets, they went up to the village. It was by this time quite dark; the houses were all lit up, and the drinking-shops crowded with the teamsters, who seemed bent on making a night of it, this being the last village through which they would pass until their arrival at Santa Fé.

They slept as usual, wrapped up in their buffalo-robes by the side of the boats, as all agreed that this was preferable to a close room in a Mexican house.

They were all a-foot as soon as daylight broke, and went up and breakfasted at a fonda, Tom enjoying the Mexican cookery after the simple diet he had been accustomed to. Then they went to the stable where the horses, which were strong serviceable-looking animals, had been placed, and put on their saddles and bridles.

The pack-horses were then laden with flour, tea, sugar, bacon, and other necessaries. By the time all was ready the caravan was just starting. Harry had spoken the afternoon before to two of its leaders, and said that he and four companions would be glad to ride with them to Santa Fé. Permission was readily granted, the traders being pleased at the accession of five well-armed men; for although Indian raids were comparatively rare along this trail, there was still a certain amount of danger involved in the journey. Some hours were occupied in crossing the river in two heavy ferry-boats, and the process would have been still longer had not half the waggons been sent across on the previous afternoon.

The long journey was made without incident, and no Indians were met with. A few deer were shot, but as it was now late in the autumn the scanty herbage on the plains was all withered up, and the game had for the most part moved away into deep valleys where they could obtain food. The tale of their passage of the canons was told more than once, but although it was listened to with interest, Harry perceived that it was not really believed. That they had been hunting, had been attacked by Indians, had made canoes and passed through some of the canons was credible enough, but that they should have traversed the whole of the lower course of the Colorado, seemed to the traders, who were all men experienced in the country, simply incredible. The party stopped at Santa Fé a few days, and then started north, travelling through the Mexican villages, and finally striking across to Denver. At Santa Fé they had converted the contents of their bags into money, which had been equally shared among them. The Indians were not willing to accept more than the recognized monthly pay, but Harry would not hear of it.

"This has been no ordinary business, Leaping Horse," he said warmly; "we have all been as brothers together, and for weeks have looked death in the face every hour, and we must share all round alike in the gold we have brought back. Gold is just as useful to an Indian as it is to a white man, and when you add this to the hoard you spoke of, you will have enough to buy as many horses and blankets as you can use all your lifetime, and to settle down in your wigwam and take a wife to yourself whenever you choose. I fancy from what you said, Hunting Dog has his eye on one of the maidens of your tribe. Well, he can buy her father's favour now. The time is coming, chief, when the Indians of the plains will have to take to white men's ways. The buffaloes are fast dying out, and in a few years it will be impossible to live by hunting, and the Indians will have to keep cattle and build houses and live as we do. With his money Hunting Dog could buy a tidy ranche with a few hundred head of cattle. Of course, he can hunt as much as he likes so long as there is any game left, but he will find that as his cattle increase, he will have plenty to look after at home."

"We will take the gold if my brother wishes it," the chief replied gravely. "He is wise, and though now it seems to Leaping Horse that red-skins have no need of gold, it may be that some day he and

Hunting Dog may be glad that they have done as their brother wished."

"Thank you, Leaping Horse. It will make my heart glad when I may be far away from you across the great salt water to know that there will always be comfort in my brother's wigwam."

On arriving at Denver they went straight to the Empire. As they entered the saloon Pete Hoskings looked hard at them.

"Straight Harry, by thunder!" he shouted; "and Jerry Curtis, and young Tom; though I would not have known him if he hadn't been with the others. Well, this air a good sight for the eyes, and to-morrow Christmas-day. I had begun to be afeard that something had gone wrong with you, I looked for news from you nigh three months ago. I got the message you sent me in the spring, and I have asked every old hand who came along east since the end of August, if there had been any news of you, and I began to fear that you had been rubbed out by the Utes."

"We have had a near escape of it, Pete; but it is a long story. Can you put us all up? You know Leaping Horse, don't you? The other is his nephew."

"I should think I do know Leaping Horse," Pete said warmly, and went across and shook the Indian's hand heartily.

"I was looking at you three, and did not notice who you had with you. In that letter the chap brought me, you said that the chief was going with you, and Sam Hicks and Ben Gulston. I did not know them so well; that is, I never worked with them, though they have stopped here many a time."

"They have gone under, Pete. Sam was drowned in the Colorado, Ben shot by the Navahoes. We have all had some close calls, I can tell you. Well now, can you put us up?"

"You need not ask such a question as that, Harry," Pete said in an aggrieved tone, "when you know very well that if the place was chock-full, I would clear the crowd out to make room for you. There are three beds in the room over this that will do for you three; and there is a room beside it as Leaping Horse and his nephew can have, though I reckon they won't care to sleep on the beds."

"No more shall we, Pete. We have been fifteen months and more sleeping in the open, and we would rather have our buffalo-robes and blankets than the softest bed in the world."

"You must have had a cold time of it the last three months up in those Ute hills, where you said you were going."

"We left there five months ago, Pete. We have been down as low as Fort Mojarve, and then crossed with a caravan of traders to Santa Fé."

Pete began pouring out the liquor.

"Oh, you won't take one, chief, nor the young brave. Yes; I remember you do not touch the fire-water, and you may be sure I won't press you. Well, luck to you all, and right glad I am to see you again. Ah! here is my bartender. Now we will get a good fire lit in another room and hurry up supper, and then we will talk it all over. You have put your horses up, I suppose?"

"Yes; we knew you had no accommodation that way, Pete."

The room into which Pete now led them was not his own sanctum, but one used occasionally when a party of miners coming in from the hills wanted to have a feast by themselves, or when customers wished to talk over private business. There was a table capable of seating some twelve people, a great stove, and some benches. A negro soon lighted a large fire; then, aided by a boy, laid the table, and it was not long before they sat down to a good meal. When it was over, Pete said:

"Lend me a hand, Jerry, to push this table aside, then we will bring the benches round the stove and hear all about it. I told the bar-tender that I am not to be disturbed, and that if anyone wants to see me he is to say that he has got to wait till to-morrow, for that I am engaged on important business. Here are brandy and whisky, and tobacco and cigars, and coffee for the chief and his nephew."

"I think you may say for all of us, Pete," Harry said. "After being a year without spirits, Jerry, Tom, and I have agreed to keep without them. We wouldn't say no to you when you asked us to take a drink, and we have not sworn off, but Jerry and I have agreed that we have both been all the better without them, and mean to keep to it; and as for Tom, he prefers coffee."

"Do as you please," Pete said; "I am always glad to hear men say no. I have made a lot of money out of it, but I have seen so many fellows ruined by it that I am always pleased to see a man give up drink."

"There is one thing, Pete," Tom said, "before we begin. We left our bundles of robes and blankets in the next room, if you don't mind I would a deal rather spread them out here—and I am sure the chief and Hunting Dog would— and squat down on them, instead of sitting on these benches. It is a long story uncle will have to tell you."

"We will fetch ours too," Harry agreed. "Benches are all well enough for sitting at the table to eat one's dinner, but why a man should sit on them when he can sit on the ground is more than I can make out."

Pete nodded. "I will have my rocking-chair in," he said, "and then we shall be fixed up for the evening."

The arrangements were soon made; pipes were lighted; the landlord sat in his chair at some little distance back from the front of the stove; Tom and the two Indians sat on their rugs on one side; Harry and Jerry Curtis completed the semicircle on the other.

"Well, in the first place, Pete," Harry began, "you will be glad to hear that we have struck it rich—the biggest thing I have ever seen. It is up in the Ute country. We have staked out a claim for you next our own. There are about five hundred pounds of samples lying at Fort Bridger, and a bit of the rock we crushed, panned out five hundred ounces to the ton."

"You don't say!" Pete exclaimed. "If there is much of that stuff, Harry, you have got a bonanza."

"There is a good bit of it anyhow, Pete. It is a true vein, and though it is not all like that, it keeps good enough. Fifty feet back we found it run twenty ounces. That is on the surface, we can't say how it goes down in depth. Where we struck it on the face it was about fourteen feet high, and the lode kept its width for that depth anyhow."

"That air good enough," the landlord said. "Now, what do you reckon on doing?"

"The place is among the hills, Pete, and the Utes are hostile, and went very nigh rubbing us all out. We reckon it ought to be worked by a party of thirty men at least. They ought to be well armed, and must build a sort of fort. I don't think the Utes would venture to attack them if they were of that strength. There is a little stream runs close to the vein, and if it were dammed up it would drive a couple of stamps, which, with a concentrator and tables and blankets, would be quite enough for such stuff as that. I reckon fifteen men will be quite enough to work, and to hold the fort. The other fifteen men would include three or four hunters, and the rest would go backwards and forwards to Bridger for supplies, and to take the gold down. They would be seven or eight days away at a time; and if there should be trouble with the red-skins they would always be back before those at the fort were really pressed. But we should not be alone long, the news that a rich thing had been struck would bring scores of miners up in no time.

"We have taken up our own ten claims, which will include, of course, the rich part. Then we have taken up the next eight or ten claims for our friends. As I said, we put yours next to ours. We have not registered them yet, but that will be the first job; and of course you and the others will each have to put a man on your claims to hold them. The lode shows on the other side of the creek, though not so rich; still plenty good enough to work. But as we shall practically get all the water, the lode cannot be worked by anyone but ourselves. Still the gravel is rich all down the creek, as rich as anything I have seen in California, and will be sure to be taken up by miners as soon as we are at work. So there will be no real danger of trouble from the Indians then. What we propose is this. We don't what to sell out, we think it is good enough to hold, but we want to get a company to find the money for getting up the machinery, building a strong block-house with a palisade, laying in stores, and working the place. Jerry, Tom, and I would of course be in command, at any rate for the first year or so, when the rich stuff was being worked."

"How much money do you think it will want, and what share do you think of giving, Harry?"

"Well, I should say fifty thousand dollars, though I believe half that would be enough. Not a penny would be required after the first ton of rock goes through the stamps. But we should have to take the stamps and ironwork from the railway terminus to Bridger, and then down.

We might calculate on a month or six weeks in getting up the fort, making the leat and water-wheel, putting up the machinery, and laying down the flumes. Say two months from the time we leave Bridger to the time we begin to work. There would be the pay of the men all that time, the cost of transporting stores, and all that sort of thing; so it would be better to say fifty thousand dollars. What share ought we to offer for that?"

"Well, if you could bring that five hundredweight of stuff here and get it crushed up, and it turns out as good as you say, I could get you the money in twenty-four hours. I would not mind going half of it myself, and I should say that a quarter share would be more than good enough."

"Well, we thought of a third, Pete."

"Well, if you say a third you may consider that part of the business is done. You won't be able to apply for claims in the names of Sam and Ben, and if you did it would be no good, because they could not assign them over to the company. There are eight claims without them, and the one you have put down in my name is nine. Well, I can get say eleven men in this place, who will give you an assignment of their claims for five dollars apiece. That is done every day. I just say to them, I am registering a share in your name in the Tom Cat Mine, write an assignment to me of it and I am good for five dollars' worth of liquor, take it out as you like. The thing is as easy as falling off a log. Well, what are you thinking of doing next?"

"We shall buy a light waggon and team to-morrow or next day and drive straight over to Bridger, then we shall go to Salt Lake City and register our claims at the mining-office there. We need not give the locality very precisely. Indeed, we could not describe it ourselves so that anyone could find it, and nobody would go looking for it before spring comes and the snow clears. Besides, there are scores of wild-cat claims registered every year. Until they turn out good no one thinks anything of them. When we have got that done we will go back to Bridger, and fetch the rock over here. We will write to-morrow to Pittsburg for the mining outfit, for all the ironwork of the stamps, the concentrator, and everything required, with axes, picks, and shovels, blasting tools and powder, to be sent as far as they have got the railway."

"But they will want the money with the order, Harry," Pete said in a tone of surprise.

"They will have the money. We washed the gravel for a couple of months before the Utes lit on us, and after buying horses and a fresh outfit for us all at Fort Mojarve, we have between us got something like five thousand dollars in gold and greenbacks."

"Jee-hoshaphat!" Pete exclaimed; "that was good indeed for two months' work. Well, look here, there is no hurry for a few days about your starting back to Bridger. Here we are now, nearly at the end of December. It will take you a month to get there, say another fortnight to go on to Salt Lake City and register your claim and get back to Bridger, then it would be a month getting back here again; that would take you to the middle of March. Well, you see it would be pretty nigh the end of April before you were back at Bridger, then you would have to get your waggons and your men, and that would be too late altogether.

"You have got to pick your miners carefully, I can tell you; and it is not a job to be done in a hurry. When they see what gold there is in the rock they will soon set to work washing the gravel, and the day they do they will chuck up your work altogether. I will tell you what I would rather do, and that is, pick up green hands from the east. There are scores of them here now; men who have come as far as this, and can't start west till the snows melt. You need not think anything more about the money. You tell me what you crushed is a fair sample of that five hundred pounds, and that is quite good enough for me, and the gravel being so rich is another proof of what the lode was when the stream cut through it. I can put the twenty-five thousand dollars down, and there are plenty of men here who will take my word for the affair and plank their money down too. If there weren't I would put a mortgage on my houses, so that matter is done. To-morrow I will get the men whose names you are to give in for a claim each; it will be time in another two months to begin to look about for some steady chaps from the east, farmers' sons and such like. That is, if you think that plan is a good one. I mean to see this thing through, and I shall go with you myself, and we three can do the blasting."

"We shall be wanted to look after the stamps and pans," Harry said. "We had best get three or four old hands for the rock."

"Yes, that is best," Pete said. "Between us it is hard if we can't lay our hands upon men we can trust, and who will give us their word to stay with us if we offer them six dollars a day."

"We might offer them ten dollars," Harry said, "without hurting ourselves; but we can say six dollars to begin with, and put some more on afterwards."

"There is old Mat Morgan," Jerry put in. "I don't know whether he is about here now. I would trust him. He is getting old for prospecting among the hills now, but he is as good a miner as ever swung a sledge-hammer, and as straight as they make them."

"Yes, he is a good man," Pete agreed. And after some talk they settled upon three others, all of whom, Pete said, were either in the town or would be coming in shortly.

"Now, you stop here for a week or two, or a month if you like, Harry, then you can go to Salt Lake City as you propose, and then go back to Bridger. If as you pass through you send me five-and-twenty pounds of that rock by express, it will make it easier for me to arrange the money affair. When you get back you might crush the rest up and send me word what it has panned out, then later on you can go down again to Salt Lake City and buy the waggons and flour and bacon, and take them back to Bridger. When March comes in, I will start from here with some waggons. We want them to take the machinery, and powder and tools, and the tea and coffee and things like that, of which we will make a list, on to Bridger, with the four men we pick out, if I can get them all; if not, some others in their place, and a score of young emigrants. I shall have no difficulty in picking out sober, steady chaps, for in a place like this I can find out about their habits before I engage them. However, there will be plenty of time to settle all those points. Now, let us hear all about your adventures. I have not heard about you since Tom left, except that he wrote me a short letter from Bridger saying that you had passed the winter up among the mountains by the

Big Wind River. That you had had troubles with the Indians, and hadn't been able to do much trapping or looking for gold."

"Well, we will tell it between us," Harry said, "for it is a long yarn."

It was, indeed, past midnight before the story was all told. Long before it was finished the two Indians had taken up their rugs and gone up to their room, and although the other three had taken by turns to tell the tale of their adventures, they were all hoarse with speaking by the time they got through. Pete had often stopped them to ask question at various points where the narrators had been inclined to cut the story short.

"That beats all," he said, when they brought it to an end. "Only to think that you have gone down the Grand Canon. I would not have minded being with you when you were fighting the 'Rappahoes or the Utes, but I would not try going down the canons for all the gold in California. Well, look here, boys, I know that what you tell me is gospel truth, and all the men who know you well, will believe every word you say, but I would not tell the tale to strangers, for they would look on you as the all-firedest liars in creation."

"We have learnt that already, Pete," Harry laughed, "and we mean to keep it to ourselves, at any rate till we have got the mine at work. People may not believe the story of a man in a red shirt, and, mind you, I have heard a good many powerful lies told round a miner's fire, but when it is known we have got a wonderfully rich gold mine, I fancy it will be different. The men would say, if fellows are sharp enough to find a bonanza, it stands to reason they may be sharp enough to find their way down a canon. Now, let us be off to bed, for the heat of the stove has made me so sleepy that for the last hour I have hardly been able to keep my eyes open, and have scarcely heard a word of what Jerry and Tom have been saying."

They only remained a few days at Denver. After the life they had been leading they were very speedily tired of that of the town, and at the end of a week they started on horseback, with a light waggon drawn by a good team, to carry their stores for the journey and to serve as a sleeping-place. There had been no question about the Indians accompanying them, this was regarded as a matter of course. It was by no means a pleasant journey. They had frequent snow-storms and biting wind, and had sometimes to work for hours to get the waggon out of deep snow, which had filled up gullies and converted them into traps. After a stay of three days at Fort Bridger to rest the animals, they went on to Utah, having forwarded the sample of quartz to Pete Hoskings.

A fortnight was spent at Salt Lake City. Waggons, bullocks, and stores were purchased, and Harry arranged with some teamsters to bring the waggons out to Fort Bridger as soon as the snow cleared from the ground.

Chapter XIX.
A Fortune

On their return to Fort Bridger Harry and his companions pounded up the quartz that had been left there, and found that its average equalled that of the piece they had tried at the mine. The gold was packed in a box and sent to Pete Hoskings. A letter came back in return from him, saying that five of his friends had put in five thousand dollars each, and that he should start with the stores and machinery as soon as the track was clear of snow. The season was an early one, and in the middle of April he arrived with four large waggons and twenty active-looking young emigrants, and four miners, all of whom were known to Harry. There was a good deal of talk at Bridger about the expedition, and many offered to take service in it. But when Harry said that the lode they were going to prospect was in the heart of the Ute country, and that he himself had been twice attacked by the red-skins, the eagerness to accompany him abated considerably.

The fact, too, that it was a vein that would have to be worked by machinery, was in itself sufficient to deter solitary miners from trying to follow it up. Scarce a miner but had located a score of claims in different parts of the country, and these being absolutely useless to them, without capital to work them with, they would gladly have disposed of them for a few dollars. It was not, therefore, worth while to risk a perilous journey merely on the chance of being able to find another vein in the neighbourhood of that worked by Harry and the men who had gone into it with him. There was, however, some surprise among the old hands when Pete Hoskings arrived with the waggons.

"What! Have you cut the saloon, Pete, and are you going in for mining again?" one of them said as he alighted from his horse.

Pete gave a portentous wink.

"I guess I know what I am doing, Joe Radley. I am looking after the interests of a few speculators at Denver, who have an idea that they are going to get rich all of a sudden. I was sick of the city, and it just suited me to take a run and to get out of the place for a few months."

"Do you think it is rich, Pete?"

"One never can say," Hoskings replied with a grin. "We are not greenhorns any of us, and we know there is no saying how things are going to turn out. Straight Harry has had a run of bad luck for the last two years, and I am glad to give him a shoulder up, you know. I reckon he won't come badly off any way it turns out."

It was not much, but it was quite enough to send a rumour round the fort that Pete Hoskings had been puffing up a wild-cat mine in Denver for the sake of getting Straight Harry appointed boss of the expedition to test it.

Everything was ready at Bridger, and they delayed but twenty-four hours there. The teams had arrived from Salt Lake City with the stores a week before, and the eight waggons set off together. Pete, the three partners, the two Indians, and the four miners were all mounted. There were eight other horses ridden by as many of the young fellows Pete had brought with him, the rest walked on foot. They marched directly for the mine, as with such a force it was not necessary to make a detour over the bad lands. At the first halting-place some long cases Pete had brought with him were opened, and a musket handed to each of the emigrants, together with a packet of ammunition.

"Now," Pete said, "if the Utes meddle with us we will give them fits. But I reckon they will know better than to interfere with us."

The rate of progress with the heavy waggons was necessarily very much slower than that at which the party had travelled on their previous journey, and it was not until the afternoon of the eighth day after starting, that they came down into the valley. A halt was made at the former camping-place in the grove of trees, and the next morning Pete and the miners went up with Harry and his friends to choose a spot for the fort, and to examine the lode. As soon as the earth was scraped away from the spot from which the rock had been taken, exclamations of astonishment broke from the miners. They had been told by Pete that Harry had struck it rich, but all were astonished at the numerous particles and flakes of gold that protruded from the rock. Pete had forwarded early in the spring to Harry the list of the claimants to the mine, and the latter and Tom had ridden over to Salt Lake City a few days before the waggons came up from there to register the claims at the mining-office, and the first step was to stake out these claims upon the lode.

"It doesn't run like this far," Harry said to the miners, "and I reckon that beyond our ground it doesn't run above two ounces to the ton, so I don't think it is worth while your taking up claims beyond. Of course, you can do so if you like, and we will allow you an hour off every few days during the season to work your claims enough to keep possession, and of an evening you can do a bit of washing down below. You will find it good-pay dirt everywhere. At least we did as far as we tried it."

They now fixed on the site for the fort. It was upon the top of the bank, some twenty yards above the lode, and it was settled there should be a strong double palisade running down from it to the stream, so that in case of siege they could fetch water without being exposed to the bullets of an enemy taking post higher up the creek. Among the men from Denver were two or three experienced carpenters, and a blacksmith, for whose use a portable forge had been brought in the waggons.

The party returned to breakfast, and as soon as this was over the teams were put in and the waggons were brought up and unloaded, the stores being protected from wet by the canvas that formed the tilts. Some of the men accustomed to the use of the axe had been left in the valley to fell trees, and as soon as the waggons were unloaded they were sent down to bring up timber. All worked hard, and at the end of the week a log-hut fifty feet long and twenty-five feet wide had been erected. The walls were five feet high, and the roof was formed of the trunks of young trees squared, and laid side by side.

As rain fell seldom in that region it was not considered necessary to place shingles over them, as this could, in case of need, be done later on. The door opened out into the passage between the palisades down to the water, and the windows were all placed on the same side, loopholes being cut at short intervals round the other three sides. Another fortnight completed the preparations for work. The stamps were erected, with the water-wheel to work them; the stream dammed a hundred yards up, and a leat constructed to bring the water down to the wheel.

The waggons were formed up in a square. In this the horses were shut every night, four of the men by turns keeping guard there. During the last few days the miners had been at work blasting the quartz, and as soon as the stamps and machinery were in position they were ready to begin. The men were all told off to various duties, some to carry the rock down to the stamps, others to break it up into convenient sizes; two men fed the stamps, others attended to the concentrator and blankets, supervised by Harry. It was the duty of some to take the horses down to the valley and guard them while they were feeding, and bring them back at night. Two men were to bake and cook, Pete Hoskings taking this special department under his care. Jerry worked with the miners, and Tom was his uncle's assistant.

The stamps were to be kept going night and day, and each could crush a ton in twenty-four hours. To their great satisfaction each of the men was allowed one day a week to himself, during which he could prospect for other lodes or wash gravel as he pleased. The old cradle was found where it had been left, and as five of the men were off duty each day, they formed themselves into gangs and worked the cradle by turns, adding very considerably to the liberal pay they received. The two Indians hunted, and seldom returned without game of some sort or other. As the quicksilver in the concentrator was squeezed by Harry or Tom, and the blankets washed by them, none but themselves knew what the returns were. They and their partners were, however, more than satisfied with the result, for although the lode was found to pinch in as they got lower, it maintained for the first six weeks the extraordinary average of that they had first crushed.

At the end of that time the Indians reported that they had seen traces of the Utes having visited the valley. The number of men who went down with the horses was at once doubled, one or other of the Indians staying down with them, preceding them in the morning by half an hour to see that the valley was clear. A week later the horses were seen coming back again a quarter of an hour after they had started. The men caught up their guns, which were always placed handy for them while at work, and ran out to meet the returning party. "What is it, Hunting Dog?"

"A large war-party," the Indian replied. "Three hundred or more."

The horses were driven into the inclosure, half the men took their places among the waggons, and the others, clustered round the hut, prepared to enter it as soon as the Indians made their appearance.

The partners had already arranged what course to take if the Indians should come down on them, and were for all reasons most anxious that hostilities should if possible be avoided.

Presently the Indians were seen approaching at a gallop. As soon as they caught sight of the log-house and the inclosure of waggons they reined in their horses. The men had been ordered to show themselves, and the sight of some forty white men all armed with rifles brought the Indians to a dead stand-still.

Pete Hoskings went forward a little and waved a white cloth, and then Harry and the chief, leaving their rifles behind them stepped up to his side and held their arms aloft. There was a short consultation among the Indians, and then two chiefs dismounted, handed their rifles and spears to their men, and in turn advanced. Harry and Leaping Horse went forward until they met the chiefs halfway between the two parties. Harry began the conversation.

"Why do my red brothers wish to fight?" he asked. "We are doing them no harm. We are digging in the hills. Why should we not be friends?"

"The white men killed many of the Utes when they were here last year," one of the chiefs replied. "Why do they come upon the Utes' land?"

"It was the fault of the Utes," Harry said. "The white men wished only to work in peace. The Utes tried to take their scalps, and the white men were forced against their will to fight. No one can be blamed for defending his life. We wish for peace, but, as the Utes can see, we are quite ready to defend ourselves. There are forty rifles loaded and ready, and, as you may see, a strong house. We have no fear. Last time we were but few, but the Utes found that it was not easy to kill us. Now we are many, and how many of the Utes would die before they took our scalps? Nevertheless we wish for peace. The land is the land of the Utes, and although we are strong and could hold it if we chose, we do not wish to take it by force from our red brothers. We are ready to pay for the right to live and work quietly. Let the chiefs go back to their friends and talk together, and say how many blankets and how many guns and what weight of ammunition and tobacco they will be content with. Then if they do not ask too much, the white men will, so long as they remain here, pay that amount each year in order that they may live in peace with the Utes."

The two Indians glanced at each other. "My white brother is wise," one said. "Why did he not tell the Utes so last year?"

"Because you never gave us time, chief. If you had done so we would have said the same to you then, and your young men would be with you now; but you came as enemies upon us, and when the rifle is speaking the voice is silent."

"I will speak with my braves," the chief said gravely. And turning round they walked back to their party, while Harry and the chief returned to the huts.

"What do you think, chief? Will it be peace?"

Leaping Horse nodded. "Too many rifles," he said. "The Utes will know they could never take block-house."

It was nearly two hours before the two Utes advanced as before, and Harry and the Seneca went out to meet them.

"My white brother's words are good," the chief said. "The Utes are great warriors, but they do not wish to fight against the white men who come as friends. The chiefs have talked with their braves, and the hatchets will be buried. This is what the Utes ask that the white men who have taken their land shall pay them."

Harry had arranged that the chief, who spoke the Ute language more perfectly than he did, should take charge of the bargaining. On the list being given Leaping Horse assumed an expression of stolid indifference.

"The land must be very dear in the Ute country," he said. "Do my brothers suppose that the white men are mad that they ask such terms? Peace would be too dear if bought at such a price. They are willing to deal liberally with the Utes, but not to give as much as would buy twenty hills. They will give this." And he enumerated a list of articles, amounting to about one quarter of the Indians' demands.

The bargaining now went on in earnest, and finally it was settled that a quantity of goods, amounting to about half the Indians' first demand, should be accepted, and both parties returned to their friends well satisfied.

A certain amount of goods had been brought out with a view to such a contingency, and half the amount claimed was handed over to the Utes. They had, indeed, more than enough to satisfy the demands, but Leaping Horse had suggested to Harry that only a portion should be given, as otherwise the Indians might suppose that their wealth was boundless. It would be better to promise to deliver the rest in three months' time. A dozen of the principal men of the Utes came over. The goods were examined and accepted, the calumet of peace was smoked and a solemn covenant of friendship entered into, and by the next morning the Indians had disappeared.

One end of the hut had been partitioned off for the use of the leaders of the party, and the gold obtained each day was carried by them there and deposited in a strong iron box, of which several had been brought by Pete Hoskings from Denver.

The day after the Indians left, a waggon was sent off under the escort of eight mounted labourers to Bridger, and this continued to make the journey backward and forward regularly with the boxes of gold, Jerry and Pete Hoskings taking it by turns to command the escort. Harry and Pete had had a talk with the officer in command at Bridger on the evening before they had started on the expedition.

"You think you are going to send in a large quantity of gold?" the officer asked.

"If the mines are such as we think, Major, we may be sending down two or three hundredweight a month."

"Of course, the gold will be perfectly safe as long as it is in the fort, but if it gets known how much there is, you will want a strong convoy to take it across to the railway, and it would not be safe even then. Of course, the bulk is nothing. I should say at any rate you had better get it in here with as little fuss as possible."

"If you will keep it here for awhile," Pete said, "we will think over afterwards how it is to be taken further."

The officer nodded. "It mayn't turn out as difficult a business as you think," he said with a smile. "You are both old hands enough to know that mines very seldom turn out as rich as they are expected to do."

"We both know that," Pete Hoskings agreed. "I dunno as I ever did hear of a mine that turned out anything nigh as good as it ought to have done from samples, but I reckon that this is going to be an exception."

When within a few miles of the fort the escort always placed their rifles in the waggon and rode on some distance ahead of it, only one or two with their leader remaining by it. The boxes, which were of no great size, were covered by a sack or two thrown down in the corner of the waggon, and on its arrival in the fort it was taken first to the store, where a considerable quantity of provisions, flour, molasses, bacon, tea and sugar, currants and raisins, and other articles were purchased and placed in it. This was the ostensible purpose of the journey to the fort. Late in the evening Jerry or Pete, whichever happened to be the leader, and one of the men, carried the boxes across to the Major's quarters and stored them in a cellar beneath it.

There was a real need of provisions at the mine, for the population of the valley rapidly increased as the season went on. The upper part of the bed of the stream had been staked out into claims, the miners and other men each taking up one, but below them the ground was of course open to all, and although not nearly so rich as the upper gravel it was good enough to pay fairly for working. A stout palisading now surrounded the ground taken up by the machinery and the mine itself, and no one except those engaged by the company were allowed to enter here. Considerable surprise was felt in the camp when the first two or three miners came up and staked out claims on the stream.

"I wonder how they could have heard of it," Tom said to his uncle.

"The fact that we are remaining out here is enough to show that we are doing something, anyhow. The men who go in are always strictly ordered to say no word about what our luck is, but the mere fact that they hold their tongues —and you may be sure they are questioned sharply—is enough to excite curiosity, and these men have come to find out and see what the country is like, and to prospect the hills round where we are working. You will see a lot of them here before long."

As more came up it was determined to open a store. In the first place it furnished an explanation for the waggon going down so often, and in the second the fact that they were ready to sell provisions at cost prices would deter others from coming and setting up stores. There was no liquor kept on the mine, and Pete and Harry were very anxious that no places for its sale should be opened in the valley.

During the winter and spring Tom had received several letters from his sisters. They expressed themselves as very grateful for the money that he and their uncle had sent on their return to Denver, but begged them to send no more, as the school was flourishing and they were perfectly able to meet all their expenses.

"It is very good of you, Tom," Carry said. "Of course, we are all very pleased to know that you have been able to send the money, because it relieves our anxiety about you; but we really don't want it, and it makes us afraid that you are stinting yourself. Besides, even if you are not, it would be much better for you to keep the money, as you may find some opportunity of using it to your advantage, while here it would only lie in the bank and do no good. It would be different if we had nothing to fall back upon in case of anything happening, such as some of us getting ill, or our having a case of fever in the school, or anything of that sort, but as we have only used fifty pounds of mother's money we have plenty to go on with for a very long time; so that really we would very much rather you did not send us any over. Now that we know your address and can write to you at Fort Bridger, it seems to bring you close to us. But we have had two very anxious times; especially the first, when we did not hear of you for six months. The second time was not so bad, as you had told us that it might be a long time before we should hear, and we were prepared for it, but I do hope it will never be so long again."

There had been some discussion as to whether the mine should be shut down in winter, but it was soon decided that work should go on regularly. Six more stamps were ordered to be sent from the east, with a steam-engine powerful enough to work the whole battery, and in September this and other machinery had reached the mine. Fresh buildings had been erected—a storehouse, a house for the officers, and a shed covering the whole of the machinery and yard. By the time this was all ready and in place the valley below was deserted, the gravel having been washed out to the bed-rock. No other lodes of sufficient richness to work had been discovered by the prospectors, and with winter at hand there was no inducement for them to stay longer there.

Only two or three of the men at the mine wished to leave when their engagement for the season terminated. All had been well paid, and had in addition made money at gold-washing. Their food had been excellent, and their comforts attended to in all ways. Accordingly, with these exceptions all were ready to renew their engagements.

An arrangement was made with the Major at Fort Bridger for an escort under a subaltern officer to proceed with two waggons with the treasure to Denver. Pete Hoskings and Jerry were to remain as managers of the mine throughout the winter. Harry and Tom had made up their minds to go to England and to return in the spring. The ore was now very much poorer than it had been at first. The lode had pinched out below and they had worked some distance along it. The falling-off, however, was only relative; the mine was still an extraordinarily rich one, although it contained little more than a tenth of the gold that had been extracted from the first hundred and fifty tons crushed.

None but Harry, Pete Hoskings, Jerry, and Tom had any idea of the amount of gold extracted in less than six months, although the miners were well aware that the amount must be very large. It was so indeed, for after repaying the amount expended in preliminary expenses, together with the new machinery, the wages of the men, provisions, and all outgoings, they calculated the treasure sent down to be worth one hundred and twenty-eight thousand pounds, while the mine if sold would fetch at least double that sum. After a hearty farewell to Pete and Jerry, Harry and Tom with the two Indians rode with the last waggon down to Bridger. The iron boxes had all been sewn up in deer-skins when they were sent down, and at night they were placed in the waggons by Harry and his companions. Over them were placed the provisions for the journey, as it was just as well that even the soldiers should not suspect the amount of treasure they were escorting.

They encountered some severe snow-storms by the way, but reached Denver without incident. The place had wonderfully changed since Tom had arrived there more than two years before. It had trebled in size; broad streets and handsome houses had been erected, and the town had spread in all directions. They drove straight to the bank, to which Pete Hoskings had sent down a letter a fortnight before they had started, and the boxes were taken out of the waggon and carried down into the vaults of the bank. A handsome present was made to each of the soldiers of the escort, a brace of revolvers was given by Harry to the subaltern, and the handsomest watch and chain that could be purchased in Denver was sent by him to the Major, with an inscription expressing the thanks of the company to him for his kindness.

"Well, Tom, I am thankful that that is off my mind," Harry said. "I have had a good many troubles in the course of my life, but this is the first time that money has ever been a care to me. Well, we are rich men, Tom, and we shall be richer, for the mine will run another two or three years before it finishes up the lode as far as we have traced it, and as we have now filed claims for a quarter of a mile farther back, it may be good for aught I know for another ten years. Not so good as it has been this year, but good enough to give handsome profits. Have you calculated what our share is?"

"No, uncle. I know it must be a lot, but I have never thought about what each share will be."

"Well, to begin with, a third of it goes to Pete Hoskings and his friends, that leaves eighty-five thousand. The remainder is divided into seven shares; I was to have two, the Indians three between them, you one, and Jerry one. His share is then about twelve thousand, which leaves seventy-three thousand between you and me. Of course, we shall divide equally."

"No, indeed, uncle; that would be ridiculous. I have been of very little use through it all, and I certainly ought not to have as much as Jerry. You and the chief discovered it, and it was entirely owing to you that any of the rest of us have a share of the profits, and of course your arrangement with the two Indians is only because the chief is so fond of you."

"Partly that, Tom; but chiefly because it is in accordance with red-skin customs. They are hunters, fighters, and guides, but they are not miners, and they never go in for shares in an enterprise of this sort. It went very much against the grain for Leaping Horse to take that three or four hundred pounds that came to him at the end of the last expedition, and he would be seriously offended if I were to press upon him more than his ordinary payment now; he would say that he has been simply hunting this year, that he has run no risks, and has had nothing to do with the mine. To-morrow morning we will go out to see what there is in the way of horse-flesh in Denver, and will buy him and Hunting Dog the two best horses in the town, whatever they may cost, with saddles, bridles, new blankets, and so on. If I can get anything special in the way of rifles I shall get a couple of them, and if not I shall get them in New York, and send them to him at Bridger. These are presents he would value infinitely more than all the gold we have stowed away in the bank to-day. He is going back to his tribe for the winter, and he and Hunting Dog will be at the mine before us next spring."

In the morning Harry was two hours at the bank, where he saw the gold weighed out, and received a receipt for the value, which came to within a hundred pounds of what they had calculated, as the dust had been very carefully weighed each time it was sent off. In accordance with the arrangement he had made with Pete Hoskings and Jerry the amount of their respective shares was placed to their credit at the bank. Drawing a thousand pounds in cash, he received a draft for the rest upon a firm at New York, where he would be able to exchange it for one on London. He then inquired at the hotel as to who was considered to possess the best horses in the town, and as money was no object to him, he succeeded in persuading the owners to sell two splendid animals; these with the saddles were sent to the hotel. He then bought two finely finished Sharpe's rifles of long range, and two brace of silver-mounted revolvers.

"Now, Tom," he said, "I shall give one of these outfits to the chief and you give the other to Hunting Dog; he has been your special chum since we started, and the presents will come better from you than from me. I expect them here in half an hour; I told them I should be busy all the morning."

The two Indians were delighted with their presents, even the chief being moved out of his usual impassive demeanour. "My white brothers are too good. Leaping Horse knows that Straight Harry is his friend; he does not want presents to show him that; but he will value them because he loves his white brothers, even more than for themselves." As for Hunting Dog, he was for a long time incredulous that the splendid horse, the rifle and pistols could really be for him, and he was so exuberant in his delight that it was not until Leaping Horse frowned at him severely that he subsided into silent admiration of the gifts.

"Here are papers, chief, that you and Hunting Dog had better keep: they are the receipts for the two horses, and two forms that I have had witnessed by a lawyer, saying that we have given you the horses in token of our gratitude for the services that you have rendered; possibly you may find them useful. You may fall in with rough fellows who may make a pretence that the horses have been stolen. Oh, yes! I know that you can hold your own; still, it may avoid trouble."

They had now no further use for their horses, so these were sold for a few pounds. They purchased a stock of clothes sufficient only for their journey to England.

"You may as well put your revolver in your pocket, Tom," Harry said as they prepared to start the next day. "I have sewn up the draft in the lining of my coat, but sometimes a train gets held up and robbed, and as we have six hundred pounds in gold and notes in our wallets, I certainly should not give it up without a fight."

The Indians accompanied them to the station. "Now, chief, you take my advice and look out for a nice wife before next spring. You are forty now, and it is high time you thought of settling down."

"Leaping Horse will think over it," the Seneca said gravely. "It may be that in the spring he will have a wigwam in the valley."

A few minutes later the train started east, and five days later they reached New York. A steamer left the next day for England, and in this they secured two first-class berths; and although Tom had managed very well on his way out, he thoroughly enjoyed the vastly superior comfort of the homeward trip. They went straight through to Southampton, for, as Harry said, they could run up to London and get their clothes any day; and he saw that Tom was in a fever of excitement to get home. Harriet came to the door of the little house at Southsea when they knocked. She looked surprised at seeing two gentlemen standing there. In the two years and a half that had passed since Tom had left he had altered greatly. He had gone through much toil and hardship, and the bronze of the previous summer's sun was not yet off his cheeks; he had grown four or five inches, and the man's work that he had been doing had made almost a man of him.

"Don't you know me, Harriet?" Tom said.

The girl at once recognized the voice, and with a loud cry of delight threw her arms round his neck. The cry brought Carry out from the parlour. "Why, Harriet," she exclaimed, "have you gone mad?"

"Don't you see it's Tom?" Harriet said, turning round, laughing and crying together.

"It is Tom, sure enough, Carry; you need not look so incredulous; and this is Uncle Harry."

There were a few minutes of wild joy, then they calmed down and assembled in the sitting-room.

"It is lucky the girls have all gone home to dinner," Carry said, "or they would certainly have carried the news to their friends that we were all mad. It is a half-holiday too, nothing could be more fortunate. Now we want to hear everything. Tom's letters were so short and unsatisfactory, uncle, that he told us next to nothing, except that you had found a mine, and that you were both working there, and that it was satisfactory."

"Well, my dears, that is the pith of the thing," Harry said. "The first thing for you to do is to send round notes to the mothers of these children saying that from unforeseen circumstances you have retired from the profession, and that the school has finally closed from this afternoon." There was a general exclamation from the girls:

"What do you mean, uncle?"

"I mean what I say, girls. Tom and I have made our fortunes, and there is no occasion for you to go on teaching any longer. We have not yet made any plans for the future, but at any rate the first step is, that there is to be no more teaching."

"But are you quite, quite sure, uncle?" Carry said doubtfully. "We are getting on very nicely now, and it would be a pity to lose the connection."

Harry and Tom both laughed.

"Well, my girl," the former said, "that is of course a point to be thought of. But as Tom and I have over thirty-five thousand pounds apiece, and the mine will bring us in a good round sum for some years to come, I think we can afford to run the risk of the connection going."

After that it was a long while before they settled down to talk quietly again.

A week later they all went up to London for a month, while what Harry called "outfits" were purchased for the girls, as well as for him and Tom, and all the sights of London visited. Before their story came to an end, the grand consultation as to future plans had been held, and a handsome house purchased at Blackheath.

Tom did not return to Utah in the spring; his uncle strongly advised him not to do so.

"I shall go back myself, Tom; partly because I should feel like a fish out of water with nothing to do here, partly because I promised the chief to go back for a bit every year. I am beginning to feel dull already, and am looking forward to the trip across the water, but it will certainly be better for you to stay at home. You left school early, you see, and it would be a good thing for you to get a man to come and read with you for two or three hours a day for the next year or two. We have settled that the three younger girls are to go to school; and I don't see why you, Carry, and Janet, should not go, in the first place, for two or three months on to the Continent. They have had a dull life since you have been away, and the trip will be a treat for them, and perhaps do you some good also. It will be time enough to settle down to reading when you come back."

The mine returned large profits that year, the increased amount stamped making up to some extent for the falling off in the value of the ore, and the shares of the various proprietors were more than half what they had been at the end of the first season's work. The third year it fell off considerably. There was a further decrease the year after, and the fifth year it barely paid its expenses, and it was decided to abandon it. Harry Wade went over every season for many years, but spent only the first at the mine. After that he went hunting expeditions with Leaping Horse, who, to his amusement, had met him at his first return to the mine with a pretty squaw, and Hunting Dog had also brought a wife with him. Two wigwams were erected that year near the mine, but after that they returned to their tribe, of which Leaping Horse became the leading chief.

Tom's sisters all in due time married, each being presented on her wedding-day with a cheque for ten thousand pounds, as a joint present from her uncle and brother.

Tom himself did not remain a bachelor, but six years after his return to England took a wife to himself, and the house at Blackheath was none too large for his family. Harry Wade's home is with Tom, and he is still hale and hearty. Up to the last few years he paid occasional visits to America, and stayed for a while with his red brother Leaping Horse, when they lamented together over the disappearance of game and the extinction of the buffalo. Hunting Dog had, at Harry's urgent advice, settled down in the ways of civilization, taking up a ranche and breeding cattle, of which he now owns a large herd. Jerry Curtis and Pete Hoskings made a journey together to Europe after the closing of the mine. They stayed for a month at Blackheath, and ten years later Tom received a lawyer's letter from Denver saying that Peter Hoskings was dead, and that he had left his large house and other property in Denver to Mr. Thomas Wade's children. Jerry still lives at the age of seventy-five in that city.

THE END

Titles in Alphabetical Order

Original Publisher and Date of Publication

All But Lost. A Novel. (Vol. I, Vol. II, Vol. III).
Tinsley Brothers, 1869.

At Aboukir and Acre, A Story of Napoleon's Invasion of Egypt.
Blackie and Son Ltd.,1899.

At Agincourt, A Tale of the White Hoods of Paris.
Blackie and Son Ltd., 1897.

At the Point of the Bayonet, A Tale of the Mahratta War.
Blackie and Son Ltd., 1902.

Beric the Briton, A Story of the Roman Invasion.
Blackie and Son Ltd., 1893.

Bonnie Prince Charlie, A Tale of Fontenoy and Culloden.
Blackie and Son Ltd.,1888.

Both Sides the Border, A Tale of Hotspur and Glendower.
Blackie and Son Ltd., 1899.

Bravest of the Brave, The; or, With Peterborough in Spain.
Blackie and Son Ltd.,1887.

By Conduct and Courage, A Story of Nelson's Days.
Blackie and Son Ltd., 1905.

By England's Aid, or, The Freeing of the Netherlands, 1585 - 1604.
Blackie and Son Ltd., 1891.

By Pike and Dyke, A Tale of the Rise of the Dutch Republic.
Blackie and Son Ltd., 1890.

By Right of Conquest, or, With Cortez in Mexico.
Blackie and Son Ltd., 1891.

By Sheer Pluck, A Tale of the Ashanti War.
Blackie and Son Ltd., 1884.

Captain Bayley's Heir, A Tale of the Gold Fields of California.
Blackie and Son Ltd., 1889.

Cat of Bubastes, A Tale of Ancient Egypt.
Blackie and Son Ltd., 1889.

Chapter of Adventures, A, or, Through the Bombardment of Alexandria.
Blackie and Son Ltd., 1891.

Colonel Thorndyke's Secret.
Chatto & Windus, 1898.

Condemned as a Nihilist, A Story of Escape from Siberia.
Blackie and Son Ltd., 1893.

Cornet of Horse, The; A Tale of Marlborough's Wars.
Sampson Low, 1881.

Curse of Carne's Hold, A Tale of Adventure.
Spencer Blackett & Hallam, 1889.

Dash for Khartoum, A Tale of the Nile Expedition.
Blackie and Son Ltd., 1892.

Dorothy's Double, The Story of a Great Deception.
Chatto & Windus, 1894.

Dragon and the Raven, or, The Days of King Alfred.
Blackie and Son Ltd., 1886.

Facing Death, or, The Hero of the Vaughan Pit - A Tale of the Coal Mines.
Blackie and Son Ltd., 1882.

Final Reckoning, A Tale of Bush Life in Australia.
Blackie and Son Ltd., 1887.

For Name and Fame, or, Through Afgan Passes.
Blackie and Son Ltd., 1886.

For the Temple, A Tale of the Fall of Jerusalem.
Blackie and Son Ltd., 1888.

Friends Though Divided, A Tale of the Civil War.
Griffith & Farran, 1883.

Gabriel Allen M.P.
Spencer Blackett, (1888).

Held Fast for England, A Tale of the Siege of Gibraltar (1779 - 83).
Blackie and Son Ltd., 1892.

Hidden Foe, A.
Sampson Low, Marston, and Company, 1891.

In Freedom's Cause, A Story of Wallace and Bruce.
Blackie and Son Ltd., 1885.

In Greek Waters, A Story of the Grecian War of Independence (1821 - 1827).
Blackie and Son Ltd., 1893.

In the Hands of the Cave Dwellers.
Harper & Brothers, 1900.

In the Heart of the Rockies, A Story of Adventure in Colorado.
Blackie and Son Ltd., 1895.

In the Irish Brigade, A Tale of War in Flanders and Spain.
Blackie and Son Ltd., 1901.

In the Reign of Terror, The Adventures of a Westminster Boy.
Blackie and Son Ltd., 1888.

In Times of Peril, A Tale of India.
Griffith & Farran, 1881.

Jack Archer, A Tale of the Crimea.
Sampson Low, Marston, Searle, & Rivington, 1883.

Jacobite Exile, A, Being the Adventures of a Young Englishman in the Service of Charles XII of Sweden.
Blackie and Son Ltd., 1894.

John Hawke's Fortune, A Story of Monmouth's Rebellion.
Blackie and Son Ltd., 1901.

Knight of the White Cross, A, A Tale of the Siege of Rhodes.
Blackie and Son Ltd., 1896.

Lion of St. Mark, The, A Story of Venice in the Fourteenth Century.
Blackie and Son Ltd., 1889.

Lion of the North, The, A Tale of the Times of Gustavus Adolphus and the Wars of Religion.
Blackie and Son Ltd., 1886.

Lost Heir, The.
James Bowden, 1899.

Maori and Settler, A Tale of the New Zealand War.
Blackie and Son Ltd., 1891.

March on London, A, Being a Story of Wat Tyler's Insurrection.
Blackie and Son Ltd., 1898.

March to Coomassie.
Tinsley Brothers, 1874.

March to Magdala.
Tinsley Brothers, 1868.

No Surrender! A Tale of the Rising in La Vendée.
Blackie and Son Ltd., 1900.

On the Irrawaddy, A Story of the First Burmese War.
Blackie and Son Ltd., 1897.

One of the 28th, A Tale of Waterloo.
Blackie and Son Ltd., 1890.

Orange and Green, A Tale of the Boyne and Limerick.
Blackie and Son Ltd., 1888.

Out on the Pampas, The Young Settlers.
Griffith & Farran, 1871.

Out With Garibaldi, A Story of the Liberation of Italy.
Blackie and Son Ltd., 1901.

Queen Victoria, Scenes from her Life and Reign.
Blackie and Son Ltd., 1901.

Queen's Cup, A Novel.
Chatto & Windus, 1897.

Redskin and Cow-Boy, A Tale of the Western Plains.
Blackie and Son Ltd., 1892.

Roving Commission, A , Or Through the Black Insurrection of Hayti.
Blackie and Son Ltd., 1900.

Rujub, the Juggler.
Chatto & Windus, 1893.

Search for a Secret, A.
Tinsley Brothers, 1867.

Sovereign Reader, Scenes from the Life and Reign of Queen Victoria.
Blackie and Son Ltd., (1887).

St. Bartholomew's Eve, A Tale of the Huguenot Wars.
Blackie and Son Ltd., 1894.

St. George for England, A Tale of Cressy and Poitiers.
Blackie and Son Ltd., 1885.

Sturdy and Strong, Or, How George Andrews Made His Way.
Blackie and Son Ltd., 1888.

Those Other Animals.
Henry & Co., (1891).

Through Russian Snows, A Story of Napoleon's Retreat from Moscow.
Blackie and Son Ltd., 1896.

Through the Fray, A Tale of the Luddite Riots.
Blackie and Son Ltd., 1886.

*Through the Sikh War, A Tale of the Conquest of the Punjaub
[or Punjab].*
Blackie and Son Ltd., 1894.

Through Three Campaigns, A Story of Chitral, Tirah, and Ashantee.
Blackie and Son Ltd., 1904.

Tiger of Mysore, A Story of the War with Tippoo Saib.
Blackie and Son Ltd., 1896.

To Herat and Cabul, A Story of the First Afghan War.
Blackie and Son Ltd., 1902.

Treasure of the Incas, The, A Tale of Adventure in Peru.
Blackie and Son Ltd., 1903.

True to the Old Flag, A Tale of the American War of Independence.
Blackie and Son Ltd., 1885.

Under Drake's Flag, A Tale of the Spanish Main.
Blackie and Son Ltd., 1883.

Under Wellington's Command, A Tale of the Peninsular War.
Blackie and Son Ltd., 1889.

*When London Burned, A Story of Restoration Times and the
Great Fire.*
Blackie and Son Ltd., 1895.

Winning His Spurs, A Tale of the Crusades.
Sampson Low, 1882.

With Buller in Natal, or, A Born Leader.
Blackie and Son Ltd., 1901.

With Clive in India, or The Beginnings of an Empire.
Blackie and Son Ltd., 1884.

With Cochrane the Dauntless, A Tale of the Exploits of Lord Cochrane in South American Waters.
Blackie and Son Ltd., 1897.

With Frederick The Great, A Tale/Story of the Seven Years War.
Blackie and Son Ltd., 1898.

With Kitchener in the Soudan, A Story of Atbara and Omdurman.
Blackie and Son Ltd., 1903.

With Lee in Virginia, A Story of the American Civil War.
Blackie and Son Ltd., 1890.

With Moore at Corunna, A Tale of the Peninsular War.
Blackie and Son Ltd., 1898.

With Roberts to Pretoria, A Tale of the South African War.
Blackie and Son Ltd., 1902.

With the Allies to Pekin, A Story of the Relief of the Legations.
Blackie and Son Ltd., 1904.

With the British Legion, A Story of the Carlist Wars.
Blackie and Son Ltd., 1903.

With Wolfe in Canada, Or, The Winning of a Continent.
Blackie and Son Ltd., 1887.

Woman of the Commune, A, A Tale of Two Sieges of Paris.
F. V. White & Co., 1895.

Won by the Sword, A Story of the Thirty Years' War.
Blackie and Son Ltd., 1900.

Wulf The Saxon, A Story of the Norman Conquest.
Blackie and Son Ltd., 1895.

Young Buglers, A Tale of the Peninsular War.
Griffith & Farran, 1880.

Young Carthaginian, A Struggle for Empire.
Blackie and Son Ltd., 1887.

Young Colonists, The, A Tale/Story of the Zulu and Boer Wars.
George Routledge and Sons, 1885.

*Young Franc-Tireurs and Their Adventure in the
Franco-Prussian War, The.*
Griffith & Farran, 1872.